About the Author

Clare Connelly was ~~brought up~~ among a family of av~~id readers, and spent~~ her childhood up a tre~~e with a book.~~ Clare is married to h~~er real-life hero~~ and they live in a bungalow near ~~the sea with~~ their two children. She is frequently found staring into space – a surefire sign that she's in the world of her characters. She has a penchant for French food and ice-cold champagne, and Mills & Boon novels continue to be her favourite ever books. Writing for Modern is a long-held dream. Clare can be contacted via clareconnelly.com or at her Facebook page.

After leaving her convent school, **Miranda Lee** briefly studied the cello before moving to Sydney, where she embraced the emerging world of computers. Her career as a programmer ended after she married, had three daughters and bought a small acreage in a semi-rural community. She yearned to find a creative career from which she could earn money. When her sister suggested writing romances, it seemed like a good idea. She could do it at home, and it might even be fun! She never looked back.

Maya Blake's writing dream started at thirteen. She eventually realised her dream when she received 'The Call' in 2012. Maya lives in England with her husband, kids and an endless supply of books. Contact Maya: mayabauthor.blogspot.com, twitter.com/mayablake, facebook.com/maya.blake.94

Confessions

June 2022
Confessions of the Nanny

July 2022
Confessions of the Boss

August 2022
Confessions of
the Billionaire

September 2022
Confessions of the Playboy

October 2022
Confessions of the Maid

November 2022
Confessions of
the Mistress

Confessions of the Playboy

CLARE CONNELLY

MIRANDA LEE

MAYA BLAKE

MILLS & BOON

First Published in Great Britain 2022
By Mills & Boon, an imprint of HarperCollins*Publishers*
1 London Bridge Street, London, SE1 9GF

www.harpercollins.co.uk

HarperCollins*Publishers*
1st Floor, Watermarque Building,
Ringsend Road, Dublin 4, Ireland

CONFESSIONS OF THE PLAYBOY

ISBN 978-0-263-30583-8

MIX
Paper | Supporting
responsible forestry
FSC™ C007454

This book is produced from independently certified FSC™ paper to ensure responsible forest management.

For more information visit: www.harpercollins.co.uk/green

Printed and Bound in Spain using 100% Renewable electricity at CPI Black Print, Barcelona

HER WEDDING
NIGHT SURRENDER

CLARE CONNELLY

For Kylie Adams, who has supported and
encouraged me from the start.

PROLOGUE

'So, LET ME get this straight.' Pietro stared across his desk at the man he'd idolised for the better part of two decades. 'You're actually asking that I marry your daughter—a woman thirteen years my junior, a woman I barely know. And why, exactly, do you suppose I'll say yes?'

Across from him Col shifted in his chair, his own gaze direct. 'Emmeline is a beautiful and intelligent woman. Why are you so offended by my suggestion?'

Pietro's scepticism on that score wasn't something he wished to communicate to his friend. Nor the belief he held that Emmeline was either painfully shy or vapid.

'I have no intention of marrying anyone,' Pietro said, neatly sidestepping the question. 'Ever.'

'Even better. Marrying Emmeline isn't going to skittle any lingering love affair for you.'

Pietro's lips were a gash, scored across his face. He spoke emphatically and with the kind of iron-like command that had his corporate opponents running scared. 'There will be no marriage.'

Col smiled at the swift rebuke. Apparently the commanding tone that Pietro's business adversaries feared was inconsequential to Col.

'I love you, Pietro. Like a son. You and Emmeline are the most important people in my life. I *need* you to marry her.'

'Why? Where has this come from?' Pietro leaned forward, analysing every flicker of the older man's face.

'I've been thinking about it for a few weeks.'

'Why?' Pietro pushed, certain now that he wasn't seeing the full picture.

Col exhaled slowly and his eyes dropped away from Pietro's. 'Emmeline wants to go to university. She's found a place in Rome. I've told her she may come here to study, with my blessing. But only so long as she marries you.'

'And she has agreed?' Pietro snapped scathingly, his impression of Emmeline as a limpet who'd signed her life away on a dotted line increasing.

'It took some discussion,' Col admitted gruffly. 'But, yes, she agreed.' His eyes held a defiant glint in their depths. 'Emmeline would do anything I ask of her. She's always been a good girl.'

A good girl? Pietro had to concentrate hard to stop himself rolling his eyes. Good girls were boring. Predictable. Dull. The description served only to reinforce his dim opinion of the Senator's daughter.

'So?' Pietro laughed, the sound rich with disbelief. 'I can keep an eye on your daughter without marrying her!'

'Damn it!' Col shouted, the words an angry curse on his lips. 'That's not enough.'

'Why not?' Pietro narrowed his eyes. 'What am I missing?'

Col's glare was defiant, his expression rich with displeasure. But after a burning moment of silence he nodded. Just once, but it was enough to signal a surrender of sorts.

'What I'm about to tell you stays in this room.'

Perplexed, Pietro jerked his head in agreement.

'Swear it, Pietro. Swear you will keep my confidence.'

'Of course.'

Pietro had no concept of what he was agreeing to, at that point, so it was easy to go along with the Senator's insistence.

'There are only two people other than myself who know what I'm about to tell you. Not even Emmeline knows.'

A *frisson* of anticipation drummed along Pietro's spine. He stayed silent, waiting for the Senator to continue.

'There's no easy way to say this. I'm dying.'

Pietro froze. He felt his body go into a kind of shocked

stasis. 'What?' he heard himself query after a long moment, and the word was almost sucked out of him.

'Dying. My oncologist thinks I've probably got a few months in me yet.'

He leaned forward, and the determination in his gaze sent shivers running down Pietro's spine.

'They won't be *good* months, though. I want Emmeline as far away from me as possible. I want her happy. Safe. Protected. I want her blissfully unaware of what's happening to me.'

Pietro felt as though a slab of bricks had landed on his chest and was determinedly squeezing all the air out of him. He'd lost his own beloved father to cancer twenty years earlier. The idea of going through that again turned his blood to ice.

'That can't be right.' He ran a palm over his eyes and stared at the Senator with renewed interest. He looked so well. Just as always. 'Have you had a second opinion?'

'Don't need one.' Col shrugged. 'I saw the X-rays. Cancer everywhere.'

Pietro swore in his own tongue. It had been a long time since he'd felt so powerless. 'I'm sorry.'

'I don't want your apology. I want your help. Damn it, I'm *begging* you for it.'

Inwardly, Pietro groaned. He would do almost anything for the older man. But marrying his daughter...?

'Surely Emmeline would prefer to find her own partner...'

'Who?' Col scoffed. 'Some fortune-hunter? She's going to be worth billions of dollars when I die. *Billions.* Not to mention inheriting the estate and the oil rig off Texas. And she's got no experience with the world.' He grunted angrily. 'That's *my* fault. After her mother died I wanted to protect her. I wanted to keep her away from all that was ugly. I did a damned good job. But now I find myself with a twenty-two-year-old daughter who's about to be orphaned—and, hell, Pietro, I need to know that someone will look after her.'

'I will,' he assured Col, meaning it.

'The occasional email won't cut it. I need her living under your roof. Emmeline *needs* looking after.'

'You say she doesn't know about the cancer?'

'Absolutely not. And she's not going to.'

'What are you talking about?'

'I want to spare her this pain. I owe her that much.'

Pietro felt frustration gnawing through him. Of all the requests he'd expected, this was nowhere on the list he'd prepared.

'It's the only thing I've ever asked of you, Pietro. Promise me you'll do this. For *me*.'

CHAPTER ONE

'YOU DON'T LIKE ME, do you?'

She regarded the handsome Italian thoughtfully, taking in his expensive suit, thick dark hair, dark chestnut eyes and lips that looked as if they were made to curse and kiss. Lower, there was the cleft in his chin, then broad shoulders and a muscled chest. Yes, even though he was wearing that suit she knew it would be muscled. There wasn't an ounce of spare flesh on him—just toned, honed body.

A shiver ran down her spine as she wondered just how the hell she was going to go through with this.

Marriage to this man? Talk about a baptism of fire. No experience—and she had very little anyway—could have prepared her for this.

He didn't answer. Had he even heard? She'd asked the question quietly, in a sort of stage whisper.

She sucked in a breath and focussed on him anew. 'I said—'

'I know what you said.'

His voice was accented. Thick with spiced consonants and mystery. He drummed his fingers—long fingers, with neat nails and a sprinkling of hair over the knuckles—on the arm of his chair.

'It's late. Would you like a coffee? Something stronger?'

Emmeline shook her head and her hair, which was long and lay flat down her back, moved a little, like a shimmering curtain. 'I'm fine.'

He compressed his lips and stood, moving across the room with a stride that spoke of raw, feral power. She watched as he took the glass lid off a decanter and tilted it, filling a round highball tumbler with amber liquid. He threw at least half of it back in one go and then spun the glass in his hand, his fingers moving easily around its circumference as he rotated it purposefully.

'I know this all seems crazy…' Emmeline murmured, her eyes large as they found his.

The force of meeting his gaze startled her and she looked away again just as quickly.

His lips curled in an expression of derisive acknowledgement. *'Un po,'* he agreed. 'A little.'

'The thing is, I don't want to upset my father. I've never been able to bear the idea of hurting him.'

Her eyes flicked to his again, and this time she held his gaze, forcing herself to be brave. If she wanted this man to be part of her plan, her bid for freedom, then she needed him to know she wasn't afraid. Even though the charcoal depths of his eyes made her stomach flip and churn, she kept her courage.

'Since my mother died he's wrapped me up in cotton wool. And I've let him.'

She bit down into her lower lip. Contrary to his first impression, it was a full, pleasingly shaped lip, Pietro realised distractedly, before throwing back another measure of Scotch.

Emmeline's sigh was a soft exhalation. 'I've felt for years that I should assert myself more. That I should insist on the freedoms and privileges that any other person my age would have.'

'So? Why have you not?'

For Pietro's part, the very idea of Emmeline's rarefied existence was abhorrent. Virtually from infancy he had bucked against restraint of any kind. He had always wanted more of everything—particularly independence and maturity.

'It's hard to explain.' *Even to herself!*

She had struggled for years to come to terms with the life she was leading—*choosing* to lead, in many ways.

'After Mom's suicide he fell apart. Keeping me safe,

knowing I was protected—it became an obsession for him. I couldn't bear to see him hurt again like he was when she died.'

Pietro froze, his body stiff, his expression unknowingly wary. The expression in Emmeline's face touched something deep inside him, tilting him way off balance.

'Yes,' she said, answering his unspoken question, interpreting his silence only as surprise. 'I do know how she died.'

Her face drained of colour and she crossed her slender legs in the opposite direction, her hands neatly clasped in her lap.

'Your father went to great lengths to…to protect you from the truth.'

'Yes.' Her smile was twisted, lop-sided. 'I just told you—protecting me from *everything* has become somewhat of an obsession to him.'

When had Emmeline come to realise that her father's protection was hurting her? That his well-intentioned benevolence was making her miss out on so much in life?

'How did you find out?'

The gravelled question dragged her back to their conversation, and to a dark time in her life that she tried her hardest not to think about.

'I was fifteen—not five,' she said with a lift of her shoulders, her expression carefully neutral. 'He wrapped me up as best he could, but I still went to school and kids can be pretty brutal. She drove into a tree, sure—but it was no accident.'

Her eyes showed all the emotion that her face was concealing. Perhaps under normal circumstances he might have comforted her. But these weren't normal circumstances and she wasn't a normal woman. She was to be his bride, if he agreed to go along with this.

As if he had any choice! The loyalty and affection he felt for Col, combined with the older man's terminal diagnosis, presented him with a black and white scenario.

'I don't think he ever got over losing her, and he's terrified of something happening to me. As much as this all seems crazy, I can see why he feels as he does.' She cleared her throat. This next part was where she really had to be strong. 'So, yes. I think we *should* get married.'

The laugh that escaped his lips was a short, sharp sound of reproach. 'You don't think I'm the kind of man who'd like to ask that question myself?'

'Oh…'

Her eyes narrowed speculatively and there was a direct confidence in her gaze that unsettled him slightly.

'I think you're the kind of man who has no intention of asking that question *ever*. Of *anyone*.' She cleared her throat again. 'If the gossip pages are to be believed, you're more interested in installing a revolving door to your bedroom than settling down.'

His smile was laced with icy disdain. 'Is that so?'

'Your…*exploits* are hardly a tightly guarded secret.'

She bit down on her lip again, her eyes dropping to the floor. The lighting was dim, but he could see the flush of pink in her cheeks.

'No,' he agreed softly.

The word should have been a warning, but Emmeline had no experience with men at all. And definitely not with men like Pietro Morelli.

'I don't propose you stop…um…that…' She waved a hand in the air, the dainty bangles she wore jingling like windchimes on the eve of a storm.

'Don't you? My, my—what an accommodating wife you'll be.'

'I won't *really* be your wife,' she pointed out quickly. 'I mean, we'll be married, but it will be just a means to an end. I imagine we can live perfectly separate lives.'

She tilted her head to the side thoughtfully, recalling the details she'd seen of his sprawling mansion on the outskirts of Rome.

'Your house is enormous. We'll probably hardly see one another.'

He rubbed a hand over his stubbled chin, somewhat mollified by her realism in the face of such a ludicrous suggestion. At least she wasn't getting carried away with fairy tale fantasies, imagining herself as a Disney princess and he as her long-awaited Prince Charming.

'And that wouldn't bother you?' he drawled, his eyes raking over her from the top of her bent head to the curved body and crossed legs.

She was the picture of boring, high-society America. No fashion, no sense of style or personality—just a beige trouser suit with a cream blouse and a pearl choker wrapped around her slender, pale neck. Why would *any* twenty-two-year-old choose to style themselves in such a fashion?

'Of course not,' she said, the words showing her surprise. 'I just told you—it wouldn't be a real marriage. My father will be comforted by knowing that we're married—he's so old-fashioned—but I don't think he expects it to be some great big love-match. It's a dynastic marriage, pure and simple.'

'A dynastic marriage?' he heard himself repeat.

'Yes. It's hard for people like us to settle down. To meet a person who's interested in us rather than our fortunes.'

She shrugged her shoulders and Pietro had the impression that Col had been fundamentally wrong about Emmeline. She didn't strike Pietro as particularly vulnerable. If anything, she had an incisive grasp of the situation that he hadn't expected.

'I definitely don't want your money. In fact I don't want anything from you. Just the freedom our marriage offers me.'

Why did that bother him? Her calm insistence that she would take his name and nothing else?

'My mother would like grandchildren,' he was surprised

to hear himself say. Baiting her, perhaps? Or trying to unsettle her?

She laughed—a sound that caught him off-guard completely. It was a musical laugh, full of the colour that was otherwise lacking from her.

'She probably already has several, given your reputation.'

Dark colour slashed across his cheeks. 'Are you suggesting I have unacknowledged children running about the place?'

She shrugged. 'Well, I guess it's a possibility you should consider.'

His eyes narrowed thoughtfully. She had more spark than he'd appreciated. It was hidden deep beneath the veneer of cultured, polite society heiress, but her intelligence and acerbic wit were obvious now that he was actually in a conversation with her.

'There aren't,' he said with finality. 'The responsibility of parenthood is not one I would abandon.'

Yes, she could tell that about this man. He had a sombre, ultra-responsible air.

'Then your mother may have to live with disappointment. At least she'll have the satisfaction of not seeing her son in the society pages for all the wrong reasons every weekend.'

She stood up, pacing across the room thoughtfully, reminding him powerfully of his own back and forth with Col earlier that same evening.

'You would need to be far more discreet, though. I'm not marrying you just to be embarrassed or ashamed. The outside world would have to think it was a normal marriage. I suppose we'd have to attend some events together, be seen out in public from time to time—that kind of thing. But within the walls of your home you can do what you want and with whom.'

'So if you were to walk into this room and find me having sex with one of my lovers you would not be concerned?'

Her heart *kerthunked* but she kept her expression neutral. 'Only from a sanitation perspective.'

He bit back a smile at her prim response. 'I see.'

'Daddy seems to think a quick wedding is for the best, and if we were to get married within the month I'd have time to enrol in a couple of subjects for next semester...'

'Subjects?' he asked, a frown marring his handsome face for a moment. Then he remembered her plans to study in Rome. The revelation of Col's cancer had thrown everything else from his mind, particularly Emmeline's reasons for pursuing this marriage.

'Yes. University. I presumed Dad told you?'

'He did,' Pietro agreed.

'Well, then, you see? I'm not going to be in your hair. I'll be out doing my own thing much of the time.'

'And there we may have a problem,' he said thoughtfully. 'While I appreciate your generosity in agreeing that my social life shouldn't be disrupted, I would have no such tolerance for you in return.'

Emmeline tilted her head to one side, her eyes meeting his with obvious confusion. 'What do you mean?'

'I won't marry a woman who wants to go out with other men. Who wants to sleep with other men.'

Emmeline pulled a face full of surprise. The possibility hadn't even occurred to her, but his hard-line stance wrought instant confusion. 'Why not?'

His eyes narrowed dangerously. 'Because it might create the impression that I can't satisfy my wife.'

'Oh, heaven forbid anyone should cast aspersions on your big macho libido,' she said, with a roll of her caramel eyes.

'That is a deal-breaker for me, *cara*.'

She darted her tongue out and licked her lower lip. She hadn't planned to go out looking for a boyfriend. The thought had really never entered her head. But, as she spoke to him now, the injustice of his being allowed to continue sleeping his way around Rome but having no such opportunity herself seemed manifestly unreasonable.

'Then maybe you should abstain as well,' she murmured, tapping a finger on the side of her mouth.

'That's not a very clever suggestion, is it?'

'Why not? It seems only fair.'

He prowled towards her. Yes, *prowled*. She felt like a bird pinned under a rock, with an enormous growling lion circling her, waiting for his moment of attack.

'Because I like sex,' he said, when he was only a step away from her. 'I am a red-blooded male and it's a part of my life. So if you force me to give up sex with other women that leaves only you…'

He left the rest of the sentence unfinished, hanging in the air between them like a plank she would definitely never walk.

'Okay…okay.' She lifted her hands in surrender, but it was too late to stem the wave of sensations that were besieging her body. 'No sex.' Her voice was thready. 'I mean, sex is fine for *you*.' She closed her eyes softly. 'And I'll talk to you if I meet someone I like…deal?'

He compressed his lips, his eyes studying her face. Her cheeks were flushed, her eyes wide, her lips slightly tremulous. Fascinating. Was that because she was annoyed? Or were more pleasurable emotions fuelling her physical response?

'*Si.*'

She expelled a shaking breath, nodding slowly. 'So we'll get married?'

'There are a few other matters to consider,' he said quietly, the words thickened by emotion.

'Such as?'

'Your appearance.'

She froze, her eyes shocked into clashing with his. Arcs of electricity shimmied and sparked between them. 'You mean how I look?'

His lips twisted into a tight, displeased smile. 'That is generally what a person's appearance means, is it not?'

She nodded, moving further away from him. She needed breathing room if she was going to keep a level head about her—particularly given this subject matter.

'What about it?'

'No one is going to believe I chose to marry you.'

He said it simply. So simply that she believed he hadn't meant to wound her.

'Why not?' She narrowed her eyes, hoping her face wasn't showing the effects of the cruelty his words were lashing her with.

'Because you're nothing like the kind of women I date. And, as you so rightly pointed out, there's more than enough images of me with that kind of woman available to anyone who cares to search for my name on the internet.'

As Emmeline had. And she'd seen glamazon after glamazon in those online images: tall, thin, voluptuous, and all stunning. Pietro Morelli had a 'type', all right.

'I like how I look,' she said, but her mind cursed her for the lie it was. Concealing her body and playing down her looks was a habit that had formed many years earlier, and she wasn't sure she had any desire to revise it.

'It would not take much effort,' he said quietly, his eyes moving over her dispassionately, assessingly.

A distant memory flashed before him of the first time he'd seen her, and the quick, instinctive desire that had warmed his blood before he'd remembered how young she was. She was naturally beautiful; why did she hide her looks?

Fire and outrage burned in her blood. 'No.'

He compressed his lips, hiding the amusement that shifted through him at her determined recalcitrance. 'If I'm going to go through with this I expect you to start dressing as if you actually have a figure and some kind of budget for clothing. It is what people will expect of my wife.'

She stared at him, agog. 'You're joking?'

'No, *carissima*. It's no joke.' His eyes roamed her face analytically. 'This is Roma. Find a boutique and worship your body, then I'll consider it.'

His arrogance and his grim, scathing indictment infuriated her, but the realisation of her dream, the closeness of her escape were things so close she could smell freedom and liberation and she wasn't going to let her appearance stop her.

Not for the first time, though, she felt the sharp needling of injustice at the lengths she had to go to in order to earn what most people perceived as a God-given right. What if she refused? Refused not just his request that she start to pay attention to her looks but also her father's suggestion that they marry? What if she took a credit card and just ran away?

It wasn't as if she hadn't thought about it. But the thought of what it would do to her father had always brought her swiftly back into line. She couldn't hurt him. But here she had a way to be independent *and* make her father happy. She just had to tick a few boxes along the way.

'Fine.' Determination and resilience still glinted in her eyes.

'Good.' He nodded crisply.

He reached into his pocket and pulled something out. Something small and white. When he handed it to her she saw it was a business card with a woman's name on it: *Elizabetta Ronimi*.

'This is my secretary's number. She will organise the details with you. Any time in the next month is fine for me.'

'You want *me* to organise our wedding?'

He shrugged, as though it didn't matter one bit to him. 'I presumed you'd hire someone to do it, actually, but you'll need to speak to Elizabetta regarding my availability and to co-ordinate your move to my villa. *Si?*'

'*Si,*' she mumbled wearily. 'I suppose that makes sense.'

'Good.'

She stared at him for several seconds before the penny dropped that she was being dismissed. Colour warmed her cheeks as she moved towards the chair she'd occupied and scooped up her clutch purse.

'I'll have Remi take you home.'

'Remi?'

'My driver.'

'Oh, right.' She nodded, but then shook her head. 'I can grab a cab,' she murmured.

He stopped her on the threshold to the room, his hand curving around her elbow. Warmth spiralled through her body, making her blood pound. Her gut twisted with something like anticipation and her mouth was dry.

'He will soon be your driver too, *cara*. Go with him.'

She didn't want to argue. She wanted to get out of there by the quickest means possible.

'Thank you.'

'*Non ce di che,*' he said softly. 'See you soon, Mrs Morelli.'

Emmeline's eyes swept shut as she stepped out of his office, one single question pounding through her brain.

What the hell have I just agreed to do?

CHAPTER TWO

THE SUN WAS high in the sky and beating down over Rome, but Emmeline barely felt it. She was cold to the centre of her being, anxiety throbbing through her.

In the end it had taken five weeks to get all the paperwork in order, including a swift visa application for Italy, helped in no small part by the last name that had always opened doors for her.

But who was this woman looking back at her now? She had a growing sense of desperation as she studied her own reflection, doubt tangling in her gut.

'Aren't you glad we went with the Vera?' Sophie asked, wrapping an arm around her best friend's shoulders, her own expression not showing even a hint of doubt. 'You're a vision.'

Emmeline nodded slowly. Sophie was right. The dress was exquisite. A nod to nineteen-twenties glamour, with cap sleeves and a fitted silhouette, its beading was perfect, and the shoes she'd chosen gave her an extra lift of height—not that she needed it.

Her hair had been styled in a similarly vintage look, pulled to one side and curled lightly, then held in place with a diamond clip that had belonged to Grandma Bovington. At her throat she wore a small diamond necklace, and vintage earrings completed the look. Her make-up was the work of some kind of magician, because the woman staring back at Emmeline actually looked...*nice*.

Beautiful?

Yes, beautiful.

'I guess we should get going.'

'Well, yeah, we're a little late—but that's your preroga-
tive on your wedding day, isn't it?'

Emmeline grimaced, lifted her head in a brief nod.

'Honey, you're going to need to work on your happy
face,' Sophie said quietly. 'Your dad's never gonna believe
this isn't torture for you if you don't cheer up.'

'It's not torture,' she said hastily.

Though she'd kept the truth behind this hasty marriage
to herself, Sophie knew Emmeline well enough to put two
and two together and get a glaringly clear picture of four.

'It had better not be. I've seen your groom already and—
whoo!' She made an exaggerated fanning motion across her
face. 'He is hotter than a spit roast in hell.'

Emmeline could just imagine. Pietro Morelli on *any*
given day of the week was more attractive than a single
human being had any right to be, but on his wedding day…?
Well, if he'd gone to half the trouble and expense she had
then she knew she'd better start bracing herself.

'Suit?'

'Yes. But it's how he wears it!'

Sophie grinned, and it occurred to Emmeline that Sophie was far more the type of Pietro's usual love interest.
With silky blonde hair that had been styled into a volumi-
nous bun on the top of her head and in the emerald-green
sheath they'd chosen for her bridesmaid's dress, there was
no hiding her generous curves in all the right places and
legs that went on forever.

Sophie was also a political daughter—though of a congressman rather than a senator—and yet she had a completely different attitude to life and love than Emmeline.
She'd always dated freely, travelled wherever and whenever she wanted. For every measure of obsessive attention
Col had suffocated Emmeline with, Sophie had been given
a corresponding quantity of freedom and benign neglect.

Emmeline had read her emails from Sophie with rapt

envy, studying the photographs and closing her eyes, imagining herself alongside her friend. What had Paris on a spring evening smelled like? And how had Argentina been in the summer? And what about that time she'd travelled on a yacht around the Mediterranean, stopping in the French Riviera for a month just because it had taken her fancy?

But all that was ahead of Emmeline now. Soon it would be *her*!

This marriage was crazy in no small part, but it was also the smartest thing she'd ever done. Marriage to Pietro was freedom—freedom to live her own life without hurting her father. Freedom to explore, travel, to *live*—away from Annersty and yet not carrying the burden of having let her father down.

Was there any other way? A way that would give her *true* freedom? The kind of freedom that *wasn't* purchased by marriage? The freedom of knowing she could live her own life?

She bit down on her lower lip, her eyes unknowingly haunted. Of course there was. She could have packed a bag and announced that she was leaving home at any time.

So why hadn't she? Because she'd been with her father when her mother had died. She'd seen the way it had killed a part of his heart, withered it forever, and she didn't dare do the same to him. She couldn't hurt him.

She was making the right decision. She'd get what she wanted, albeit in a not particularly easy way, and her father would be placated. And then, eventually, she'd divorce Pietro and all would be well.

A renewed glint of determination shifted through her eyes. 'Let's go.'

Sophie nodded her approval. 'Attagirl. That's better.'

She sashayed to the door of the small room at the back of the ancient chapel, craning her head out and nodding.

Music began to play—loud and beautiful. A mix of

organ, strings and woodwind. It was Pachelbel's *Canon in D*, a piece that Emmeline had always loved.

She watched as Sophie disappeared ahead of her, counted the ten seconds Maria her wedding co-ordinator had advised and then stepped out of the anteroom into the back of the chapel.

It was packed. The pews were crammed full of well-dressed guests. Many of her father's political friends had come, a few of her schoolfriends, and apparently all of Italy's upper echelons of society had turned out to get a look at the woman who'd finally brought renowned bachelor and commitment-phobe Pietro Morelli to his knees.

She moved along the back of the church, behind the last row of guests, smiling as she caught the eye of someone she vaguely remembered having met once or twice on her visits to the Capitol.

The smile clung to her lips as she saw her father waiting for her. His eyes were moist with unshed tears, his body slim and lean in a fine suit. He wrapped her in a bear hug, almost squashing her, and then kissed her cheek.

His eyes, when he pulled back, searched hers. 'Ready?'

She nodded, smiling brightly at him. She wouldn't let him think she had doubts. Having agreed to this, she wouldn't let him live with any kind of guilt over the fact that he'd pressured her into marrying a man she didn't know—a man called Pietro Morelli, no less!

'Good.' He nodded. 'I'm glad.'

He turned his body slightly and she turned with him, towards the front of the church. She looked past the acres and acres of guests, standing and staring with undisguised curiosity, and there was her groom.

Oh, boy.

Sophie really hadn't been exaggerating. In fact she might have waxed a little more lyrical about just how freaking gorgeous her groom looked. *All other Italian pin-ups—eat your heart out.*

His skin was darker than it had been a few weeks ago, as though he'd been out in the sun a lot. Emmeline tried not to imagine him sunbaking on the Riviera, with a suitably gorgeous companion all too willing to rub oil over his body. Was it an all-over tan? Of course he'd have a private spot to go around in the altogether...

Her father was walking, and she had no choice but to walk with him. One foot in front of the other. But as she got closer her trepidation doubled. Up close to Pietro, she was reminded powerfully of that handsome face with its permanent scowl and the dark, intelligent eyes, his chiselled jaw and symmetrical features. The broad body that she somehow just *knew* would be hard and warm.

His eyes met hers and there was something in them—challenge? Admiration? No, not that. But his look was intent. He stared at her long and slow, uncaring of the hundreds of guests assembled, nor the priest who was waiting patiently.

Col extended a hand and Pietro shook it. This evidence of their firm, long-held friendship gave Emmeline a much-needed boost. A timely reminder that he wasn't a wolf—well, not *just* a wolf. He was someone who had every reason and every intention to be just what they'd agreed. A convenient husband. He was simply a very handsome means to a definitely necessary end.

'*Cara,*' he murmured, low and deep, in a husky greeting that set her pulse firing and spread goosebumps over her flesh. He leaned in close, whispering to her through the veil that covered her face. 'This is more like it.'

Her heart turned over at the compliment, but something like impatience groaned in her chest—impatience that he might think she'd gone to all this effort for *him*; impatience at the fact that he was right.

She arched a brow and met his eyes without showing a hint of her turmoil. 'I thought about wearing a suit, but, you know... This seemed more appropriate.'

'Definitely. I almost wish I was going to be the one to remove it.' He straightened, the hit having met its mark.

Her cheeks glowed with warm embarrassment at his comment, and the effect it had had on her body.

Traitorous flesh.

Her nipples peaked, straining against the soft fabric of her bodice, and an image of him doing just that spooked into her mind. His suit would be rumpled, his jacket discarded, the tie gone, the shirt half unbuttoned with its sleeves pushed up to expose his tanned forearms. There were seemingly a thousand buttons on her dress—probably actually only fifty—and it had taken Sophie the better part of a half-hour to pull the dress together. Would he move slowly or quickly?

She swallowed, staring straight ahead.

The service itself was surprisingly swift. A simple recitation of vows, just as she'd seen in dozens of movies and television shows, preceded by the question about whether or not anyone objected.

That part had had Emmeline holding her breath, waiting, wondering—and strangely hoping no one would say *Yes, this is a sham!* She'd waited, watching intently as the priest's eyes had skimmed over the congregation.

Finally he turned to the couple, smiling brightly.

'Then without further ado, I now pronounce you man and wife.'

Not *husband* and wife, she noted in the small part of her brain still capable of rational thought. 'Husband' and wife would suggest that he too had been altered in some significant way by what they'd just done. 'Man' and wife made all the changes hers.

'You may now kiss your bride.'

She winced unknowingly. *Your* bride. A possessive phrase that spoke of ownership and rankled. Well, what had she expected? She'd chosen this path to freedom because it was easy. Because it meant she wouldn't have to upset her father. She deserved to feel a little objectified.

Her small facial expression of displeasure was easy for Pietro to discern. Seeing it pass across her face like a storm cloud, he wrapped an arm around her waist, drawing her closer to his body quickly, easily, giving her no chance to question his actions. His eyes briefly met hers and there was sardonic amusement at the heart of his gaze.

She tilted her chin defiantly, inadvertently giving him the perfect angle of access. He dropped his lips to hers, pressing them against her mouth, separating her lips easily and sliding his tongue inside.

It was an invasion of every single one of her senses.

Did he know it was her first kiss? Yes, her first kiss—at the age of twenty-two and on her wedding day. Shame made her toes curl and yet desire heated her up, right to the base of her abdomen. His fingers on her back feathered across her nerve-endings, and she made a small whimper low in her throat that only her groom could possibly have heard.

He broke the kiss, his eyes meeting hers laughingly.

Was he laughing at her?

Her heart was racing, banging against her ribs so hard she thought it might crack them. Her breath was burning inside her body and she stared at him in a tangle of confusion. It took at least ten seconds for her to remember where she was and who she was with.

'I would slap you if all these people weren't watching us,' she muttered under her breath, pasting a tight smile to her face.

His lip lifted in sardonic mockery. 'Or would you rip my clothes off?' he pondered.

But before she could respond, he reached down and took her hand in his.

'They *are* watching, so keep pretending this is the happiest day of your life.'

By the time they'd reached the end of the aisle, having

paused several times to accept good wishes and hugs of congratulation, Emmeline's mouth was aching from the forced smile she'd adopted.

A crowd had formed beyond the church and there was a throng of paparazzi. Inwardly, Emmeline trembled at the idea of being photographed. Her husband apparently had no such qualms.

'Ready?' he asked, pausing just inside the door, sparing a quick glance at her face.

Then again, why *would* he hesitate? This was his life. If the number of photographs of him on the internet proved anything it was that he was followed and snapped often. He probably couldn't walk down the street without someone taking his picture.

But Emmeline's life hadn't been like that. A handful of society events had led to her picture sometimes being splashed in the papers, though not often. She was too drab. Boring. Ugly. Why print a picture of Emmeline Bovington unless it was to compare her unfavourably to the renowned beauty her mother had been?

She closed her eyes, sucking in a deep breath, and was unaware of the way Pietro's eyes had caught the deceptive action.

He studied her thoughtfully. He'd seen panic before, and he saw it now. Was this idea *so* unpalatable to her? Hell, she'd suggested it and her father had railroaded him. If anyone should be panicking it was Pietro.

Her hesitation annoyed him—probably more than it should. He stepped out through the door, holding her hand and bringing her with him into the brightness of the Italian afternoon. The steps towards the street were empty, but beneath them was a large crowd, and as they erupted from the church applause broke out. Rose petals were thrown high into the air. The noise was deafening.

He smiled, lifting a hand in acknowledgement, and turned towards his bride.

There it was again.

Panic.

Blinding, devastating panic.

Impatience crumpled his common sense and quickly ate up his judgement. He caught her around the waist and this time he tipped her back in a swoon worthy of an old black and white Hollywood movie.

His lips on hers were an assault; it was a kiss that gave voice to his annoyance when he wasn't otherwise able to. Her hands curled around his neck, her fingers tangling in the hair at his neck, and she made that noise again. That little whimper of confusion that made him hard all over.

That annoyed him even more, and he pressed his hands into her back, lifting her higher, pressing his arousal against her abdomen, leaving her in little doubt of just what kind of man she'd married.

It lasted only seconds, but when he eased her back to stand and pulled away from her the crowd broke out into thunderous applause.

Her eyes were thunderous too. Thunderously pissed off. He could practically hear the storm brewing.

Good. Let Little Miss Refined work on *that.*

'I swear to God, kiss me again and I'll wait until you're asleep and do some serious damage to you,' she said angrily, but her smile was plastered on again seconds later as Col came up behind them.

'I know I wanted this for you both, but seeing you together…' He shook his head wistfully, tears in his eyes. 'I could die a happy man right now.'

Emmeline laughed, not noticing the way her husband had stiffened at her side. 'God, Daddy, don't say that. You'll tempt the heavens.'

'Che sera, sera,' Col said with a shrug.

Emmeline dismissed that attitude. Her father was clearly thrilled that the wedding had taken place, and she wasn't going to take that away from him. Now there were several family photographs to pose for.

Emmeline had met Pietro's mother Ria a few times over the years, and it was easy enough to make conversation with her. His brother Rafe was similarly easy. At least five years younger, Emmeline wondered why *he* hadn't been suggested as a possible groom by her father. He boasted the same pedigree and was equally handsome. Less established in his career, it was true, but with their family fortune what did that matter?

'So, you're now my sister-in-law, eh?'

She returned Rafe's smile, and felt herself relaxing as they posed in the sunshine for the requisite shots.

Nonetheless, it was a relief when the photographer declared she had enough 'for now' and they were free to return to their guests. For Emmeline, that meant Sophie and a hint of normality.

'Ah, the woman of the hour.' Sophie grinned, passing her half-finished champagne flute to Emmeline.

'Don't remind me.' She took a sip, and then another, closing her eyes as the cold bubbles washed down her throat.

'So, Maria was just running through the details with me.'

'Ugh—there's still more, isn't there?'

Sophie laughed softly. 'The reception. But don't worry—that's just a cocktail party at a gorgeous restaurant overlooking the river.'

'Okay, I can cope with that.'

'Then you and Pietro will take your leave—insert catcalling and whistling—and the rest of us young, hip and happening people will have an open bar at some club that's just opened. Apparently your husband had something to do with the financing of it.' Sophie shrugged. 'Sounds kind of fun.'

Emmeline pulled a face. 'Not to me. I can't think of anything worse.'

'Yes, well… I'm sure you'll have your hands full anyway…'

Emmeline sent her friend a scathing look. 'Yeah, right.'

'Hmm, I saw the way you guys kissed. I know passion when I see it.'

Emmeline practically choked on her champagne. She coughed to cover it, lifting a hand to her mouth.

'Trust me—that's not what this is.'

'Then you need to get to a hospital, because if you can be in the same room as that guy and not need CPR then you are some kind of cold fish.'

'Or just a very sensible woman,' she said quietly.

The formalities seemed to last forever. Speeches. The cutting of the cake. Their first dance as a couple…

Emmeline stood in Pietro's arms, trying her hardest to pretend not to be affected by her husband's touch when a single look had the power to turn her blood to lava.

'So…' he drawled, the single word imbued with more cynicism than she'd known was possible. 'You are my wife.'

The sentence brought a smile to her face, but it wasn't a smile of pleasure.

'Don't sound so thrilled about it.'

He slowed the movement of their bodies, his eyes scanning the crowd. 'I can name three people who are beside themselves,' he said coldly.

She followed the direction of his gaze. Her father and his mother stood to one side, each of them beaming with obvious pleasure.

'Yeah, I guess this is a dream come true for Daddy,' she said with a small shake of her head.

There was a look of frustration in her eyes that Pietro thought about probing. But the last thing he wanted was to get to know his inconvenient bride any better.

'And for my mother,' he said simply. 'I'm sure she's imagining a lifetime of calm now that I've apparently hung up my bachelor shoes.'

'*Apparently.*' She repeated the word, rolling it around in

her mouth, wondering about the practicalities of what they'd agreed to. The idea that he'd be free to see other women so long as he was discreet.

It didn't bother her. At least that was what Emmeline told herself. And yet a pervasive sense of confusion filled her.

They would be living under the same roof, seeing each other in the hallways, the kitchen, the lounge, the pool. Despite her protestation that they'd be like flatmates, was it possible that she would be able to ignore her husband at such close quarters?

From the first moment she'd seen him she'd found him worryingly distracting, and the years hadn't stilled that awareness.

And now they were married…

'You are as stiff as a board,' he complained. 'Did you never learn to dance?'

Her cheeks flushed pink and the look she cast him was laced with hurt. 'I was lost in thought,' she mumbled, making an effort to pay attention to her husband.

'Dancing does not require your mind. It is something you feel in your body. It is a seduction.'

He rolled his hips and colour darkened her cheekbones. His body was every bit as fascinating as she'd imagined. All hard edges and planes, strong and dominating, tempting and forbidden in equal measure.

It would be playing with fire ever to touch him in earnest. This was different—a dance at their wedding was unavoidable. But Emmeline had to keep her distance or she'd risk treading a very dangerous path.

'Relax,' he murmured, dropping his head towards hers. 'Or I will kiss whatever it is you are thinking out of your mind.'

She started, losing her footing altogether. She might have fallen if he hadn't wrapped his arms more tightly around her waist, bringing her dangerously close to his body.

'Don't you dare,' she snapped.

His laugh was like gasoline to a naked flame.

'Then smile. Relax. At least pretend you are enjoying yourself.' He dropped his mouth to her ear and whispered, 'Everyone is watching us, you know.'

She swallowed, her eyes scanning the room over his shoulder. The room was indeed full of wedding guests dressed in beautiful clothes, all smiling and nodding as he spun her around the dance floor.

Emmeline's heart sank.

Pretending to be married to Pietro Morelli was going to require a hell of a lot more patience and performance than she'd envisaged.

It was late in the night and Emmeline stifled another yawn. Sophie had found a group of friends—as always—and was charming them with her wit and hilarity. Emmeline listened, laughing occasionally, though she knew all the stories so well they might as well have been her own. Still, sitting with Sophie and pretending to laugh at her hijinks was better than watching her husband.

Her eyes lifted in his direction unconsciously.

He was still talking to her. The redhead.

Emmeline's frown was instinctive—a response to the visual stimulus of seeing a stunning woman so close to the man she, Emmeline, had married only hours earlier.

The woman had auburn hair that tumbled down her back in wild disarray, and she was short and curvaceous, but not plump. Just the perfect kind of curvy—all enormous rounded boobs and butt, tiny waist and lean legs. Her skin was honey-coloured and her lips were painted bright red. Her nails, too. She wore a cream dress—wasn't it considered bad manners to wear white to someone else's wedding?—and gold shoes.

Who *was* she?

Pietro leaned closer, his lips moving as he whispered in the woman's ear, and the woman nodded, lifting a hand to his chest as she dragged her eyes higher, meeting his. From all the way across the room Emmeline could feel the sexual tension between them.

She stood without thinking, her eyes meeting Sophie's apologetically. *I'll be right back,* she mouthed.

Sophie barely missed a beat. She carried on with the story of the time she'd got caught flying from Thailand to London with very illegal monkey droppings in her handbag—she'd been sold them at a market and told they would bring good luck…whoops!—and Emmeline walked deliberately across the room towards her groom and the woman she could only presume to be a lover—past or future. She didn't know, and she told herself she definitely didn't care.

She was only a step away when Pietro shifted his attention from the redhead, his eyes meeting Emmeline's almost as though he didn't recognise her at first. And then his slow-dawning expression of comprehension was followed by a flash of irritation.

He took a small step away from the other woman, his face once more unreadable.

'Emmeline,' he murmured.

'Pietro.' Her eyes didn't so much as flicker towards the woman by his side. 'I need you a moment.'

His lips twitched—with amusement or annoyance, she couldn't have said. He walked towards her, putting a hand in the small of her back and guiding her to the dance floor.

Before she could guess his intentions he spun her around, dragging her into his arms and moving his hips. Dancing. Yes, he was dancing. *Again.*

She stayed perfectly still, her face showing confusion. 'I don't want to dance any more.'

'No, but you want to speak to me. It is easier to do that if we dance. So dance.'

'I…' Emmeline shook her head. 'No.'

He slowed his movements and stared at her for a long, hard second. 'Why not?'

'Because it's not my…thing,' she mumbled, looking away.

Mortification filled her. So many things she'd never really done. Experiences she'd blindly accepted that she would never enjoy. She'd made her peace with that. But now, surrounded by so many people who'd all lived with such freedoms as a matter of course, wasn't it natural that she was beginning to resent the strictures of her upbringing?

Her voice was a whisper when she added, 'As you so wisely pointed out.'

'Then let me show you,' he said.

And his hands around her waist were strong and insistent, so that her body moved of its own accord. No, not of its own accord; she was a puppet and he her master.

Just as she remembered—just as she'd felt hours earlier—every bit of him was firm. His chest felt as if it was cast from stone. He was warm too, and up close like this she could smell his masculine fragrance. It was doing odd flip-floppy things to her gut.

'You told me you'd be discreet,' Emmeline said, trying desperately to salvage her brain from the ruins of her mind. 'But you looked like you were about to start making out with that woman a moment ago.'

'Bianca?' he said, looking over his shoulder towards the redhead. Her eyes were on them. And her eyes were *not* happy. 'She's a…a friend.'

'Yeah, I can see that,' Emmeline responded, wishing she wasn't so distracted by the closeness of him, the smell. What was it? Pine? Citrus? *Him?*

'Are you jealous?'

'Yes, absolutely,' she said with a sarcastic heavenwards flick of her eyes. She leaned closer, lowering her voice to a whisper. 'We have a deal. I just don't want our wedding guests to see you with another woman. What you do in *pri-*

vate is up to you.' She let the words sink in and then stopped moving. 'I'd like to go home now.'

Pietro wasn't used to being ashamed. He was a grown man and he'd lived his own life for a very long time. But something about her calm delivery of the sermon he really did deserve made a kernel of doubt lodge in his chest.

He knew he should apologise. He'd been flirting with Bianca and Emmeline was right: doing that on their wedding day wasn't just stupid, it was downright disrespectful. To his bride, sure, and more importantly to their parents.

He stepped away from her, his expression a mask of cold disdain that covered far less palatable emotions. 'Do you need anything?'

'No.'

'To say goodbye to anyone?'

She looked towards Sophie, enthralling her newfound friends, and shook her head. 'I'd rather just go. *Now.*'

Silence sat between them and she waited, half worried he was going to insist on doing a tour of the room to issue formal farewells.

But after a moment, he nodded. 'Okay. Let's go, then.'

He put a hand on her back but she walked away, moving ahead of him, making it obvious she didn't need him to guide her from the venue. She'd walk on her own two feet.

She hadn't made this deal with the devil to finally find her freedom only to trade it back for this man.

Emmeline Morelli was her own woman, and seeing her husband fawning all over someone else had simply underscored how important it was for her to remember that.

CHAPTER THREE

SHE'D EXPECTED A LIMOUSINE, but instead Pietro directed her to a low, sexy black Jaguar, parked right at the front of the restaurant.

He reached for the front passenger door, unlocking it at the same time, and Emmeline sat down quickly, stupidly holding her breath for some unknown reason. What did she think would happen if she breathed him in again?

He closed the door with a bang and a moment later was in the driver's seat. The car throbbed to life with a low, stomach-churning purr, and he pulled out into the traffic with the consummate ease of a man who'd grown up in these streets and knew them well.

Silence stretched between them and it was far from comfortable. The car had a manual transmission and required frequent gear changes from the man with his hand curved around the leather gearstick, his strong legs spread wide as he revved the engine, his arm moving with the gears.

There was an athleticism in his movements even when simply driving a car.

Emmeline ground her teeth together and focussed on the passing view of starlit Rome. Her new home.

She hadn't thought about what it would mean to leave Georgia behind. At most she'd contemplated the sadness that would come from not seeing her father so often. But there was so much more than that. Annersty was the plantation she'd called home all her life, in the town where she'd grown up, with all the people she knew...

'Tell me what you see for yourself, in the future, pumpkin?' her father had asked her.

'I don't know, Daddy. *This*. I like it here...'

'But one day I won't *be* here.'

His voice had been soft, yet it had cut like glass through her flesh.

'*One* day,' he'd said to calm her, and the words had been reassuring, referring to a time that was distant-seeming. 'But I'd want to know you've got a family of your own to make you happy.'

'I hardly know Pietro—and what I do know I don't think I like.'

He'd given a laugh of genuine amusement. 'He's a good man. Do you think I'd be pushing for this if I didn't thoroughly believe that?'

Her eyes had met his and she'd seen the truth in them. She'd nodded then, sealing her fate with that single gesture.

A soft sigh escaped her lips. She had agreed to this and there was no sense in getting all remorseful now. She'd married Pietro Morelli and they both knew it was a marriage in name only. She held that reassurance close like a talisman.

Yet what was that vitriolic acidity in her gut? It frothed angrily when she remembered the way he'd been looking at that redhead—Bianca—as though he wanted to lick her all over.

An angrier sigh pressed from her lips and Pietro turned his head, studying her in the intermittent light cast by the streetlamps they drove beneath. She looked pretty damned good, despite his assertion weeks earlier that she was far from the kind of woman he was attracted to. It wasn't as though she'd made any major changes—only it was the first time he'd seen her in a dress, wearing make-up, heels, and with her hair done in a style other than a plain ponytail.

He fought the urge to ask her how she was feeling. It wasn't his business and he sure as hell didn't care.

He pressed his foot harder onto the accelerator, chewing up the miles to his home.

The gates swung open as they approached and he eased the car along the curving drive, pulling it up outside the garage. His fleet of vehicles was housed inside and his mechanic would be waiting to give the Jaguar a once-over. He cut the engine and turned to say something to his bride, though he wasn't sure what.

There was no point, in any event. Her hand was on the door and she was pushing it outwards before he could articulate a thing.

She stood tall and proud, her eyes running over the façade of the building, studying it as if for the first time.

'Nothing's changed,' he said, the words darker than the night that surrounded them.

She flashed him a tight smile. 'Yes, it has.' Her eyes looked bigger somehow, and the moon was drawing out flecks of amber and gold from amongst their caramel depths. 'I live here now.'

Pietro's expression was grim, and Emmeline flinched inwardly. Her own shock at the fact that they were now married was dwarfed only by his, and yet he made a decent show of pretending normality.

'I'll show you to your room. Come.'

She thought about making a joke—wasn't it a tradition to carry a bride over the threshold of her new home?—but the tightness of his back as he walked away, the firm angle of his head, showed how little he wanted to laugh about this situation.

Emmeline followed, her gaze wandering over the façade of his house as she went. It was an impressive building. If she had found her host…no, her *husband*…less intimidating she would have asked him a little about it. Still, a place like this had to be in the history books; she could do her own research. Especially once she was at uni and had access to a fantastic library.

She breathed in, imagining the scent of all those books. Renewed purpose reassured her. There was a reason she'd married him. She had to keep that firmly in mind and then all would be well.

'It's late. I won't give you the tour now. Tomorrow the housekeeper will show you where things are.' He stood with his hands in his pockets, his attention focussed squarely ahead.

'That's fine, only…'

'Si?' It was an impatient huff.

'Um…where am I supposed to sleep?'

His expression contorted with irritation but he moved forward, down a long corridor, then turned left and took her up a flight of stairs.

'These rooms are for your use.'

He pushed a door inwards, showing her a practical space that had been set up with a desk, a bookshelf and a tread-mill. The latter made her smile, though she covered it with a yawn.

'Very good.'

'There is a bathroom through there. And your bedroom is here.'

He nodded towards a third and final door and she turned the handle and pushed the door inwards, her eyes scanning the room with interest.

It was not dissimilar to a particularly lovely five-star hotel. A king-size bed made up with nondescript white bed linen and silvery grey throw cushions, a white armchair near the window and yet another book case, and double doors that presumably concealed a wardrobe.

With increasing interest she stepped into the room, the thick beige carpet soft underfoot.

'No books?' she murmured, eyeing the almost empty shelf. The sole book in its midst was a tourist guide to Rome and she refused to believe its placement had anything to do with her husband. He wasn't thoughtful like that.

'This has been used as guest accommodation in the past,' he said softly. 'The décor is neutral in order to accommodate the guests I've had staying here. You are free to add your own touches—furnish it with whatever books you wish.'

She fluttered her eyelids exaggeratedly. 'Even if I want to paint the walls lime-green?'

His smile was dismissive. 'Your choice. It is not as if I will ever be in here to see it.'

She laughed, but there was a thunderous rolling in her gut that she didn't want to analyse. Anxiety, she told herself. She had taken herself out of the comfiest little nest in the world and dropped herself like a stone into the deep end of a raging river.

'So, hot pink then?' she joked, walking towards the window.

She hadn't noticed at first, but as she got closer she saw that it was in fact French doors, and beyond the window was a small Juliet balcony.

Her heart fluttered as she turned the handle and opened the door, feeling a warm breeze breathe in off the city. They were far enough away that she could make out Rome's landmarks with ease, see their place within the cityscape.

'Your suitcases are in the wardrobe,' he said, definitely impatient now, calling her attention back to the important business of getting settled. 'I wasn't sure if you'd find it invasive for the housekeeper to unpack for you. Let me know if you'd like me to send her up…'

Emmeline waved a hand in the air dismissively. 'I can manage.'

'Fine.' A curt nod. 'My room is down at the other end of the hallway. Last door on the right-hand side. If you need me.'

As in, *Don't bother me unless you're on fire, your room is falling away from the building, and there is no one else you can think of to call.*

'Okay.' She smiled—out of habit rather than happiness.

He paused on the threshold for a moment, his eyes glittering like onyx in his handsome face. *'Buonanotte, cara.'*

'Goodnight.' The word came out as a husky farewell. She cleared her throat but he was gone.

Emmeline stretched her arms over her head and then moved towards the door to her room, pushing it shut all the way until it clicked in place.

This was her home now.

She shouldn't think of herself as a guest, nor of this arrangement as temporary. She'd married him—for better or for worse—and, while she wasn't stupid enough to imagine they'd stay married forever, this was certainly her place in life for the next little while.

The doors did open on to a wardrobe, as she'd suspected, and her two suitcases sat in the centre. She'd unpack in the morning, she thought, when she had more energy. She pushed one open and pulled out a pair of cotton pyjamas and the prospectus for her university course, putting them on the foot of the bed.

Her feet were aching, her body was weary, her mind was numb. What she needed was a hot shower and the pleasant oblivion of sleep.

She reached around to the back of her dress and groaned out loud. The buttons. The damned *buttons*.

The mirrors in the wardrobe showed exactly what her predicament was. There were what seemed like hundreds of the things; they'd taken Sophie an age to do up, and without help Emmeline would never get out of her dress.

Obviously she could sleep in it. Sure, it was heavy and fitted, and she wouldn't exactly be comfortable, but it would save her any embarrassment and she could simply ask one of the staff to help her the following morning.

Or... a little voice in the back of her mind prompted.

She grimaced. Yes, yes. *Or...*

She pulled the door inwards and peered down the corridor. It was longer than she'd appreciated at first, and somewhere at the end of it was the man she'd married.

Refusing to admit to herself that she was actually a little bit scared, she stepped into the hallway and walked down it, paying scant attention to the artwork that marked the walls at regular intervals. At the end of the corridor she waited outside the last door on the right, taking a moment to ball her courage together.

She lifted her hand and knocked—so timidly that she knew there was no way he would have heard the sound.

Shaking herself, she knocked harder:

Once.

Twice.

Her hand was poised to knock a third time, and then the door seemed to be sucked inwards. Pietro stood on the other side, his face unforgiving of the interruption.

'Yes?' It was short. Frustrated.

'I...' Emmeline swallowed. 'Am I interrupting?'

'Do you need something?'

Her eyes clashed with his—angry gold against unreadable black.

'This is in no way an invitation...'

His lips flickered for the briefest second into a genuine smile. It was so fast she thought she might have imagined it.

'Fine. What is it?'

She spun around, facing the wall of the corridor directly opposite. 'There's a billion buttons and I can't undo them. I guess wedding dresses are designed with the fact in mind that a bride won't be undressing alone...'

'Apparently,' he murmured, moving closer.

She knew that because she could feel him, even though he didn't touch her. His warmth seemed to be wrapping around her like an opportunistic vine up an abandoned wall.

'Would you mind?' she asked quietly, keeping her attention focussed on the bland whiteness of the hallway wall.

'And if I did?'

'I suppose I could find some scissors somewhere...' she pondered.

'No need.'

And then, even though she'd come to his room for this express purpose, the sensation of his fingertips brushing against her back made her shiver. Her nipples strained against the fabric of her gown in a new and unexpected sensation.

'Are you cold?'

The question caught her off-guard. She bit down on her lip, willing her body to behave, her pulse to quiet, her heart to settle. But her body had its own ideas, and it continued to squirm, delighting in his closeness and his touch.

'I'm fine.'

His laugh was soft, his breath warm. It ran across her back like a wildfire she should have paid better attention to.

He pushed at the first button, flicking it open expertly. *One down, nine hundred thousand to go*, she thought bleakly. He dragged his fingers down to the next button and her stomach rolled with awareness.

Emmeline sucked in a deep breath.

He wasn't *trying* to turn her on; this was just how he was. The man oozed sensuality from every pore of his gorgeous, perfectly tempting body.

Still, as he undid the second button and moved on to the third the dress parted an inch at the top, and she was sure it wasn't an accident that his fingertips moved across her skin as he lowered them to button number four.

He worked slowly, and for every second she stood in front of him she felt as if her nerves were being pulled tight, stretched and tormented. At button number twenty he wasn't even halfway down her back, and a fever-pitch of heat was slamming through her.

Had he undone enough for her to take the dress off? She wasn't sure, at this stage, that she much cared if the dress got torn, so long as she could get it off without subjecting herself to another moment of…*this*.

Oh, maybe one more moment, she conceded weakly, sucking in a deep breath as his fingers grazed the flesh near where her bra should be. She hadn't needed one in the dress; its boning was sufficient.

Lower still, and the next two buttons came apart slowly. His fingers were achingly close to her lower back, to the inches of flesh that dipped towards her rear.

No man had ever seen her there, let alone touched her. His fingers lingered on her flesh, not moving downwards, just stroking her skin. Her pulse hammered and her eyes drifted shut on a tidal wave of imagining and longing, on hormonal needs that had long ago been relegated to the back of her mind.

'I... I...' The word stammered out as a dubious whisper. 'I can cope from here,' she said quietly, even though her body screamed in silent rejection of her comment.

He ignored her. His hands moved lower, to the next button, pushing it through its beaded loop, separating the fabric, and then his fingers were back, lingering on the flesh exposed by the undone dress.

'That's enough,' she said again, with more strength to her words, and she backed them up by moving a step forward, away from him, and slowly turning around.

His eyes almost electrified her. They were full of something—some strange emotion she couldn't process. His jaw was clenched tight and there was displeasure lingering in the harsh curves of his lips.

'Thank you,' she said softly, unaware of how pink her cheeks were, how enormous her pupils, how full her lower lip from the way she'd been savaging it with her teeth.

His eyes dropped to her mouth, and unknowingly she darted her tongue out and licked its edges. His own lips flickered in a small sign that he'd seen the nervous gesture, before his gaze travelled lower, to the curve of her breasts no longer held firm by the dress.

'Did you want to join me, *cara*?' he drawled, those eyes lifting back to hers with something like *knowing* buried in their depths.

She shook her head quickly from side to side, but still

she didn't move. Her throat was dry, parched, and it stung as though razorblades had been dragged along it.

'I think you do.'

His smile flickered again, but it was a harsh smile, thoroughly without pleasure.

'I think your nipples are tight and aching for my touch. I think your skin is covered in goosebumps because you want me to kiss you all over. I think you came to me tonight because you're curious about whether sleeping with me would feel like that kiss outside the chapel.'

She stifled a groan. 'But...'

'But?' he prompted, reaching out a hand and capturing hers, lifting it to his lips.

She had expected a kiss, but instead he dug his teeth into the ball of her thumb and arrows of heat and need shot through her, making her knees shake and her back sway.

She couldn't speak. She could barely think. Sensation and feeling were all that was left in her.

'But you are a virgin?' he prompted, her inexperience not even a question.

Was it emblazoned on her skin somewhere? Like the opposite of a scarlet letter and something only he could see?

'And you are saving yourself for someone you love?' He dropped her hand and let out a harsh sound of laughter. 'Rather a shame, given you've just married *me*.'

His eyes returned to hers with renewed speculation.

'How do women like you even *exist* in this day and age?'

There was anger in the question—an anger she didn't understand.

'Women like me?' She was surprised that her voice came out smooth and calm—cold, even.

'A virgin at twenty-two! Did your father lock you up in some kind of a chastity belt? Build a moat around Annersty?'

Emmeline shook her head. 'Neither.'

'So you just aren't interested in boys? In sex?'

Emmeline grimaced, her cheeks flushing darker. 'I guess not.'

'Your body's reaction to me would dispute that.'

'You're imagining it.'

His laugh was soft. 'Careful, Mrs Morelli. One touch and you melt like butter in my hands. Imagine if I pinned you back against that wall and kissed you as though I wanted so much more from you…'

The image filled her with a sense of strange confusion. She *wanted* him to do that. At least a part of her did. A crazy part. The part that had no pride and no rational ability to think.

'I'm sure I'd be very disappointing after the women you're used to,' she said stiffly, sounding so prim that she cringed inwardly.

He didn't say anything. His hand lifted and reached for the cap sleeve of her wedding dress, and slowly he guided it lower. So slowly that she had plenty of opportunities to say something. To object. But she didn't. She watched him with hooded eyes as he drifted it downwards, the fabric a torment as it pulled over the skin at her décolletage and then lower, exposing one of her breasts to the night air— and to his eyes.

They were neat breasts—not huge. But nor were they tiny—and they were firm. His eyes studied her, but she couldn't tell what he was thinking.

'Has a man ever touched you here?' he asked, the question gravelled.

She shook her head, biting down on her lip.

'Do you want *me* to touch you?'

A slick of moist heat formed between her legs and her eyes were anguished as they met his. She nodded. Just a tiny, almost involuntary movement of her head, accompanied by a mask of abject fear on her face.

He laughed softly, dropping his hands to her waist and yanking her closer. His body was hard all over, and she could feel the hint of his arousal through the fabric of her dress. A moan was thick in her throat.

'And I thought this wasn't an invitation,' he said with sardonic mockery, dropping his head so quickly she couldn't anticipate his intention, moving his mouth over the swell of her nipple and rolling his tongue over its unsuspecting tip.

She cried out at the stark feeling of pleasure. It came out of nowhere and it practically cut her off at the knees. His face was stubbled, and the contrast of his rough chin across her soft breast, and the warm wetness of his mouth, the lashing of his tongue...

She was melting—just as he'd said she would.

Swirling need pounded inside her, creating a vortex of responses she'd never imagined possible. Her body was experiencing its first awakening, and any thought of words or sense had fallen from her mind. There was only this.

She could hear herself mumbling incoherently, needing more than he was giving. A wave was building and she had no idea when and how it would crash. Only knew that it was imperative she stay on it, surf it right to its conclusion.

He dragged his lips higher and she cried out at this abandonment of her nipple. But his hand lifted up and cupped her breast, his thumb and forefinger taking the place of his mouth, twisting and plucking at its sensitised nerve-endings until she was crying out over and over, a fever-pitch of sensation rioting inside her.

His other hand pushed her forward, holding her tight against him as his lips sought hers, kissing her as his hands moved over her, and she cried into his mouth as the feelings became too much, her awareness of him too great.

'Oh, God, please...' she groaned into his mouth, with no idea of what she was asking for, only knowing that she needed *something*. Something he alone could give her.

He pulled away, lifting his head at the same moment as he dropped his hand and stepped backwards. His look was one she couldn't fathom. His chest was moving rapidly, his jaw clenched, but she couldn't understand why he'd stopped. Arousal was a raging river in her bloodstream.

'Go to your room, Emmeline.'

The way he said her name was like warm butter on hot toast. It dripped over her body.

Did he mean *with him*? Was he going to come with her? Her confusion was muddied by the way her body was crying out for him.

'I'm not interested in breaking in virgins.'

He turned away from her, stalking into his own room and picking up the glass of Scotch that was resting on the bedside table.

Her jaw dropped. She stared at him, confused and bereft. 'I'm sorry?'

'No need to apologise,' he said, with a shrug of those broad shoulders.

His hair was tousled. Had *she* done that? Had she run her fingers through it so that it now stood at odd angles, all messy and gorgeous?

'I'm not… I wasn't apologising,' she said, her voice thick with emotion. 'I don't understand why you stopped. I don't—'

His accent was coarse when he was angry. 'I'm not interested in sleeping with you. It would complicate things and undoubtedly be unsatisfying, for me.'

She drew in a harsh breath, her eyes flashing with pain.

'Don't be offended,' he murmured. 'I'm just used to more experienced lovers.'

Mortification curled her toes, flushing away any lingering desire. She spun on her heel, walking quickly down the corridor. It was only when she reached her room that she realised she'd come the whole way with her breast still uncovered.

Pietro stared into his whisky, his expression grim.

That had been a mistake. He could still taste her on h'

lips, smell her on his clothes, hear her sweet little moans of fierce, hot need as though she were still with him. Worse, he could *feel* her—like a phantom of the night he *could* be having if only he hadn't pulled things to a stop.

He was hungry for her…hard for her.

Col's daughter.

A groan permeated the silence of the room and bounced off the walls, condemning him as it echoed back. He'd married her to save her. He'd married her because he'd felt obliged to help his friend out.

Desiring his wife had never been part of the equation.

And he had to damned well do a better job of remembering that.

CHAPTER FOUR

IT WASN'T AS though she'd lived a particularly active and busy life. Confined to Annersty, her company had been made up predominantly of the staff, her father and the schoolfriends she'd caught up with from time to time for lunch.

But life in the villa was utterly silent.

A week after their wedding, and she'd barely seen her groom.

Thank God! The less she saw him, the less she'd need to remember what a fool she'd been in his arms. What a weak, willing, stupid *idiot*. Shame over that night still had the ability to make her blush.

She wandered further along the citrus grove, reaching up and plucking an orange blossom from a tree as she passed, bringing it to her nose and smelling its sweet fragrance.

Oh, they'd seen each other a few times. Once the next day, when she'd been walking around the villa like a lost lamb having escaped slaughter.

He'd come out of a room which she'd subsequently learned was his home office, full of enough technology to power a spaceship. Their eyes had met and he'd arched a brow—a simple gesture that had conveyed derision and scepticism. She'd dipped her head forward and moved past him, her heart pounding, her cheeks burning, her whole body confounded by mortification.

Two days had passed before she'd seen him again, that time in the evening. He'd walked in through the front door just as she was passing. And he'd looked tired. World-weary. He'd loosened his tie so he could undo his top button, and his jacket had been removed. She'd managed a tight smile and a nod of acknowledgement before she'd scurried away, and even kept her head up as she'd gone.

There were oranges growing in this part of the citrus grove, and further down the gently sloping lawn were lemons and limes. Beyond them were quinces and then olives.

It was a perfect Mediterranean garden—just as she'd always fantasised such a spot would be. She paused at the end of the row, turning around and looking down the hill towards Rome. The sky was streaked with orange and peach: a hint of the sunset that was to follow.

The warmth was quite delicious. She felt it on her skin and smiled. Her first genuine smile since before the wedding.

University would help. She needed activity. Something to do to keep her mind busy. Distracted from *him*. Her husband. And the treacherous way her body had responded to him.

She needed to remember her reasons for embarking on this charade! For the first time in her life she had a semblance of independent freedom, and she didn't want to waste it by pining for a man who didn't even like her. Hell, he barely seemed to notice she existed.

This marriage wasn't about lust and need. It wasn't about him.

It was about *her*. It was her vehicle to going out into the world at last.

A whisper of discontent breezed through her but, as always, Emmeline ignored it. She had stayed at Annersty, stayed under the same roof as her father, because it had been the *right* thing to do. Just as marrying Pietro to assuage her father's obvious concerns was the *right* thing to do.

And the fact that it spoke of a lack of faith in her own abilities? That it spoke of her being infantilised to an unbearable degree? She wouldn't think about that. She *couldn't*. For she knew where that path would take her, and criticising her father, whom she adored, was not something she would countenance.

All that mattered was that she had left home—*finally*. She was in Rome. A smile tickled at her lips and once more she felt the sunshine warm her skin.

At twenty-two, she'd finally done it!

Her phone buzzed, startling her out of her reverie. She lifted it from the back pocket of her jeans and Pietro's face stared back at her from the screen.

Her heart pounded as she swiped the screen across. 'Hello?'

'Emmeline.'

There it was again. The warm butter oozing over her skin. She closed her eyes and sank to the ground so that she could give him the full force of her concentration.

'Are you there?'

'Oh.' She blinked her eyes open and nodded. 'Yes. What is it?'

'Your father is coming for dinner tonight. Seven o'clock.'

Silence prickled between them. Then, 'Daddy's coming…*here*?'

'*Certamente*. Naturally I presumed you'd want to see him again before he leaves for the States.'

Emmeline nodded, but consternation ran through her. She *had* intended to see her father again—only for coffee the following morning, when it could be just the two of them.

'Right.' She bit down on her lip.

'My assistant will let Signora Verdi know,' he said, referring to the housekeeper Emmeline had met once or twice. A matronly woman who filled her with a sense of awe.

'Fine,' she said, a little too sharply.

'Though he knows our marriage was arranged to serve a purpose, I think it would be good for him to see that we are…getting along.'

Emmeline's stomach churned. *But we're not.*

'Do you?' she asked.

'*Si*. He loves you very much,' Pietro said, but his tone was weary. Impatient. 'Seeing you happy will make *him* happy.'

'So you want me to fake it?' she snapped, before she could catch back the sarcastic rejoinder.

'I want you to think of your *father*,' he said softly. 'As you've proved yourself so very good at in the past.'

'What's that supposed to mean?'

'You married me to make him happy.'

A woman's voice filtered through into the call and acid spiked Emmeline's blood. She couldn't make out what the woman said, but the tone was low. *Personal*.

Jealousy—unmistakable—pricked at her flesh.

'I'll be home by six. And, Emmeline? Perhaps wear a dress.'

Outrage simmered in her blood as she disconnected the call. Wear a damned *dress*? He actually thought he could boss her into wearing whatever the hell *he* wanted? What *he* thought would be appropriate? True, since their wedding she'd gone back to the clothes she felt most comfortable in, and they were hardly the kind of clothes that would set the world on fire. But of all the rude, misogynistic, barbaric things to say!

She stood up, her hands shaking as she jammed the phone back in her pocket and stared out at Rome.

She'd show him, wouldn't she?

At ten minutes past six Emmeline walked into the formal dining room, intending to pour herself a stiff drink to steel her nerves. What she hadn't expected was to see her husband already at the bar, shaking a cocktail mixer.

She froze on the threshold, taking a deep breath. She had only a second to compose her face into a mask of calm before he looked up. And when their eyes met she was thrilled to bits that she'd put her plan into action.

It had involved hours of shopping—her least favourite activity by a mile—but the effect was worth it.

The dress was exquisite. It had the advantage of looking as though it had been made for her—in a silk fabric that clung to her breasts and hips and stopped several inches shy of her knee—and it had batwing sleeves that fell to halfway down her hands, giving her a sense of comfort. The front had a deep vee—far deeper than she'd worn in her life before. She'd teamed it with a pair of espadrilles, which made the look a little more casual for an at-home dinner.

'I'll have what you're having,' she murmured, with a veneer of confidence she was far from feeling.

He began to shake the drink once more with a tight nod. 'Nice dress.'

The compliment made heat flood through her body. 'Thanks.'

'It makes it almost impossible to remember that you're a sweet and innocent little virgin bride.'

Emmeline fought her natural reaction of embarrassment, which he must have been trying to goad her towards. She saw beyond it. Her eyes narrowed and she moved closer, watching as he poured the martini into a glass and curling her fingers around its stem before he could even offer it to her.

'That bothers you?'

'It confuses me,' he corrected, reaching for more bottles of alcohol and sloshing it into the mixer. 'Particularly when you are dressed like this.'

'So one's choice of attire is an indicator of sexual inclination?'

'No. But dressed like this you are…irresistible.'

She sipped her drink to hide her reaction, and then spluttered as the alcohol burned its way down her throat. 'Ugh—that's strong.'

'It's a martini,' he pointed out seriously. 'It's meant to be strong.'

She nodded, taking another sip, and this time it went down more easily.

'Why do you dress like you do?' He returned to their previous conversation.

'Why is it any of your business?' she fired back, her eyes holding his even when she wanted to look away.

'It interests me. You are an attractive woman who goes out of her way to hide her assets. It makes no sense.'

Emmeline turned away from him, surprised by how easily he'd surmised the truth of her situation. 'Not everyone thinks their worth is derived from their appeal to the opposite sex.'

He made a sound of disagreement. 'But to take pride in one's appearance isn't just about meeting someone, or attracting a lover. It's a sign of self-love to want to look your best.'

'I don't agree,' she murmured, even though she'd never really thought beyond the opinions she'd formed in her teenage years.

'But don't you feel *better* in this dress?'

He walked towards her, a glass in his hand, his eyes holding hers. She stared at him, refusing to cower even as nerves fluttered inside her.

'Don't you *like* the way you look tonight?'

'I don't like the way you're looking at me as though you want to rip it off,' she said thickly, sipping her drink.

His laugh was a slow, sensual cord, wrapping around her. And was she imagining there was something like tension in the harmless sound? The air in her lungs was burning, exploding…

'We've already discussed that. I'm not interested in being the man who teaches you to feel.'

He lifted a finger and ran it across her lower lip, then dragged it lower, and lower still, to the fabric that joined at the centre of her chest. Then lower to her navel. She gasped as he ran it over her womanhood and paused, lingering there, padding his thumb across a part of her body that no man had ever touched.

'Though I'd be lying if I said that right now it doesn't hold at least *some* appeal.' His words appeared to be almost dragged from him, as though against his will.

Confusion and doubt were back. Uncertainty. Her insides were swirling and without her knowledge her body swayed forward.

'I wonder if you would orgasm quickly...' he murmured distractedly, and a sharp swell of need made her groan.

She nodded—but what was she even nodding at?

His lips twisted into a hard-fought smile and he pulled his hand away. She made a small whimper of anger, and before she knew what she was doing her free hand had curled around his wrist, catching it and dragging him back.

'Careful, *cara*. I don't think you want to play with a man like me.'

'Why are you tormenting me, then?' she asked thickly, holding his hand still and pushing herself against him, her eyes wide, her body screaming with need. 'Why stir me up and then walk away? Is that *fun* for you? Do you *like* seeing me like this?'

'Fun? No. As for why I like doing this... I can't say. I suppose I'm a little like a cat with a ball of wool. The idea of a twenty-two-year-old virgin is not something I can understand. You fascinate me and I just don't seem able to help myself.'

'Then don't,' she whispered, sipping the last of her drink. 'Please.' She lifted her arms around his neck, and her lips sought his. *'Please.'*

'You're Col's daughter.' The words were gravelled. Dark and husky.

'And yet you married me.' She ground her hips against him, her eyes showing her every need and desire.

He swore into her mouth in his own language, and then his hand was running down her thigh, finding the hem of her dress and lifting it, pushing aside the fabric of her silky underwear. He brushed his fingers over her throbbing heat and she gasped, the sensation unlike anything she could have imagined.

'I'm not the right man for you to want,' he said.

And he was so right. But sensual need had overtaken any vestige of common sense.

'Shut up,' she said hungrily, and he laughed against her lips.

'Shut up and do this?' he asked, pushing aside the fabric of her underwear.

Her heart skidded to a stop. All she could do was wait. Wait for what came next.

If Emmeline had been capable of rational thought she might have cared a little more that they were in a room anyone could have walked into at any point. But she didn't. Fortunately her husband had his wits about him, and Pietro used his body to guide her back, so that she collided with a wall near enough to a corner to provide some cover.

His finger invaded her heat gently at first, nudging inside, preparing her slowly for the unfamiliar sensation. She whimpered as he pushed deeper, a cry catching in her throat as she throbbed around him, her muscles tensing and squeezing.

'God,' she groaned, grinding her hips, and he laughed softly, moving his finger in a swirling motion while his thumb found the cluster of nerves at her entrance and teased it.

Her blood was boiling beneath her skin like liquid iron. She breathed out hungrily, the rasping sounds punctuating the silence of the room, and then she bit down on her lip as the sensations began to overflow, making her face blotchy with heat and sweat bead on her brow. She curled her fingers into his hair, holding him tight, and scrunched up her eyes.

The overload of feeling was something she hadn't prepared for. Waves of arousal and satisfaction ebbed through her, rocking her to the core. She stayed perfectly still, letting them pound against her nerve-endings, and then she tilted her head back, resting it against the wall as her breathing slowed to normal.

He eased his finger out of her wet, pulsing core, and she made a small sound of surprise at the unwelcome abandonment. When she opened her eyes he was staring down at her, his cheeks slashed with dark colour, his eyes silently assessing.

The world stopped spinning.

Everything stopped except her breathing and her awakening.

She lifted a hand, curled her fingers into his shirt, needing him for support. She held him while she caught her breath—in and out, in and out—and he watched her the whole time.

Finally, after long moments of silent, stretching heat, he spoke.

'You are far too sensual to have been uninterested in sex. Were you forbidden from dating?'

Her mind was still reeling from what had just happened. 'I need a minute...'

She bit down on her lip but couldn't stop the smile that spread across her face. She was beautiful at any time, really, but like this she was angelic.

'What the hell was *that*?'

His frown showed confusion. 'What?'

'I... I just... *Wow*.'

His groan was somehow scathing. 'Tell me you have at least *touched* yourself?'

Should she have? God, she supposed she *should* have had at least a passing curiosity in her own sexual development. Shame that she hadn't ever explored this side of herself made her flush to the roots of her hair.

'I...'

'What the hell happened to you?' he muttered. 'How can you have ignored these feelings? This desire?'

She swallowed, but the insulting tone of his voice was making her defensive. 'Not everyone sees sex as the be-all and end-all…'

'Yes, they do,' he disputed, a rough smile in his voice. 'At least anyone who's had really great sex does.' He shook his head. 'I wish I'd known this about you before agreeing to this damned marriage,' he said angrily. 'You *need* to have sex. And fast. But not with me.'

Her heart turned over in her chest. 'Why not with you?' she prompted.

His eyes flashed with rich frustration. 'I told you. Educating virgins isn't my thing. I'm not looking for the complications of that.'

'Even with your *wife*?' she responded archly.

'Not a *real* wife, remember?'

She bit down on her lip and nodded. 'So? What am I meant to do?'

'Well, you've waited twenty-two years. I guess a few more won't kill you.'

But it might kill *him*, Pietro thought as he turned his back on her. Walking away as though he was completely unaffected was damned near impossible with the raging hard-on between his legs.

A virgin. And yet so gorgeous and wanton and sensual. God, he wanted to take her to his bed. Despite what he'd said, the idea of teaching Emmeline Morelli *just* what her body was capable of stirred all kinds of animalistic masculine fantasies in his mind.

Being the first man to move inside her… Hell, the need to possess her was so savage it was beneath him.

He couldn't do it.

He'd married her because he loved Col Bovington like a father, and he would resist the urge to sleep with Emmeline for that exact reason.

No matter how damned much he was tempted.

He was the adult. The *experienced* adult. He had to control this beast of desire that was burning between them or he'd never forgive himself.

'I've always liked Rome.'

Col's voice had a wistful note. Or maybe Pietro was imagining things, because, in the back of his mind—much as it must be in Col's—was one single question: was this the last time Col would come to Italy? Was this the last time he'd look down on this ancient city?

'It's a city like no other.' Pride pierced Pietro's statement.

'Si,' Col agreed, a smile on his face. His eyes scanned the skyline, taking in the glistening lights of the city in the distance set against the inky black sky. 'How is she?'

Guilt slashed through Col. A feeling that was as unwelcome as it was foreign.

'Is she settling in? Happy? Adjusting?'

Pietro could close his eyes and remember the way her body had felt. The way her body had closed around his finger. The sounds she'd made as she'd come—hard.

He clamped his teeth together and focussed on the cupola of *il Vaticano*, willing his libido to remember where he was and with whom.

'It's still very early,' he said noncommittally.

'But you *are* getting along?' Col pushed.

Pietro expelled a breath. 'Sure.'

If you could count barely seeing each other and then him making her come for no reason other than he'd wanted to the second he'd seen her.

'Good.' If Col had doubts he didn't express them.

Pietro propped an elbow on the bannister and turned to face his friend slowly, weighing his words with caution. 'I think you need to tell her the truth.'

'About what?' Col joked.

It fell flat.

'She's stronger than you think.' God, Pietro hoped that was true. 'She'll cope with it. What she *won't* cope with is discovering you've lied to her.'

'I know her better than anyone.'

Col's words held a warning and Pietro heeded it. Not because he was afraid, but because the older man was probably right. Col had drawn a line in the sand and Pietro had no intention of walking over it.

He sighed gruffly. 'Then *consider* talking to her.'

'I can't. I need her to have more in her life than me.' His eyes shifted to Pietro and his skin looked pale all over. 'If she knows she'll come home.'

'So? Let her.'

'No. *Damn it!* The whole point of this is… I don't want her to nurse me. She deserves better than that.'

Pietro was very still, watchful. Waiting. 'You don't want her to nurse you? She's your daughter. When my father was sick—'

'It's not the same.' Col seemed to wince at the abruptness of his answer. 'I'm sorry, Pietro. I don't mean to belittle what you went through. But it's not the same.'

'Why not?'

'Because she is my only child. She will be orphaned when I die. Because she adores me and idolises me and I will not have her seeing me weakened and bedridden.' His jaw clenched firmly. 'I love her too much for that.'

An aeroplane passed overhead, leaving a trail of white cloud shimmering against the night sky. Pietro stared at it for a moment, wondering about the plane's destination and the people that occupied its belly. He wondered too at Col's 'love'. *Was* it love that could so easily lie? *Could* you love someone and deny them an opportunity to say goodbye?

'Did you think he looked tired?' Emmeline asked when Pietro returned to the lounge room, having said farewell to the American Senator.

The question caught him off-guard in its directness and perception. Then again, she was the much-adored daughter of the man—of course she'd notice small changes.

'Perhaps.' He sidestepped the question with surprising difficulty, his gaze resting on Emmeline's face.

She was distracted, toying with the hem of her dress, her fingers running over its silky edge as she nodded slowly. He knew what that dress felt like because he'd held it in his hands. He'd touched it and run his fingers over it and then he'd found her heart and driven her crazy against the wall.

'He did. I suppose it's jetlag… Or something.' She shook her head. 'I don't know.'

He sucked himself back into the conversation with difficulty, his arousal straining against the fabric of his pants. It was unwanted. So was the guilt that was sledging through him. Guilt at deceiving her despite the fact he owed his loyalty to Col and not to Emmeline.

'I'm going out,' he murmured, speaking the words before he'd even realised what he'd intended.

'Out?' She frowned, flicking a glance to the slim wristwatch she wore. 'It's after ten.'

His laugh was softly mocking. 'In Roma that is still early, *cara*.'

Her cheeks darkened, and her eyes were huge in her face as she looked at him. Her pretty face twisted into an expression he didn't recognise, but then it was gone. She was herself again. Unfazed, uninterested.

'Fine,' she said. 'Thank you for tonight.'

'You're *thanking* me?' he said with disbelief. 'I invited your father here for my own purposes as much as yours.'

Her smile was a twist of pale pink lips and then she stood, moving towards him.

'I didn't mean for that.'

As she passed him he caught a hint of her vanilla and rosebud fragrance and his gut clenched with barely controlled need. The desire to snake his hand out and catch her around the waist, to pull her to him and make her come again, filled him like an explosion. His head turned as she left the room, following her by instinct. The way that dress pulled against the curves of her arse as she walked…the way her long legs glided as if she was in a damned ballet…

He needed to get out of the house before he did something really rash. Like give in to temptation and invite his wife to his bed…

CHAPTER FIVE

HIS BEDROOM WAS far enough away from hers that she wouldn't necessarily hear when he came home each night. But somehow in the month they'd been married her ears had trained themselves to hear the slightest noise.

Like the opening of his bedroom door and the shutting of it a second later.

She heard the tell-tale click and her eyes drifted to the bedside table. She reached for her phone, checking the time. It was just after two.

How did he do that so often and still look so damned fresh the next day?

She tried not to think about who he'd been with and where. Though she didn't need to be a genius to work it out.

He'd made no effort to hide his virility, and they'd agreed before marrying that he'd continue his life as before. And he was doing that. It was Emmeline's fault that it no longer sat well with her.

She turned over in the bed, flipping on to her other side so she could stare out of the window. It was still warm, with the breeze that drifted in offering a hint of relief—but not much. The day had been sticky.

Was there only one woman in his life? Was it the beautiful redhead from the wedding?

She closed her eyes and the woman's face came to mind. She'd been stunning—but so clearly cosmetically enhanced she should have borne her surgeon's signature somewhere on her body. Was that the kind of woman he went for?

Emmeline would never be like that.

She blinked her eyes open but it was too late. An image

of her mother had seared into her brain and she made a small sound in the dark room.

Patrice Bovington had been beautiful too. Stunning without cosmetic enhancement. But that hadn't stopped her from seeing her doctor regularly, having a little Botox dabbed into her forehead, a tad of filler in her lips. Over the years she'd changed, but so subtly that it was only in looking back at photos that Emmeline could recognise the fact that beautifying herself had become an unhealthy obsession for her mother.

And a foolish one too. For there would always someone more beautiful, more svelte, younger. Why make one's appearance the hallmark of one's self-esteem?

'You could almost be pretty if you put some effort in.'

She sat upright in the bed, the fever in her blood burning out of control. Did he *know* that looking pretty had led to all the problems she'd had with her mother? Guilt made her stomach flop as she remembered their last argument. The day before Patrice had driven her Mercedes convertible into an enormous elm around the corner from the house.

Emmeline rolled back to her other side, staring at the wall now. But it was no good. Her mind was wide awake, her legs restless, her body warm.

She sat up, then pushed her feet out of the bed.

She'd only swum a handful of times since arriving at the villa. Both times when she'd known Pietro was out of the house.

And now he was fast asleep—probably exhausted from seducing some beautiful woman all evening.

Emmeline changed into her swimsuit quietly. If she could hear the sound of *his* door clicking open and shut then he could certainly hear hers. She tiptoed out into the corridor, pausing for a second, her breath offensively loud in the silent evening.

The stairs were around ten steps away. She moved quietly but quickly, like some kind of night-time ninja.

She'd just wrapped her fingers around the top of the bannister when his door was flung open.

He stood there in a pair of shorts, otherwise naked, his
scowl landing on her as though she'd driven a herd of el-
ephants through the house.

'Did I wake you?' she whispered, not sure why she was
keeping her voice down given the fact they were the only
two in the house.

'No. I was up.' His eyes dropped to the swimsuit that was
clearly on display, his frown deepening. 'It appears we've
had the same idea.'

'Oh.' She didn't dare look at his shorts but, yes, she supposed they *could* be swimming trunks. 'It's a hot night...'
she finished lamely.

His grunt was an agreement of sorts.

She prevaricated on the steps for a moment, contemplating going back to her room and then deciding against
it. When he began to move towards her, though, her pulse
kicked up a notch. Her breath was held in her throat.

'What are you doing?'

He looked at her as though she'd gone mad. 'Going for
a swim. We just discussed this.'

'Oh. I thought...' She closed her eyes and breathed in
deeply; it was a mistake. The smell of him filled her, reminding her of how it had felt when he'd touched her so
intimately.

'The pool is more than big enough for the both of us.'

He was right, of course, and now she felt like an even bigger idiot. It was bad enough that he thought her some kind
of inexperienced prim virgin. Worse when she confirmed
those thoughts by acting just like one.

'I know that,' she snapped, resuming her journey down
the stairs, moving quickly to stay ahead of him.

At the bottom she moved ahead—not waiting for him,
not wanting him to think that she saw this as a joint venture.

He wanted to swim and she wanted to swim. That didn't mean they would be swimming *together*.

The air on the deck was noticeably cooler, but it was still a sultry, muggy night. It felt as though a huge bandage was pressing down on Rome, holding in its heat, making breathing difficult.

Emmeline dropped her towel onto a lounger and turned towards the pool—just as Pietro dived into the water, his body strong and flexed as he hit the surface and went underneath.

He was like a god, tanned and muscular, as if he'd been carved from stone. She watched the water separate as if to welcome him and then conceal him again, almost by magic. Her breath was held again inside her lungs—waiting, apparently, for the moment he reappeared at the other end of the pool when she let out a slow sigh.

'Well?' He turned to face her. 'Are you joining me, Mrs Morelli?'

Her eyes met his, and if she'd known about the look of anguished surrender in them she would have tried harder to conceal her feelings. But she didn't.

The moonlight sliced through her as she moved to the water's edge and dipped her toe in. As she'd hoped, it was deliciously cool.

She sat on the edge and then eased herself into the water. It reached up to her waist and enveloped her in its thick, luxuriant relief.

She didn't swim. Rather she walked across the pool, her face deliberately averted from his. He might have found it entertaining if he hadn't already been frustrated beyond belief. The idea of a cold swim had been essentially to serve the same purpose a cold shower might have. Instead his wife was swimming with him, her pert breasts outlined by the light cast from the moon, her enigmatic, aristocratic face tilted angrily away from him.

Was she angry with him? And, if so, why did he like the

idea so much? Why did he want to inspire that hot, fierce temper in her?

He dived underwater and swam the length of the pool, pretending not to notice as he passed her by and splashed water in her general direction.

When he surfaced she'd moved to the other end of the pool.

Was she hiding from him? The idea of her being the mouse to his cat was like a red rag to a bull. He dived underwater again and swam beneath the surface, stealthy and silent, and had the pleasure of seeing surprise on her face when he lifted himself up right beside her.

'Nice evening?' she murmured, her eyes scanning his face, her anger flashing more visibly now.

'Not really,' he said noncommittally.

Without developing some kind of mystical psychic ability she had no idea what he meant by that. She turned her head away, her eyes soaking in the view of Rome in the distance without really seeing it. Even at this early hour of the morning the city was alive, its buildings outlined with light, all its ancient stories winding around themselves, whispering through the walls to those who wanted to listen.

'Do you do this often?' He turned to face her, his body achingly close.

'No.'

'Nor do I. Strange that we both had the same idea tonight.'

'Not really. It's been muggy as hell today,' she pointed out logically. 'I couldn't sleep.'

He nodded, but his eyes were speculative. 'And in general?' he prompted.

God, she looked young like this—bathed in moonlight and the salt water of his pool.

Her eyes were blank. 'What do you mean?'

He compressed his lips. 'Are you settling in well to Rome?'

'Oh.' She was grateful for the night, grateful that it hid her blush. 'Yes. I've sent off my enrolment forms. I'll start university next term.'

'What will you study?'

'Psychology.' She looked away from his intense gaze, feeling that he saw way too much. 'It's always interested me.'

'I see.' He frowned thoughtfully. 'I would have imagined you doing history, or perhaps English literature.'

She lifted a hand and ran it over the water's surface, feeling its thick undulations beneath her fingertips.

'Why? Because I'm bookish? Because I look as though I'd be perfectly at home under bags of dust in an ancient library?'

His smile was perfunctory. 'No.'

He moved closer towards her, and again she had the sense that he was chasing her. Ridiculous when they were simply floating at the same end of the pool. Besides, why would a man like Pietro Morelli chase her?

'Because the last time I saw you, you spent the entire night staring at very old paintings as though they were the beginning and end of your existence.'

Emmeline's smile was genuine. 'I'd never seen works of art like that before. The Dutch Masters have always fascinated me.'

'So you can see, then, why I thought of history—perhaps art history—as your university subject of choice?'

'Oh, I *love* art.' She nodded. 'And old things in general.' She tilted her head back into the water, wetting her hair. It draped down her back like a silken curtain. 'But I've wanted to do psychology for almost as long as I can remember.'

Not quite true. She could recall the exact moment when it had dawned on her that a lot of people's minds needed fixing.

Apparently Pietro was drawing the same conclusion. 'When did you learn the truth about your mother's death?'

'I thought I told you?' she murmured quietly, feeling the night wrapping around them like a blanket. 'I knew at the time.'

'I'm sorry you had to experience that loss. And so young.'

Emmeline rarely spoke about her mother. Her father never wanted to talk about her, and Emmeline didn't really have anyone else to confide in about something of that nature. But, perhaps because Pietro had known Patrice, Emmeline felt her strongly held borders dropping.

'She'd been unhappy for a long time. I didn't expect her to die, but it wasn't a complete surprise, somehow.'

'Unhappy how?' Pietro pushed, moving closer.

His recollections of Patrice were vague. She'd been drop-dead gorgeous, and kind enough. Perhaps there'd been a coldness to her, a sense of disconnection. He'd been a young man when he'd last seen her and his thoughts weren't easy to recall.

'Oh, you know…' Emmeline's smile was uneven, her eyes not quite meeting his.

'No, I don't. That's why I asked you.'

How could Emmeline answer? There'd been that morning when she'd come downstairs to find her mother passed out, two empty bottles of gin at her feet, her make-up ruined by her tears. And there'd been all the little nips and tucks, of course. But the biggest clue had been the control she'd begun to exert over Emmeline.

Even as a teenager Emmeline had known it wasn't right—that there was something unhealthy about her mother's desire to infantilise Emmeline, to keep her from experimenting with clothes and fashion. Discouraging Emmeline's attempts on improving her image had been one thing, but knowingly pushing her towards unflattering hairstyles and prohibiting her from anything except the wardrobe she, Patrice, had selected…

It had taken years for Emmeline to understand her mother's motivations and they'd left her reeling.

'Lots of things,' she said vaguely, shaking her head.

Perhaps it was the raw pain in his wife's voice that stalled Pietro from pushing further. For whatever reason, he let the matter go for a moment.

'Psychology will no doubt be very interesting,' he said quietly. 'When do you begin?'

'A month.'

He nodded. 'There's still time for you to adapt to life here, then.'

'I think I'm just about adapted,' she said quietly.

He was so close now that when he moved the water rippled in response and it almost felt as though he was touching her. She knew she should put some distance between them, but she'd hardly seen him for a month. This nearness was like a highly addictive form of crack cocaine.

'You have been bunkered here in the villa,' he said softly. 'It's time for you to start coming out with me. You are my wife. There are events. Functions. Things to attend.'

'Oh.' She bit down on her lip and uncertainty glimmered in her eyes. She had been the one who'd suggested they needed to keep up a certain public persona. But now the idea filled her with doubts. 'I don't know if that's really necessary…'

'Not all the time, no. But there are certain things you can no longer avoid.'

'I haven't been *avoiding* anything.'

As soon as she said it she knew it was a lie. She *had* been holed up in his house as much as possible—reading, emailing, reading some more. Keeping her ears permanently trained on noises that might herald Pietro's arrival so that she could scamper away.

'My bank organises a banquet every summer. It is a Midsummer's Eve theme—very beautiful and enjoyable. You'll come with me.'

She arched a brow, instantly resenting his imperious tone. 'Oh, I will, will I?'

'*Si.*'

His fingers brushed against hers underwater. Surely it wasn't an accident? Her heart didn't think it was. It pounded hard against the fabric of her being with a thundering beat that he must be able to hear.

'I usually take a date. That would raise eyebrows this year.'

She smiled, but it was a distracted smile. He'd been late home almost every night in the month since they had been married. It was impossible to believe he hadn't been seen out with different women in that time.

The thought made her heart race, but for a less palatable reason now. *Jealousy.* Not because she cared for him or wanted him, she hastened to reassure herself. But because he was *hers.* Her husband. And she didn't particularly want people thinking that he was straying from the marital bed already.

Marital bed.

What a joke.

Longing surged inside her.

The need he had awoken was at fever-pitch.

She controlled it as best she could, but her mind continued to toss up images of just what it would be like to be made love to by a man like her husband.

The reality wouldn't live up to her fantasies, Emmeline was certain.

'It's Friday night,' he murmured.

Her eyes clashed with his and the longing was back, begging her to do something—anything—to indulge it.

'You want me to go?' she asked quietly.

'I think you should come, *si.*'

She bit down on her lip, and then spoke before she could question the wisdom of her proposition.

'Well,' she said thoughtfully, 'there's something I want too. I suggest we…trade.'

'Oh? And what is it that you want, Mrs Morelli?'

Say the words... Say the words... her courage pushed angrily.

'I want you to sleep with me.'

They blurted out of her on the warm breeze that rushed past.

Pietro barely reacted. Just a tightening around his lips showed that he'd heard her proposition and was digesting it.

'I told you—'

Emmeline waved a hand in the air. 'That you're not interested in being my first lover,' she said, with a shrug of her shoulders. 'But it's too late for that. You've shown me what my body can feel and I want to know more.'

'I'm not a damned *teacher*.'

'No. You're my husband.'

His eyes narrowed, and his breath was clearly tearing from his body.

'I'm not going to sleep with you,' he said with an angry shake of his head.

God, she was Col's *daughter*, and he'd married her to ease the mind of his dying friend.

But surely Col knew enough of Pietro's ways to know that this was a possibility.

Why was Pietro fighting it so hard?

The last month had been a living torture as he'd forced himself to keep his distance, never sure if the flame between them would burst out of control.

'I'll go to this...this banquet with you. And whatever else you want me to attend. But I need to know what it feels like.'

'Why now?' he asked, the question thick in his throat.

'I didn't *mean* to not sleep with anyone. I just never met a guy I was interested in. Honestly, I started to think I was kind of...sexually not all *there*. All my friends have been in relationships forever.' She bit down on her lip.

'You lost your mother at a vulnerable time in your life,' he said gently.

'Yes, that's true. It changed who I am.' Her clear amber gaze held his for a long moment. 'Life sort of got away from me. I feel like I've spent the last seven years in a sort of stasis and now I'm ready to start living again. I want to wake up.'

Be brave. Be brave.

She closed the distance between them, surprising him when she wrapped her arms around his neck. 'I want *you* to wake me up.'

His eyes were lightly mocking as they stared back down at her, but he didn't push her away. He didn't remove her touch.

'I'm not Prince Charming, Sleeping Beauty.' The words were cold. Determined.

'I know that.' She blinked her eyes. 'I don't need you to be.'

'I wouldn't have married you if I'd known,' he said with an angry shake of his head. 'You deserve to find someone yourself. Someone you care about.'

'She'll be vulnerable to fortune-hunters.'

Yes, Emmeline—the sweet, naïve virgin heiress—sure as hell would have been vulnerable. She might as well have had a target on her back for some guy to come along and sweep her off her feet.

All Col's reasons for pursuing this marriage were blindingly clear to Pietro. What had at one point seemed ridiculously absurd now made absolute sense. Even without the fortune she would inherit, her youthful innocence would mark her as the easiest target for no-good bastards on the lookout for an easy buck.

'This isn't about happily-ever-after,' Emmeline said with a grim determination. 'I'm twenty-two, and until our wedding day I'd never even kissed a guy.'

She dropped her eyes, the admission making her insides squirm with embarrassment.

'I feel like some dusty old antique no one's wanted to

pick up off the shelf.' Her throat moved as she swallowed. 'But when you look at me it's like… I *get* it. I get what everyone's talking about. I understand—finally—the appeal of sex. And I don't want to die a virgin.'

He couldn't help but laugh softly at her dramatic end note. 'You are not going to die a virgin. You are still young.'

'Yes, but…if not now, when? *Who?*'

An excellent question.

Suddenly the idea of someone else taking this precious gift was anathema to Pietro. The red-blooded man that was thick in his blood had begun to see his wife as *his*. Not just a bride of convenience, but a woman in *his* home, under *his* protection. Was he to let her go one day, knowing some other man would take what he, Pietro, had so nobly declined?

He groaned softly, knowing then that the devil was on his shoulder and he was listening to his urgings. He was listening when he should be speaking sense, reminding her of what they were.

'You are too young for me,' he said, with a finality that his hard-as-stone cock wasn't happy with. 'And too inexperienced.'

He reached up, wrapping his hands around her wrists, pulling them away from his neck. As he glided them through the water, resting them at her sides, her pert breasts pressed into him.

His arousal jerked and for the briefest moment his will-power left him. How easy it would be to do what she wanted! She was handing herself to him on a silver platter.

But he'd regret it.

One way or another he'd conquer this desire—because nothing and no one *ever* got the best of Pietro Morelli.

CHAPTER SIX

Dio. Since when had she started wearing skirts like that?

Pietro stared out of the villa window, his concentration sapped by the image of his wife in a scrap of denim that barely covered her arse and a simple white strappy top.

Without a bra.

The pert outlines of her breasts were clearly visible, as were the hardened nubs of her nipples, straining at the fabric. She was tapping a pen against her mouth, her eyes intent on the book she had propped on her knees. But his eyes were lost on her lips. Lips that were slightly parted, full and pink, glistening as though she'd just licked them.

'I'm twenty-two and until our wedding day I'd never kissed a guy.'

A fierce burst of possession tore through him. Those lips had welcomed his claim on them, had sought his mouth and kissed him back. They'd parted for his invasion.

She'd tasted so sweet.

His eyes swept closed as he remembered the way she'd come to him on their wedding night, all pink-cheeked and nervous. The way she'd stood like a rabbit caught in bright headlights—which was exactly what she'd been! How could she have understood the onslaught of sensual heat that was flaring up between them?

Even for Pietro it was proving difficult to process. And impossible to ignore, apparently. Did she have any idea what her presence was doing to him? Here in his house… his virgin bride?

His for the taking.

The idea spread like wildfire through his body. It took

every ounce of his willpower not to give in to temptation and act on it.

But it would be so wrong. Other women were for meaningless sex. She was *different*. Not someone he could desire. She was someone he needed to protect. Yes, as a brother would protect his sister.

Ugh. Not as a brother!

She tossed her dark hair over one shoulder and her eyes lifted almost unconsciously. She was clearly lost in thought, her mind wandering as her eyes did the same.

Pietro jerked his own head down, returning his concentration to the marketing reports he'd been given that morning. Or at least pretending to.

But it was incredibly dull reading, and his wife was just metres away, her long legs calling to him...

With a noise of impatience he scraped his chair back and strode towards the glass doors, his expression grim.

'Are you wearing suntan lotion?' he asked, pushing the door open wider as he stepped through it.

Emmeline's frown showed that she'd been deep in thought—that his question had seemed to come from a long way away.

'Are you wearing suntan lotion?'

Her face showed bemusement. 'No. But it's after five. I'm sure I'll be—'

'The Roman sun still has bite.' He turned on his heel and disappeared, returning a moment later with a small yellow tube. 'Here.'

He tossed it down on the lounger and she picked it up, unscrewing the lid slowly. His eyes followed her progress and he crossed his arms over his chest, his manner imposing.

He had been imposing even *before* Emmeline had factored in her embarrassing confession and request in the pool last night. No. Not last night: in the early hours of that same morning.

The colour in her cheeks now had nothing to do with the fact that she'd been reading by the pool for hours. Though why she'd chosen to return to the scene of the crime was beyond Emmeline. In that moment, confronted by the ghost of what a fool she'd been, she wished she was anywhere else.

She flicked the cap off the bottle and squeezed some cream into her hands, then rubbed it over her exposed arms and the vee of her neck.

Pietro watched, but his temper wasn't improved by the display. Nor was it improved when she placed more cream into her palm and reached down to spread it over her legs. Legs that were long, tanned and smooth…

He looked away from her, his arms still crossed.

But he could see her in his mind. As she'd been in the pool early that morning—her hair like a shimmering black veil, her eyes enormous, her lips curved into a smile.

Her question hadn't been unreasonable. Hell, he'd backed her up against a wall and slid a finger into her wet heat until she'd come in his arms. Of *course* she was curious.

He'd stirred something inside her and now he was preventing her from experimenting. From exploring that side of her.

It wasn't fair.

Was she annoyed that he'd turned her down?

'The thing is,' he said, as though their conversation from the night before was still going, had simply been paused for a few hours while they slept and he worked. 'You're my wife, and if we were to sleep together it would be too complicated…'

Her eyes flew to his face, the statement knocking her off balance completely. She hadn't expected this, but she managed to pick up the threads of their negotiation as though it were just that—a simple business deal.

'Complicated how?'

'I have nothing to offer.' He spoke stiffly, his shoulders

squared. 'I'm not interested in a relationship, and I suspect you'll blur those lines if I do what you ask of me.'

She nodded slowly and then shrugged her shoulders. 'Sure.'

Her easy acceptance was insulting. 'If you came to want more from me I can promise you I wouldn't offer it.'

She bit down on her lip and shrugged once more. 'Whatever. It's not important. Forget I mentioned it.'

He looked away once more. *Why* did she have such beautiful legs? Out of nowhere he pictured them wrapped around his waist as he pulled her closer, pressing into her.

His arousal throbbed painfully.

'I know I can't hold a candle to your usual…um…lovers. It was stupid of me to even suggest it.'

'You are *very* different,' he agreed softly.

Her battered pride was almost debilitating in its intensity. He didn't need to *tell* her how different she was. She'd seen the photos. He'd all but told her that she wasn't attractive. God, she'd thrown herself at his feet! Of all the foolish, embarrassing, childish, stupid things to do!

Regret washed over her heart. But pride was beating its drum, forcing her to remember who she was and what she wanted in life. This marriage was a stepping stone for Emmeline—a brick path to freedom.

'I think I just got carried away last night. The moon… The water… The heat…' Her smile was dismissive. 'It won't happen again.'

She briefly met his eyes and then looked back to her book, pretending fascination with the page she was on even as the words swam before her eyes.

It won't happen again.

'That is for the best, *cara*.'

He spun on his heel and stalked back inside the villa before he gave in to temptation and pulled her to her feet, roughly against his chest, and plundered those sweet lips that had been tempting him all afternoon.

* * *

Rafe let out a low whistle, his eyes locked on some point across the room. Pietro followed his brother's gaze, though he knew what he'd see.

His wife, Emmeline Morelli, looking as if she'd walked out of a goddamned *Vogue* photo-shoot. Her dress was beautiful, but every woman at this event was draped in couture and dripping with diamonds. It was Emmeline he saw.

Her long dark hair had been set in loose curls that waved around her back, and the dress itself was a sort of Grecian style, in a cream fabric that gathered beneath her breasts then fell in floaty, gauzy swathes to her feet, which were clad in shimmering gold sandals. She wore a snake bracelet on her upper arm, and a circle of gold around her head.

She looked like a very beautiful, very sexy fairy. Something the two men she had been locked in conversation with for the past twenty minutes seemed eminently aware of. Her face was animated as they spoke, her eyes illuminated and her laugh frequent.

Hot, white need snaked through him.

'Married life seems to agree with Mrs Morelli,' Rafe said, and grinned, grabbing a glass of wine from a tray being walked past by a waiter.

'*Si,*' Pietro agreed, willing himself to look away but finding it almost impossible.

'And you?' Rafe turned to study his brother, a smile twitching at the corners of his lips. 'I would ask how *you're* finding the leap into married life, but I can see for myself that it is no hardship.'

Pietro's expression was shuttered.

'No comment, eh?' Rafe laughed good-naturedly.

A muscle jerked in Pietro's jaw. 'There are too many of these twinkling lights,' he snapped, changing the subject. 'I feel like they are everywhere I look.'

Rafe's laugh was annoying Pietro. *Everything* was annoying him. Who the hell *were* those men? Had she met them before? It was possible that they had dealings in America…that they knew Col. Perhaps she'd hosted them at the plantation. Maybe they were old friends.

A groan of resentment died in his throat. He nodded dismissively at his brother. 'I'll speak to you later.'

Pietro moved quickly, cutting through the crowd, ignoring any attempt to draw him into conversation. But there were so many people between him and his wife and he was the man of the hour, in huge demand.

He spent a few minutes in curt exchange with a board member, and then smiled briefly at his cousin Lorena before getting within striking range of his wife.

He paused, watching her up close for a few seconds, seeing the way her face moved while in conversation.

Guilt was not something he was used to and yet he felt it now. Her father was one of his most valued friends, and yet he'd hardly taken the time to speak to Emmeline. What was making her laugh like that? What did she find funny?

He compressed his lips and moved closer, but at the moment of his approach the two men stepped away—not before one of them pressed a kiss against Emmeline's cheek and almost earned an angry rebuke from Pietro.

'Oh, Pietro.' She blinked up at him, her expression shifting swiftly from enthusiasm to confusion.

His chest felt as if it had been rolled over by a car. He manoeuvred his body, placing himself between Emmeline and the crowd, her back almost touching the wall, so that both of them would be reminded of the night he'd made her come.

Her breath snagged in her throat. She stared up at him, a pulse beating wildly in her throat.

'Who were those men?'

A frown tugged at her lips, but only for a second. Then the enthusiasm was back in her eyes, apparently irrepressible.

'Oh, they're professors at the university! One of them is

a lecturer in the psychology department. It's going to be so helpful to have people there I know already.'

Great. She'd continue to see people who looked at her as though she was an ice cream they wanted to lick regularly.

Anger made common sense impossible. 'You should be with me,' he grunted angrily. 'Not talking to strange men.'

'They weren't *strange* men—they were perfectly nice. And staying with you at something like this is impossible,' she responded curtly. 'Everyone wants to talk to *you*, not me.'

'I don't care; you're my wife.'

'Yes, your *wife*. Not an accessory,' she pointed out softly, keeping her voice low purely out of recognition of the fact that there were people everywhere.

'We agreed that we wouldn't draw attention to our relationship or lack thereof. I will *not* have people gossip that my wife's interest is straying.'

She blinked up at him, her face pale. 'You must be kidding me! Your ego is wounded because I was talking to two probably married professors from the university I'm going to attend?'

'You weren't just *talking.* You were…'

'What? You think I was *flirting*?' she said with disbelief. 'You're unbelievable.'

'Forse,' he acknowledged. 'Nevertheless, I want you to stay with me tonight.'

Emmeline glared up at him angrily. She might have moved hell and high water to please her father, but that was where her submissive tendencies ended.

'No way.' To her chagrin, tears sparkled on her eyelashes. She blinked them away angrily. 'Right now you're the last person I want to see.'

And then, with her back up against the wall—literally—he placed a hand on her hip and stroked her flesh gently, teasing her, making her pulse throb.

'Why do I find that so hard to believe?' he asked throatily, the words a hoarse demand.

'Don't.'

She bit down on her lower lip, and there was such a look of need in her eyes and confusion in her face that he almost dropped his hand.

Almost…but not quite. 'Don't what?'

Don't use this against me, she thought, her heart hurting. This desire she wasn't used to was tormenting her enough already.

He moved a little closer, dropping his head by degrees, so that when he spoke his words were whispered into her ear. 'Go and wait for me in the car. It's time for us to leave.'

'We've only been here an hour,' she pointed out huskily, her body attuned to every shift in his.

'Fifty-nine minutes too long,' he responded.

'Why are we leaving?'

Because I don't want to watch you being drooled over by any other man.

Because I want to make love to you.

Because you're mine.

He shook his head. 'It's time. I'll be out as soon as possible.'

But it was not so easy for Pietro to depart. By the time he'd said goodbye to the more influential of the guests Emmeline had been cooling her heels in the car for almost a half-hour, and it was clear that she was in a foul mood.

'Am I being punished for enjoying a conversation?' she demanded, the second he was in the driver's seat.

'No.' He revved the car to life and floored the accelerator.

He shifted a sidelong look her way. Her jaw was clenched, her hands gripped tightly in her lap, her body vibrating with barely suppressed anger.

'I went to a lot of effort to come to this damned thing tonight because you told me you wanted me to! No, you told me I *had* to! I don't appreciate being frog-marched out like some errant schoolgirl.'

Oh, God. The last thing he needed was to picture his wife as a schoolgirl. *Hell.* She *had* been a schoolgirl the first time he'd seen her, around the time of Patrice's funeral. She'd appeared in the hallway in a navy blue dress, with a blazer that fell to her hips, and even then Pietro had known she had the potential to be trouble for him.

He had unconsciously stayed away from the plantation after that, avoiding her as much as he could. It hadn't always been possible—there'd been a few dinners and parties, in the intervening years—but for the most part he'd kept a very wise distance.

Something about Col Bovington's daughter had sent all his warning sensors haywire, and now he knew how right his instincts had been.

'I was having a good time,' she continued angrily, her gaze focussed on the streets of Rome as they drove.

She didn't know it well enough yet to recognise that they were heading out of the city—away from his villa.

'I'm glad,' he said quietly. 'But those men were all over you and you were encouraging them.'

'How can you *say* that? We were just talking.'

'Believe me, *cara*, with you in that dress no man will be "just talking" to you.'

Her jaw dropped and she whipped around to face him, her face lashed by pain. 'It's a *nice* dress. A *respectable* dress.'

'You look good enough to eat—and I'm sure as hell not the only man who thought so.'

Emmeline's face drained of all colour, and all the fight seemed to leave her in one second.

Pietro didn't notice.

'You're my *wife*! It doesn't matter that our marriage is unconventional. I will not have you dragging my name through the mud...'

'Your name…' She rolled her eyes, but her words were just a whisper. 'For such a powerful, successful guy, you've got major insecurity about your reputation.'

He slammed his palm into the steering wheel, anger coursing through him. It wasn't about that! Didn't she understand? He had *no* insecurities; his virility left him little room for doubt on that score. It was just a stupid excuse. Something he could say that would achieve the desired result—which was what? Her total isolation? *Dio.* What kind of barbaric son-of-a-bitch was he turning into?

'*You* said I should change how I look.'

She was shivering now—a reaction Pietro finally recognised, though he couldn't understand it. Unconsciously he drove faster, turning the car onto the highway and picking up speed.

'You said that I had to be what people would expect of your wife. Haven't I done that?'

He gripped the steering wheel tighter, his eyes focussed on the night sky ahead. She'd done it—only far too well for his liking.

'You would have complained if I'd come to that thing tonight wearing something I was comfortable in—something I usually wear. Now you're complaining because I'm dressed like any of those other women who were there.' She shook her head from side to side. 'That's not fair.'

It wasn't—she was right. But nothing about this was fair! He'd been *happy* before marrying Emmeline. Happy in his life…happy with the endless parade of women he'd taken to his bed.

And now?

He had no damned idea.

'Where are we going?' she asked, as if waking from a dream and suddenly realising that they were well outside the city.

'Not much further,' he promised, his eyes flicking to the

clock in the centre of the dashboard, willing the distance to shorten. 'Close your eyes, *cara*.'

'I'm too angry to sleep,' she snapped, but she did sit back in her seat, and a moment later her eyes fluttered closed.

Her steady, rhythmic breathing informed him that she'd drifted off despite her protestations. He drove the rest of the way in a silent car, but his thoughts were still screaming at him.

What he was planning was stupid, crazy, and he'd decided firmly against it. But after seeing her with those men... He no longer had a choice.

He pulled the car through the electric gates to the farmhouse and then crept up the gravelled driveway.

Though no one lived there, he had a team who kept it permanently tidy and stocked.

His headlights illuminated the pots of geraniums and lavender that stood on either side of the green-painted door.

He went inside, checking from room to room, leaving the bedroom until last. It was an enormous space, with an old iron bed in the middle. The floor was tiled and the shutters were closed over the windows, making it pitch-black. In the morning light would filter through the cracks, and when the shutters were open a stunning view of the countryside would open up, with the ocean glistening beyond the rolling hills.

It didn't take him long to make the room ready, and then he went back to the car.

Emmeline was still asleep, and he knew the kindest thing to do would be to carry her inside and leave her to sleep.

But fire was raging through his body, tormenting him as much as it was her, and there was only one answer to that.

He opened her door and crouched down, hesitating for a second before pressing his lips to hers.

In her drowsy state, she opened her mouth to receive his and moaned, lifting her hands to curl them around his neck, her fingers twisting in the dark hair at his nape.

'Pietro…' she moaned, and he undid her seatbelt then lifted her out of the car in one easy movement. He cradled her against his chest, carrying her with grim determination into the house. He moved up the stairs at the front, through the corridor and then up the flight of internal stairs.

'Where are we?' she asked, looking around and then, as if remembering that she was annoyed with him, pushing at his chest. 'I can walk.'

'I'm aware of that.'

He shouldered the door of the bedroom open and Emmeline looked around, a soft gasp escaping her lips. Dozens of candles had been lit, casting a golden glow in the room.

The *bedroom*.

Music was coming from somewhere, a lilting song in his native language that did something strange to her heartbeat.

He placed her down on her feet with care and then straightened, catching her face between his hands. 'You have two choices, Emmeline.'

'And what are those?'

'You may use this room to sleep,' he said softly, stroking her cheek. 'Or we will be together here tonight. Your first time. *Our* first time.'

He dropped his lips to hers softly, studying her, waiting. He felt as if he'd been waiting an eternity already…

CHAPTER SEVEN

THE AIR STRETCHED between them, thin and tense. Emmeline's heart was rabbiting about in her chest. She'd wanted this for a *really* long time. Since their wedding? Or since her father had first suggested this hare-brained idea?

The thought of marriage to the charismatic tycoon she'd adored from afar for as long as she could remember had scared the heck out of her—mainly because she'd known she'd find it impossible not to fall head over heels in lust with the confirmed bachelor.

And love? Would sleeping with him blur the lines of what they were, just as he'd said? And was she brave enough to reject him when he was offering something she wanted so badly?

She blinked up at him, doubt making her voice quiet. 'I'm not tired.'

He expelled a breath he hadn't realised he'd been holding.

'Thank God for that.'

And now his patience deserted him.

He balled a hand into her hair, tilting her head back to allow him access, and kissed her as she'd never been kissed before. His tongue duelled with hers, lashing her with his need, and his body was hard and erect as he pushed her backwards onto the bed. She fell and he went with her, lying on top of her as his kiss pressed her head into the mattress and her body writhed beneath him.

A fever of need was spinning from her womanhood through her whole body, making her pant with desperate hunger. And he understood it. It burned in him, too.

'This is so beautiful,' she gasped, watching the candlelight flickering against the wall, casting shadows that did something to her insides.

'*Si.*'

His hands pushed at the fabric of her dress, lifting it higher, moving it up her body, exposing her long legs to him so that he groaned into her mouth as he felt the expanse of her thigh.

'*You* are beautiful,' he added, dragging his mouth lower, teasing the flesh at the base of her neck.

After a lifetime of not wanting to be beautiful it was strange for her to find those words so seductive, so pleasing. She swallowed.

He flicked the pulse point in her neck that was pounding hard and fast, his tongue a call to arms she couldn't ignore. Her hands pushed at his jacket and he groaned low in his throat as she arched her back at the same time, needing more, so much more, wanting her to touch him, to feel him.

Despite her complete inexperience she was driven by an ancient feminine dance, the power of which had been implanted into her soul at birth.

She rolled her hips, cursing the fabric between them. But his length was hard and it pressed against the sensitive flesh of her need. He thrust it towards her as though they were naked. He ground it against her and heat rose inside her. Her eyes had stars dancing in front of them and her breasts were tight, her nipples straining against the fabric of her dress, desperate for attention.

He ran his palms over her flesh and she cried out at the unexpected touch. As he ground his arousal tighter, harder, faster, his hands moved over her breasts and an orgasm split through her, its intensity almost ripping her apart.

She arched her back, moaning, crying out, her hands pushing at his shirt as the strength of the feelings he'd stirred made breathing, speaking, *anything* almost impossible.

But Pietro wasn't close to finishing. He was going to

make this a night Emmeline Morelli would never forget. A
night worthy of her first time.

As her breath softened and her cheeks glowed pink he
crawled down her body, his hands worshipping her through
the dress, his mouth running over the soft folds of fabric until they connected with her underpants. They were
simple white cotton, and that brought a smile to his face.
He liked to imagine her in them. That alone would fuel
his fantasies for years to come. But for now they served
no purpose.

He slid them down her body, over the shoes she still wore,
discarding them at the foot of the bed. She was writhing,
her body still on fire. He traced circles along her legs with
his fingers, moving towards her thighs.

She gasped, and the sound made him smile.

'You want me to touch you here?' he said softly, padding a thumb over the sensitive cluster of nerve-endings.

'I want everything,' she moaned.

His erection jerked hard in his pants. As hard as it could,
anyway, when it was already taking up more room than was
left inside the fabric.

'You are going to get it,' he promised darkly.

His hands were gently insistent as they separated her
legs, pushing them wide apart to reveal her whole self to
him. Before she could guess what he intended to do he ran
his tongue across her seam.

She cried out into the room as new pleasures began to
swirl around her, but he held her legs still, keeping her open
to him. Keeping her right where he wanted her.

It was both an invasion and a sensual adventure. The intimacy of the act should have embarrassed her, or shamed her,
but it did neither. She tilted her head back and stared at the
ceiling as his tongue lashed her sensitive nerve-endings and
euphoric delight careened over her body. She was at the top
of a rollercoaster and the ride was only just getting started.

Emmeline didn't try to control herself as cry after hoarse

cry came from her mouth. She couldn't. She was completely subjected to the pleasure he was creating. He was her master.

'I want you to come,' he said against her body, and the words were a command that started a fever inside her.

She reached up and grabbed the duvet in her fingers, wrapping her hands around it and arching her back as his tongue moved faster, deeper, harder. Finally the muscles deep inside her squeezed hard, wet and desperate, and then, overjoyed, she felt pleasure fill her. It rioted through her, ricocheting off her body.

'God…' she whimpered at the candles in the room, shivering and yet covered in perspiration at the same time. 'I can't believe you just did that.'

His laugh was slightly unsteady as he dragged his mouth higher, over her flat stomach to her gently rounded breasts. He flicked one nipple with his tongue and then moved his mouth to the other, clamping his teeth over it just hard enough to make her cry out with renewed awareness.

'Why can you not believe it?' he prompted, his smile lazily indolent, his eyes hooded as his head came level with hers.

'I just… You kissed me…down there.'

'Down *here*, you mean?'

He curved a hand possessively over her womanhood and she sucked her lip between her teeth, nodding slowly.

'I want to do that again and again,' he promised, the heel of his hand pressing on her flesh just hard enough to keep the tremors of sensation going.

'Okay.' She smiled up at him, her body strangely lethargic in the midst of the passion he'd stirred up.

His laugh was a rumble…a coarse sound. He stood up, and for a moment she was assailed by loneliness and concern. *Was he stopping?*

But his fingers flicked at his buttons, loosening his shirt, pushing it off his body to reveal the full expanse of his tanned naked chest. She'd seen him like this before—in the pool—and the memory of that had burned itself into her fantasies.

But this was different.

He was undressing for *her* now. Undressing with his eyes hooked to her body, his fingers moving with determined speed as he slid the clothes from his body until he was in just a pair of black briefs. His arousal was evident through the fabric, straining against it, pushing outwards so her eyes couldn't help but be drawn to it.

'Am I right in thinking you have not *seen* a man before, Emmeline?'

The question was asked impassively, with no judgement, but Emmeline's face flushed with blood. Embarrassment made her look away and swallow.

'Of course I've seen a man,' she said quietly.

'Naked?' he prompted.

She shook her head, still unable to meet his eyes.

'Come here.'

Her heart thundered inside her body but she stood, closing the small distance between the bed and him. Even her own nakedness didn't shame her, though she'd never been this way before.

As if instinctively understanding her thoughts, he caught her around the waist. There was something in his expression—a confusion, a newness—that made her breath hitch in her throat. He drew her against the hard planes of his body and she made a soft sound of anticipation as his arousal pressed against her.

'I didn't want to marry you,' he said thickly. 'But now I can't think of anything I want more than what we are about to do. You are…uniquely beautiful.'

The words made her heart flutter; it felt weightless, without gravity, and she felt it might lift out of her body altogether.

'I'm not.' She shook her head.

'You try to disguise your beauty,' he corrected. 'And I cannot understand why, when most women do everything they can to enhance what they have.'

For a moment pain lanced her. A pain so deep, so embedded, that it had always been a part of her.

'It's who I am,' she said quietly.

'I want to get to know who you are,' he murmured. 'I didn't want to marry you, but you're my wife. And I'm glad.'

Her stomach churned and emotions ransacked her body, filling her heart with something new.

A sense of belonging.

He caught her hands and lifted them to his underpants. 'Undress me.'

Her eyes flew to his; doubt and uncertainty warring with temptation. 'I've never done this…' she babbled.

He laughed softly. 'I'm aware of that.'

She drew her brows together, her face a mask of doubt. 'I thought educating virgins wasn't your thing?'

'Not just any virgin,' he said in a gravelled tone. '*You*, Mrs Morelli.'

'What if I'm not…? What if this isn't…?' She closed her eyes, forcing herself to think clearly and speak what was on her mind. 'You told me you're used to experienced lovers. What if I'm terrible in bed?'

That unfamiliar stroke of guilt slashed through him anew. *He'd* said that. In fact he'd said words to that effect several times. Why had he been such a bastard to her?

'Tonight I want to show you what your body is capable of,' he said thickly, pulling her closer and making her gasp when his arousal throbbed hard against her body.

He felt her knees tremble. Her eyes were huge in her face, all honey and caramel, awash with far too many thoughts and doubts. Doubts *he'd* put there. Doubts he wanted to remove one by one, kiss by kiss.

'I'm scared,' she said, with such simple honesty it broke his heart.

'I know.' He kissed the tip of her nose.

His tenderness made her heart swell. Her fingers moved of their own accord, pushing at his underwear, lowering it over the hard line of his erection and then down, over his thighs. He stepped back, moving out of his underwear as he guided her to the bed.

She fell backwards, but he didn't immediately join her. Instead he reached into the drawer beside the bed and pulled out a foiled square.

'Protection,' he said with a half-smile.

'Ah. No grandkids.'

She nodded, her wink reminding him of the first day they'd discussed this marriage. When she'd been so sure of herself. Sure that she was getting a convenient husband, a ticket to her university studies and to…freedom. The word lodged in his mind as incongruous, as it had done back then.

'Not tonight.' He grinned.

Their eyes met and the air sparked with something neither had ever felt before. Though Pietro had slept with more women than he could easily remember, he'd never taken a woman's virginity. Even as a young man he had gravitated towards experienced lovers. This was new ground for them both.

How could he reassure her? Drive that doubt from her mind properly?

A strange sense of uncertainty ached in his gut. But she pushed up on her elbows and stared at him.

'I want this,' she said with soft confidence. 'I don't care what happens next. I want to *feel* this.'

He nodded and lowered himself onto the bed, kissing her slowly, sensually, marvelling at the feeling of flesh on flesh. Her naked breasts were flattened by his hair-roughened torso. His arousal was close to her—so close he could take her. The way she was trembling beneath him was a reaction to the newness of this, even as her eyes looked at him as though he was the air she needed to sustain life.

He dragged his mouth lower, rolling one of her nipples with his tongue while his hand slid down and splayed her legs wide, giving him more room, more access.

'You tell me if you need time,' he said thickly, not even sure the command made sense.

But she understood. She understood as though he'd spoken in a language made just for them.

She nodded and he lifted his head, one hand cupping her cheek as he kissed her hard. His tongue was passion and flame and she writhed beneath him, lifting her hips, searching for him, welcoming his invasion.

And God knew he wanted that too.

He pushed into her gently, gliding only his tip into her warm, tight core, giving her time to adjust to each incremental sensation as he filled her anew.

She moaned into his mouth as he moved, and all his control was required to stop himself taking her as he wanted to—hard and fast. He pulled out slowly, then pushed in deeper, before removing himself again. As he did so each time he took more and more of her and her muscles relaxed, welcoming him deeper, without restraint, without reserve, until he was pressing against the barrier of her innocence.

He kissed her, holding her tight as he thrust past it, removing it forever, imprinting himself on her as the first lover of her life. The first man who'd touched her like this.

Finally his whole length was sheathed by her, wrapped up in her, squeezed by her, and he paused, giving them both a moment to adjust to how it felt. He pushed his face higher so he could see her properly, could read her face. He saw wetness in her eyes and something turned in his gut.

'You're in pain.'

He moved to pull out of her but she shook her head and wrapped her legs around his waist.

'No, no, it's…' She shook her head and her smile was tight. Self-conscious. 'It's fine.'

Perfect, she amended inwardly. Everything about the

moment was more perfect than she could ever have fantasised or hoped. It was sublime.

'"Fine" is a good starting point,' he said darkly. 'But it
requires improvement.'

And then he moved quickly, his body thrusting into her
and pulling out, each movement sparking an electrical current beneath her skin until she was almost out of breath. The
assault on her senses was unlike anything she'd expected.
Even when he'd touched her and brought her to orgasm it
had been different from this. Now every nerve-ending in
her body was twitching, as though he was stirring her from
the inside out.

And he was, she realised, arching her back as the feelings began to overtake everything.

The galaxy was bright and hot and she was intimately
aware of her part in it: like flotsam, bright and floating,
powerless and yet powerful. A contradiction in her heart.

She dug her nails into his shoulders as wave after wave
of pleasure swallowed her, devoured her, making her eyes
leak hot tears she didn't even feel. Only when he caught one
with his tongue and traced it up her cheek did she realise
she was crying—but she couldn't stop.

She was incandescent, the explosion of her pleasure like
a fire in her blood. He held her as she came, held her tight,
reassured her, whispered to her in Italian, his words stirring
her up more, hotter, faster. She clung to him as the tornado
swirled around her, held him as though he alone could save
her, and then she cried out, sweat beading on her brow as
the storm broke.

Pleasure saturated the room, thickened her breath. She
clung to him until the craziness slowed and she was once
more herself.

But she was not herself. She'd never be herself again.
She had shaved off pieces of her being and handed them to
him, bound them into his soul and his flesh, uniting herself
with him even if he didn't want that.

She fell back onto the bed. The beauty of what they'd shared was incredible. Yet it was almost immediately eclipsed by a sense of guilt. Of self-doubt.

She'd just experienced the most unimaginable delight and he…he'd simply had a good workout.

'I'm sorry,' she muttered, turning her face away and staring at one of the flickering candles. 'I told you I wouldn't be any good at this.'

'Hey.'

He caught her face in his hand and turned her back to look at him, even though she couldn't bear to see the pity and disappointment in his eyes.

'What are you talking about?'

'Nothing,' she muttered.

It was impossible to give voice to the embarrassment that was quickly usurping her delight. Uncertainty and inexperience were horrible accomplices, and they dogged her every thought.

'Cara…' He spoke quietly, bringing his mouth to her earlobe and pulling it between his teeth, wobbling the flesh and breathing warm air over her delicate pulse-points so that she shivered anew. 'Do you feel this?'

He thrust into her again, deeper, harder, his body like a rock.

'Yes, but you didn't—' She bit down on her lip.

His laugh was soft recrimination. 'I did not finish because I didn't want this to be over. Believe me, it is taking every ounce of my willpower not to.'

Her eyes clashed with his, trying to read truth in his statement.

'You answer my needs perfectly,' he promised.

She wasn't sure she believed him, but then he began to move once more and she was lost to thought. She arched her back, her body held by his, and this time as he rocked her to new heights of awareness and fulfilment his mouth tormented her breasts, so there were fires raging in every part of her body.

She ran her fingers over him, wanting to touch and feel every inch of him, to enjoy his body as he was hers. And as she began to fall apart at the seams, a tumbling mess of sensation and feeling, a tangle of emotions, he kissed her, his mouth holding hers as he made her world shift once more.

Only this time he came with her.

Feeling him throb inside her, feeling his body racked by a pleasure he couldn't control and knowing it was being with *her* that was doing that to him made an ancient feminine power rock her. She held him tight and kissed him back, her mouth moving over his as he lost control of himself, as though she felt he needed some kind of reassurance.

Later she would find that instinct absurd, but in that moment it filled her, made her desperate to comfort him somehow.

He swore in his own language, the harsh epithet filling her mouth and her soul.

'You were worried I wouldn't enjoy myself?'

He rolled away from her, pulling out of her and sitting up in one motion. His face was angled down towards her, his smile bemused.

'How do you feel?'

Emmeline blinked up at him and stretched her body. She was covered in a fine sheen of perspiration and her nipples were taut; there was a red rash on the parts of her body his stubble had grazed, including her thighs, and at the top of her legs. She arched her back, tossing her arms over her head and stretching like a cat in the sunshine.

'I feel...*whole*.' She smiled and closed her eyes, her breathing soon deep and soporific.

He studied her for a moment, hearing the reality of what they'd done banging on a door in his mind—one he was going to ignore for as long as possible.

'Tell me,' he said thickly, running a finger over her abdomen up to the swell of her breast.

'What?' She flicked her gaze to him.

'Explain to me why you haven't done that before.'

'Maybe I was waiting for you,' she murmured, the words incongruous in their sweetness. She broke the spell by smiling teasingly. 'Or maybe I just didn't meet anyone who tempted me.' She pushed up on one elbow, her eyes not shying away from his. 'Is that so strange?'

'Yes.' He shook his head. 'Yet it also makes sense.'

Her eyes dropped to the sheet between them. 'I'm glad you made an exception to your "no virgins" rule for me.'

His laugh was a soft caress. 'That was rude of me.'

'It was *honest* of you,' she corrected, stretching again, her body lean and long and begging for his touch.

He cupped her breast possessively, his eyes simmering with tension as they locked to hers. 'Do you need anything? Food? Water? Wine? Tea?'

She shook her head slowly. How could she need anything when he'd just made her feel like that?

She smothered a yawn with the back of her hand and he smiled.

'Sleep, then.'

'Mmm…but then I might think this was all a dream.'

He covered her with the duvet that was folded across the bottom of the bed. 'Which will give me the perfect opportunity to remind you otherwise,' he said, with a deep husk to his words.

Her eyes were closed, her breathing even, but she was still awake. He watched as she breathed in and out, her face calm, her cheeks still pink from the heat of their lovemaking. He watched as the smile dropped and her wakefulness gave way to slumber…as her breathing grew deeper and steadier and her eyes began to dance behind their lids. Her lashes were two sweeping fans across her cheeks.

And still he watched. Without realising it he was being

pulled into a spell; it wrapped around him, holding him immobile.

There were mysteries surrounding his bride. Mysteries of her choice. Her being. The contradiction that lived deep inside her. She was stunningly beautiful and yet she did everything she could to hide that fact. She had lived like a prisoner for years—a prisoner of her father's love and concern, but a prisoner nonetheless—and yet she was brave and spirited, strong and independent. Why had she sacrificed her independence for so long?

She was sensual and desirable and yet she'd never even been kissed. How had she subjugated that side of her nature for so many years? She was twenty-two years old but she lived like a Victorian. Most women her age had their heads buried in their smartphones, sending glamorous selfies to their social media followers. She read books by the pool and covered herself from head to toe. *Why?*

These were questions to which he badly wanted answers, but there were other overriding questions that poisoned the perfection of the moment.

How would she react when she learned the truth about her father's health? Would she be able to forgive him for keeping it from her?

And, most importantly of all, why did the idea of lying to her, disappointing her, inadvertently hurting her with his dishonesty, make his skin crawl all over?

CHAPTER EIGHT

HER BODY THROBBED in an unusual new way. She stretched in bed, and wondered at the strangeness of everything. Not just her body, but the smells that enveloped her. Sort of citrus and lavender, clean and fresh. And the sounds—or lack of sounds. No busy motorways or bustle of a nearby city.

Her eyes blinked open, big pools of gold in the darkened room—dark save for the flickering of a couple of candles and the glow of a laptop screen beside her.

'*Ciao.*'

His voice was a warm breath across her body. She looked up at Pietro—her husband…her lover—and a lazy smile curved her lips.

'I had the strangest dream,' she murmured, pushing up onto one elbow so that the duvet fell from her body, uncovering her breasts for his proprietorial inspection.

He dropped his eyes to the display, unashamed of enjoying her nakedness. 'Are you sure it was a dream?' he prompted, folding his laptop closed and placing it carelessly on the bedside table nearest to him.

'It must have been,' she said softly. 'It was too perfect to be anything else.'

She was so beautifully unsophisticated. He couldn't remember the last time he'd been with a woman who didn't dissemble in some way. Her honesty was as refreshing as her body was tempting.

He brought his frame over hers, so large against her slender fragility that Emmeline couldn't help but feel safe in his presence. As though nothing and no one could hurt her if he was by her side.

The thought evaporated when his lips touched hers, his kiss perfection in the midst of her body's awakening.

'I want you again,' he said.

Her smile was broad. 'Good.'

He dropped his eyes for a moment. Something was clearly bothering him.

'I want you too,' she reassured him.

His laugh was a kernel of sound—a husk in the night. 'I hated seeing you with those men.'

She blinked, having no idea at first who he was talking about. Then, 'I was just talking.'

'I know that.' His smile was self-deprecating. 'It is possible that I overreacted.'

She burst out laughing. 'Is that some kind of extremely hesitant apology?'

He ran a hand over her hair, stroking its dark glossy length thoughtfully. 'Yes.'

'Apology accepted. But, Pietro? You can't really expect me never to speak to another man…'

'*Lo so.* I know.'

'Good. Because I came to Rome to find my feet—to be myself. I can't do that with you getting all shouty every time I have an innocent conversation with someone…'

'I know.'

He lifted himself up and straddled her, the strength of his want for her evidenced by the rock-hard arousal that was already pressed against her abdomen.

'But I will bring you to my bed each night and make it impossible for you to even *think* of another man.'

He dropped his head, placing a kiss on her temple.

'I will be all you think of and your body will crave mine.'

He thrust into her without warning and she cried out at the sweetness of his invasion, the possession that she was already hooked on.

'Starting now.'

'Starting a couple of hours ago,' she corrected breathily.

He grinned. 'Yes.'

He made love to her as though she was his only lover—as though he'd been dreaming of her for years. As though he needed her and only her. He made love to her with an intensity that blew her mind and filled her with the kind of sensual heat she hadn't believed could possibly exist.

She refused to acknowledge the truth: that she was one of many lovers for him and he was her only.

Afterwards, as she lay with her head resting on his chest, listening to the strong, fast beating of his heart and feeling the steady rise and fall of his chest, all was silent in the bedroom.

Except for the rather loud and insistent rumble of her stomach.

She burst out laughing, self-conscious but mostly amused. 'Apparently I'm starving.' She sat up straight, turning her face towards his. 'I hardly ate today,' she said after a moment, thinking back to her shopping trip and then the time she'd spent styling her hair and applying make-up.

'Why not?'

He stroked a hand over her back as though it was the most natural thing in the world, and his touch stirred a deep sense of rightness right down in the bottom of her soul.

She chewed on her lower lip. 'Just busy, I guess. I don't suppose there's anything here though…?'

'If so then someone's going to find themselves out of a job tomorrow.'

'Why?' she asked, looking around the darkened room. Only a few candles remained alight, flickering lazily against the white walls.

'Because I retain a full-time housekeeper to maintain this estate.'

'Estate? What *is* this place?'

His hand stilled on her back and then resumed its contact, as though he couldn't bear not to touch her. 'It is what you would call a bolthole,' he said after a small pause. 'My own little slice of the world.'

'Why would you need a bolthole, Mr Morelli? Is it for when your hordes of admirers and past lovers get too much?'

It was meant to tease him, but his face flashed with true annoyance. 'There is significant media intrusion in my life—something you might have noted if you'd been with me more.' He winced at the way that had sounded and shook his head. 'Sorry. I'm sure you're no stranger to that sort of invasion.'

'No,' she agreed, and she wasn't offended or upset—only interested. 'Though staying on the plantation as often as I did meant I wasn't really a figure of much interest,' she said quietly, conveniently glossing over the articles that had been so painful to her teenaged heart. The articles that had so callously compared her boring appearance to her mother's legendary beauty.

'You're lucky,' he said, taking her statement at face value. 'For years I was followed everywhere I went, with paparazzi eager to catch a photograph of the kind of mess I'd get into next.'

His wink hid genuine pain; she wasn't sure how she knew that, but she did.

'Including your escapade with that very much married Brazilian model?'

He grunted. 'Apparently.'

She expelled a soft breath—a sigh that meant nothing. It simply escaped her lips without her knowledge.

'I didn't know she was married,' he surprised her by saying gruffly. 'We didn't have that kind of relationship.'

She nodded thoughtfully. 'What kind of relationship *did* you have?'

He looked at her thoughtfully for a moment and then pushed out of the bed, striding across the room and grabbing a pair of shorts.

'You don't want to talk about it?' she asked as he pulled them up his body, leaving them low on his hips.

'I'm happy to talk about it if you would like. But let's get you something to eat as we speak, hmm? I don't want your energy fading.'

She hid her smile and stood, keeping a sheet wrapped around her as she moved.

His laugh was mocking. 'Why are you covering yourself?'

She sent him a droll look. 'Because I'm naked.'

'And you are worried I might see you?' He crossed the room, dislodging the sheet from beneath her arms, dropping his head to kiss her shoulder. 'Really? After what we've shared?'

Her cheeks flushed pink and something inside Pietro twisted painfully. So her innocence wasn't just a question of virginity. It was simply *her*. She had a sweetness, a naivety that was so unusual he doubted he'd ever seen anything like it.

'*You're* wearing something.'

'Yes, but I don't look like you.' He grinned, pulling her close. 'I want to *see* you.'

'Believe me, I feel the exact same way.'

His laugh was a little off-kilter, but he stepped backwards and slowly slid his briefs from his body so that he was completely naked.

'Better?'

Emmeline felt as though she'd eaten a cup of sawdust—her mouth was completely dry. 'Uh-huh.'

He laughed, kissing her cheek, and then reached for her hand. He laced his fingers through hers and she grinned.

'What?' he asked.

'First time I've held hands with a guy. Other than my father.'

He pulled a face that perfectly covered the way his heart

was rabbiting about like a wild thing in his chest. 'I don't want to think of your father right now.'

Or the fact that he had cancer. Was dying and lying to his only daughter. Nor the fact that he was using Pietro to cover that lie.

Emmeline's laugh covered the unpleasantness of his thoughts. 'Sorry. It's just this is all so strange.'

'Si. Quest'e verita.'

He pulled her after him, out through the door and down the stairs, and for the first time Emmeline spared a thought for the dwelling they were in. It was a very unassuming rustic farmhouse. Large terracotta tiles lined the hallway and the walls were cream. The furniture was nice, but certainly not designer.

'It came like this.' He answered her unspoken question.

'When did you buy it?'

He squeezed her hand. 'Here.'

He guided her into a kitchen and lifted her hand to his lips, kissing it before releasing her fingers from his grip. He opened the fridge and she watched, waiting.

'Five years ago.'

'Why?'

He thought about not answering, but what was the point in that?

'I'd broken up with a girlfriend. The press thought we would get married. So did she, I suppose. It was a messy split. Acrimonious. Bitter. Public.' He grimaced. 'I learned a lot from that experience. Most of all the importance of having somewhere to go when things get heated. I should have taken the time to calm down.'

'You didn't?'

He shook his head, pulling a box out of the fridge and opening it. 'I stayed in Rome.'

'That was bad?'

He laughed. 'I did a lot of drinking to forget her. A *lot*. It was not a good phase of my life.'

'I'm sorry,' she murmured, hating the lash of jealousy that whipped her spine.

'Don't be. We are still friends, and I realised that I needed somewhere all to myself. No one knows about this farmhouse. It's owned by my corporation, but I never bring anyone here.'

Pleasure soared at the fact that she'd made the cut, but there was envy too. 'How...*admirable* that you're still friends.'

His eyes met hers, his smile making her feel as though she'd been sledged in the gut. 'Jealous?'

'Not at all.' She looked away, hating how transparent she must be to him. Unfortunately she had no experience in pretending not to give a crap about her husband's past. Especially when his past must so radically outstrip her own experience.

'Why does that annoy me?' he mused, lifting a piece of meat out of the container and placing it on a dark timber chopping board. He reached for a knife; it glinted in the light.

'I don't know,' she said softly, distracted by the motion of the knife as it cut easily through the meat. 'Even with this place you're still in the press more than I can ever imagine.'

'And you are *never* in it,' he said thoughtfully, placing the pieces of sliced beef onto a plate and then turning back to the fridge.

'Well, there's nothing interesting about me,' she said softly.

'That isn't true.' A frown tugged at his lips. 'You are an anachronism.'

'I know.'

She couldn't help it. She reached over and lifted a piece of meat, placing it into her mouth just as he turned around.

Her eyes met his and she shrugged. 'I'm starving,' she said through a full mouth.

He grinned. 'I'm glad to see you eating. You need energy.'

Her pulse raced. 'Do I?'

'Oh, yes, *cara*.'

He paused, his eyes scanning her face so intently that she froze.

'What is it?'

'When you smile like that you look so much like your mother.'

Something flashed in her expression. Something that was definitely not pride or pleasure. It was doubt. Guilt. Pain.

Curiosity flared in his gut. 'That annoys you?'

'Of course not,' she said stiffly. 'My mother was very beautiful. I'm flattered.'

'No, you're not.'

'Why do you say that?'

'Because I know you,' he said simply.

And her stomach flopped because she didn't doubt he was being honest.

'So why do you not want to look like Patrice?'

'You'll never be like me! Take this off! Wipe it all off! It's too much rouge, too much mascara. You look like a porn star gone wrong.'

Emmeline shuddered, her smile as fake as the night was dark. 'You're wrong,' she insisted, even as the memory scratched its fingers over her spine.

'I'm never wrong.' His eyes sparked with hers. 'But I can be patient.'

He placed a handful of strawberries on the plate, then a wedge of cheese and some bread.

But I can be patient.

Did he have some mysterious super-ability to know just what she needed to hear?

'It's complicated,' she said, after a moment of silence had passed.

'Family stuff often is.'

His smile showed a depth of experience that she understood.

'Are your parents pleased you've "settled down"?' She made inverted commas with her fingers and he lifted his broad shoulders.

'I suppose so. Rafe thinks you're quite irresistible,' he added as an afterthought. 'I think he's more than a little jealous that your father chose *me* as your groom *du jour*.'

Emmeline made a sound of amusement and lifted a strawberry to her lips. Strangely, she was not remotely self-conscious in her nudity. Everything about that moment felt right.

'Have you ever been in love?'

Except that.

The question came from her lips completely unexpectedly, uninvited and unwanted. He stared at her for a moment, his expression unreadable.

'No.'

'Seriously?'

She reached for the plate but his hand caught hers, lifting it to his lips. He pressed a kiss against her palm and then took her finger into his mouth, sucking on it for a moment. Her stomach rolled.

'Seriously,' he murmured, coming around the kitchen bench to stand opposite her.

'But you've been with so many women.'

'Sex isn't love, *cara*.'

Just like that the floor between them seemed to open up; a huge hole formed and it was dark and wide...an expanse of confusion and heartache that she couldn't traverse.

Sex isn't love.

And it wasn't.

Sex was just a physical act. A biological function. A hormonal need.

Nothing more. Why had she asked that stupid question?

'What about that woman you broke up with? The one the press went into a frenzy over?'

'Which one?' he muttered, arching his dark brows.

'Five years ago—before you bought this place.'

'Bianca,' he said quietly. 'I cared for her. I still do.'

Jealousy was no longer just a flame in her blood; it was a torrent of lava bubbling through her, burning her whole.

'Bianca as in that beautiful redhead you were all over at our wedding?'

Contrition sparked inside him—and regret too. He'd forgotten that Emmeline knew her name. It was a stupid, foolish oversight that Pietro would never ordinarily have made.

'That was wrong of me.'

'You can say that again,' she snapped, reaching for a pistachio nut as a distraction. 'You're still seeing her?'

Her insides ached. Her body still throbbed with his possession, her nerve-endings were vibrating with the awakening he'd inspired, and she was jealous. So, *so* jealous.

'No.'

Emmeline stood up. She felt strange. Strange and achy.

'It's none of my business,' she said quietly, moving around to the other side of the kitchen bench—ostensibly to grab some more food, but in reality because she needed space.

'Of course it is. You're my wife.'

'But this isn't a *real* marriage, remember? We have a deal. You're free to…to do what you want.'

He stared at her long and hard. 'You don't think that's changed now, Emmeline?'

Doubts flickered inside her. 'What are you saying?'

'I don't want to see anyone else.'

He hadn't even realised that himself, but as he stared at his beautiful bride he knew it was the truth. And he knew she deserved to know it.

'I want to sleep with *you*. A lot. I want to be married to you. And I know we are doing this all the wrong way around, but I want to get to know you. There is so much of you that is a mystery to me, and for some reason I have become obsessed with uncovering all your secrets.'

He came around to her side of the bench and dug his hands into her hips.

'Every. Single. One.'

'This place is so beautiful.' She stared out at the rolling hills of the countryside, her eyes clinging to the fruit orchard in the foreground before moving on and landing on the glistening ocean. 'I don't know how you can ever leave.'

'Business,' he said simply. 'My office can't actually function for that long without me.' He thought of the emails his assistants had been forwarding and grimaced. 'I have to get back.'

Emmeline sighed. 'Today?'

'Now,' he agreed.

Or soon, he amended, sitting on the spot of grass beside her. After three days in the countryside he wasn't sure he could put off the reality of life for a moment longer. He wanted to, though.

'But it's so nice,' she said again, tilting her head to look at him.

She rested her cheek on her knees, which were bent against her chest, and he had to fight against reaching out and touching her. It was his 'go to' impulse now, and he suspected he might need some kind of 'Emmeline patch' to get through a day in the office without her.

How had he ever thought her ordinary and dull to look at? She was so breathtakingly beautiful that he derided himself for not having noticed. It didn't matter what she wore—these past three days she'd gone around in old shirts of his and she'd looked sexier than any woman he'd ever known.

No, she was simply Emmeline.

He saw every expression that crossed her face—includ-

ing the slight flicker of regret that shifted her lips downwards now.

'You can stay here,' he said quietly. 'I can come back on
the weekend. If you'd prefer it…'

'No.'

The response was instantaneous. How could she stay
away from him? Her addiction was firmly entrenched. She
couldn't remember a time when his body hadn't taken over
hers.

'We'll come back some other time.'

She stood a little jerkily, wiping her hands across her
knees.

He followed her and got to his feet, then caught her
around her waist. 'I'm glad we came here.'

'Me too.'

Her smile was bright, but there was something in her
expression that he didn't like. An uncertainty he wanted
to erase.

Only he had no idea how.

He'd spent three days with her but he hadn't uncovered a
single secret. Instead, he'd got to know her body intimately.
He'd become acquainted with every single one of her noises,
every single movement her body made that signalled pleasure, need, desire, an ache. He'd learned to read her body
like a book, and yet her mind was still an enigmatic tangle
of uncertainty…

'You seem nervous.'

She flicked her gaze to him, wondering at his perceptive
abilities. 'I guess I am.'

Her smile was tight. Forced. Anxious.

Pietro slowed the car down, then pulled off to the side
of the road. Emmeline's gaze followed a young child skip-
ping down the street, his mother walking behind, her arms
crossed, her eyes amused.

'What is it?'

Emmeline shifted her gaze from the child—his mother was next to him now, her smile contagious.

'Honestly?'

'Si, certamente.'

'It's stupid.'

'I doubt it,' he said reassuringly, his voice low and husky.

The statement was a balm to her doubts. Still, she hesitated before she spoke.

'What happened back there…' She bit down on her lip and cast a glance over her shoulder, towards the road they'd just travelled at speed. 'The closer we get to Rome, the more it feels like a fantasy. Like it never really happened. Like it won't happen again.'

'How can you say that?' he asked, a genuine smile of bemusement on his face. 'I was there. It happened. It happened a *lot*.'

Pink spread through her cheeks and she looked away, uncomfortable and disconcerted. 'But it doesn't feel real, somehow.'

He expelled a soft sigh. 'It *was* real.'

She nodded, but her uncertainty was palpable. 'I guess it's just…the last time we were in Rome everything was still so weird between us.'

His laugh caressed her skin.

He pulled back into the traffic, his attention focussed ahead. 'A lot's happened since then.'

And it had—but the fundamental truth hadn't changed, except in one crucial way. It was weighing on him more and more, heavy around his neck. Knowing that her father was dying and that she had no idea was an enormous deceit now. They'd crossed a line; they were lovers.

But Pietro wasn't overly concerned. Of the many things he excelled at, one of his strengths was managing people and situations. He just had to manage this situation tightly. Starting with his father-in-law.

CHAPTER NINE

'YOU DO NOT sound well,' he drawled down the phone, wondering at the sense of anger he felt towards this man he'd always admired and respected. A man he loved. A man who had helped him remember himself after the despair of losing his own father.

Col's cough was a loud crackle. 'I'm fine. The goddamned nurse is here, taking my temperature.'

'Rectally?' Pietro's response was filled with impatience. He softened it with a small laugh. 'Because you sound cranky as all hell.'

'I am. I'm a damned prisoner in this room.' Another cough. 'How's my girl, Pietro? Are you looking after her?'

Again, a surge of annoyance raged through Pietro's chest. 'She doesn't appear to need much looking after. Emmeline is stronger than I'd appreciated.'

Col's laugh was broken by a wheeze. 'Ah. I see you've come up against her stubborn side. Try not to judge her too harshly for it. She inherited that from me.'

'Mmm…' Pietro nodded, rubbing his palm over his stubble. He should have shaved. The pink marks of his possession had become regular fixtures on Emmeline's skin.

'Is there a problem?' Col's question was imbued with the strength that was part and parcel of the man.

'*Si.*'

'What is it? She's happy, isn't she? You told me you'd look after her…'

'She's happy,' Pietro agreed, thinking of her flushed face lying beneath him, her eyes fevered, her brow covered in perspiration. Then he thought of her uncertainty as they'd driven back to Rome the day before. The way she'd seemed pursued by ghosts unseen.

'So? What is it?'

'She deserves to know the truth about your health,' Pietro said heavily. 'She isn't going to understand why you haven't told her. You must give her a chance to see you. To say goodbye.'

A wheeze. Then another. Pietro waited, but his loyalty was shifting from the dying man to his daughter—the woman who loved her father and had no idea his life was ending.

'You can't tell her.'

It wasn't the response Pietro had expected. He shifted his weight to the other foot and braced an arm against the glass window that overlooked the city. In the distance he could make out the hill that screened his villa from sight. Was she there, looking out on the same blanket of stars he was? Was she staring up at the sky, wondering about him, missing him, wanting him?

His body throbbed with a need he fully intended to indulge. *Soon.*

'Someone has to,' he said, with a soft insistence that was no less firm for being quietly spoken. 'She deserves to know.'

'You aren't to say anything.'

Col's voice was raised, and in the background Pietro heard someone—a woman—telling him to calm down.

But Col was working himself up, his tone harsh. 'If I'd wanted her to know I'd have damned well told her. She's my daughter, Pietro. You've known her for a month—I've known her all her life. I know what she needs, damn it. You can't ruin this.'

'She deserves a chance to say goodbye.'

'No.' It was emphatic. 'I'm already gone. The man she thought I was…the man I used to be…that's not me now.'

There was a thick, throaty cough, then the scuffling sound of the phone dropping to the floor.

Pietro spoke quickly. 'Col? *Col?*'

A woman's voice came more clearly into the earpiece as the phone was lifted. 'Hello?'

Pietro expelled an angry breath. 'Yes?'

'I'm sorry, Senator Bovington needs to rest now. This conversation will have to wait.' The nurse lowered her voice. 'And next time please take more care not to upset the Senator.'

The call was disconnected before Pietro could ask to speak to Col for a moment longer. He shoved his cell phone back into his pocket and paced to the other side of his room.

And he swore, loudly, into the empty office, his temper ignited more than ever before.

The confidence he'd worn into the office earlier was morphing into doubt. Emmeline deserved to know the truth, but it wasn't Pietro's confidence to break. Perhaps with anyone else, he would, but Col was like a second father to him. He wouldn't share this secret until he had Col's permission. He couldn't.

But the knowledge that he was lying to Emmeline was a weight on his chest, and he found himself hesitant to go home to her that evening. The idea of looking at her, kissing her, making love to her, knowing that he was sitting on such a fundamental secret, made his situation unpalatable, to say the least.

He dialled Rafe's number on autopilot.

'*Ciao?*' Rafe answered, the single word slightly rushed and breathless.

'Are you free for dinner?'

'What time is it?'

Pietro gazed down at his gold wristwatch. 'After seven.'

'*Dio.* Already?'

'*Si.*'

'Okay. Dinner in an hour?' He named a restaurant near his own apartment. 'Is Emmeline joining us?'

Pietro's spine ached with rejection but he shook his head. 'Not tonight. She has…something on.'

Rafe was silent for a moment. 'You've always been a bad liar. I'll meet you soon.'

He disconnected the call before Pietro could refute the claim. Then he flicked his cell phone from one hand to the other and finally loaded up a blank message.

I have a meeting to attend. I'll be late. I'm sorry.

He grimaced as he sent it. Rafe was right; Pietro was a God-awful liar.

He saw the little dots appear that showed she was typing a message, but they went away again almost instantly, without any message appearing. He frowned, waited a few more moments and then put his phone back into his pocket.

Rafe was waiting at the restaurant when Pietro appeared.

'So?' he asked, nodding towards the martini that was sitting at the empty place on the table. 'What's going on?'

Pietro took the seat and threw back half the drink in one go. 'I need your complete discretion,' he said quietly, his tone showing the seriousness of his mood. 'This is a…a *private* matter.'

'Of course.' Rafe was clearly resisting the urge to joke about feeling like an extra from a bad World War Two resistance movie. He must sense it was not the time.

'Col's sick.'

'Col? Col Bovington?'

'Yes. Who else?' Pietro hissed.

'What do you mean, sick?'

'He has cancer; it's terminal.' He paused, in deference to the memories he knew would be besieging Rafe of the cancer that had taken their own father. 'He has months to live. Perhaps only weeks.'

'Poor Emmeline. She must be beside herself. I know how close they are.'

'Yes.' Pietro nodded angrily, his jaw clenched as he reached for his drink and twisted it in his hand. 'The thing is, she doesn't know.'

'She doesn't *know*?' Rafe repeated with disbelief, his dark eyes latching on to his brother's. 'What the hell do you mean?'

'Col wanted it that way,' Pietro responded with a defensive lift of his shoulders. 'And when I agreed to keep it from her I didn't… I hardly knew her,' he finished lamely. 'I didn't think it would be any hardship not to tell her the truth. I didn't care about her at all.'

'And now?' Rafe pushed.

The newness of what he was feeling was something Pietro wasn't willing to ruin by discussing it, though. He kept his answer vague.

'I know her well enough to know that she'd want the truth. She wouldn't want Col going through this alone. She'd want to be with him at the end.'

'Perhaps.' Rafe nodded. 'But Col is obviously seeking to protect her from the grief of watching a much-loved parent die…'

'We've been through that. But aren't you glad we got a chance to say goodbye to our father? To honour him? To ease his suffering?'

'We aren't Emmeline. If Col is right—and you must assume he knows his own daughter—then you'd be hurting her for no reason. And Col would never forgive you.'

'No. I gave him my word.' Pietro's response was stony. Cold. His heart was iced over by the thought of how that promise was betraying Emmeline. 'Until he frees me from that obligation I must keep it.'

'It sounds to me as though you've made your decision,' Rafe murmured gently. 'So what do we need to discuss?'

Pietro glowered. What he needed was for someone to absolve him of guilt, to tell him he was making the right decision. But no one could do that—and very possibly he wasn't.

'*Niente.*'

Emmeline turned the page of her book, having no idea what she'd just read. In truth, she'd covered several chapters, but she couldn't have recounted a single incident that had taken place.

Where was he?

And who was he with?

Her heart twisted in her chest as she thought of her husband with someone else. What assurance did she have that he wasn't still seeing Bianca, or any number of his past lovers?

Doubts filled her, making her feel nauseous and exhausted.

She should have gone to bed; it was late. But waiting for him to come home had become an obsession. She didn't want to fall asleep—to have him return at some point in the middle of the night and for her body to respond to his when he might well have been…

God. Was he sleeping with someone else?

A car's engine throbbed outside the door, low and rumbling, and her tummy flopped as her eyes looked to the clock. It was just after midnight.

Butterflies danced inside her, beating their wings against the walls of her chest, and her fingers were shaking as she flipped another page.

The door was pushed inwards and she waited, her eyes trained on the corridor beyond. Waiting, watching. He didn't see her at first. His head was bent, his manner weary. He stood dragging a hand through his hair, staring into space.

'Oh. You're home!' she said, in an admirable imitation of surprise.

He started. His eyes flew to Emmeline's and she knew

she wasn't imagining the darkening of his expression. The look of something in his face that might well be guilt.

'I didn't expect you to be awake, *cara.*'

'I've been reading. I guess the book engrossed me,' she lied. *What was it even called?* She folded it closed carefully, without attempting to stand. 'Did you have a good night?'

There it was again! That expression of uncertainty. Of wrongdoing. Her stomach churned and she looked away, unable to meet his eyes but knowing she had to speak honestly about how she felt. She needed to know where she stood.

'Have you been with another woman?' The question was a whisper. A soft, tremulous slice of doubt in the beautiful lounge of his villa.

'Oh, Emmeline…' He moved quickly to her and crouched down at her feet. 'No. Of course I haven't.' He put a hand on her knee, drawing her attention to his face. 'I had dinner with Rafe.'

'Yes.' She nodded jerkily. 'I know. He called hours ago, to say you'd left your jacket at the restaurant. He said he'd drop it by later in the week.'

Hours ago. Pietro understood then why his wife was so uncertain.

'I had to go back to the office to finish something,' he lied.

He'd needed to think. And he hadn't been sure he could face his wife with the knowledge he held—the lie he was keeping from her. What had seemed so simple was now burning through his body, making each breath painful.

'You can't seriously think I would be seeing anyone else?'

'I don't know,' she said softly, her eyes not able to meet his. 'I mean, I knew what I was getting when I married you…'

'No, you didn't. Neither of us did,' he said simply. 'I thought I was marrying the boring, spoiled daughter of a dear friend. I didn't expect my wife to be *you*. I thought I'd want to carry on with my life as before…'

'But you don't?' she pushed, her eyes huge as finally they met his.

'Not even a little bit,' he promised. He stood, holding a hand to her. 'You have to trust me, Emmeline.'

Guilt coursed through him. How could he ask that of her?

Emmeline bit down on her lip. She trusted Pietro with her life, sure, but her heart…? And it was her heart that was involved now. Her whole heart. It had tripped into a state of love without her knowledge, and definitely without her permission, and she couldn't say with any certainty that he wouldn't break it.

Not intentionally, but just by virtue of the man he was.

'Trust me,' he said again, cupping her face. 'I don't want anyone else.'

'It's crazy,' she said softly, doubt in her features. 'We only just met…'

He dropped his mouth to hers, kissing her with all the passion in his soul. She moaned into his mouth, wrapping her arms around his neck. So much for not responding, she thought with an inward snort of derision. She couldn't be in the same room as her husband and not feel as though a match had been struck.

'We've known each other for years.'

He kissed the words into her mouth and they filled up her soul.

'But not really.' She pulled away, resting her head on his chest, listening to his heart.

'I remember the first time I saw you,' he said quietly. 'I'd come for your mother's funeral. You were a teenager, and I think even then I knew that I was looking at you in all the wrong ways.' His smile was apologetic. 'You had just come home from school, do you remember?'

Remember? Of course she remembered. Her father's

handsome young friend had looked at her and a fire had lit in her blood.

'Yep.' She cleared her throat. 'You were the most gorgeous person I'd ever seen,' she said with mock seriousness. 'You fuelled *all* my teenage fantasies.'

His laugh was a soft rumble. 'No wonder you never met a boy you liked,' he teased. 'Who could live up to *me*?'

It was a joke, but Emmeline was falling back in time, her mind tripping over those painful years in her life.

She covered the direction of her thoughts with a flippant response. 'Who indeed?'

'I thought at the time that it was strange you were still at school. Your mother had just passed away, and yet you were carrying on with your life…'

'People handle grief in different ways,' she said softly. 'I needed to be around friends. The familiar. Sophie was a godsend.'

'How come you've never told your father what you know about Patrice's death?'

She looked up at him, her eyes awash with emotions. A part of him—the part of him that wanted his wife to be happy and at ease—felt he should back off. But the rest of him—the part that so desperately needed answers—pushed on with his line of enquiry.

'He thinks you believe she simply crashed.'

'She did crash.' Emmeline's smile was tight, her tone dismissive.

'But she drove into that tree on purpose.'

'Probably drunk,' Emmeline said, with the anger she tried so hard to keep a tight rein on taking over for a moment.

She stepped away from Pietro, pacing towards the window that overlooked the city. Her eyes studied its beautiful glow but she hardly saw it.

'Why do you say that?'

'Because she was always drunk at the end.' Emmeline

bit down on her lip but the words were bubbling out of her almost against her will.

Pietro frowned. 'Your father has never mentioned that. There was no hint of it in the media.'

'Of course there wasn't,' Emmeline said wearily. 'Daddy controls the local press, for the most part. *And* the coroner's office.'

Emmeline spun around to face Pietro, bracing her back against the glass window behind her.

'If she'd hit another car, hurt someone, then I don't think even Daddy would have been able to keep it hushed up. But as it was only Mom died, and no one could have gained anything from seeing our family name disgraced.' She swallowed, her throat a slender pale column that was somehow so vulnerable Pietro ached.

'How do you know about her drinking?' Pietro murmured.

Emmeline swallowed, looking away. Years of silence kept her lips glued shut even now.

'How do you *know*?' he insisted, staring at her lowered face, waiting for her to speak.

'Because she couldn't hide it towards the end. She was a drunk. A *mean* drunk,' she added quietly.

Pietro's eyes narrowed. 'Mean, how?'

Emmeline expelled a shaking sigh. 'Just mean.'

'To you?' he prompted.

'Of course. With Daddy away at the Capitol for much of the time, I was the only one around to *be* mean to. Well, other than the servants—but they were paid well and put up with it.' Emmeline swallowed back the sting of tears and pressed her palms to her eyes. 'I could never do anything right by her.'

She shook her head angrily.

'Everything about me offended her. Especially as I got older. I remember there was one dinner and Congressman Nantuckan made some throwaway comment about how beautiful I was, that I was going to be every bit as pretty as my mom when I grew up. I must have been all of twelve. He was probably just being kind,' she said, shaking her head. 'But Mom was furious. *Furious*. As though I'd planned some elaborate betrayal and laced her dinner with cyanide.'

A dark and displeasing image was forming for Pietro, but he took care not to react visibly. 'What did she do?'

'Nothing. Not straight away, anyhow. Mom would never show her hand publicly. But once everyone left she pulled all the clothes out of my wardrobe. She told me I was on the right track to becoming an A-grade whore if I didn't watch out. She—'

Emmeline gasped as a sob escaped her, and lifted a hand to her mouth to block it.

'I'm so sorry,' she said, shaking her head desperately. 'I never talk about this! But I've ripped off the Band-Aid and I don't seem able to stop…'

'I don't want you to stop,' he assured her, fighting the urge to close the distance between them. He wanted to comfort her, but he suspected that it would cause her to stop sharing, and he desperately wanted to understand more about her life.

She nodded, but her hands were shaking, and finally Pietro gave up on maintaining his distance. He walked to the bar and poured a stiff measure of Scotch, then carried it to his wife. She curled her fingers around it, sniffed it before taking a tiny sip. Her face contorted with disgust and she passed the glass straight back.

'*Yuck.*'

His smile was indulgent, but impatience burned inside him. 'You were twelve, and on the cusp of changing from a girl into a young woman…?' he prompted.

She nodded, pulling at the necklace she always wore.

'She couldn't stand that. When I was young she was such an attentive, affectionate mother. We were very close. But from around ten or eleven, as I shot up and started to develop a more mature body… Mom saw it as some kind of act of defiance. She started to see me as competition, hated the time I spent with Daddy. When people came to the house she'd send me to my room. I wasn't allowed to wear anything that drew attention to myself. Cosmetics were forbidden. So was dying my hair or having it cut into a style.'

'Yet you were still beautiful,' he said softly. 'And anyone would have been able to see that.'

Emmeline's eyes met his with mockery. '*You* didn't. You specifically told me that I didn't look good enough to be your wife.'

He groaned—a sound of deep regret. He *had* said that. 'Emmeline, I saw you as a teenager. I wasn't thinking straight the night you came to my office. And, if anything, I suppose I was…annoyed.'

'Annoyed?' she prompted.

'*Si.* Annoyed that you went to such effort to cover up your natural beauty.'

'Even after she died it was a habit. I don't know… I guess I got very mixed up. Any time I would even *think* about wearing something other than what she'd chosen for me I'd hear her voice, hear the things she'd called me, and I'd know I could never do it.' Emmeline blinked, her enormous eyes round and golden in her face. 'When you told me I needed to change how I looked…'

'I was a bastard to say that to you,' he said gruffly.

'Yes. An *arrogant* bastard,' she agreed, although the words were softened by her smile. 'But you freed me, in a weird way. It was almost as if I'd been waiting for someone to shake me out of that mind-set. To remind me that she was gone and the power she'd exerted over me had gone with her. There was an article in the papers not long after she died. It compared me to her and the headline was *Dull Heiress Can't Hold a Candle to Dead Mother.* Can you believe that?'

His snort was derisive. 'Ridiculous journalists.'

'Yes, and a ridiculous story. They'd taken a heap of long-lens shots of me leaving school, playing baseball— you know, generally the worst, most unflattering pictures. A normal girl would have been devastated by that.'

'You weren't?'

'No. I saw it as a tick of approval. I was doing just what I was supposed to. Mom would have been proud of me.' She shook her head again. 'It took me a long time to unwrap those thoughts and see them for the idiocy they were. For many years I couldn't gain that perspective...'

His eyes swept closed and he processed what she was telling him. He thought of the way he'd criticised her appearance—first telling her she was too conservative and then accusing her of looking too 'available' when she'd dressed as he'd suggested.

'You are beautiful to me no matter what you wear—and to any man. Your mother was playing a foolish and futile game, trying to hide you like that.'

'She wasn't exactly firing on all cylinders,' Emmeline pointed out with a grimace.

'I cannot believe your father wasn't aware...'

'He doted on her,' Emmeline said wistfully. 'There was a significant age gap between them, as you know. She was his precious, darling wife.' She shook her head bitterly from side to side. 'He had no idea.'

'I can't understand that.'

Emmeline shrugged. 'I think it's quite common. A lot of people who love someone with a dependency issue fool themselves into thinking nothing's wrong. They don't want to admit the truth, so they don't.'

'But—'

'I know.' She lifted a finger to his lips, her smile distracting. 'It doesn't make sense.' She dropped her finger lower, digging the tip into the cleft of his chin. 'The first thing that's gone right for me is actually...um...'

'Yes?' he prompted, the word a gravelled husk.

'This. Marrying you. It must seem crazy to an outsider but here…with you… I feel so alive. For the first time in a long time I'm myself again. Thank you.'

Guilt was heavy in his chest.

Tell her. Tell her now.

He wanted to so badly, and there was only one way to stop the words galloping from his mouth. He crushed his lips to hers, taking possession of her mouth with his, pressing her against the window, making her his once more. Here, like this, everything made sense.

Nothing and no one—no truth kept or lie uncovered—could hurt what they were.

CHAPTER TEN

THE NIGHTCLUB WAS full to overflowing and the music was low-key, electronic. It thumped around the walls. The lighting was dim. Even dancing with her husband, his arms wrapped around her waist, she couldn't make out his face properly.

'So this is where our wedding guests came?'

He nodded. 'I believe so.'

His hands dipped lower, curving over her rear, holding her against the hint of his arousal. Her eyes flared with temptation and desire.

'It's nice…' She wrinkled her nose as she looked around, studying the walls that were painted a dark charcoal and featured beautiful black and white prints of Italian scenes.

'I am going to take a stab in the dark and say it's not your usual scene,' he teased, kissing the top of her head.

'Not exactly!' She laughed. 'But that doesn't mean I can't learn to like it.'

'There is no need. I don't come here often.'

'But you have something to do with it?'

'I financed it,' he agreed.

'Uh-huh. That would be why they treated you like some kind of god when you walked in here.'

'Or it could have been because of the incredibly beautiful woman on my arm.'

She shook her head, her smile dismissive. 'I'm sure I'm not the first woman in a nice dress you've brought through those doors.'

He slowed for a moment, hating it that she was right— hating it that his past was as colourful as it was. Not once had he questioned the wisdom of the way he lived, but now, married to Emmeline, he wished more than anything that he *hadn't* slept with any pretty woman who'd caught his eye. He wanted to give her more than that, but he couldn't exactly wind back time.

'Have you spoken to your father lately?'

'Ah…' She expelled a soft sigh. 'A change of subject, I see. I take it that means I'm the hundredth woman you've come here with, or something?'

He compressed his lips, angry with himself and, perversely, with Emmeline for pushing this line of enquiry. 'Does it matter?'

She blinked up at him and shook her head. 'I guess not.'

She looked away, but the pleasant fog of sweet desire that had wrapped around them dissipated. A line had been drawn and she'd stepped back over it, warily.

'I was just thinking,' he said gently, 'that I wish I had come into this relationship with less baggage.'

'Fewer ex-lovers, you mean?' she murmured, moving in time to the music even as most of her mind was distracted by the idea of Pietro *ever* making love to someone else.

'Si, certo.'

'But why?' she asked softly, and stopped moving, staring up at him.

'You deserve better than someone like me.'

He was surprised to hear himself admit that. Until that moment Pietro would have classified himself as supremely confident and self-assured.

'But perhaps you wouldn't be such a sensational lover without all those women you've been with before,' she quipped, winking up at him.

His laugh was gruff. 'So practice makes perfect?'

'Yes. But now you get to practice with just me.'

'And you are perfect,' he said quietly.

He kissed her gently then, and the world stopped spinning, the music stopped playing. Everything was quiet and still—a moment out of time. A moment that resonated with all the love in Emmeline's heart.

And in his too?

She didn't dare hope that he loved her. She knew that what they were was changing, morphing, shifting every day. That he looked at her as though he'd never seen a woman before. That he held her after they'd made love until she fell asleep. That he was always holding her, still, in the soft light of morning.

She knew that he was choosing to work fewer hours in his office and instead spending time in the villa. Oftentimes he was propping up a laptop, but generally near her. By the pool, in the lounge, in their bedroom.

And that was the other thing. Since they'd come back from the farmhouse she hadn't slept in her own room once. His room was becoming 'their' room.

Still… Getting close to one another was one thing. Falling in love was quite another. Emmeline wasn't going to get her hopes up. Life had taught her that there was safety in low expectations and it was a hard lesson to shake.

The song came to an end, fading seamlessly into another.

'Are you hungry?' he murmured into her ear.

She looked up at him, her eyes meeting his with sensual heat. 'Not for food,' she said quietly.

His laugh set her pulse firing. 'Then let's get out of here.' He squeezed her hand. 'I just have to see Leon—the owner. Want to come?'

'Not particularly.' She smiled at him and he smiled back, and the world was quiet again, spinning softly around them as if Emmeline and Pietro existed in their own little space. 'I'll wait in the car.'

'Five minutes,' he promised, holding up his hand and flexing his fingers.

She nodded, watching as he cut through the crowd effortlessly. Or did it part for him? Either way, he moved unencumbered through the hundreds of dancing guests. Once he was out of sight she turned and made her way in the opposite direction, towards the doors of the nightclub.

'Emmeline.'

The sound of her name had her pausing, turning, a blank smile on her face as her eyes scanned the crowd. She didn't see anyone she knew at first, and was about to resume her progress towards the door when a beautiful redhead came into view.

And then she knew instantly who was looking back at her.

'Bianca.'

The woman's smile was bone-chilling. 'You know who I am? Good. That saves me the trouble of introductions.'

'I saw you pawing my husband at our wedding,' Emmeline heard herself say, and instantly wished she could pull the words back. They were rude and unnecessary, and the last thing she wanted was to make a scene.

'Being pawed *by* your husband is a more accurate description,' Bianca commented, with a purr in the words.

'Yes, well… That's ancient history,' Emmeline said, lifting her slender shoulders in what she hoped looked like an unaffected shrug.

'If that's what you want to believe,' Bianca said, her smile tight, her lips bright red. 'You know, I could *never* put up with a husband who was so easily tempted away. But then, yours is hardly a *conventional* marriage, is it?'

Emmeline's doubts, already so close to the surface, began to wrap around her anew. Her brain—logical, calm, cool—knew that Bianca had every reason to be unkind. That her gloating attitude was probably just a cruel manipulation aimed at hurting Emmeline. But the muddiness of what she actually was to Pietro, and the truth of what she *wanted* to be, made her heart ache.

'I almost wish *I* had married him,' Bianca said, tapping a fingertip along the side of her lips. 'But this way I get to have my cake and eat it too.' Her laugh was a soft cackle.

'I don't understand…'

'I get the best parts of Pietro—without the press intrusion and the expectations of being Mrs Pietro Morelli… You're good cover for him and me.'

Emmeline felt as if she was drowning.

She stared at Bianca and shook her head. 'I don't know if you're telling me the truth, or just trying to upset me, but either way it's time for me to go.' She blinked her enormous eyes, the hurt in them impossible to conceal. 'Please don't come near me again.'

'It's not *you* I want to be near,' Bianca purred as a parting shot.

Emmeline spun and made a beeline for the door, bursting through it and into the night air with an overwhelming sense of relief.

Pietro was only seconds behind her, his breath loud, as though he'd just run a marathon. 'Was that Bianca I saw talking to you?'

Emmeline didn't have time to hide the hurt in her eyes. She nodded bleakly, then looked around for their car.

A muscle jerked in Pietro's cheek just as a camera flash went off. He swore angrily and put a hand in the small of Emmeline's back, guiding her away from the nightclub towards his car. He opened her door without saying a word, then moved to the driver's side.

He revved the engine as soon as she was buckled in, and pulled out into the empty street. The silence prickled between them, angry and accusatory.

'What did she say to you?' he asked finally, as they cleared the more built-up streets of the city and went on their way to his villa.

'Nothing.' She frowned, then closed her eyes. 'I don't know if it matters.'

Pietro gripped the steering wheel until his knuckles glowed white. 'Tell me what she said.'

Emmeline swallowed, her mind reeling. She had gone

from the euphoria of being with Pietro to feeling as if everything was a sinister ruse.

'She told me our marriage was a convenient cover for your relationship with her. She implied that you and she are still very much a thing.' Emmeline shook her head. 'She knows that our marriage isn't conventional.'

The words were a sharp accusation and Pietro swore.

'That last part is true,' he said thickly. 'I shouldn't have said anything to her but I was…angry. I was wrong to expose you to that kind of gossip.'

'Yes, you were,' Emmeline muttered, her heart plummeting. 'I'm sure she's told anyone who cares to listen,' she added, mortified.

'I don't care. It's not true any more. You *know* how much everything has changed between us.'

He reached down and put a hand on her knee but she jerked away. Her eyes lifted to his and the pain and uncertainty in them had him swearing and veering the car off the road, pulling to a rapid halt in a space marked for buses.

'Please listen, *cara.* You know the truth about Bianca and me because I have told you. She has always wanted more from me than I have to give. She is very jealous of you.'

'I know that,' Emmeline said quietly. 'And I know she wanted to hurt me tonight and obviously cares very much for you. But it makes me wonder… What do I know about *you*?'

'You know *everything* about me.' He groaned. 'Please believe me, Emmeline. I have never had with any woman what I have with you. This is special, and different, and you and I are both finding our way with it. Don't let outsiders—someone like Bianca—cause problems for us.' He pressed a finger beneath her chin, lifting her face to his. 'I won't let you. I won't let *her.*'

'I wish you didn't have such a long list of ex-lovers,' she muttered.

'None of them matters to me. Not a bit.'

Her eyes clashed with his; she wanted to believe him so badly. 'Have you been with her since we married?'

He shook his head.

'In that first month?' she persisted, holding his gaze. 'When we weren't sleeping together? I hardly saw you, and you were home late almost every night.'

He shook his head. 'I had dinner with her once. But that's all. I think I *wanted* to sleep with her. To prove to myself that our wedding hadn't changed anything. But the truth is I'd kissed you by then and I no longer wanted any other woman.'

Her heart turned over in her chest. Was it true? Did she believe him? It took such a leap of faith for her to trust anyone—especially given the strange circumstances. But gradually she found herself relenting.

'Why were you always so late?'

'You need to ask?'

His smile was like sunshine on a rainy afternoon. She felt its warmth penetrating the storm and could have wept with relief.

'I didn't trust myself not to touch you,' he said thickly. 'It was bad enough on our wedding night, when I kissed you and touched you and tasted your sweetness for myself. But after the night you wore that dress…' He groaned. 'I knew I was in serious trouble.'

The truth in his words filled her. 'Why couldn't you touch me?'

His smile was lopsided. And sexy as hell.

'Because you were meant to be a bride of convenience. Ours was an arranged marriage. I wasn't supposed to be craving you. To be dreaming about you…obsessing over you.' His sigh was exaggerated. 'And yet I was. I *am*. I suppose initially I resented that. I wanted to prove to myself that I could resist you. Spoiler alert: I couldn't.'

She expelled a soft sigh, but the memory of Bianca was still too fresh for her to relax completely.

'I don't want to see her again,' Emmeline muttered.

His eyes glinted with a heated emotion she couldn't interpret.

'Believe me, you will *never* see that woman again.'

'Can we go home now?'

He nodded, and inside he felt as though he'd been spared from Death Row with a minute left on the clock.

He dropped his head and kissed her slowly, gently. 'Don't let anyone come between us, *cara*. I cannot change the man I was, but you are changing everything about the man I *am*. The man I want to be.'

Her stomach squeezed with happiness. Because she knew he was telling the truth.

She trusted him implicitly.

It wasn't long before they found their way back to each other's bodies, exploring every inch available and sating their appetites.

'You are crying,' he whispered, chasing a tear up her cheek, depositing it back in the corner of her eye.

She laughed through a sob, shaking her head, wrapping her hands around his waist. 'I'm sorry. It's just so perfect. I don't know what happened—what I did to deserve this—but it's just...'

He smiled—a smile that tipped her world off its axis—and then he thrust deeper, and she moaned into the cool night air, her body moving with his. They were completely in sync, completely together.

He kissed her as he ground into her and she wrapped her legs around his back, holding him close, needing him in her core. His tongue lashed hers and together they spiralled off the edge of the earth in a tangle of limbs, sheets, sweat and cries.

Afterwards he stroked her hair, his eyes smiling down into hers. He rolled onto his back, pulling her with him, holding her tight, and she listened to the beating of his heart for a long time. She thought for a moment that he'd fallen asleep, but after a long time he spoke.

His voice was a gravelled husk in the night. 'Have you spoken to your father lately?'

'No.'

She shook her head and her hair tickled his nose. He patted it down flat and then stroked her naked back, feeling every bone of her spine, knotting down to the curve of her rear.

Tell her. Tell her.

But the moment was so perfect. Some time he might find a way to be honest with his wife. But on this night, with the sound of their lovemaking still heavy in the air, he couldn't bring himself to do it. To ruin what they'd just shared.

'You don't speak often? That's interesting. I would have thought you'd find being apart from him more of an adjustment.'

Emmeline shrugged. 'I lived on the plantation but my father was often away. I did try to call him a few days ago and he emailed back. Something about house guests.' She shrugged. 'That will mean he's out showing off the horses, the cattle, his shooting prowess.' She wiggled her brows—he felt the movement against his chest. 'Knowing Daddy, he's never been happier.'

Pietro groaned inwardly. The lie was tightening around his chest.

'My father speaks of you often, you know,' she murmured, apparently having no clue that her husband was in a self-induced hell of sorts. 'He adores you.'

Pietro's smile was tight. 'It's mutual.'

'Why?' She pushed up on her elbows to study him. 'Why are you so close?'

That bleak time from his past sat like a weight on his chest. 'I've always admired him.'

'That's not the same thing.'

'No,' he agreed. 'Years ago, I was in negotiations with

your father. I was buying some commercial real estate of
his—just off the Champs Elysées. I was devastated by my
father's death—I got the call about it while we were in a
meeting—and your father... Col...supported me. Not just
that day, but afterwards too. I'd always admired him as a
businessman, a politician, but as a friend he was irreplaceable.' He shrugged. 'He was a rock when I badly needed
one.'

As Pietro spoke the words they reverberated around his
soul. Col had been his rock when there'd been no imperative on him to be any such thing. He had been strength and
resilience, and he had imparted those qualities to Pietro.

How could he be anything but loyal to the statesman
now, in his own time of need? Pietro owed Col his alle-
giance, even though lying to Emmeline was beginning to
poison him.

'That's just like him.' Emmeline smiled. 'He's so self-
less...'

CHAPTER ELEVEN

'GOOD MORNING, MRS MORELLI.'

He dragged a finger down her body, finding her womanhood and brushing against it possessively. She writhed beneath him, remembering the way they'd made love the night before. Her body still throbbed from the strength of that pleasure.

'Buongiorno.' She blinked up at him.

'Do you know what today is?'

Her smile was irrepressible. 'My first day at university.' She grinned. *'Yay!'*

He laughed. '"Yay"?'

'Uh-huh. Yay. Just…*yay*.'

He dropped his head and kissed her gently. 'Which means we have been married two months.'

'And it feels like two weeks.' She stretched her arms over her head. 'Time really does fly when you're having fun.'

His wife—his beautiful wife—stared up at him with all the goodness in her soul and he felt as though the sun was beaming right through his chest.

'Are you nervous?'

'Nervous? God, no. I'm excited. I have been wanting to study for so long, Pietro. I can't believe I've put this off. I feel like there's a whole world out there—a world of learning and knowing—and finally it's going to be mine.'

She sat up excitedly, pushing the covers off her naked body and stepping out of the bed. He watched as she strolled across the room, uncaring of her nakedness. She pulled a pair of jeans off a hanger, and then a cream blouse, and took his favourite pair of briefs from her underwear drawer.

He groaned across the room. 'Not those.'

The smile she threw over her shoulder was pure imp-ish cheek. 'Oh, yes. You can imagine me in them all day.'

'I'll imagine stripping them *off* you all day,' he corrected.

'That too.' She winked, sashaying into the adjoining bathroom and switching the fan on with the light.

The noise droned in the background and Pietro fell back against the mattress, staring up at the ceiling fan that was spinning lazily overhead.

The sense that he was betraying her had lessened. So, too, the feeling that he was living on borrowed time. After several more attempts at getting Col to tell the truth to his daughter Pietro had been forced to accept that the secret was there and that it existed beyond Pietro's control. They would deal with the fallout when it happened.

It never once occurred to him that there might be a fallout bigger than they could handle, because he and Emmeline had become a single, unified force. The idea of anything happening to them that they couldn't handle was impos-sible to contemplate.

He listened to the running of the shower and the soft singing that she did without even realising. Smiled wider when he caught the tone-deaf notes she seemed always to miss.

He stepped out of bed, strode across the room and pushed the door inwards. Steam swirled around him. She had her eyes closed, her face lifted towards the showerhead, and water was raining over her face and down her back. She hummed now, quietly, and he grinned as he pulled the shower door open and brought his mouth down on hers without warning.

Her eyes flew open and then she surrendered to the kiss, moaning as he pushed her back against the cold tiles, groan-ing as his body pinned hers and water ran over them both, down their faces and into their mouths.

'Remember what I said the night you were talking to those two professors?'

He asked the question as he brought his mouth down to take a nipple between his teeth and roll it gently, as he moved his hand lower, brushing over her feminine core, before he transferred his mouth to her other breast.

'No...' she moaned, rolling her hips, inviting him in. Needing him again.

How was it always like this for them? Would it ever not be? She felt as if an explosion had caught her in its midst, powerful and fierce.

'I will bring you to my bed every night, so that no other man ever, *ever* interests you.'

The passion in his words was wrapping around her, squeezing her, filling her with all the love in the world. 'You already do that,' she said huskily.

'It never hurts to take precautions, though, does it?'

She laughed, but any hint of amusement died inside her as he dragged his lips lower, falling to his knees so that he could kiss her in her most sensitive, private place. His tongue ran along her seam and her knees quivered as sensations began to drown her, to make thought impossible.

'I can't believe there was a time when you were not mine,' he said against her flesh, and she moaned, running her fingers through his hair as pleasure spiralled in her belly, driving through her, making her blood heat and her heart pound.

'I need you!' she cried out as an orgasm began to unfurl, spreading through her limbs, making them weak and aching.

'I'm glad.'

He didn't stop, though. His fingers dug into her hips and he held her where he needed her, his tongue dictating the speed of her release, and the intensity too. She cried out into the shower as the orgasm unfolded, her mind exploding, every conscious thought obliterated by the havoc he wreaked on her body.

He kissed her quivering flesh as he stood, but didn't

give her even a moment to recover. His hands spun her easily—she was weakened by the total meltdown of her bodily awareness—and he bent her at the hips. Holding her steady, he drove into her from behind and felt her tremble as his possession was complete—the ultimate coming together.

He throbbed inside her, his fingers massaging her wet, soapy breasts, his arousal rubbing against her sensitive nerve-endings, squeezed by her tight, wet muscles. He spoke in Italian—words that meant nothing and everything. He bent forward, kissing her back as he moved, stroking her, touching her, and finally, when her muscles squeezed him with all their need, he emptied himself into her, the feeling of ownership more complete than ever before. She owned him, and she was his.

Emmeline pressed her flushed face against the shower tiles, her mind reeling.

'I am going to find it very hard to concentrate today,' she said thickly, rolling her hips as he continued to pulse inside her, his length experiencing the aftershocks of the earthquake of their coming together.

'That makes two of us.'

He ran a finger down her back before easing himself out of her, away from her, releasing them from the agony and ecstasy of what they had been. She stood and turned to face him, and her eyes were so vibrant and her smile so broad that a dull ache spread through his chest.

He'd been fooling himself in pretending the lie didn't matter.

It did. Of course it did.

He ran a hand over her hair, wet and dark. 'Emmeline…?' he said softly, studying her cautiously.

'Mmm?' She wrapped her hands around his waist, holding him close to her body.

How could he tell her now? On her first day at university? It would derail her completely, and he'd already done his best to do that. No, he couldn't do it today.

But Col Bovington was going downhill, and enough was enough.

Pietro had an obligation to his wife. Soon, when the time was right, he would tell her.

Having made the resolution, he felt a thousand times better. As if simply by deciding to do something he had in some way enacted a small step of the deed.

Absolution was close at hand.

Emmeline hummed as she moved about the kitchen. There was a pile of textbooks in the corner, opened to the page she had most recently been reading. She cast a gaze over the *papas di pomodoro,* smelling the piquant sweetness of the tomatoes and the undertones of basil and garlic, then shifted her focus to the quails that were roasting in the oven.

It was the first time she'd cooked dinner for Pietro's family and she wanted everything to be perfect.

He'd laughed when she'd said as much. 'I have a housekeeper, a chef and a valet. Why do you not leave the food to them? You have too much on your mind already,' he had said, nodding towards the books that were littered around the house.

'I've only been at uni a week; it's still early days.' She'd smiled back. 'Besides, I want to. I like to cook and I think... I don't know... It just feels like something nice to do.'

Of course now she was regretting that impulse, as time marched on and food simmered and she worried that she would have nothing ready by the time they arrived.

There was nothing she could do but wait. The quail in *confit* needed an extra hour before they would be ready to remove. The soup was the entrée. There were olives, breads and cheeses ready to serve as antipasti.

She rubbed her hands together, checking the table for the tenth time. She'd set it with a simple white cloth and put several vases of old-fashioned roses in the centre. Sprigs of orange blossom lent them a beautiful fragrance. Plus, they reminded Emmeline of his farmhouse—the place where their relationship had come alive.

She smiled as she leaned down and breathed in deeply—then her back pocket vibrated. She reached down and fished her cell phone out, relieved and surprised in equal measure to see a text from her dad. She'd left several messages for him in the last week, and apart from a brief email she'd heard nothing.

Hi, Pumpkin. Sorry I've been hard to catch lately. I've got the flu and it's kept me in bed all week. Are you doing good? Love, Daddy.

A smile tickled her lips. It was something he had often asked her when she was younger.

I'm doing real good, Daddy. Uni is amazing.

She ran her finger over the phone, wondering what she should say about her husband and settling for, Married life suits me. Come over and visit soon?

She thrust her phone into her pocket and continued with her preparations. But as she showered and changed she couldn't help but let a kernel of worry infiltrate her happiness.

Her dad wasn't a young man. For the flu to have kept him in bed all week sounded serious. That and the fact that she hadn't spoken to him in rather a long time had her mind unpleasantly distracted.

She chose a black silk slip dress, teamed it with a long string of pearls and a pair of black ballet flats, then quickly applied basic make-up.

Pietro appeared just as she was bent forward, slashing mascara over her brows, and his eyes locked to her rear before she straightened and spun around.

'If it isn't my favourite husband,' she murmured, her eyes clashing with his in the mirror.

'Your *only* husband?' he prompted.

'For now.'

She winked and turned her attention back to the mirror, ignoring the serious tremble that assaulted her heart. Initially she'd felt their marriage would be of short duration. That she'd wean herself off life at Annersty, let her father adjust to her departure and then move on. For good. But now...?

'I have something for you,' he said softly.

Curious, she spun around, scanning his outfit, his hands, and seeing nothing.

'It's downstairs.'

'What is it?'

'Come and see,' he murmured, holding a hand out to her.

Emmeline walked to him, wanting to peel her dress off as she went, to expose her nakedness to him. She followed behind him, her curiosity increasing with each step, until they reached the front door.

He lifted his hand to cover her eyes. 'Wait a moment.'

She bit down on her lip, held her breath and listened as the heavy timber door was pulled inwards. Then his hand dropped from her eyes and she blinked, focussing beyond him.

A sleek black car sat before her. A Bentley with a soft roof that looked as if it would turn the car into a convertible.

'It's...it's beautiful,' she murmured. 'I don't understand...'

'Well, *cara*, you are a Roman now. You go to university here. You live here.'

He moved to the car and opened the driver's door; she followed, a frown etched in her face.

'Do you know what I have been thinking about lately?'

'What?'

'When we first discussed marrying, I remember you

saying something about wanting only the freedom it offered.' He cleared his throat. 'I didn't understand it at the time. I still don't. But I know I want to give you everything in this world, and a car seems like an important step to true freedom.'

Unexpected tears sparkled on Emmeline's lashes. 'Stop doing this to me!' She groaned, a laugh breaking the seriousness of her mood. 'You're *too* perfect.'

'*Cara*, I'm not…'

Something flickered in his face—something that briefly made her heart skid to a stop before she pushed the doubts away.

He *was* perfect. She had no reason to worry that he'd ever disappoint her or let her down. He was her match in all ways.

'Thank you,' she said softly.

'Hop in,' he replied, and grinned.

She smiled brightly as she slid behind the wheel. 'You know, I'm not actually a great driver…'

His laugh was husky. 'Then I shall have to teach you.'

As he'd already taught her so much. 'The thing is, I get bored,' she said honestly. 'I find it all a bit dreary.'

'Not here, you won't. Roman roads are fun. They are designed to test you.'

'I love my car. Even if I just sit in it to study.' She grinned at him.

A plume of dust from further down the driveway heralded the arrival of another car, and Emmeline stepped out with true regret. As she did so she saw a university parking permit on the dashboard, and that single gesture of thoughtfulness meant more to her than the extravagant gift of such an expensive car.

'I love it,' she said again, walking around the bonnet and pressing a kiss to his cheek.

His eyes latched to hers and she had the strangest feeling that he wanted to say something else. That something was bothering him.

'Is everything okay?' she asked searchingly, her eyes scanning his face.

'Ciao, ragazzi!'

Pietro's mother stepped from the car, a vision in green, her hair styled in a topknot, a large gold necklace at her throat and a pair of gold espadrilles snaking up her legs. She sashayed towards them as though the driveway were actually a chic fashion show catwalk.

'Mother,' Pietro drawled, kissing Ria on both cheeks before she transferred her attention to Emmeline.

'Ah! My lovely daughter-in-law,' she said in her heavily accented English. 'Still too skinny, I see,' she said, with a disapproval that Emmeline guessed was only half joking.

'Mother,' Pietro scolded warningly. 'That is enough.'

'What? I want grandchildren. Can you blame me?'

Emmeline's heart squeezed painfully. The truth was, the image of a baby had begun to fill her dreams. How sweet it would be to grow their own little person in her body—to hold it and feed it and cuddle it and love it.

Maybe one day that would happen. But for now Emmeline was having her first taste of life as a normal adult woman and she wasn't ready to sacrifice her independence yet. Her life with Pietro was perfect and new, and she didn't want to add a baby into the mix.

Yet.

Her eyes met Pietro's over Ria's head and she smiled; she knew he understood. He wanted her to be happy. To be free.

Her eyes drifted to the car, and as they walked into his home, she saw the number plate: *Mrs M.*

Her smile stretched broader, making her cheeks hurt.

Rafe arrived only a few minutes after his mother. They were sitting at the table sipping rosé wine, when he strode in, relaxed in pale trousers and a T-shirt.

'Ah, Rafe. Off the yacht, I see,' Ria said critically, but her smile showed nothing but maternal pride.

'*Ciao*, Mamma.' He grinned, doing the rounds and saying hello to his family. 'This smells wonderful. So you cook, too?' he demanded of Emmeline.

'A few dishes,' she said with false modesty.

Emmeline had always loved cooking. She'd spent as much time in the kitchen as possible—especially when Patrice had been on the war path. It had been the perfect bolthole. A spot where she could make dishes and enjoy the therapy that cooking and baking offered. She'd mastered croissants from scratch at the age of fifteen—just before her mother had died.

'Tell me again why *I* did not get to marry you,' Rafe grumbled good-naturedly, taking the empty seat beside Emmeline.

'Hush,' Ria said, reaching across and batting at Rafe's hand. 'She is your brother's wife.'

'Still… A man can dream.' Rafe winked at Emmeline, then reached for a handful of *grissini*.

'Leave some for the rest of us,' Pietro drawled, taking the seat on the other side of Emmeline and passing a glass of wine to his brother.

Beneath the table, Pietro's hand found Emmeline's knee and he squeezed it. She turned to face him. Their eyes met and sparks flew that Emmeline was sure everyone must surely see.

She smiled softly and then focussed on the story Ria was telling. Or tried to. But beneath the table Pietro's fingers moved steadily higher, until they were brushing her thigh, teasing her, comforting her, simply *being* with her.

'I'll get the soup,' she said after a moment, scraping her chair back and moving towards the kitchen.

'Would you like a hand, darling?' Ria called after her.

Emmeline shook her head. 'I'm in control.'

In truth, a moment to herself was essential. A single

touch from her husband was enough to set her pulse skittering and stay that way. Was it possible that if she stayed married to him she was going to end up having a stroke?

The thought made her smile, but it also made something strange shift inside her.

If she stayed married to him?

Where had that come from?

She lifted four bowls out of the cupboard and ladled delicious soup into them, thinking about the arrangement they'd come to. Discomfort was like ice inside her. They'd never really talked about how long they'd stay married for. But everything had changed. The deal they'd made was surely redundant now. She was in love, and she was pretty damned sure he was too.

Which meant *what*, exactly? That they'd live happily ever after? Was that even what he wanted?

Uncertainty brought her happiness down a notch. Perhaps they needed to have a talk about that? A *Where are we going?* conversation...

She grated some fresh parmesan over the top of the soup, adding a glug of oil and few leaves of basil.

The thing was, they'd done everything in reverse. From her extensive experience with books and movies Emmeline had gathered that generally two people met, discovered they were attracted to one another, dated, fell in love and slept together, then moved in together or got married. But at some point before that crucial last step they discussed what they wanted. Where their future was going.

Could they discuss that now? Or would it be weird? Everything was so good she didn't want to ruin it.

With a small noise of frustration she lifted two bowls and moved through the kitchen and back into the dining room.

'Let me give you a hand,' Pietro said, as though he'd only just realised his wife would be ferrying four bowls on her own.

'Thanks,' she murmured, depositing the first in front of Ria before following her husband back to the kitchen. As she walked through the door he caught her around the waist and pulled her to him.

'I want to take you upstairs *now…*' He groaned. 'Why is my family here?'

She laughed, but her heart was thundering, her pulse racing. 'I don't know. It was a terrible idea. Let's send them away.'

'Definitely.' He kissed her hard and fast. 'A down payment,' he said with a wink.

'Good. I'll expect payment in full later.'

'How much later?' He groaned again, his expression impatient.

She kissed his cheek. 'Not long, I hope.'

The soup was a hit. She had been anxious about cooking such a quintessentially Italian dish for her husband's family, but they seemed genuinely to love it, and Emmeline had to admit it was one of her best. The quail was perfect, too. Served with some crispy potatoes and garlic-roasted green beans, it was an excellent mix of flavours and textures.

Pietro took over hosting after dinner, making espresso martinis in the lounge area that they progressed to.

Pietro had given her a car. That *meant* something. Not to mention his sweet sentiments about her wanting freedom. This marriage was so much more than either of them had anticipated. It was real.

'You're quiet,' Rafe remarked, taking the seat beside hers. *Whoops.*

'And you look concerned. Is everything okay?'

Emmeline hardly wanted to have a deep and meaningful conversation about her marriage with her brother-in-law, so she scrambled for the easiest explanation she could offer.

'Oh, you know…' She smiled at him, her mind turning over quickly. 'It's my dad. He's not well, and it's hard to be over here and so worried about him,' she said with a shake of her head.

Rafe's surprise was obvious, but Emmeline didn't understand it, of course. 'He *told* you?'

'Of course he told me,' Emmeline said with a small frown of her own. 'It's hardly a secret.'

'Oh, thank God. I know Pietro's been tearing himself up about all this. It must be a weight off his mind that you know.'

Emmeline's look was quizzical. It was just the flu, and she'd only recently found out about it herself. 'How does Pietro know?' she asked quietly.

Rafe froze, apparently sensing that they were speaking at cross purposes. He sipped his martini, his eyes scanning the room. 'Um…'

'How does Pietro know what?'

Pietro appeared at that moment, devastatingly handsome in the suit that she loved so much. But Emmeline hardly noticed.

'How do you know my father is sick?'

CHAPTER TWELVE

SILENCE STRETCHED LIKE a piece of elastic. Then it stretched some more.

Emmeline tried to make two and two add up to four but it wasn't possible.

'Rafe just said you've known for a while. That it's been tearing you up,' she murmured. None of this was making sense.

Rafe swore, standing up and setting his martini glass down in one movement. He tossed Pietro a look of deep apology. 'I thought she knew.'

Emmeline stood up too, the movement unknowingly fluid. 'Knew *what*?' Her voice was louder. More demanding. The fear in it was obvious.

'Emmeline?'

Ria appeared at her side, and only with every single ounce of self-control in her body did Emmeline manage to calm herself. To offer her a tight, terse smile. But her eyes were haunted, her skin pale.

'Thank you for a lovely dinner. I think I should leave you to it now,' Ria said.

'Me too,' Rafe added quickly. 'Don't see us out.'

Pietro glared at his brother before dragging his attention back to his wife. It was quite possibly the worst manner in which this news could have been dropped.

'What the *hell* is going on?'

Pietro expelled a long, slow sigh. 'Sit down, *cara*.'

'I don't want a damned seat,' she responded caustically, her eyes flying around the room as if answers might suddenly appear. 'Well?' She tapped her foot, her arms folded across her slender chest.

'Rafe seemed to think you knew—'

'Daddy has the flu,' she answered sharply. 'But that's not what you're talking about, is it? Pietro? What's wrong with him?'

Fear was written across her beautiful face; her eyes were haunted by it.

'Your father *is* sick,' he confirmed.

Emmeline made a grunting noise of impatient displeasure. 'I've gathered that. What's wrong with him?'

A muscle jerked in Pietro's cheek.

'Is it serious?'

'Si, cara.'

'Oh, God.' She reached behind her for the sofa, collapsing into it wearily. 'What is it?'

Pietro crouched before her, his hands taking hers. 'He has cancer. Advanced and incurable.' He rubbed a thumb over her hand, across the soft flesh of her palm. His heart hurt with the pain in hers. 'I'm sorry.'

Tears fell down her cheeks, but shock was numbing her to their balm. 'I don't understand. When…? How…? Why didn't he tell me?'

'He wanted you to be happy. He wanted to *know* you were happy, to die knowing that you weren't going to be left stranded by the loss of your father. He wanted to know that you have other things in your life. Other people.'

'You,' she said quietly, pulling her hands free and rubbing them along her thighs. 'When did you find out?'

Pietro reached up and touched her cheek but she jerked away from him.

'When?'

It was a primal grunt. She was skinning the situation alive, trying to boil it down to just bones and fact.

'The day he came to see me.'

Surprise resonated through the room as though an atom bomb had been dropped. 'Before we were married?' she responded angrily, her voice high pitched and stringy. '*Be-*

fore we were married? You've known this whole time. Oh, my God.'

She stood up jerkily, looking around the room as though she didn't recognise it. As though it were simply a set and she an actress—a character in a play with no real meaning, no real plot. Nothing was real.

She blinked, clearing the confusion from her mind and trying her hardest to hone in on what mattered. There would be time to come to terms with Pietro's betrayal. But in that moment more was at stake.

'How bad is it?'

'He's dying,' Pietro said, the words thick and guttural. He stood slowly, but didn't attempt to move towards her. 'He told me it was a matter of months. If that.'

'No. I don't believe you.'

She stared at him, all her grief and confusion and the bereft state of her soul silently communicating themselves to Pietro.

'My father is… He's never sick.'

Pietro's expression was bleak. 'The cancer is through-out his body.'

The words were like strange sharp objects. She could barely comprehend them. Her daddy was ill? Why had he sent her away? Was he in pain? Was he lonely? The thought of him going through something like cancer without anyone to hold his hand brought a lump to her throat.

'And you let me stay here with you, knowing I had no idea? Knowing that my whole world—' She stabbed her hand into her chest, her eyes wild in her face. '—my father, my only family, was dying on the other side of the world? How *dare* you make that decision for me? How *dare* you lie to me like that?'

'He wanted it this way.'

'It doesn't matter! You should have *told* me!' she roared, turning her back and stalking out of the lounge.

She took the stairs two at a time, pacing down the corridor and into his room, which they'd been sharing for weeks. She pulled clothes out of the closet at random. Jeans, a few skirts, shirts… She had more clothes at home—she didn't need to pack much.

Home. Annersty. The words whispered through her with sombre realism.

'I couldn't tell you,' he said with muted anger in his words. 'What are you doing?'

'*Why* couldn't you?' She spun around to face him, her eyes accusing.

'He made me promise and I owed it to him to keep that promise.'

'Even knowing how it would hurt me?'

'I didn't want to do that,' he said thickly. 'You must believe this is true. I was in an impossible situation…'

'Damn it, Pietro.' The words reverberated around their room. 'Don't you *dare* talk to me about impossible situations! This wasn't impossible. It should have been easy.'

'Your father—'

'Yes, yes…' She waved a hand in the air, cutting him off. 'You've told me. He didn't want me to know. But what did *you* think?'

He froze, the question so direct that he hadn't expected it.

'You must have thought about it. Did you think I wouldn't care? Did you think I'd be able to forgive you this?' She zipped her suitcase with such ferocity that her nail snagged in its closure and she swore under her breath. 'You've been sitting on a time bomb.' She dashed a hand over her eyes, wiping away her tears.

He made a visible effort to pull himself together, straightening his shoulders and wiping his expression clean. 'You want to go to him?'

Her eyes bore into his. 'Of *course* I do. I would have gone to him weeks ago if anyone had told me what the hell was going on.'

'Good…fine,' he murmured. 'I'll organise my plane…'

'No.' She reached for her phone with fingers that shook. 'I'll book myself on the next available flight.'

Her meaning was clear. She didn't want his help.

'I have a jet at the airport. It will take hardly any time to fuel…'

'I don't want your stupid jet,' she snapped. 'I just want to get to him.'

'This is the fastest way,' he promised. 'I know you're angry, but let me do this.'

Emmeline looked away, panic and worry making her uncertain.

Pietro's voice came to her as if from a long way away. He spoke into his phone in his own language, ordering the flight preparations to begin. In some part of her mind she was glad. She was furious with him—furious in a way she doubted she'd ever forgive—but she wasn't sure she could face this completely alone.

He disconnected the call and she spoke without meeting his eyes. 'When?'

'Now. Come. I'll drive.'

She kept her eyes averted as he lifted her suitcase easily, carrying it down the stairs and past the car he'd given her only hours earlier. She ignored the anguish that churned her gut.

Mrs M. What a joke. She'd been nothing to him. Was this why he'd married her? To keep this lie? To deceive her?

All her ideas that their marriage had begun to mean something real were obviously just stupid, childish fantasies. There was no way that he loved her as she loved him. If he'd cared for her at all he would have found a way to break the truth to her sooner.

She stared out of the window as he took the car to Fiumuncino, the countryside passing in a blur that eventually gave way to the built-up cityscape and then more industrial outlying buildings. Finally, it pulled up at a small air terminal.

'Here.' He nodded towards a hangar that was guarded by a single soldier.

It wasn't Emmeline's first time flying in a private jet—her father's was permanently stationed in the States—so it was no surprise for her to be ushered through a private building and customs area before being whisked across the deserted Tarmac to a jet bearing a golden 'M' on its tail.

He handed her suitcase to an attendant, but it wasn't until he climbed the stairs with her that it occurred to Emmeline he might be coming along for the trip. That she might have given herself a rather long flight with a man she never wanted to speak to again.

'What are you doing?' she asked, her words as cold as ice as she paused at the top of the plane's steps.

'What do you think?' He walked deeper into the plane, pausing at an armchair and waiting for her to follow.

She shot him a pointed look, but moved towards him. Fine. If he wanted to join her—to sit with her—then she'd make him sing for his supper. He could damned well give her some answers to the questions that were crashing around inside her.

'So he told you before you and I had even agreed to the marriage?' she said, sitting down in the armchair and buckling her seatbelt in place.

Her fingers were trembling so she clasped them firmly in her lap. Shock was a wave that was spreading around her, swallowing her in its depths.

'He bullied you into marrying me,' she murmured, her eyes locking on the view beyond the window. She had to focus on this conversation or she'd fall apart.

A muscle jerked in Pietro's cheek at her characterisation of their marriage. 'He asked me to help him.'

She pulled a face. 'To help him *manage* me? God! This was meant to be *my* decision. My first step to freedom.'

There was a throb of anxious silence, and if Emmeline had lifted her eyes to Pietro's face she would have seen the aching sympathy there. But she couldn't look at him. His face was now inextricably linked with betrayal.

'He was worried about how you'd cope. He didn't want you to see him unwell.'

Emmeline stared out of the window, the lump in her throat growing bigger by the minute. Was he in pain? Was the housekeeper Miss Mavis looking after him? Was he scared? Tears filled her eyes and she didn't bother to blink them away.

'I didn't agree with his decision, but I had to honour it.'

She whipped her head around, barely able to see him through the fog of her grief. 'Don't *say* that. You can't have it both ways! If you didn't agree with his decision then you should have *told* me.'

'I wanted to tell you.' A frown was etched across his face. 'I'd decided I would tell you one day, when the time was right.'

Her laugh was a harsh sound of fury. 'You just said he has months, maybe weeks, to live. What were you waiting for?'

'Excuse me, *signor*? *Signora*?' An attendant practically tiptoed down the centre of the plane, her expression professional. 'We're ready for take-off. Can I get you anything to eat? Drink?'

'No,' he snapped curtly.

'Yes. Scotch. Neat,' Emmeline demanded. 'And some aspirin.'

'Yes, *signora*.'

Pietro leaned forward and put a hand on her knee once privacy had been restored. 'This changes *niente*—nothing about what we are.'

'Like hell it does!' Her disbelief was a force-field of shock. 'You have been lying to me this whole time. *This whole time*.' She sat back in her seat, all the fight in her evaporating as quickly as it had appeared.

When the attendant appeared with her drink she threw it back, then lifted the aspirin.

'Don't take those,' he murmured. 'You've just had a ton of alcohol…'

She glared at him angrily and tossed the pills into her mouth. 'Go to hell.'

She woke somewhere off the coast of the States. Her head was pounding, her eyes were scratchy and there was a heaviness in her heart that didn't initially make sense. She was disorientated and confused.

She blinked her eyes open and looked forward.

Straight into the brooding stare of her husband.

The smile that was always so quick to come to her lips when she saw him did not come.

Sadness and grief sludged through her instead, and then it all came rushing back. The lie. The secrecy. The betrayal. Her father's cancer.

The fact that he was going to die.

And she hadn't been with him.

Instead she'd been living in Italy, believing everything was amazing, pretending she was normal, truly thinking herself to be happy.

'You told me I could trust you,' she said, so quietly he had to strain to hear the words. 'Do you remember?'

'*Si.*'

'You were talking about Bianca and the other women. But I took it to mean you were generally trustworthy.'

'Your father trusted me,' he said softly, darkly, the words slicing through her resolve.

The betrayal—by both the men she loved—cut her to the quick.

'I can't believe he told you and not me. How dare he? How dare *you*?'

'He was concerned that you would be very vulnerable when he is no longer with us. You will inherit an enormous fortune, and he felt you hadn't had the experience necessary to remain safe from less desirable elements. He wanted to know you were protected. Is that so awful?'

'Yes!' she spat angrily. 'He was afraid of wild dogs and so he sent me to live with a wolf.'

Pietro's eyes flashed with suppressed frustration.

'Don't you *get* it? I will never believe anything you say again. You begged me to trust you and I did. Apparently I was just as naïve and stupid as Daddy thought.'

She glared out of the window, her heart thumping hard when land appeared below. She was back in her country—or the airspace above it, at least—and she never planned to leave it again.

She was home. At least, that was what she told herself.

'Oh, sugar.' Miss Mavis pulled the door inwards, her face lined with tears. Her middle was comfortingly round and she pulled Emmeline against her, holding her tight. 'I'm so sorry.'

Emmeline was aware of everything in that instance. Miss Mavis's sweet scent—like lemon and sugar and butter all rolled into one—the sound of an aeroplane droning overhead, the way Pietro stiffened at her side, and the way her own heart lurched and rolled with the certainty that it was too late.

'I came as soon as I heard. How is he?'

'Oh, Miss Emmeline...'

Miss Mavis's face crumpled and Emmeline knew. She just *knew*. Even the light was different as it glistened across the front of Annersty. The sun was bleak, mourning his loss.

'When?'

The quiet question came from behind her—a voice as much stained by grief as her heart was. And she didn't doubt the truth of his sadness. Pietro had loved Col like a father. Had loved him enough to marry her just to give Col some semblance of reassurance at the end of his life.

'An hour ago,' Miss Mavis sobbed. 'We tried to call you, but your phone…'

Miss Mavis, whom Emmeline had known from five years of age, was like family. She ran a hand over Emmeline's back, holding her tight, comforting her.

'Can I see him?' Emmeline whispered, sounding like the little girl she'd been the year Mavis was hired.

'Of course you can.'

Miss Mavis stepped inwards and Emmeline followed, but then she spun around, her eyes fiercely accusing as they locked to Pietro's.

'Don't.'

She lifted a hand to emphasise her point, then fixed her gaze somewhere over his shoulder. She didn't want to look at the pallor of his face, the haunted eyes. She didn't want to think about the fact that he'd lost someone he loved as well. That he was possibly as wrenched apart by sadness as she was.

'Don't you dare come into my house.'

He flinched as though she'd hit him. *'Cara…'*

'No. Don't you dare.'

Miss Mavis's hand on her back offered strength and comfort. She was feeling more and more like herself again.

'If I'd never married you I would have been with him. *I would have been with him.*'

Pietro braced a hand on the side of the door but otherwise made no effort to move inside. 'It's not what he wanted.'

'He was wrong. *You* were wrong.' She shook her head angrily. 'You should have told me. I should have been here. I'll never forgive you for this.'

She stepped backwards and slammed the door shut, sobbing as it latched into place.

CHAPTER THIRTEEN

ON THE THIRD day after her father died—the morning of the funeral—she found a note stuffed in a book. It had fallen beneath his bed, and she'd pulled it out, was unfolding it slowly, when a knock at his door startled her. She spun guiltily, jamming the piece of paper into her vintage Dior clutch.

Pietro stood in the opening, dressed in a black suit, his dark hair styled back from his face, and he looked so strong and handsome, so supportive and sexy, that she wanted to throw herself across the room and take every bit of strength he was willing to give her.

But she didn't. Because he'd destroyed what they were. Or maybe what they'd never been. The illusion of their marriage seemed like a dream now—one she would never have again. He'd kept his distance since they'd arrived at Annersty, and yet he'd always been there. Dealing with the lawyers, the servants, the mourners who arrived unannounced.

'It's time to go,' he said quietly, his face lined with sympathy and sorrow.

The childish urge to tell him to stay the hell away from the funeral evaporated in the midst of what she knew her father would have wanted and expected. Col had loved Pietro, and she knew her husband well enough to know that it was mutual.

'I'm not going with you.' She settled for that instead.

'Yes, you are.'

He pushed the door shut, leaving him on the bedroom side of it, and walked towards her. She froze like a deer in the headlights—as she had on their wedding night.

She tilted her chin defiantly, remembering all that had happened since that night. Changes had been wrought on her personality and her confidence—changes that couldn't be undone now.

'We *will* go together because if we arrive separately it will cause gossip and scandal.'

'Oh, heaven forbid anyone should cast aspersions on the great Pietro Morelli's marriage—'

'I don't give a damn what the papers say about *me*,' he interrupted firmly, his expression showing grim sympathy, 'but your father, on this day, deserves the focus to be on him. I will not provide the media with any distraction from the greatness he achieved in his long career of public service.'

'Oh, God.' She gripped his shirt for support as her body weakened, a wave of nausea rolling over her at the recognition of what this day was. 'I can't do this.'

'Yes, you can.'

'I can't!' she sobbed, shaking her head from side to side. 'I can't bury him. I can't. *I can't.*'

'Hush…hush.'

He stroked her back, her hair, held her tight, whispered words in his own language—words she didn't try to translate. She didn't need to understand what he was saying to feel comforted.

'I'm here with you.'

And he was. He stayed by Emmeline's side throughout the awful, necessary ordeal. As she said goodbye to the hundreds of lawmakers, donors and friends who'd come to pay their final respects. Pietro's mother and brother were there too, and it was strange to see them here in the church at Annersty. Her new family merging with her old.

Only they weren't her family.

And Pietro wasn't really her husband.

The funeral was a time to say goodbye to more than just Col. It was an ending of all things.

Late that night, when everyone had left and it was just Emmeline and her grief, Pietro found her on her knees in a room that he quickly surmised had been hers as a girl.

'What are you doing here?' she asked without looking, the tone of weary defeat thick in her words.

He crouched down beside her and handed her a mug. 'Coffee?'

She took it, her eyes red-rimmed. 'Thank you.' She curled her fingers around it and sat down on her bottom, staring around the room. 'I was just wishing I could lift a corner of the blanket of time and slip beneath it.' Her smile was vague. 'I want to be a little girl again.'

'The room is very…pink.'

She nodded. 'My favourite colour.'

'I'm surprised,' he said quietly. 'I would have thought perhaps green or red.'

Emmeline wrinkled her nose. 'Nope. Pink. Rainbow. Sparkles.'

She sipped her drink and then pushed herself up to stand, pacing over to the window.

'It was a nice funeral.'

'It was. A fitting service for a man like your father.'

Silence filled the room. A sad, throbbing ache of quiet that spread darkness through Emmeline's soul. She wanted to lift the blanket of time and go back days, not just years. She wanted to be back in Rome, lying in Pietro's arms, hot and slumberous from having made love to him all night, smiling as though the world were a simple place.

But she couldn't go back. Time was a one-way train and it had scooped her up, deposited her on tracks she didn't want to be on. Yet here she was, bound by grief and betrayal, and her destination was fixed.

'There's no point you being here,' she said softly. 'You should go back to Rome.'

'No.' A quiet word of determination. 'I'm not leaving you.'

She turned to face him, her expression blank. 'I don't want you here. Daddy was wrong to think I couldn't cope with this. And he was wrong to think you and he should keep it from me. It's all wrong. Everything we are has been a mistake.'

'It's not the time to make this decision,' he said stonily. 'You have buried your father today.'

'I know what the hell I've done today!' she snapped. 'Tomorrow, the next day—it doesn't matter. Nothing's going to change how I feel.' She sucked in a breath, her lungs burning with hurt. 'If you care about me at all, you'll go. Please.'

His eyes were impossible to read as they locked to hers. He stared at her for a long moment and then nodded softly, turning on his heel and leaving. He pulled the door shut with a soft click but Emmeline was as startled as though he'd slammed it.

Well? She'd been emphatic. What had she expected? That he'd sweep her off her feet and carry her to bed? Lie her down and stroke her back until she fell asleep?

That spoke of an intimacy that had been a lie. How could anything make sense when trust was broken between them? And, no matter what he said or did, he'd broken their trust in the most vital of ways. Robbing her of the chance to be with her father in his last months. To love him and care for him.

She had another sip of coffee, her eyes following the moonlight that danced over the rolling hills of the estate. The trees she'd always loved…the hills she'd rolled down as a young girl.

Strange that she no longer felt the same ties to Annersty she had at one time believed unbreakable. It was no longer the home she saw when she closed her eyes. Instead, her mind was filled with visions of fruit orchards and a tumbling down farmhouse.

She blinked her eyes open, determined not to let her traitorous thoughts go there.

Emmeline slept fitfully, her dreams punctuated by loneliness and grief, her mind heavy with sadness and need. When she woke she was pale, and there were bags under her eyes. She didn't bother to hide them. It was only the housekeeping staff here, and Miss Mavis had seen her in all modes over the years.

Emmeline pulled on a pair of jeans and a sweater. It wasn't a particularly cold day, but she was cold inside.

When Emmeline had finished senior school, and decided not to attend college so she could keep an eye on her father, she'd moved out of her old bedroom and into a larger suite of rooms. It had been more appropriate, given the fact she'd been of an age when most people were moving out of their parental homes for good. She had a large bedroom, a walk-in wardrobe, a beautiful bathroom that had always made her feel as though she was in an old-fashioned book like *Gone with the Wind*, and beyond that a sitting room and office that had a beautiful view over the lake in the East Lawn.

Her eyes were focussed on that window as she crossed the sitting room, seeking out the view that had always provided such a balm to her soul, so it wasn't until she heard a movement that she realised she wasn't alone.

Pietro was on the sofa, scruffy as hell and even more physically beautiful for his air of dishevelment. He wore the trousers from the suit he'd had on at the funeral, and the shirt too. The jacket had been discarded somewhere. He'd pushed his shirtsleeves up and his hair was thick and tousled, as though she'd been dragging her fingers through it all night even though she knew she'd never do so again.

She froze, her eyes unable to do anything but drink him in. To stare at him as though he was the answer to every question that had made her toss and turn all night.

'Buongiorno.'

His voice was gravelled perfection. She sucked in a breath, steadying herself, blinking her eyes to clear the image of him as the man she loved. How could she forgive him? He was her father's friend. And a liar.

'What are you doing here?'

He stood, and if she had ever seen him in the boardroom

she would have recognised the look of unshakable determination that set his face.

'I'm staying with you.'

'I told you to go.' It was a bleak rejoinder.

The wind ran around the house, wuthering against the walls and shaking the glass behind her. She jumped as it banged loudly in its ancient timber frame.

He stood, crossing the room so that he stood before her. He didn't touch her, but he looked at her so intently that he might as well have.

'I love you,' he said simply. 'If you are here then I am here.'

She made a noise of exasperation. 'You don't need to pretend any more! Daddy's dead. It's over. You did what you were supposed to do. We can let this charade go.'

She wrapped her arms around her chest, hugging herself tight.

If anything, his expression simply assumed an air of even greater determination. 'You need to eat something.'

'I'm not hungry.'

'You look terrible.'

Her eyes flashed with pent-up emotion. 'Just as I did when we first became engaged? This is who I *am*, Pietro. You might have tried the Cinderella treatment on me but I'm just this person. Here.'

It took all his strength not to respond angrily. He *was* angry! Bitterly so. But he smiled gently instead.

'I mean you look like you *feel* terrible. You look as though you haven't slept. You look as though you have lost weight even in the few days we have been in America. Please, come and eat something.'

'This is *my* house,' she said coldly. 'I'll do what I damned well please.'

She stalked out of her suite, her shoulders square, her gaze focussed on the stairs ahead. But her heart was breaking and her eyes were leaking hot, salty tears of misery...

* * *

Days passed in a strange fog. Pietro was always there. Sleeping on the definitely too short sofa just outside her bedroom, keeping his distance but also watching her constantly. After a week she stopped wanting him to go. She stopped wishing he would go. Or rather she began to accept that she was glad he'd stayed.

Her world had been rocked off its axis with Col's death, and having Pietro with her offered comfort that she knew she couldn't get from anyone else. Even Sophie, with her cheery visits and bottles of wine, couldn't erase the throbbing ache deep in her heart.

Emmeline didn't speak to Pietro. Not beyond the obligatory morning greeting and an occasional comment about the weather. But his constant presence was doing something strange inside her. Something she needed and resented in equal measure. She was starting to feel like herself again, and she hated it that it was because of Pietro.

A month after Col's death Emmeline came home to find her father's lawyer in the lounge, locked in conversation with Pietro.

'We've discussed this,' Pietro was saying firmly. 'The estate passes in its entirety to Emmeline.'

Emmeline paused on the threshold, a frown on her face, before sweeping into the room. Pietro's expression was wary, his concern obvious. Emmeline knew why. She had continued to lose weight and she didn't have any to spare.

She ignored his concern and smiled politely at Mr Svenson. 'Can I help you with something, Clarke?'

'Oh…um…er…'

'It's handled,' Pietro said firmly, standing.

Clarke Svenson followed his lead, smiling kindly at Emmeline as he moved as quickly as possible towards the door.

As soon as they were alone, Emmeline whipped around to face her husband. 'What was that all about?'

Pietro expelled a sigh and reached down for his coffee

cup. He took a sip and she realised, with a sudden flash of guilt, that he hardly looked his best either. He looked tired, and she hated the way her heart twisted in acknowledgement of the fact.

'There are the usual scum looking to get in on your father's will. Long-lost second cousins twice removed—that sort of thing.' He rolled his eyes. 'It's being handled.'

Her eyes were round in her face. 'By you?'

'*Si*. Someone has to evaluate the claims on their merits.' He moved towards her, slowly, cautiously, as though she were a skittish horse he needed to calm.

She nodded, but without understanding. 'And you've been doing that?'

'*Si.*'

'Why?'

'Because I'm your husband,' he said softly. 'Because you needed me to.'

His eyes ran across her face and he took a step closer, but she shook her head.

'And because my father expected you to,' she added softly.

So much of what they were came back to that, and Emmeline couldn't shake the feeling that she'd been traded. That she was not so much an asset as a bad debt that her father had needed to hand off before he'd died.

Her grief was never-ending.

'We must talk,' he murmured gently.

'I know. But I'm not… I can't… I can't. Not… I'm not… ready.'

'Okay—that's okay. I understand.'

'God, *stop* being so understanding. Stop being so kind. I don't want you here, picking up all these pieces. No matter how kind you are now, nothing can change what happened.'

He ground his teeth together, his eyes clashing with hers. 'I hated lying to you.'

'That's *bull*. You aren't the kind of man who would do anything he hated.'

'It was the perfect rock and a hard place,' he said with understated determination. 'Your father made me swear I wouldn't tell you…'

'How did you think I'd forgive this?' she asked. 'How did you think we'd move past it?'

'I don't know,' he said honestly. 'But I knew we would. I know we *will*.'

'How? How *can* we?'

'Because I am me, and you are you, and together we have found something so special, so unique, that it is irreplaceable.' His eyes forced hers to meet his, and the challenge was impossible to ignore. 'I worried about you not knowing. I worried about you finding out and about you losing your father. I worried about your anger and your hurt. But I never once thought it would be the end for us.'

He stared at her still, his eyes begging her to see, to understand.

'Can you look at me now and think there is a life which we don't share?'

'It was all a lie.' She was numb.

'Nothing about what we are was a lie.'

'Yes, it was! You were my… You woke me up, remember? With you I became a proper, full person. I felt whole and mature, and the most like myself I've ever felt. And really you were just an extension of Daddy. Managing me and infantilising me out of a mistaken belief that I can't look after myself. I thought you saw me as an equal, but instead I was your obligation.'

'At first,' he said, the words a thick concession. 'But you dressed me down at our wedding and I knew that Col was wrong about you. You were naïve, yes, but not weak. Not incapable of handling yourself.'

He reached out and took her hand in his, and his relief at her letting him hold it was immense.

'I'm not here to protect you. I'm here because I need you—and right now you need me. That's marriage.' He stroked the soft flesh of her inner wrist. 'I want more than anything to be married to you. Not because your father sought it, but because of who you are and what we have come to mean to one another.'

The words were like little blades, scraping against the walls she'd been building brick by brick around her heart.

And yet she wasn't ready.

She couldn't forgive him.

'It's too soon. Too much.' She blinked away tears and pulled her hand back to herself. 'If you'd slept with another woman I would find it easier to forgive.'

His laugh was a harsh sound of disbelief. 'You are grieving, and I am trying to give you the space you need. I do not want to crowd you. And I certainly don't want to fight with you. But ask yourself this question: What could I have done differently? I spoke to your father weekly, urging him to tell you about his illness. He was adamant that you should not know.'

'You spoke to him *weekly*?' If anything her sense of betrayal yawned wider.

'He wanted to be reassured you were happy.'

'Oh, *what* a good friend you were!' she snapped, but the indignation of her words was somewhat marred by the sob that strangled them. 'You went above and beyond to make me happy.'

A frown was etched over his handsome face.

'You made it so obvious that you weren't attracted to me, and still you seduced me. You made me think I was *very* happy.'

'None of that had anything to do with your father.'

She rolled her eyes. 'It was *all* because of him. He pulled the strings—just like he did with me my whole life.' She stamped her foot. 'You were supposed to be *mine*. Rome was meant to be *mine*.'

'I didn't marry you with any expectations that it would become a real marriage. That was all *us*. I fell in love with you, Emmeline. Not because of Col but because of you and me.'

The words were sucking her in—so sweet, so exactly what she needed to hear that she rejected them instantly.

'No.'

She held a hand up in the air. To silence him? Or slap him?

'Lying to me about Dad, keeping his secret—that's completely incompatible with love. Love is honesty and truth. It's trust.'

'In a perfectly black and white world, perhaps. But nothing about this was simple. My loyalties were split from the moment I met you. I made him a promise before I even properly knew you. I felt obligated to stick to it. That's the man you love.'

She blinked, felt her heart bricking itself up, its walls forming more easily now they had well-worn foundations.

'I don't love you,' she mumbled tightly. 'I never did. I see that now. I loved Rome. I loved sex. But you? No. I don't even *like* you.'

She spun on her heel and walked quickly from the lounge, waiting until she was in her own room before she let out the sob that was burning inside her.

That night, her dreams were terrifying.

Her mother stood behind Emmeline, her face pinched, dressed all in black.

'See? This is what you deserve, Emmeline. You are alone. All alone. Nobody will be there for you. And that's as it should be.'

It was the crying that woke him. Emmeline had been tossing and turning and crying out in her sleep almost nightly for the whole month they'd been at Annersty. But this was different.

Her sobbing was loud, and when she began to say, 'Go away! Go away! Go away!' again and again in her sleep he felt a cold ache throb through him.

He'd stayed because he'd believed it to be what she needed. But was it possible he was hurting her more with his presence?

I don't even like you.

That was possibly more damning than her insistence that she was angry. It was such a cold denial of all that they were.

Torn between going to her and letting her settle herself, he was just standing to move into her bedroom when she went quiet. All returned to normal.

Pietro took up his cramped space on the sofa, his mind an agony of indecision. Torn between what she needed and what he wanted, he knew there was only one option open to him.

If she needed him to go so she could have the space to realise what they were, then he had to give it to her.

CHAPTER FOURTEEN

EMMELINE STARED AT herself in the mirror with a frown. The dress was beautiful. Her hair was neat. Her make-up flawless.

But she looked wrong. Different. Something was missing. The tan she'd acquired in Rome? The smile that had permanently framed her face? The glint she'd become used to seeing in her eyes—one of utter happiness?

No matter.

She wasn't that girl any more.

She blinked and stepped away from the disappointing image in the mirror. She had no time for maudlin self-reflections. She was late.

Thankfully Sophie was permanently at least fifteen minutes behind schedule, but Emmeline still felt stressed as she lifted her vintage clutch and tucked it under her arm. She pulled her bedroom door inwards, and the lurch of emptiness as she crossed the threshold and stepped into the small area that Pietro had used as a makeshift bedroom was like falling into a pit of quicksand.

There was nothing left of him. Not even the faint hint of citrus and pine that had lingered a day or two after he'd told her he would go if that was what she'd really wanted.

The horrible truth was she *hadn't* wanted that—not really. She'd nodded as he'd said the words, seeing that his mind was apparently made up, but her heart had been screaming. Begging him to stay, willing him to ignore everything she'd said and just be with her.

He'd driven away only an hour after they'd spoken, and the sense of grief and loss had almost eclipsed anything she'd felt since her father had died.

He'd messaged her every second day over the fortnight since he'd left but she hadn't replied. Not because she'd wanted to be childish or to punish him, but because she had no idea what to say. How to express feelings that she couldn't even comprehend herself. The grief, the betrayal, the disbelief. The worry that he'd been pushed into a marriage he'd never wanted. That she'd been falling in love while he'd been making do. The worry that she'd never be able to trust that there had been truth in *any* of their inter-actions.

She slipped behind the wheel of her car, her expression bleak as she started the engine and began to make her way into town.

The Bowerbird Lounge was doing a roaring trade, de-spite the fact it was a grey November day. The tables outside featured patrons wrapped in brightly coloured blankets, and the heaters beneath the awnings were on and glowing warm.

As she'd expected, Sophie was nowhere to be seen, but their reserved table was available so Emmeline took a seat and ordered a Diet Coke. She enjoyed people-watching. With her dark sunglasses firmly in place, she gave herself the freedom of scanning the room, watching the guests and catching snippets of conversation.

Ten minutes later her phone began to buzz and she reached into her clutch, pulling it out and answering it when she saw Sophie's face beaming back at her from the screen.

'Hey, hon, I'm just looking for a space. I'll be a few min-utes, okay?'

'That's fine,' Emmeline murmured.

'Seriously… What the hell? There's no spaces on this whole damn block.' Sophie made a grunting noise of com-plaint and Emmeline smiled, tinkering with the clip on her purse.

A piece of the lining, old and fine, ran across her finger-tip. She tried to pull it straight, then realised it wasn't the lining at all. It was a piece of paper, folded several times, with her name on the front.

Her heart was pounding so hard and fast that she could no longer hear the din of the restaurant. She disconnected the call and dropped her phone to the table, her fingers shaking as she unfolded the letter. The letter she'd thrust into her bag on the morning of the funeral and forgotten about.

How had she forgotten? Disbelief raged inside her as she sat, ready to read whatever the note contained.

Her dad's handwriting was barely recognisable to Emmeline. It was spidery and fine, weak and pale.

Pumpkin…

Emmeline felt tears sting her eyes. She could hear Col's voice so clearly. She sucked in a deep breath and kept reading.

At the end of one's life I suppose it's natural to reflect. On choices, decisions, roads not taken. Having you as a daughter is the best thing I've ever done, but I wonder now if I've done it all wrong. Have I failed you? More than likely. That's hard for me to admit, because I have always tried to do everything in my power to make your life a good and rich one.

I didn't want to lose you so I kept you close, and I got in the way of you living your own life. I've been selfish.

These last few months…knowing you to be in Rome, on the brink of so much excitement in your life, so happy with Pietro… I have finally seen you as you should have been all along. Your happiness and independence is the most precious gift I have ever received. I wish I could have helped you find them sooner.

I know my death will have come as a surprise. But while I know you are shocked, you must know that I wanted it this way. Please don't be angry with me for keeping my diagnosis from you. I wanted to spare you as much pain as possible, and I know you would have deferred your own pleasure and adventures to stay close to me. You've done far too much of that already.

Pietro disagreed with my decision, but he was faithful to the last. I am grateful to him for upholding my confidence even when he felt strongly that you would prefer to know the truth. Sparing you the pain of seeing me as I've become is my last gift to you— and it is *a gift, Pumpkin. I am not this man.*

I hope you can both forgive me for making him stay the course. Or perhaps I have been selfish to the last.

Be happy together. He is a good man and he loves you very much.

As do I.
Forever,
Daddy

Emeline didn't realise she was sobbing until the young girl at the table beside her reached across with a tissue.

'Oh, I'm sorry…'

Emmeline stood up, the table jerking loudly as she moved. She wove through the restaurant and caught Sophie just as she was bursting through the door.

'I have to go,' Emmeline said quickly. 'I'm sorry.'

'Is everything okay?'

Emmeline shook her head, then nodded, her face showing all the confusion that was rich in her heart. 'I… I don't know.'

She handed the letter to Sophie and wrapped her arms around herself as her best friend scanned its contents.

Afterwards, she lifted her eyes to Emmeline's face, trying very hard not to react. 'Where did you get this?'

Emmeline's voice was a sob. 'It was…it was in his book. I found it on the day of the funeral but I… I put it in my clutch and I just found it now. I didn't even think about it again. I suppose I presumed it was just… I don't know. Why didn't I read it sooner?'

Sophie tsked sympathetically. 'Would it have changed anything?'

Emmeline's expression bore anguish. Sophie knew the truth of the situation now—including her real reasons for marrying Pietro.

'How can he have thought it was the right decision?'

Sophie expelled a soft breath. 'Your father was a very proud man.'

'God, I know that. I *know* that! But he was also selfish.' Her voice cracked as she spoke the condemnation. Hot guilt at betraying him spread like wildfire through her body. 'He had *no right* to decide to cut me out.'

'He wanted you to be happy.'

'So he sent me away?'

Sophie sighed. 'Imagine if you'd stayed. You'd have nursed your father and you'd have been by his side when he died, sure. You'd have seen a great, strong man become weak and no longer in control of his body. And when he died you'd have been alone. Bereft. Miserable. Instead you have a new life. A life you love.'

'A life my father *chose* for me,' Emmeline scoffed. 'Don't you *see*, Sophie? I should have been free to find my own way!'

'If you had every choice in the world before you, would you want anything other than what you had with Pietro? Would you have chosen any differently for yourself?'

Emmeline's heart skidded at the mere mention of her husband's name. It spurred an ache deep inside her gut, for it was not just a random collection of letters. It was a call that her body instinctively wanted to answer. It was a promise and a denial. It was everything.

'You can choose now, Emmeline. It's not too late. You have the world at your feet. What do you want to do?'

Pietro was on fire, and then he was ice-cold. His brow beaded with perspiration as once again he read the letters at the top of the document. Did he miraculously expect them to alter in some way? To rearrange themselves and say something else.

PETITION FOR DIVORCE
Emmeline Morelli v Pietro Morelli

He swore, using every curse he knew, and then repeated them for good measure, scraping his chair back and moving to the door of his office even as he wrenched his phone from his pocket. For the second time in two months he ordered his jet to be made ready at a moment's notice, the urgency in his voice instantly communicating itself to his unflappable assistant.

He stared at the document for the entire drive to the airport, and then again as the plane lifted off. It was a straight-up divorce petition. No dispute over assets or ongoing entitlements, despite his considerable wealth—then again, her own fortune was formidable. She had no need to make a claim on his.

But it bothered him because everything about the document spoke of a woman who wanted to wrap their marriage up swiftly—to bring it to an official conclusion in the fastest possible way.

Did she really think he'd sign the damned thing? Without so much as a conversation?

His plane touched down in the early evening and Elizabetta, with her usual efficiency, had organised a driver to collect him. He stared broodingly out of the window as the car cut through the miles between the airport and Annersty.

But when it pulled up at the front of the grand estate the

adrenalin that had brought him the whole way to Georgia seemed to disappear. He swore under his breath and pushed himself out of the car, the divorce papers clutched in his hand.

Miss Mavis answered the door and her smile was warm. Precisely the opposite of what he expected from Emmeline.

He was unable to dredge up more than a grimace of acknowledgement. 'Is she home?'

'Yes, sir.' Miss Mavis stepped back, holding the door wide open. 'She's swimming, I believe.'

'Swimming?' He arched a brow. Well, he hadn't expected *that*.

He stormed through the house, anger taking the place of adrenalin. How dared she end their marriage like this? Without the courtesy of so much as a phone call? Hell, she hadn't even answered his text messages!

As he got closer to the indoor swimming pool the sound of her splashing made him slow. He tried—and failed—to get a grip on his temper. The doors were made of glass. He saw her even before he'd shouldered into the marble-floored room. She was moving slowly through the water, her stroke elegant, her legs languid as they kicked along the length of the pool.

Desire kicked hard in his gut; he forced himself to ignore it.

He ground his teeth together and began to stride on at the side of the water, all the way to the end of the pool. He reached it before she did, and crouched down so that when her fingertips grazed the tiled edge he was able to reach down and touch them. He'd meant simply to alert her to his presence, but the moment he felt her soft flesh beneath his a visceral ache overtook his body—a need to touch more than her fingers, more than her hand.

He straightened in physical rejection of the idea.

She emerged from the water and all he could do was stare at her. Her face was wiped clean of make-up, her hair was slicked back, and her expression showed nothing but shock. He felt something like a stabbing pain in his gut. She was so young, so innocent and so beautiful.

If she wanted a divorce, what kind of bastard was he to fight it? Didn't she deserve her freedom? True freedom? Not the kind that was bargained for and arranged by her father, but the freedom that came of being a young woman who had her own place in the world.

All the fight and the anger he'd brought with him, the disbelief that she wanted to end their marriage, evaporated.

He had to let her go.

He had to do what Col hadn't been able to.

He had to acknowledge that she was a mature woman with every damned right to make her own choices in life.

'Pietro.'

It was a groan and it broke through his resolve. Her eyes dropped to the document in his hands and at the moment of recognition she blanched. Her eyes held desperate anguish as they met his.

'You got the papers.'

'Si, cara.'

Why did she look as though he was killing kittens in front of her? This was *her* choice. *Her* decision.

He looked away, the sight of her making him want more than anything to argue with her. To use any tool at his disposal—yes, even sex—to get her to agree to give their marriage another chance.

But she'd been railroaded enough for a lifetime.

'You didn't have to hand-deliver them.'

Her words were so quiet. So pained. God, how he wanted to swoop down and take that pain away.

'That wasn't my intention.' He stepped back from the water's edge, feeling utter disbelief at what he was about to do.

'Wasn't it?'

The water made a rippling sound as she lifted her arms

out of it and braced her forearms against the coping, then pressed her chin into the back of one hand.

'So why *did* you come?'

He shook his head, forcing himself to look at her. But the pain was back—an ache that seemed to rip through him when he met her eyes. The change in her was marked. The happiness that had seemed to shimmer out of her pores in Rome was utterly absent now.

'I was surprised to receive these,' he said, without answering her question.

'Why should you be?'

Visibly, she seemed to tighten her resolve, to assume a mask of unconcern. How did he know it to be a mask? Because he *knew*. He knew everything about her.

'Our reasons for marrying are gone now. He's dead.' Her voice cracked. 'You're free.'

Pietro's head whipped back to hers. He crouched down. Urgency perforated his tone and he spoke before thinking. 'What do you mean, I'm *free*?'

'You did everything he wanted. You were a very good friend to my father. But it seems only fair to absolve you of this responsibility.'

Now it was Emmeline whose eyes were jerking away, refusing to hold his.

Pietro's mind moved quickly, rapidly sifting through her statement, trying to comprehend her words.

'You're divorcing me because you want to free me from our marriage?' He held the papers up. 'This is for *me*?'

She opened her mouth, surprise obvious in her face. She shook her head, and her eyes showed panic. 'I… It's the right thing to do.'

'*Why* is it, *cara*? Do you think I no longer love you?'

Tears sparkled on her lashes, mixing with the water of the pool. 'Please…don't. Don't say those things. It's not fair.'

His gut whooshed to the floor. She was right. Hadn't he just been telling himself that? And yet…

'I'll sign the papers, Emmeline. If that's what you really want. But I want to hear you say it.'

'Say what?' The words were a whisper and yet they echoed around the pool room.

'Tell me you don't love me.' He crouched down once more. 'Look in my eyes, see all the love I feel for you there, and tell me you don't feel the same.' The words were so deep, so gravelled. 'Tell me you don't want to live in Rome with me, as my wife, that you don't want to be in my bed, that you don't want to continue your studies. Tell me that you want to end our marriage. That *you* want that.'

Her sob was heartbreaking but he didn't withdraw.

'I don't want to be married to you. Not like this.'

Her addendum at the end was a lifeline in the midst of a turbulent, terrifying ocean.

'Not like what?'

'Not because of him. Not because you felt forced to protect me. Don't you see? I'm not the girl he thought I was. The girl *you* thought I was.'

'I know that,' he agreed urgently. 'You never were. I married you because Col asked me to, yes. But I want to stay married to you because of how I feel. How *you* feel. Because of what we *are*.'

Tears ran down her cheeks. She bit down on her lip and looked away from him, trying—and failing—to rally her emotions into order.

'I don't think I believe you.'

The words were agonising to both of them.

'I need us to divorce. It's the only way.'

None of it made any sense. He expelled a soft sigh as he tried to comprehend his wife's viewpoint.

'Then say it.' His eyes held a silent challenge. 'Tell me you don't love me and I'll sign these papers and drop them off at your lawyer's on my way out of town.'

Her sharp intake of breath told him everything he needed to know.

'But if you love me—as I think you do—say that. Tell me that. Be honest with me.'

'Our marriage has no future,' she murmured, ignoring his question. 'I'll never trust you. I'll never believe you're not with me because of a sense of obligation...'

'My God, Emmeline! If this was about obligation do you think I would have slept with you? I tried so hard to fight that, to not want you as I did, and yet you became my obsession. Think about it, *cara*. You had given me *carte blanche* with other women. But I didn't want them. I wanted *you*. I have wanted you from the moment we married. Hell, probably from that moment in my office when you were laying down the ground rules for our marriage.'

She rejected his assertion with a skyward flicker of her eyes. 'Sure. You thought I was so sexy you told me I had to change how I looked.'

He nodded angrily. 'Yes! Because you were so obviously trying to make yourself as uninteresting as possible. And I was right about that. Because even then I knew you. I don't care what you look like, for heaven's sake. I care about how you *feel*. I want you to be happy. I want you to be happy with *me*. But if you want to be here at Annersty alone, or—*God*—with another man eventually, just tell me. Say it and I'll sign these.'

'I can't... I told you. I can't... This marriage...'

He made a sound of frustration, and before she knew what he was doing—perhaps before even Pietro knew himself—he was sliding into the pool beside her, fully dressed. He kicked his shoes off as he wrapped his arms around her waist and drew her to him. And then he kissed her, the surprised 'O' of her mouth giving him the perfect opportunity. He kissed her and she kissed him back.

At least she did for a moment, before her hands lifted to his chest and she sobbed. 'I'll never trust you.'

'Yes, you will.' He stared down at her earnestly. 'I think you already do. I think you hate what happened, and I think you're mad as hell, but I think you love me and you want to find a way to make this work. Do you think that divorcing me will make you happy?'

She stared at him, her expression one of abject fear. And then she shook her head slowly. 'But I need to know you're not trapped. That you're not with me because of him.'

'I'm not.' He arched a brow and pulled her closer, dropping his mouth so that his lips were just a millimetre from hers. 'You gave me a perfect escape clause. You sent me the divorce papers. If I didn't want to be with you do you think I would have flown halfway around the world the second I got them? No. I would have signed them, posted them and heaved a sigh of relief.'

He watched her face, watched it carefully, so that he saw the play of emotions in her features and particularly the moment comprehension seemed to overcome doubt.

'I am *yours*, Emmeline Morelli, for the rest of your life. Married or not, I will never not love you. I will never be with another woman. I will never marry again or have a family. Nothing. Because all that I am…all that I will ever be…is tied up in you.'

Her breath was held in her throat. But still he wasn't sure she understood. So he kissed her again. He kissed her and he whispered into her mouth, over and over and over, like a spell being cast just for her. *'Ti amo, mi amore. Ti amo.'*

In response Emmeline reached up, out of the pool, sliding her fingers across the tiles until they reached the divorce papers. She pulled at them and then, without breaking their kiss, dropped them into the water.

'I love you too.'

'Per sempre?' he groaned.

She nodded. 'Yes. Forever.'

EPILOGUE

Three years later

EMMELINE STOOD IN her graduation robe, clutching her degree, a beaming smile on her face. In the front row sat Pietro, so handsome, so beautiful, and beside him Rafe, Ria and Sophie. Emmeline smiled down at them, waving her fingers as Pietro snapped a photograph, then moved offstage.

Three blissful years, a university degree, and now she was on the cusp of a life that was about to change forever.

There was a swirling sense of celebration and she took part in all of it—smiling through the after-party, making polite conversation with the university professors who had been so helpful to her.

Finally, though, she was alone with her husband.

'I have something for you,' he said, with obvious pride.

'I have something for *you*,' Emmeline repeated. 'Let me go first?'

'Certo.' He grinned. 'Though it hardly seems fair. You are the one who graduated with distinction today. Surely the gifts should all be for you?'

'My gift is a present to me, too.'

She reached into her bag and pulled out an envelope, handing it to him. She watched as he lifted the flap and then looked at the front of the card. It was just a generic *I love you* gift card she'd picked up at the pharmacist. Nothing special.

But when he opened it to read the contents inside, and lifted his eyes to her face, she saw his shock and surprise and she laughed.

'This says we are going to be parents.'

'I know. I wrote it.'

His jaw dropped and he read the card again, his eyes scanning it over and over just to be sure.

'Are you serious?'

'Uh-huh.'

'But…when?'

Emmeline laughed. 'I think we've given ourselves plenty of opportunities, don't you?'

'We're going to be *parents*.'

He closed his eyes, and when he opened them they were swimming with emotion. He dragged her against his chest and kissed her, and she kissed him back, her heart soaring with love and optimism.

What they were—who they'd become—had taken a leap of faith, a mountain of trust and all the courage Emmeline possessed. And it had been worth it.

She stood in the arms of the man she adored, knowing without doubt that they would live happily. *Per sempre*.

* * * * *

THE PLAYBOY'S
RUTHLESS PURSUIT

MIRANDA LEE

To my husband, Tony,

For always being there.

CHAPTER ONE

I SHOULD BE HAPPIER, Jeremy thought as he leant back in his office chair and put his feet up on his large leather-topped desk. *My life is pretty well perfect. I'm as healthy as a horse, filthy rich and blessedly single. On top of that, I'm no longer Chief Investment Consultant at the London branch of the Barker-Whittle banking empire. What a relief!*

Working for his over-achieving father had not been Jeremy's idea of a fun occupation. Unfortunately, he'd been darned good at his job. Despite the accolades and the generous bonuses he'd earned over the years, he much preferred being his own boss. Jeremy had used some of his recently acquired wealth to buy an ailing publishing firm, which he was turning into a rather surprising success. Perverse, considering it was an accidental purchase.

Jeremy's initial aim when launching out on his own had been to go into the property development business, his first purchase last year a town house in one of Mayfair's best streets. But the publishing company leasing the building had proved difficult to deal with, the owner stubbornly insisting on staying put till his lease ran out. So Jeremy had made an offer that he couldn't refuse, thereby solving the problem, his intention having been to relocate his new business to cheaper premises whilst he renovated and converted the slightly run-down property into three luxury apartments.

But things hadn't worked out that way. He'd found himself *liking* the people who worked at Mayfair Books, all of whom were naturally worried about losing their jobs. He also liked the rooms the way they were. Slightly shabby, yes, but full of character and charm, with lots of wood-panelled walls and antique furniture. It had been clear from talking to the employees and looking at their sales figures, however, that the business itself had desperately needed updating. Whilst Jeremy had known next to nothing about the modern publishing industry, he was an intelligent and well-connected man, with loads of business contacts, one of which headed the marketing division of a rather famous London publisher.

So here he was, almost a year later, heading Barker Books, having changed the name along with the company's fortunes. They'd actually made a profit during the last quarter. He even got up every morning and happily went into his office these days, unlike his time at the bank when he'd conducted most of his business over the phone.

So work wasn't the reason for this odd feeling of discontent.

Jeremy knew it wasn't his love life, either. That was sailing along as usual, though, since buying the book business, his focus had been more on work than women.

Not that he felt sexually frustrated. He didn't. Jeremy had no trouble finding willing ladies to accompany him to the many social occasions he was constantly invited to. A man of his status and wealth was a prized guest. His partner du jour invariably accompanied him back to his bed for the night, despite Jeremy always making it clear that dating him was never going to lead to a ring on her finger. He didn't do love or, God forbid, marriage. Thankfully, most of them were good with that, because he didn't do broken hearts, either.

When the reason for his discontent continued to elude Jeremy, he was forced to give the matter deeper thought, something he usually tried to avoid at all costs. He'd never seen the benefit of self-analysis, or counselling. It had never done his older brothers any good. Jeremy knew exactly why he was the way he was. He didn't need a shrink to tell him that his aversion to love and marriage stemmed from his parents' constant divorcing and remarrying. That, plus their abandoning him to boarding school when he was just eight, where he'd been bullied endlessly.

He hated thinking about those years, so he didn't, his mind swiftly moving on to happier times. He'd thoroughly enjoyed his years at University in London, finally using his excellent brain to its full capacity. His results had thrilled his maternal grandmother, who'd promptly made him her heir, on the condition he went on to study at Oxford. Which he had, his generous private income—Gran had passed away shortly after he enrolled—providing him with the kind of lifestyle to which he'd quickly become addicted. He'd done sufficient study to easily pass his exams but, generally speaking, fun had been the order of the day, Jeremy carousing to a level that might have become a problem if he hadn't acquired two slightly more sensible friends.

Thinking of Sergio and Alex sent Jeremy's gaze to the photo of the three of them that was sitting on his desk. Harriet had taken it on the day Sergio had married his one-time stepsister in July last year, Sergio having asked both Alex and himself to be his best men. The wedding had taken place on the shores of Lake Como, in the grounds of a magnificent villa. Whilst no longer worried that Bella might be a chip off her fortune-hunting mother's block, Jeremy wasn't convinced the marriage would last. Love never lasted, did it? Still, there was nothing he could do about that. It was a shame, though, how little he saw of his best friend these days. Of *both* his best friends. He *had* seen them at Alex's wedding to Harriet in Australia back in February, but only briefly. Jeremy really missed the days when they'd all lived in London and got together regularly, back when they'd still all been bachelors and hadn't become billionaires.

Hadn't been thirty-five, either. That had been the kiss of death, their all turning thirty-five last year. That, and the super sale of their WOW wine bar franchise to an American equity company. Suddenly, everything had changed, with the Bachelor Club they'd formed back at Oxford no longer relevant. Maybe their friendship was no longer relevant, either.

With a sigh, Jeremy scraped his feet off his desk. They hit the floor with a thud, the sound echoing the hollow feeling inside his heart. Leaning forward, he picked up the photo, frowning as he studied the three faces smiling back at him.

Jeremy didn't envy his friends and their marriages, but he hated the thought that he would hardly ever see them from now on. Their priorities would be their wives and their families, not him. He would become old news, someone whom they recalled with vague fondness when they glanced through their photo albums every decade or so.

'Who's that man, Dad?' he imagined Alex's son asking. Harriet was expecting a boy.

'Oh, that's Jeremy. A chap I knew once. We went to Oxford together. He was the best man at our wedding. Gosh. Haven't seen him for years.'

Jeremy scowled as he slammed the photo face down on the desk and snatched up his phone.

'Damn it all, I'm not going to let that happen,' he ground out as he retrieved Alex's number.

Realising it would be the middle of the night in Australia—not nice to call at such an hour—Jeremy sent an email volunteering himself for godfather duty when the time came. That done, he righted the photo, placed it back in its pride of place and settled down to have a look at their current sales figures. Finding the file on his laptop, he clicked it open but didn't get far before there was a rapid *tap-tap-tap* on his door.

'Come in, Madge,' he said.

Madge entered as briskly as she did everything. In her mid-fifties, Madge was a thin, plain woman with cropped grey hair, piercing blue eyes and a schoolmarm manner.

Jeremy had hired her soon after buying the business, the previous owner's secretary having quit in a huff over the new owner's high-handed tactics. Jeremy had been impressed with Madge's no-nonsense attitude, plus her knowledge of the publishing industry. He liked her enormously, and the affection was mutual.

'We have a problem,' she said straight away.

'Which is?'

'Kenneth Jacobs can't be the auctioneer at tonight's charity auction. He has a terrible head cold. I could hardly understand him on the phone just now.'

'I see,' Jeremy said, not actually seeing at all. He knew who Kenneth Jacobs was; hard not to, since he was Jeremy's only best-selling author, having come with the deal when he'd bought the business. Kenneth wrote the grizzliest of murder mysteries, which had a huge fan base but whose forty-plus books hadn't been marketed properly. Despite knowing this, Kenneth hadn't left the publisher who'd given him his start. A crusty old bachelor, Kenneth was lazy when it came to business matters. Once Jeremy had taken the helm, he'd republished Kenneth's entire back list, with new covers, and put them all out as e-Books.

'What charity auction?' Jeremy asked, having gained the impression that he was supposed to already know.

Madge rolled her eyes. 'Truly. Just as well you have me to organise things around here. It's not easy working for a man who has a short-term memory loss.'

'I'll have you know I have a photographic memory,' Jeremy said defensively whilst his mind scrambled to remember what it was he'd forgotten.

'In that case I'll photograph everything for you in the future instead of telling you,' Madge said with her usual caustic wit.

As much as Jeremy often enjoyed Madge's dry sense of humour, on this occasion his patience was wearing a little thin.

'Do that, Madge. But for now I would appreciate it if you'd explain about this charity auction one more time, then tell me exactly how I'm supposed to fix the problem of Kenneth having a head cold.' Though by now he had a pretty good idea. Jeremy wasn't always the most intuitive of men, but he wasn't thick, either.

Madge expelled one of her exasperated sighs. 'I would have thought that the words *charity auction* were self-explanatory. But that's beside the point. You told me after the last charity dinner you went to that I wasn't to accept any more invitations to such dos. You said you'd rather slash your wrists than sit through another of those dinners where the food was below par and the speakers intolerably boring. You said you were happy to donate to whatever cause was going but you'd given up being a masochist when you stopped working for your father. You said that—'

'Yes, yes,' Jeremy broke in firmly. 'I get the picture. But that last dinner was just a meal followed by speeches, not something as interesting as an auction. Now, if you don't mind, please fill me in on the relevant details and stop with the ancient history lesson.'

Madge looked as close to sheepish as he'd ever seen her. 'Right. Well, it's being held in the ballroom of the Chelsea Hotel, and it's to raise funds for the women's refuges in the inner-city area. There's a sit-down dinner before the auction, which I'm assured will have quality food and which should raise a good sum of money since it costs a small fortune per head. I gather the place is going to be full of society's finest. Kenneth was to be the auctioneer, the last prize being the privilege of the winning bidder having their name used as a character in his next book. It's been done before, of course, by other authors. But never by Kenneth. The poor fellow is quite disappointed, as well as worried about letting Alice down. She's the girl who's organised everything. Anyway, I told him that you would do it in his stead.'

Jeremy pretended to look displeased. 'Oh, you did, did you?'

For a split second, a worried frown formed on Madge's high forehead. But then she smiled.

'You're just joking, right?'

Jeremy grinned.

Madge flushed with relief and pleasure. She adored Jeremy, envying his mother for having such a warm and wonderful son. He might be a devil where the ladies were concerned—or so she'd been told—but he was a good man and a great boss. Smart, sensible and surprisingly sensitive. She didn't doubt that one day he'd fall in love and settle down.

'You are a teaser,' she said. 'Now, do you want me to ring Alice and tell her you'll do the job as auctioneer? Or do you want to ring her yourself?'

'What do you think, Madge?'

This was another thing she liked about her boss. He often asked her opinion. And usually took it.

'I think you should ring her yourself,' she said. 'It would put her mind at rest. She seemed rather stressed. I gained the impression she was new at this job.'

'Right,' he replied, nodding. 'You'd better get me her number, then.'

Madge already had it in hand, of course.

'You are a very devious woman,' he said as she gave it to him.

'And you are a very sweet man,' she returned with a smug smile before turning and leaving him to it.

Jeremy found himself smiling as he keyed Alice's number into his phone.

'Alice Waterhouse,' she answered immediately, her voice crisp and very businesslike, its cut-glass accent betraying an education at one of those private girls' schools that turned out girls who invariably worked in jobs such as PR or fund-raising for charities before marrying someone suitable to their class.

Jeremy wasn't overly keen on girls from privileged backgrounds, which was rather hypocritical of him, given his own background. There'd been a time when he hadn't cared about such things. If a girl was pretty and keen on him, then he didn't give their character—or their upbringing—much thought. He bedded without bias or prejudice. But nowadays, he found the girls he dated who'd been born rich were seriously boring, both in bed and out. He disliked their innate sense of entitlement, plus their need to be constantly complimented and entertained. Perhaps it was the attraction of opposites, but there was something very appealing about girls who *had* to work for their living, who didn't have the fall-back position of Daddy's money.

He imagined that the plummy-voiced Alice Waterhouse was just such a daddy's girl.

'Jeremy Barker-Whittle,' he replied, well aware that whilst his own voice wasn't overly toffee-nosed, it was deep and rich and, yes, impressive. Alex and Sergio used to tell him he could have made a fortune on the radio. People who first met him over the phone were often surprised by the reality of him in the flesh. They clearly expected someone older, and possibly more rotund, with a big chest and stomach. Like an opera singer.

People did make the wrong assumptions at times.

He wondered if he was wrong about Alice Waterhouse. Then decided he wasn't.

'I'm the publisher of Kenneth Jacobs's books,' he informed her. 'It seems I'm to be your stand-in auctioneer tonight.'

'Oh, that's wonderful,' she said, not gushing but obviously relieved. 'Madge said you might do it. I have to confess I was beginning to panic. Thank you so much.'

Against his better judgment, Jeremy found himself warming to her.

'It's my pleasure,' he said. 'Truly.' Jeremy had always fancied himself a bit of a showman. He would actually enjoy playing auctioneer tonight.

'You can bring a partner, if you wish,' Alice offered. 'I allocated two places for Mr Jacobs at the main dining table. He said he didn't have anyone to bring so I was going to sit with him.'

'I won't be bringing anyone with me, either,' Jeremy admitted. He might have brought Ellen, a lawyer he dated on and off, and whose company he enjoyed. But she was overseas in Washington, working, at the moment. 'I'm a crusty old bachelor too,' he added, amused by this description of himself. 'So perhaps you would do me the honour of sitting next to me at dinner tonight.'

'That would be *my* pleasure,' she returned.

'I presume it's black tie?'

'Yes, it is. Is that a problem?'

Jeremy smiled wryly. 'No. No problem.' If there was one thing for which Jeremy could be relied upon it was to show up at social functions, properly attired. He loved fashion, and took pride in his appearance. His wardrobe held a wide array of clothes from casual to formal. His dinner suits were the best money could buy, the one he'd worn to Sergio's wedding made by one of the top tailors in Milan. He'd wear that one tonight.

When she started thanking him again, he cut her short by asking when and where they could meet up tonight. Once he had the details in hand, he said goodbye, hung up then called out to Madge.

She popped her head through the door straight away.

'Everything settled?' she asked.

'Fine. Just tell me one thing. Have you actually met this Alice?'

'No. I only talked to her over the phone.'

'So what PR company does she work for?'

Madge looked puzzled. 'She doesn't. I mean…didn't

I tell you? She works as a counsellor at a couple of the women's refuges.'

'No, Madge, you didn't mention that.'

'Sorry. Bit flustered today. Anyway, Alice explained when she first rang that they couldn't afford the fees of professional fund-raisers so she was doing it all herself. Not an easy job, I can assure you.'

'No,' Jeremy said thoughtfully. Damn, but he hated it when he was wrong about someone. He supposed it wasn't impossible that the daughters of wealthy men could be born with social consciences, plus the desire to make a difference to those less fortunate than themselves. But in his experience, it was rare.

Jeremy was impressed, and resolved to do everything in his power to make tonight's auction a success.

'I'd better get back to work,' he said, but his mind remained elsewhere. He was definitely looking forward to finding out tonight all about the enigmatic and intriguing Alice Waterhouse.

CHAPTER TWO

'THANK YOU FOR lending me this lovely cocktail dress, Fiona,' Alice said as she inspected herself in the cheval mirror. The dress was black and sleek and strapless, with a matching coat that would protect her from the chill night air till she could get inside the air-conditioned hotel. Despite summer being just over a month away, London was in the grip of a cold snap.

'My pleasure,' her flatmate replied, the words reminding Alice of the conversation she'd had earlier today with Kenneth Jacobs's publisher. What a nice man he was. And what a lovely voice. He would make a much better auctioneer than Mr Jacobs.

'I seriously wish I was going to your do tonight instead of having dinner with Alistair's parents,' Fiona added. 'But it's his mother's birthday…' Her voice trailed off as she shrugged resignedly. 'Never a good idea to get on the wrong foot with one's future mother-in-law.'

'I would imagine not,' Alice agreed, glad that she'd never have to worry about such matters. No way was she ever going to get married.

'You look lovely,' Fiona said. 'I wish I had your figure. And your height. And your hair.'

Alice was taken aback by the compliments, thinking there wasn't anything special about her figure, though she did have nice hair, naturally blonde and easy to style. As for her height, she wasn't that tall. Just under five eight. Admittedly, Fiona was on the short side. Despite that, she was a strikingly attractive girl with thick dark hair, big brown eyes and the kind of voluptuous body that men lusted after. Not that Alice wanted to be lusted after. It was the last thing she wanted.

'That dress looks much better on you than it did on me,' Fiona went on. 'When I wore it, my boobs spilled out over the top. I had men gawking at them all night. Alistair said I was never to wear it again, so if you want it, sweetie, it's yours.'

Alice hated the way Fiona called her sweetie, as if she were a kid when in fact they were both the same age. She also didn't want to be treated as if she were still the girl who'd first come to London and shown up, broke, on the doorstep. Still, it was an understandable hangover from when Alice had first come to London and shown up, broke, on the doorstep of Fiona's flat, mainly because she was the closest thing to a friend that Alice had ever had at boarding school. Not that they moved in the same circles, but they did share crushes on the same movie stars. Alice had only known Fiona's address because Fiona had told everyone at school when her billionaire father had presented her with the keys of a Kensington flat for her eighteenth birthday.

To give Fiona credit, she'd taken Alice in and let her have a room, rent-free, till Alice had been able to earn some money. Then, when Alice had said she would be moving out a few weeks later, Fiona had begged her to stay, saying she enjoyed her company. Over the seven years they'd lived together, they'd become quite close, sharing confidences the way girls did. Fiona understood why Alice was anti-men, but she still hadn't given up hope that one day Alice would meet a man she could trust—and love.

'Did I tell you that Kenneth Jacobs pulled out of doing the auctioneer job at the last minute?' Alice said as Fiona sprayed her with perfume. 'He came down with a head cold.'

'Oh, no!' Fiona exclaimed. 'What did you do?'

'I panicked at first.'

Fiona laughed. 'You? Panic? Never! You would have sorted something out.'

Fiona's blind faith in her organisational skills amused Alice. Still, anyone would seem cool, calm and collected in comparison with Fiona, who could be quite scatter-brained. And very messy. It crossed Alice's mind that Fiona might have originally asked her to stay because she did most of the housework.

'I was lucky. Kenneth put me onto this lovely lady at Barker Books and before I knew it, the owner of the company rang me back and offered to take Mr Jacobs's place.'

'That *was* lucky.'

'You've no idea how lucky. He has this absolutely gorgeous voice. He's going to make a great auctioneer. Now no more of that perfume, Fiona. I have to get my things together. The cab I ordered will be here any second. I've made arrangements to meet Mr Barker-Whittle in the foyer of the hotel at seven.'

'What?'

'I said I—'

'I know what you said,' Fiona broke in sharply. 'I hope we're not talking about *Jeremy* Barker-Whittle here.'

Alice frowned. 'Yes. That's how he introduced himself. Why? What's the matter with him?'

'He's just one of the most infamous playboys in London—that's what's the matter with him. Handsome as the devil, with more charm than any man has a right to. My sister dated him once for about five minutes, and she hasn't stopped raving about him ever since. She claims that after being with Jeremy no other man could possibly compare. Lord, but I'd never have lent you that sexy dress if I knew who you'd be sitting next to tonight.'

Whilst momentarily thrown by this news, Alice also felt peeved that Fiona would think for a moment she would fall victim to some playboy's dubious charms. Surely she knew her better than that. Now that she'd been warned about Mr

Barker-Whittle, he had not a hope in Hades of snaring her interest, no matter how handsome and charming he was. And he *was* charming, she conceded, thinking of how much she'd liked him over the phone. And yes, he was a right royal devil, calling himself a crusty old bachelor like that!

'Forewarned is forearmed, Fiona,' she pointed out. 'Now that I know he's a player, I will be on guard against any attempt by him to seduce me. Though you, of all people, should know I am immune to men of his type.'

Even as she said the words, Alice knew she was lying. She'd always found handsome devils attractive. In the movies mostly, but also in real life. There was something wickedly appealing about good-looking men of a certain reputation. She'd gone out with one once, and it had cost her dearly. Whilst still not totally immune to finding such men attractive, she felt confident she had learned her lesson. It was a pity, however, that her stand-in auctioneer was coming alone. Still, if Jeremy Barker-Whittle decided after meeting her that she would provide him with some after-auction entertainment, then he was sadly mistaken.

'But I don't get it,' Fiona said. 'Jeremy's in banking, not books.'

'Well, he's in books now,' Alice said ruefully whilst wishing that he weren't. What a pity Kenneth had to come down with a cold.

'Strange,' Fiona mused. 'Still, I suppose he can afford to be in anything he wants to be in. The Barker-Whittle family is seriously loaded. They've been in merchant banking forever.'

'You seem to know a lot about them.'

'Yes, well, as I said, Melody became obsessed with the man for a while and made it her business to find out everything she could.'

'Anything else I should know about him before tonight?' Alice asked.

'Not really. Just don't believe a word the silver-tongued scoundrel says. And don't go agreeing to go out with him.'

Alice almost laughed. As if.

'That'll be my cab,' she said when her phone pinged. 'Now you have a nice time tonight, Fiona, and don't worry about me. I'll be fine. Jeremy Barker-Whittle won't even get to first base.'

Fiona didn't look so sure. Alice recalled her friend's worried expression when she walked into the foyer of the hotel a couple of minutes past seven. *Fiona had a right to be worried*, came the instant stomach-tightening thought.

Jeremy Barker-Whittle was already there, sitting on one of the guest sofas, talking to someone on his phone. She knew it was him, despite the presence of several other males in the foyer. None of them, however, was wearing a black dinner suit. And none fitted the image she'd already formed in her mind of what one of London's most infamous playboys would look like. When Fiona had been talking about him, Alice had automatically pictured one of her favourite movie stars who'd made his reputation by playing rich bad boys. Jeremy Barker-Whittle was almost a dead ringer. Very handsome with an elegance to his face and clothes that could not be feigned. He had money written all over him, the kind of man whom other men envied and women craved.

Alice didn't crave him, but his looks certainly set her heart racing. She scooped in a deep breath, glad that he hadn't noticed her yet. It gave her the opportunity to gather her wits and her defences. And to look him over without being observed. His mid-brown hair was slightly wavy; it fell from a side part to his collar, a single lock flopping sexily across his high forehead. His nose was strong and straight and his eyes a sparkling blue. Yes, they actually sparkled. At least they did when he glanced up and spied her standing there, looking at him. He immediately put his phone away and stood up, smiling as he came over to her, bringing her attention to his mouth, with its sensual lower lip and dazzlingly white teeth. Now her stomach did a little flip-flop, reminding her starkly of her vulnerability to men who looked perfect but invariably were not.

'Please tell me that you're Alice,' he said with that incredible voice of his. Like rich dark chocolate, it actually made her name sound sexy. Which was a minor miracle. She'd always hated her name, thinking it girlish and old-fashioned.

It was difficult not to respond to his practised charm, but she managed to control herself, tapping into the reserved façade that she always used around men of his ilk.

'I am,' she admitted coolly, having resisted the unwise impulse to smile back at him. 'And I presume you're Mr Barker-Whittle?'

CHAPTER THREE

WHOA! THOUGHT JEREMY. He wasn't used to women being this cool to him, especially women who looked like Alice. It rattled him for a moment. But only a moment, his mind searching for some reason why she might be in a negative frame of mind where he was concerned. All he could think of was the way he'd described himself as a crusty old bachelor. Maybe she didn't like being deceived. She'd been warm enough to him over the phone, whereas now she was all ice.

The corner of his mouth twisted at his own pun on her name. Alice. All ice. *Very funny, Jeremy. Now see if you can use some of the infamous Barker-Whittle charm to warm up Miss Ice Princess a bit, or the evening ahead is not going to be as enjoyable as you anticipated.*

Which was a shame, given that he was partial to slender, cool-looking blondes, especially ones with gorgeous blue eyes and mouths just made for sin.

'Please, call me Jeremy,' he insisted as he subtly looked her up and down. 'No one calls me Mr Barker-Whittle, not even Madge. Especially not Madge,' he added with a laugh. 'By the way, Madge said that we should offer two character names to auction off, not just one,' he invented. 'If that's all right with you.'

'What? Oh, yes. Yes. That would be…great. Thank you.'

He'd thrown her a little, which was exactly what he'd wanted to do. For a split second she was the Alice he'd talked to on the phone. Sweet and grateful. But then that chilly mask slipped back into place.

Not that Jeremy was giving up. He had all evening to accomplish the thawing of Alice. If nothing else, he would enjoy the challenge. After all, it wasn't every day that a member of the opposite sex challenged him, especially single ones. He'd duly noted the lack of rings on either hand, a sure sign that she was neither married nor engaged. Of course, that didn't mean she didn't have a boyfriend or a partner. Though surely any boyfriend or partner worth his salt would have accompanied her here tonight. If one existed and he'd made a deliberate choice not to come, then the fool deserved to lose out. On second thought, however, Jeremy doubted there was some man waiting in the wings. That air of touch-me-not that she had about her would not encourage the average modern male.

Jeremy smiled wryly at the knowledge that he was far from average, or in the slightest deterred in his pursuit of the gorgeous Alice. She'd sparked curiosity in him from the first moment he'd heard that cut-glass voice of hers. Now that he'd met her, his curiosity was joined by desire, Jeremy resolving not to rest till she agreed to go out with him.

'You were going to show me the layout in the ballroom,' he reminded her. 'But first, let me take your coat…'

Panic churned in Alice's stomach at the thought of taking her coat off, of exposing more of herself to this man's far too sexy gaze. If he thought she hadn't noticed the way he'd looked her over, he was sadly mistaken. Alice knew men found her attractive. It was a burden most blondes with nice figures and pretty faces had to put up with. Fortunately, these days, she didn't attract too much male attention, always going to work with her hair pulled back, no make-up on and wearing jeans. Tonight, however, she was looking her very best. Silently, she cursed Fiona for lending her this revealing dress, plus spraying her with all that expensive perfume. The make-up she only had herself to blame for. But at the time, she hadn't known she'd be spending the evening in the company of a man who could make her want to be different from the woman she'd become.

At least she'd put her hair up, though not into its usual scraped-back ponytail. It was fashioned into a sleek sophisticated bun, worn slightly on one side, the latest style for formal occasions. Still, better than it being down. Pity about the dangling diamanté earrings she'd chosen to wear, however, and which swung against her bare neck when she walked. Alice contemplated telling him she would keep her coat on but he was already moving behind her and, really, she could hardly go all night with a calf-length coat flapping around her legs. Without glancing over her shoulder at him, she reached up to push the coat back off her shoulders—it wasn't the kind that had buttons—sucking in sharply when she felt his fingertips brush over the nape of her neck. A shiver ricocheted down her spine as the coat slid down her arms, presumably into his waiting hands. She was too shaken to turn and look. Too shocked.

What kind of power did this man have to make her feel like this? So swiftly and so surely. Alice had felt sexual attraction before; she hadn't always been so wary of it. She'd found the thought of sex fascinating from the time puberty hit, spending a lot of her teenage years indulging in romantic fantasies over various handsome actors. Then there'd been that charmer at college, the tall dark and handsome one she'd been attracted to despite everything, the one who'd convinced her he returned her feelings. And so she'd agreed to go out with him. More fool her!

But the attraction she'd felt on that occasion paled into insignificance compared to this highly charged feeling that was currently sweeping through Alice. It was madness, this urge she had to throw caution to the winds, to forget all the lessons she'd learned about men, to ignore Fiona's warnings and just let Jeremy Barker-Whittle have his wicked way with her. Which, of course, was what he wanted to do. He was a playboy, wasn't he? That was what playboys did.

But not with me, Alice decided as she marshalled all her willpower. *Not tonight. Not* ever.

'I'll just go over and check this in,' he said smoothly after she turned to finally look at him. 'Then we can proceed.'

He walked the same way he did everything, she noted ruefully. With style and casual elegance. Nothing hurried. Nothing awkward. Far too soon he was walking back towards her, this time his gaze openly admiring.

'Nothing beats a little black dress, does it?' he said as he took her elbow and steered her over to the bank of lifts. 'The concierge informed me that the ballroom is on the first floor,' he added, before she could ask what in hell he was doing. Not that she would have phrased it like that.

Still, she extricated her arm from his hold as soon as possible, sending him a look that held the silent but definite message that he was to keep his hands to himself. No way was she going to let him take control of the evening. Or of her. No way!

Jeremy resisted the temptation to roll his eyes. But truly, she was like a heroine out of a Victorian romance novel. Not that he'd read any, but he could imagine what such a woman would be like. All prissy and uptight, looking down her nose at men, especially ones who dared put a finger on her virginal flesh.

Alice would have been perfect for such a role, except for three factors. First, that dress. Strapless and very fitted, it gave him a clear picture of what she would look like naked. Very nice indeed, with high firm breasts, an athletically flat stomach, a deliciously small waist, long shapely legs and just enough hip and bottom for stroking. Second was the way she'd stared at him when she'd first arrived. That was not the stare of some prissy virgin. Her eyes had fairly ogled him, betraying that she'd found him as sexually attractive as he found her.

And then there was the way her whole body had quivered when his hand had brushed the back of her neck. It had been quite accidental. Jeremy wasn't in the habit of indulging in sly, lecherous touching. He never needed to. That Alice had reacted in such a way had been very telling. The woman who'd wrenched out of his hold just now should have whirled around and glared her disapproval. But she hadn't.

During the short ride up to the first floor in the lift, Jeremy concluded that Alice Waterhouse was nothing but a fraud. Her Ice Princess act with him was just that. An act. What was behind this pretence, he had no idea. But he aimed to find out.

CHAPTER FOUR

THE BALLROOM WAS INDEED, Alice already knew, on the first floor. She'd been there earlier today, checking that everything was being set up according to her instructions. She'd also taken personal responsibility for putting the name cards in place, having paid great attention to the guests' wishes when it came to seating. Each card also doubled as an auction number, being T-shaped, with the guest's name on the front and their number on the back.

Alice exited the lift first, anxious not to give Jeremy the opening to take her arm once more. She hated having to be rude, but she would be, if she had to. And she would *have* to if he kept manhandling her, his touch doing things to her body that didn't bear thinking about.

'It's just along here,' she said, and hurried down the carpeted corridor.

He kept up with her easily, his stride almost twice one of hers. Of course, he was a good six inches taller than she was, with long legs. Plus she couldn't walk all that fast in four-inch heels and a short, tight skirt.

The corridor eventually opened out into a larger space where a couple of staff members were putting the finishing touches to a bar area along one wall.

'Pre-dinner drinks are scheduled from seven-thirty onwards,' Alice said crisply as she walked over and pulled open one of the closed double doors that led into the ballroom, her eyes finally forced to meet those of her companion. 'The official time for the dinner to start is eight-thirty. I asked you to be here at seven so that you would have time to read through the list of items to be auctioned, and to discuss how you might want to proceed.'

'Proceed?' he echoed in that wonderfully rich voice of his, stepping forward to hold the door open for her.

Alice smothered a sigh. Trust him to have gallant manners. She supposed it was part of his seductive armoury to play the gentleman with women. No doubt he would pull out chairs and hold taxi doors open. And *always* wear a condom.

Alice only just managed not to gasp at this last thought. Where in heaven's name had that come from? Okay, so she found Jeremy Barker-Whittle attractive. Any woman would. He was drop-dead gorgeous. But finding him attractive was a far cry from thinking about having sex with him. Yet, as her gaze dropped from his beautiful blue eyes to his wickedly sexy mouth, she couldn't help wonder what it would be like to go to bed with him. He must be good at it, she reasoned, if Fiona's sister hadn't stopped raving about him. She'd met Fiona's sister, who was a real party girl. She'd sleep with anything in trousers, according to Fiona. So Melody must have slept with Jeremy.

'Cat got your tongue?' he said with a wry smile.

Alice blinked, swallowed, then shot him a small, stiff smile. 'Sorry. I had this sudden awful thought which distracted me.'

'Anything I should know about?'

'Not at all,' she said, thankful that she wasn't a blusher these days. She had been once, but not any longer. Working in women's refuges had toughened her up considerably. 'I've been a little OCD about the seating arrangements for dinner and it suddenly occurred to me that I might have made a mistake on one table.' Lord, but she was better at lying than she would ever have imagined. 'Still, nothing that can't be rectified,' she went on. 'Now, what I meant by how to proceed is do you want to have the whole auction after dinner, or sell off a few items between courses?'

'Definitely sell off a few items between courses. It will

keep the guests in a buying mood. And stop them from getting bored.'

'I agree. Right. Follow me.'

Jeremy followed her into the ballroom, appreciating the sight of her satin-encased derrière much more than her still less than warm demeanour. The ice in her voice and eyes might have melted a little but there was still a long way to go before he could confidently engage her in a conversation that might satisfy his curiosity over her, as well as give him an opening to ask her out. Still, he had several hours in which to achieve his goal.

Alice led him between a myriad of circular tables, each one set to a high standard with white linen tablecloths, silver cutlery, crystal glasses and beautifully appointed name cards placed at each setting. Every table had a number in the centre, which no doubt had been emailed to the guests so that they knew where to head on entering. That was what had happened at the last charity dinner Jeremy had been to, the one that had bored him to tears.

He already knew that this evening's dinner would not bore him in the slightest. In fact, Jeremy was looking forward to every intriguing second.

'It all looks splendid,' he complimented in Alice's wake.

She didn't stop or turn around, just said a cool, 'Yes, it does...' over her shoulder.

Jeremy frowned, wondering exactly what was bugging the lovely Miss Waterhouse. Surely she didn't act like this with every man she met. Was it him personally, or something else? Maybe she'd had a row with someone. The missing boyfriend perhaps?

'You organised all this by yourself?' he threw after her.

'Most of it,' she tossed back at him. 'The hotel staff were very helpful, of course.'

They arrived at the stage, which ran across the far end of the ballroom and which could be used for many purposes. Concerts. Award nights. Presentations. Whatever. Tonight it was set up with a podium in the middle, a microphone attached. There was a long wooden table behind it, which held an array of objects and a laptop computer, open, at one end. Clearly, this was where Alice would be standing, handing him items and jotting down the numbers of the winning bidder.

A man wouldn't want to be of a nervous disposition, Jeremy thought as he glanced up at the podium. Fortunately, he wasn't. But he wondered how Jacobs would have coped. Not that he knew the man well. Kenneth could be a secret exhibitionist for all he knew. Lazy did not mean shy.

There were three flights of steps, which led up onto the stage. One at each end and one in the middle. Alice stopped at the base of the one in the middle and finally turned to face him. She looked a little flushed in the face, but her eyes remained cool.

'I left the list of items for sale on the podium,' she told him. 'Perhaps you could have a look at them whilst I go check that seating.'

'Okay,' he agreed, and watched as she wound her way back through the tables, not stopping till she reached the one nearest the door, at which point he shrugged and made his way up onto the stage.

The list of items was extensive and varied. Sporting and entertainment memorabilia. Several dinners for two at five-star restaurants. A family weekend at a B&B in Weymouth. A short holiday for two in Spain. Premiere seats to a rock concert. Return flights to various European capitals. An oil painting of the Duchess of Cambridge by an up-and-coming London artist. Last but not least was the privilege of having Kenneth use a person's name—amend that to two—in his next thriller.

Jeremy didn't take long to scan the list, replacing it on the podium before taking a moment to inspect the wooden gavel, even giving it a practice bang, which echoed through the cavernous room and had several waiters lifting their heads for a moment. Not Alice, however, who was already no longer at the table near the doors. Jeremy wondered if that had just been an excuse not to remain in his company longer than strictly necessary. His teeth clenched in his jaw as he made his way down from the stage and headed for the exit. Frankly, he was beginning to feel slightly peeved. And confused. What was it about him that she didn't like? He wasn't used to women not liking him. He certainly wasn't used to being given the cold shoulder.

Jeremy soon saw that Alice wasn't outside in the pre-dinner drinks area, either. People had begun to arrive, but it wasn't crowded enough for him not to spot her. Creamy blonde hair like hers did stand out.

'Jeremy Barker-Whittle!' a male voice boomed out from just behind his shoulder. 'Fancy seeing you here.'

Jeremy turned with some reluctance to face the owner of that voice. George Peterson had been a client of his when he'd been an investment consultant. The owner of several car yards, he had entrusted Jeremy with building his considerable savings into an early retirement portfolio. Fortunately, Jeremy had obliged. George was in his late fifties, his wife around the same age, Jeremy liking the fact that George hadn't traded his wife in for a younger model as most self-made men seemed to do at some stage.

George beamed at him. 'I was talking to Mandy here about you the other day, wasn't I, love? I said whatever am I going to do now that Jeremy's no longer looking after my money? I got so nervous last month that I cashed in all my stocks and shares and put them in the bank.'

'Not such a bad move, George. Things are very volatile at the moment. Still, your money's not going to grow much sitting in the bank. Perhaps you should think about buying property.'

'See, what did I tell you, love? Jeremy's always got his finger on the pulse. So what are you up to these days, lad? Got a proper girlfriend yet or are you still playing the field?'

It was ironic that Alice came into view right at that moment, smiling and chatting with people as she worked the room, a glass of champagne in her right hand. Their eyes met and Jeremy smiled at her, at which point George's ruddy face swivelled round to see what he was smiling at.

'*Very* nice,' George said, thankfully in a low voice. 'Is she your date for tonight?'

'No,' Jeremy admitted. 'She's the lady who's organised this do. Her name's Alice Waterhouse. Alice!' he called out, and beckoned her over. 'Come and meet some very good friends of mine,' he added, smiling at the thought that she could hardly avoid him now.

'I know Alice,' Mandy piped up. 'I spoke to her on the phone when I first got her email about tonight. When I told her how much a fan I was of Kenneth Jacobs's books, she said she'd put me on the same table as him.'

Alice plastered a smile on her face and went to meet Jeremy's very good friends.

Jeremy introduced them, Alice quickly remembering her phone conversation with Mandy.

'I'm so sorry,' she said straight away, glad to be able to direct her conversation towards anyone but the very annoying Jeremy, who continued to smile at her in that smug fashion, as though they had some kind of secret relationship going on. 'Mr Jacobs can't be here tonight. He's got a dreadful cold. We're still auctioning off his prize, though. His publisher here has very kindly agreed to do the auctioneering honours tonight.' With that, she served Jeremy with a saccharine smile that didn't touch her eyes.

'*What?*' George's eyes widened with surprise. 'Is she talking about you, Jeremy?'

'She is indeed.'

'When did you become a publisher?'

'Shortly after I left banking.'

'Is there money in it?'

'Probably not,' Jeremy said drily. 'But as they say in the classics, it's not always about the money.'

George guffawed. 'That's a good one. A Barker-Whittle saying it's not about the money.'

Alice noticed that Jeremy's eyes stopped sparkling for a split second. Not that she cared.

A waiter with a tray of drinks paused next to their group, offering them flutes of champagne or orange juice. They all selected champagne, all except Alice who already had a glass, which she was not actually drinking. She couldn't afford to get tipsy, not if she had to deal with lover boy all night. Her vain attempt to avoid him till dinner hadn't worked, she conceded with a degree of frustration.

'I really should mingle,' Alice said. 'I'll see you all at dinner, since we're on the same table.'

'How lovely!' Mandy gushed.

'I'll mingle with you,' Jeremy offered immediately.

'No need to do that,' Alice blurted out in alarm. 'You should stay and look after your friends.'

'We don't need looking after, little lady,' George retorted. 'Off you go, both of you.'

The conspiratorial smirk he sent Jeremy did not escape Alice's notice. Lord knew what he'd said to the man.

'Why did George look at you like that?' she asked bluntly as she made her way through the milling crowd, Jeremy at her side.

'Like what?'

She ground to a halt and glared up at him. 'Like he was secretly playing matchmaker.'

'Can't say that I noticed.'

Alice sighed in exasperation.

'George is a bit of a romantic,' he added. 'Take no notice of him.'

She was struggling to find something to say when Jeremy was claimed by another couple who knew him, this time some television executive and his wife. And that was how it went for the next forty minutes, lots of other guests vying for his attention as if he were some kind of celebrity, all of them assuming she was his girlfriend, something he occasionally didn't deny. Not that that stopped the women from flirting with him. Neither did it stop her feeling ridiculously, irrationally jealous.

Irritated and confused, Alice had difficulty maintaining her usual calm demeanour. Finally, the urge to snap something rather rude at an over-made-up blonde whose false eyelashes were in danger of falling off she was fluttering them so much, almost overwhelmed Alice. Sucking in a deep, gathering breath, she turned to Jeremy, smiling up at him in a somewhat brittle fashion. 'Sorry, Jeremy, but I must visit the ladies' room before the evening begins. I'll see you later at the table. Ours is table number one.'

The relief she felt at exiting his presence was enormous. But the sight of her over-bright eyes in the powder-room mirror was both telling and worrying. *Be careful, Alice*, she warned herself. *Be very, very careful.*

CHAPTER FIVE

JEREMY FOUND GEORGE and his wife before entering the ballroom at twenty-five minutes past eight, chatting away with them as they made their way to table one, which was right at the front of the room near the stage. Alice was nowhere to be seen, her continued absence frustrating him. Never one to beat a dead horse, Jeremy began to accept that perhaps Alice actually *wasn't* attracted to him. But if that was the case, why had she reacted negatively a couple of times to women flirting with him? And she had. Oh, yes. He'd glimpsed definite irritation in her body language, especially when that blonde had started giving him gooey-eyed looks.

Jeremy was thinking about the reasons for Alice cutting and running when she suddenly walked out onto the stage, making her way slowly towards the podium. How magnificent she looked up there, he thought, unable to take his eyes off her. Like a young Audrey Hepburn, though with blonde hair. Talk about class! Once in position at the podium she turned on the microphone and tapped it a couple of times, bringing relative quiet to the buzzing ballroom. Once everyone was seated, she cast a wide smile around the room and began to speak in that well-educated, crystal-clear voice of hers.

'Welcome, everyone,' she began. 'First, I must thank you all for coming here tonight and supporting a cause that is dear to my heart. It is unfortunate that women's refuges are necessary in our supposedly civilised and enlightened world, but that is sadly the case. Some of you might not know this, but I work as a counsellor at a few of the inner-city refuges, and I know personally that they are all struggling to make ends meet, plus to cope with the number of women asking for help. We desperately need more refuges. More case workers. More counsellors. Of course, that all means more money, some of which we hope to raise tonight through your kindness and generosity. So please…dig deep. Trust me when I say that whatever you donate will make a huge difference to those women who have nowhere to go and no one to turn to. They need your help. Thank you.'

When Alice stopped speaking, the whole room erupted with clapping, Jeremy feeling immensely proud of her, and quite moved. What a speech! What a woman! Politicians could take a leaf out of her book when it came to inspiring people. If he hadn't been doing the auctioneering job, Jeremy would have been tempted to bid for every single item himself, making sure that the very best price would be achieved before the gavel came down. As it was, he vowed to give the charity a hefty donation of his own at the end of the night. Who knew? Maybe the gesture would make her agree to go out with him. Because he was still going to ask her, wasn't he? Nothing was surer in his mind.

When Alice sat down at the table, everyone spoke to her at once, congratulating her on her lovely words and assuring her that they would all dig deep. Jeremy couldn't get a word in edgewise. As soon as he could, he leant a little closer to her and said quietly, 'That was a seriously impressive speech, Alice. You could do fund-raising for a career, if you wanted to.'

Alice stiffened at the way her body responded to that deeply masculine voice of his, plus the warmth of his breath against her ear. Her stomach tightened, and so did her nipples, something which had never happened to her before. It was quite frightening, but also insidiously beguiling. She ached to turn to him and give him a real smile, one which told him how desperately she wanted to give in to the erotically charged spell that she suspected he was capable of casting over her. If she let him.

But to do so was to dance with the devil, the devil being men who had no conscience or morals. She'd seen first-hand what such men could do to a woman. Okay, so maybe Jeremy wasn't as bad as her sister's abusive bully of a husband. Or that vile creep she'd gone out with from college. But he was still a serial womaniser who wanted a woman for one thing and one thing only. Admittedly, since meeting him, her own traitorous mind had been filled with that same thing. Clearly, Jeremy was a Casanova extraordinaire who didn't have to lift a finger to make women swoon. His elegant looks and his natural charm did it for him. And yes, that wonderfully sexy voice of his.

Despite being sorely tempted, Alice refused to become just another of this playboy's conquests. So she schooled her face into a polite smile before turning her head to answer him. Unfortunately, she hadn't anticipated just how close Jeremy's face was. Barely centimetres separated their noses, their eyes, their mouths…

Her smile froze in place as she stared at his lips, hating herself for wondering what it would be like to be kissed by them. But she wondered just the same. And she wanted. Oh, yes, she wanted. For a long moment she almost surrendered to the crazed urge to close the gap between them. But at the last second she pulled herself together. And he, thank God, leant back into his chair.

'I couldn't be a professional fund-raiser,' she said with her usual cool reserve. 'I don't like asking anyone for money. At least this way people get something in exchange for their donation. I've been assured the food and wine will be good, but of course there won't be much choice. It's a set menu, with only two dishes in each course, served alternatively so that people can swap if they want to. That's the only way the staff could cope with so many meals.'

'It looks good to me,' Jeremy remarked as the starters arrived at their table.

Alice was glad that she had something to concentrate on other than her crazy feelings. She glanced over at Jeremy's plate—scallops cooked in a white wine sauce—then down at her own, which was a stir-fried beef dish served on Asian greens. Alice heaved a sigh of relief when everyone at the table tucked in without swapping, all of them seemingly pleased with the food. And with the wine, red or white being offered by the constantly circling waiters. Each table already had jugs of iced water and freshly squeezed orange juice if people didn't drink alcohol. Mandy, who was on her right, chose the white, as did Alice. Not that she had any intention of drinking much.

'Eat up,' Jeremy said when she just sat there with her fork in her hand, and her mind still elsewhere. 'I love a woman who enjoys her food.'

Alice rolled her eyes at him. 'I get the impression that you love *all* women.'

He just smiled, not seeming in any way offended. 'You could be right there. They are definitely the nicer sex.'

'With the emphasis on the sex part,' she retorted, thinking to herself that she was insane to start this kind of tit-for-tat conversation.

He gave her a searching look. 'You don't like men much, do you? Or is it just me?'

Guilt consumed her at the realisation of how rude she had been when in truth he had done nothing wrong. Everything had been in her overheated imagination, plus her overheated libido.

'I do apologise,' she said sincerely. 'I'm not normally this rude. It's been a long and difficult day. I do like you. Honestly. I appreciate your coming tonight and being my auctioneer. It's just that...'

'What?'

She closed her eyes and shook her head. Impossible to explain the situation without being rude again.

'Nothing,' she added, opening her eyes and throwing him a wan smile. 'I'm a little tired.'

'You don't look tired,' he said. 'You look beautiful.'

Oh, Lord. He was like the Chinese water torture. 'Please don't,' she said with a low groan.

'Please don't what? Tell you that I think you're wonderful? I'd like to ask you out, Alice. To dinner, with me paying next time.'

Alice could not believe how tempted she was to just say yes. *Yes, yes, please take me out to dinner then take me back to bed.* It shocked her, the strength of that temptation, not to mention her desire. Fiona had been so right about Jeremy. He was seriously dangerous.

'Thank you for asking me,' she answered. 'I'm flattered. But my answer has to be no.'

His eyes narrowed as they scanned her face. 'Why is that, might I ask? You just said you liked me.'

'Do I have to give you a reason? Maybe I already have a boyfriend.'

'Do you?'

'No,' she said, lifting her glass of white wine to her lips. So much for her decision not to drink. But Lord, this man would drive any woman to drink.

'Girlfriend?'

Her startled gasp sent wine splashing over the rim of her glass.

With the speed of a quarter horse jumping out of the stalls, Jeremy whipped the snow-white handkerchief out of his breast pocket and dabbed at where the wine had run down her chin and throat, heading for her cleavage.

'Don't do that,' she snapped, even as her arms broke out into goosebumps.

'Don't be ridiculous,' he countered as he continued to mop up the wine.

Both George and Mandy said something but she wasn't listening, her focus solely on where that infernal handkerchief was straying, down towards her bullet-like nipples.

Just before he reached them, his hand stopped and he put the handkerchief away. Alice was not sure if she was relieved or disappointed.

'So what's your real reason for refusing to go out with me?' he asked her quietly as she snatched up her fork and attempted to finish her starter. 'And I'd like the truth, please.'

She swallowed one meagre mouthful before putting the fork down. 'If you must know, it's because of your reputation.'

He looked bemused. 'And what reputation is that?'

'Come now, Jeremy, you must know what people say about you. You're a playboy.'

'Oh, is that all?' he said, and laughed. 'And that's your only reason?'

She blinked at him. 'You don't think that's a good enough reason?'

'I've never come across it before.'

She just stared at him, thinking that she had never come across someone quite like him before, either. He was arrogant, yes, but with a wonderfully easy-going manner, which was both disarming and seriously seductive.

'I would imagine that not many women would say no to you, Jeremy,' she said truthfully. 'But I am. Please don't make a big deal about it. I'm not interested in wasting time on a man who thinks dating is a game and women are interchangeable.'

'I couldn't imagine ever thinking you were interchangeable, Alice. I can see that you are absolutely unique.'

'Why? Because I'm saying no to you?'

When he smiled she wanted to slap him. And kiss him. And say yes to him.

Her shoulders straightened as they did whenever life put her back against the wall.

'It's time for us to go auction off a few things,' she said coolly, and stood up.

CHAPTER SIX

BY THE END of the evening, Jeremy concluded that if he ever lost all his money and didn't want to return to banking he could become an auctioneer. Whipping up enthusiasm for the items on offer came naturally to him. But then, he'd always had the gift of the gab. He especially loved the thrill of the bidding wars, plus the moment when he brought the gavel down and said, 'Sold!' The whole process had been exciting. And profitable for the women's refuges. Alice seemed very pleased with the results. They had raised over four hundred thousand pounds from the auction alone, with the profit from the dinner lifting the total to half a million. Dear old George had contributed more than his fair share, bidding determinedly against a few other bidders for the privilege of having his name—plus his darling wife's—in Kenneth's next thriller. Mandy had been over the moon.

'I can hardly believe it,' Alice said afterwards. 'I never dreamt we'd raise so much. Of course, I have you to thank, Jeremy,' she added. 'You were brilliant.'

Jeremy didn't get too carried away with her compliment. There was still a wariness in her eyes during her dealings with him. Logic told him he was probably wasting his time pursuing Alice. But logic could not compete with the desire for her that had grown with each moment he spent in her company. She possessed a heady combination of mystery and allure, of unconscious warmth one moment and frosty reserve the next. It did irk Jeremy that, for the first time in his life, his reputation as a playboy wasn't working for him. It usually whetted female interest, most women wanting to see if he could live up to his reputation as a lover. Others obviously imagined that they would be the one to ensnare his heart and make him settle down. They didn't know they were fighting a lost cause. A few went out with him just for fun. They were the ones he liked best.

Alice obviously wasn't any of those. She was a serious girl, with a serious outlook on life. He wondered if her slightly anti-men attitude came from something that had happened to her in the past, or maybe from where she worked. It could hardly endear the opposite sex to Alice if she was constantly dealing with women who'd suffered from domestic or sexual abuse from their boyfriends or husbands. He would never hurt her. He just wanted the opportunity to get to know her, and, yes, to get to *know* her. Was that so wrong?

Yes, Jeremy, came a voice he wasn't used to hearing. Possibly his conscience? *Alice is not the sort of girl who could handle a fling with a man like you. You would probably end up hurting her, whether you meant to or not.*

Rubbish, another voice argued back immediately. His male ego perhaps? *You're exactly what Alice needs. Dating you will make her lighten up a bit. You can give her a fun time, and pleasure. Lots and lots of pleasure!*

His loins prickled anew at this last thought.

Naturally, this second voice won the day, Jeremy refusing to be deterred despite Alice's earlier half-hearted rejection. She was attracted to him. He was sure of it. She just had to get to know him better…

'I have some wealthy friends who would be only too glad to make a substantial donation to your cause,' he said as he accompanied her back to the foyer of the hotel. He was thinking of Sergio and Alex, who were both generous givers to charity, Alex especially. 'I'll give them a call tomorrow and get back to you. And then there's the matter of my own personal donation.'

A startled Alice ground to a halt, throwing him what could only be described as a panicky look. 'But I don't expect you to donate a thing,' she said hurriedly. 'You've already been more than generous with your time tonight.'

'It was no hardship. I enjoyed every moment. But I didn't pay for my dinner. Neither did I buy anything at the auction. I can well afford to make a donation, Alice. I thought I might match what you raised tonight pound for pound. Now don't go thinking there any strings attached to this offer, because there aren't,' he continued before she could protest. 'So who will I send the money to?'

'What?' She seemed totally flustered.

'You have registered a proper charity, haven't you?'

'Yes, of course I have. It's called Save Our Refuges.'

'Right. I'll tell my friends.'

'The Bank of England is handling the donations for us. You can just transfer the money straight into the account. The details were on the email I sent to all the guests. But of course you weren't a guest, were you?' she added, frowning. 'I'll email Madge in the morning with all the information. But honestly, Jeremy, you don't have to donate that much money.'

'Why not? I can afford it. Besides, money doesn't go all that far these days. If you want to open more refuges you're going to need a lot more than a million pounds.'

'I suppose so...'

'Your charity will also need a few well-heeled patrons, like *moi*. You will need help, Alice, if you want to achieve the goals you set out in your speech. I'll tell you what, since you won't go out to dinner with me, why don't you drop by my office one day this week and we'll have a think tank on what other fund-raising activities you can employ? I'll see if Madge can join us. She's a smart lady and a fabulous organiser. I'm sure she'd love to be involved. How about Friday afternoon? Are you free then? If you're busy, we can make it next week some time.'

Alice still seemed reluctant, yet fiercely tempted at the same time. He could see a war going on in her eyes. But she would not, in the end, Jeremy believed, look such a gift horse in the mouth.

'I…well…yes, I suppose I can make it on Friday afternoon. But not till around four. Is that too late for you?'

'Not at all. Four would be fine.' Step one accomplished, which was to make her see that he wasn't such a bad guy. 'I'll have Madge email our address. Let her know if you can't make it and we'll reschedule.' Good to not sound desperate to see her again. Yet he *was* desperate. Weirdly, irrationally desperate. Jeremy could not envisage letting Alice just disappear from his life. He hadn't been this captivated by a woman in years. Or this challenged. She wasn't going to be an easy conquest. But, then, he didn't really want her to be a conquest. Despite his reputation as a ladies' man, Jeremy was not a rake, or a libertine. He genuinely liked women, liked their company, in bed as well as out. Seduction was not his usual game, possibly because he rarely had to employ such tactics. Getting a girl to go to bed with him had always been so damned easy.

Alice, however, was not going to be easy. Hell, he couldn't even get her to go out with him let alone go to bed with him. His pursuit of her was going to take patience, and some cunning. But he was sure she would be worth it.

His eyes ran over her one last time, imprinting her lovely face and figure in his memory bank so that he could download it into his mind at will during the next two days.

'I'll go get your coat,' he offered.

Alice could have told him that she would get it herself, but she knew that feminist defiance was useless against a man of Jeremy's nature. He might be a playboy, but he was also a gentleman of the old school who knew how to treat a woman. Alice felt both flattered and frustrated by his gallantry. She also felt flattered and frustrated by his determined pursuit of her. Clearly, he thought that making himself a patron of her charity would make her so grateful that she would finally agree to go out with him.

Silly man. She had no intention of doing so, despite the moments of sexual weakness, which he had effortlessly evoked in her tonight. But she would take his help, and his money, which was much needed by people who didn't have the resources or the resilience to help themselves. As she watched him walk over and collect her coat, she wondered if he had any idea at all what the women and children who fled to refuges had suffered. Or if he cared. Hard to imagine that a man of his wealth and background really cared about those less fortunate than himself. Or really cared about her, for that matter. She was just an attractive girl who'd dared to resist his charms and say no to him. She'd become a challenge, one which he smugly thought he'd eventually overcome. She'd seen the spark of triumph in his eyes when she'd agreed to come to his office on Friday.

Alice's mouth curved into a wry smile. If he thought she wasn't aware of his not very subtle ploy, then he was very much mistaken. Or maybe he didn't mind if she guessed how far he was prepared to go to get her, or how much he wanted her.

A shiver ran down Alice's spine at this last thought, a shiver that didn't bear too close an inspection. Because down deep, in that place reserved for unpalatable and somewhat scary truths, lay the fact that she secretly wanted him back. Perverse, really, given there was nothing to admire about Jeremy Barker-Whittle except his movie-star looks, his silver-tongued voice and his old-fashioned manners, all of which were either God-given or practised traits. He didn't show any genuine qualities that she could like and respect. Why, he'd actually *laughed* over his less than admirable reputation. What kind of man did that?

When he started walking back towards her with her coat draped elegantly over one arm, Alice steeled herself for what was to come next. She knew that if she put out her hand to take her coat he would ignore it. So she placed her purse and laptop down on a nearby armchair and waited till he got close enough before turning and lifting her arms away from her sides in expectation of his sliding the coat up them and over her shoulders. Which he did, oh, so smoothly, Alice despising the involuntary tremor that ran through her tensely held body.

'Where do you live?' he asked her as she struggled for total calm. 'Maybe we could share a taxi?'

What could she say? Silly to lie. 'I share a flat in Kensington,' she admitted as she picked up her laptop and purse.

By the time she glanced up at him, he was looking at her with surprised curiosity.

'That's where *I* live,' he said. 'In Kensington.'

'Really?' Was fate conspiring against her at every turn? She was trying to resist the man, not be thrown into his path each time. 'What a coincidence.'

'But a convenient one,' he said, smiling.

'Convenient?' she repeated somewhat archly.

'We should definitely share that taxi.'

'Well, yes, yes, I suppose so,' she said reluctantly.

Jeremy's sudden rise in temper startled him. Anger was not something he liked in others, or himself. He considered it poor form at the best of times. Only when severely provoked did he surrender to the temporary but often self-destructive comfort of fury. It had been many years since he'd lost it. Now that he thought about it, he hadn't truly lost his temper since his last year at boarding school when he'd come across one of the younger boys being bullied as he'd once been bullied. The fight that ensued had seen him almost expelled, only his father's paying for a new science block stopping that unfortunate event. Jeremy had rarely been grateful to his father for anything, but he was that day.

He'd really wanted to go on to university, and he might not have been accepted if he'd been expelled. Since then, Jeremy had steered well clear of all uncontrolled outbursts.

Occasionally, when annoyed with someone, he resorted to sarcasm. But that was as far as he usually went. The temptation to say something caustic to the ever reluctant Alice was acute, but counter-productive. So he simply smiled through clenched teeth and waved her ahead of him out towards the taxi station.

The ride from the hotel to her address in Kensington was blessedly short, with Alice sitting as far from him as possible with her knees pressed primly together, her laptop resting across her thighs, her head turned steadfastly towards the window. She didn't say a single word. Neither did he. Jeremy was half regretting his decision to pursue this girl. As intriguing as he found Alice, she wasn't worth losing any sleep over, or spending a small fortune on. His earlier assumption that she was attracted to him could be wrong. Either that, or she had some serious issues where the opposite sex was concerned. Maybe she'd been treated badly by a past boyfriend, some arrogant rich brute who'd cheated on her perhaps, leaving her bitter and cynical over men in general, and wealthy ones in particular. It would explain so much. Her chilly responses to his overtures. Her contempt of his reputation as a playboy.

By the time the cab pulled up outside her address, Jeremy felt confident that he'd hit on the reason behind her wariness where he was concerned. He couldn't have been wrong about her finding him attractive. No way.

'Thank you for tonight, Jeremy,' she said stiffly when she finally turned her head to look at him. 'You were a brilliant auctioneer, and a very pleasant dinner companion.'

He gazed deep into her eyes. 'Maybe we can do it again some time…' *But without the auction next time.*

Despite the dim light in the back of the cab, he saw the heat that suddenly flooded her cheeks, saw the startled widening of her eyes. Clearly, Alice was not used to blushing, wasn't used to having her composure rattled.

'We can discuss future auctions on Friday,' he added smoothly, his eyes still locked with hers.

'What? Oh, yes. Friday.' She seemed to have difficulty dragging her eyes away from his. Turning abruptly, she reached for the door handle before throwing an almost frightened glance over her shoulder. 'Please don't get out,' she said before he could do so. 'I'll see you at your office on Friday around four.' And she was gone, fleeing the cab with an unflattering speed, leaving Jeremy to smile ruefully at her ongoing resistance to the sexual chemistry that had just flared between them. Not just flared. It had fairly sizzled, with a heat that had left her flushed and him frustrated in a fiercely cruel fashion.

Jeremy watched her bolt up the stairs to the front door of her flat, the kind of flat that only rich girls lived in. She didn't turn back to wave at him before letting herself into the stylish town house. A light came on immediately, showing him that her flat was on the ground floor, which was always the most expensive. The upper floor and the basement flats would be cheaper. Though not much. Since investigating property prices in London more thoroughly, Jeremy knew that the most dilapidated flat in this area cost close to a million pounds.

He sat staring at the far from dilapidated town house for a few seconds before telling the driver to go on, his mind and his body in turmoil. It annoyed him that he hadn't found out a single personal detail about Alice tonight other than her lack of a boyfriend. He hadn't satisfied his rabid curiosity about her at all, let alone satisfied that other urgent need that had now arisen to torment him. Jeremy could not remember the last occasion he'd gone home alone after a date with a girl he liked. In actual fact, he couldn't recall that ever happening. Not that tonight was a proper date, he reassured his bruised male ego. Still, it rankled that for the first time in his life a girl had actually said no to him, especially one who he felt confident was sexually attracted to him.

By the time Jeremy exited the taxi in front of his stylish mews house three streets away, his resolve was firmly back in place, his ego refusing to accept her rejection. The bottom line was that he wanted Alice Waterhouse as he'd never wanted a girl before. And he meant to have her. End of story.

CHAPTER SEVEN

'NEW CLOTHES, I SEE?' Fiona said over breakfast on Friday morning, her tone very knowing.

Alice looked up from her bowl of oats, determined not to react to Fiona's continual niggling over her agreeing to Jeremy being a patron of her charity. 'Yes,' she said coolly. 'I hadn't bought anything new for ages and felt I couldn't show up at Jeremy's office in my old jeans and jacket. So I went shopping last night.'

'Your blouse is new too,' Fiona pointed out. 'And red. You never wear red.'

Alice shrugged. 'It was on sale and I liked it.'

'It's sexy.'

'Is it?'

'You know it is. So are those skinny jeans. He got to you, didn't he? I know you said you turned his dinner invitation down, but you and I both know, Alice, that he hasn't given up. His offering to be involved in your charity is just a means to an end. And you're the end.'

'I did find Jeremy attractive,' Alice admitted, privately thinking that that was the understatement of the year. 'But I still won't be going out with him.' Or so she kept telling herself. 'Look, the man is seriously rich, Fiona. It would be silly of me to cut off my nose to spite my face. If he wants to help with the charity then I'm going to let him. To refuse his support would be foolish. I don't know what you're so worried about. He's not that irresistible,' Alice added as she stood up and carried her unfinished bowl over to the sink.

'Huh. Tell that to the legions of women he's left frothing in his wake.'

Alice immediately thought of the over-made-up blonde

who would have dumped her partner on the spot if Jeremy had crooked his finger at her. The evidence of his charisma had been in her face all that night, the memory of his effect on her having stayed with Alice long after she'd fled their taxi. She could not deny that the thought of seeing him again today had inspired her shopping expedition last night. The red silk blouse *was* sexy, and hadn't been on sale.

'Want some more coffee?' she asked Fiona as she made herself some.

'Don't try to distract me with coffee, madam. I'm trying to talk some sense into you.'

Alice's patience with her friend finally ran out. Turning, she shot Fiona one of her chilly looks. 'I don't need anyone to talk sense into me, Fiona. I make my own decisions in life. Please stop warning me about Jeremy Barker-Whittle. If I ever change my mind and go out with him—and that's a big if, I can tell you—then it's no one's business but my own. Did I try to tell you not to become engaged to Alistair, despite his having the most irritating mother?'

Fiona looked a bit sheepish. 'She is irritating, isn't she?'

'Very. On top of that, what happened to your always telling me that I shouldn't be so down on men because of what just two of them did? You keep reassuring me that not all men are scoundrels. I'm beginning to think that maybe you're right. What harm would come if I had dinner with Jeremy? Or even if I went to bed with him?'

Fiona's big brown eyes rounded like saucers. 'You're thinking about going to bed with him?'

All the time, Alice thought. *Every minute of the day and night*.

'No,' she lied. 'I'm just saying it wouldn't be the end of the world.' Was it really her saying something so outrageous? So casual and carefree?

'But Jeremy *is* a scoundrel.'

'No, he's not,' Alice defended. 'He's actually very nice.

He's just a bit shallow, and spoilt. Inherited money doesn't do any man any good. But he's not nasty.'

'Oh, Lord. You're falling for him already.'

'Don't be ridiculous. I would never fall for a playboy. But he is fun to be around. I have to give him that.'

Fiona made a squawking sound. 'I don't know what to say!'

Alice had to laugh. 'Then don't say anything. Now I have to get to work. Are you going out tonight?'

'Alistair's taking me out for dinner. Some fancy French restaurant that's just opened in Soho.'

'Have fun, then. Talk to you tomorrow.'

Alice did her best to put aside thoughts of Jeremy on her way to work. Not easy when you were just walking or sitting, alone, on the Tube. Fiona's pointed comments this morning hadn't helped get the man out of her head. What had possessed her to defend him the way she had? Or to suggest that she might sleep with him at some time in the future? She knew she wouldn't. She couldn't. Aside from her ingrained distrust of the opposite sex, she was still a virgin, for pity's sake. A total ignoramus where actual sex was concerned. Jeremy would think she was some kind of weirdo if he ever found out.

By the time Alice got off the train at Hammersmith station, she'd determined to be polite and professional with Jeremy this afternoon. But she would not betray a hint of her inner feelings. If he flirted with her again, she wouldn't flirt back. If he asked her out again, she would definitely say no. Fiona had been right. He *was* a bit of a scoundrel; a man of manners but no morals. It was perverse how attractive she found him. But, then, life was perverse, wasn't it?

Alice sighed then headed for the refuge, which was in a four-bedroomed house located a few blocks from Hammersmith station. It was her favourite refuge to work in, a decent-sized place with a spacious back garden though somewhat run-down. They currently had half a dozen women staying there, along with several young children. The accommodation was cramped, but at least it was safe.

The house next door to them was still up for sale, Alice noted as she walked past. Nobody wanted to live next to a shelter, she supposed. But perhaps the charity could afford to buy it, if and when Jeremy's rich friends came through with some more donations. It would be interesting to see if he'd followed through on that. If he didn't, then she'd know that his so-called interest in helping out was nothing but a sham.

The thought dismayed her. She wanted him to be worthy of her liking him so much. Wanted him to prove Fiona wrong.

Well, she would find out the truth this afternoon, wouldn't she? Till then...

Alice steeled herself for the day ahead. Her job wasn't an easy one, most of the women she counselled too lacking in self-esteem to listen to what she was saying, let alone take her advice. But she did her best, which was all she could do. There were few easy solutions to the massive problems that faced society these days. Pasting a bright smile on her face, she let herself in the front door, almost immediately being confronted by two squealing children who were happily trying to kill each other. Girls, they were, possibly all of eight or nine.

Alice rolled her eyes as she grabbed the main aggressor by the back of her T-shirt, hauling her away from the other girl.

'Don't you think your mothers have enough problems without you two fighting and screaming like banshees?' she said firmly as she glowered down at both of them.

The girl she was holding pulled a face. 'What's a banshee?'

Alice prayed for composure. 'It's a ghost. A very scary ghost who wails at the walls whilst it haunts houses.'

'What's a wails?' the other girl asked.

Alice was very glad when their mothers appeared at the top of the stairs and called them away. Shaking her head after them, she walked slowly along the hallway and let herself into the room where she did her counselling. The sight of the mess in there showed that several of the children had been using it as a playroom overnight. Understandable, she supposed, given the lack of space, plus the fact that she did have some toys in there for the littlies who hated being separated from their mothers, even for a half-hour therapy session.

'Oh, dear,' Jane said from behind Alice's shoulder. Jane was the housekeeper and cook. A widow in her late fifties, she lived on the premises. 'Sorry about that.'

'It's all right,' Alice said, throwing the weary-looking woman a reassuring smile. 'It won't take me long to clean up.'

'You're a good girl,' Jane said, patting Alice on the shoulder before going off to do one of the million and one jobs she did in a day.

I try to be good, Alice thought as she started picking things up. *But I might not be so good after this afternoon's meeting with London's most infamous playboy.*

It was a troubling thought, yet at the same time an insidiously exciting one.

As Alice continued to clean up, her mind stayed on Jeremy. Was he really as good-looking as she remembered? And as charming? Would he ask her out again?

She hoped he would, at the same time hoping she'd have enough common sense to keep saying no. But Alice was beginning to doubt it.

He was a devil, all right. A wickedly sexy, almost irresistible devil!

CHAPTER EIGHT

'COME IN, MADGE,' Jeremy said at the sound of her familiar triple tap, a quick glance at the wall clock showing that it was twelve minutes to four, a little early for Alice, who he felt sure would keep him waiting, as she had the other night.

Madge hurried in, holding a huge tome in her hands.

'I thought you might like to know a little bit more about Alice,' she said in a conspiratorial tone, 'so I looked her up in the latest *Who's Who*.'

'And?'

'She's the younger daughter of Richard William Waterhouse, the twenty-second Earl of Weymouth. Deceased, it says. Her mother is Lily Amaryllis Waterhouse, nee Knight. They had three children, Arthur William, who died in childhood, then came Marigold Rose, followed by Alice Hyacinth.'

'Someone has a thing for floral names,' Jeremy said drily. 'Though Alice isn't a flower, is it?'

'Sweet Alice is. And I think there's a rose called Miss Alice.'

'I see,' he said. 'Is that all it says about her?'

'Pretty well. Their ancestral home is called Hilltop Manor, and is in Dorset, not far from Weymouth.'

Which wasn't all that far from his own family home in Cornwall. Maybe he could offer to drive her down there one weekend. Once she stopped playing Ice Princess and decided to become a normal girl, that was.

'Thanks, Madge. That explains the voice but not the job.'

'You didn't find out much about her the other night, did you?'

'Not much. She's not the kind of girl who would like being questioned.'

Madge's eyebrows lifted. 'Sounds intriguing.'

'That, she is. Very intriguing.'

'You like her, don't you?'

'Very much.'

'I thought you might. I mean, you're a generous man, but I wouldn't have thought that charity fund-raising on a regular basis is your thing.'

Jeremy had to smile. 'You know me too well, Madge. But personal issues aside, I do believe this is a very good cause. I would have wanted to help out regardless of how I felt about Alice.'

He noted how Madge's mouth twitched, as if she was having difficulty suppressing a smile. Or even a laugh.

'You've found me out,' he admitted. 'But for pity's sake, don't let the cat out of the bag when Alice is here. I'm trying to impress the girl, not make her even more wary of me.'

Madge looked taken aback. 'She's wary of you?'

'Either that or she's wary of all men. I asked her out and she said no.'

'No!'

'Yes. It was a definite no.'

'Maybe she already has a boyfriend.'

'She doesn't. She said so. She also said my reputation as a playboy had preceded me.'

'Oh, dear.'

Jeremy wasn't sure why he was telling Madge all this. There was nothing she could do. But it felt strangely comforting to have a sympathetic ear on the matter. He was no longer as confident of eventually bringing Alice round as he'd been the other night. Too much time had passed, filled with endless hours of doing what he hated doing. Thinking.

'I'd better get back to my desk,' Madge said. 'It's almost four.'

'When you bring Alice in, I want you to stay for a while, then I'll ask you to get us all coffee.'

Madge smiled. 'Okay.'

Alice broke her strict budget by taking a taxi to Mayfair. She hated wasting money, having spent the last few years saving madly for a flat of her own. She didn't care how small it was. She just wanted to own her own place. Hopefully, she would have enough by the time Fiona got married in August. She wouldn't, though, if she kept paying for cabs instead of taking the Tube. Still, this was a one-off…

Like buying new clothes the other night?

Guilt and excitement squirmed in her stomach as the cab turned down the street in Mayfair that housed Barker Books. It stopped outside a stylish white town house, which had a freshly painted black front door and colourful window boxes filled with flowers. After paying the driver, she climbed out and stood on the pavement for a full minute, scooping in several deep breaths in an effort to calm her galloping heart.

A young woman carrying two takeaway coffees hurried past her, running up the steps and elbowing the door open before stopping and throwing her a questioning look.

'Are you coming in here?' she asked.

'Yes,' Alice replied.

'The door's open,' the girl told her. 'It just swings shut sometimes. Who have you come to see?'

'Mr Barker-Whittle.'

'Right. Then you'll want to see Madge first. She's in the second room on your left.'

'Thanks.'

Sucking in one last gathering breath, Alice walked slowly up the steps and into the devil's lair.

Madge did her best to keep her expression neutral when Alice walked in. But she could see straight away what had captivated Jeremy. The girl was a delight to behold. Fresh faced and very pretty, with beautiful blue eyes, a cute nose and fashionably full lips. But whilst her clothes were modern and, yes, quite sexy, she wasn't wearing any make-up. On top of that, her blonde hair was pulled back into a girlish ponytail. Clearly, she'd made no effort to doll herself up for the occasion. Also clearly, she wasn't as enamoured of Jeremy as he was of her.

'You must be Alice,' Madge said as she stood up and walked around from behind her desk.

'And you must be Madge,' the girl returned with the sweetest smile. 'Thank you so much for all your help with the auction. Lord knows what I would have done if your boss hadn't put up his hand as auctioneer.'

'I gather he did a good job,' Madge said, then added drily, 'or so he informed me. Come, I'll take you to him.'

Alice's chest tightened as she followed Madge over to the heavy wooden door on which the PA knocked three times in rapid succession.

'Come in, Madge,' Jeremy called out, his deeply rich voice startling Alice anew. No man had a right to have such a voice as well as everything else. As Madge opened the door, Alice steeled herself to come face to face with his seductive physical presence, wondering not for the first time today why she was putting herself through such torture. It wasn't just to secure his patronage. The truth was she wanted to see him again. Silly Alice.

CHAPTER NINE

JEREMY'S OFFICE SHOULDN'T have surprised her. She'd already noted that the place hadn't been renovated in the modern style the way of a lot of London's town houses had been this past decade, stripping away all their old character-filled features in favour of soulless white walls and sleek lines, with recessed lighting and furniture that looked good but wasn't comfortable at all. Alice loved the wood-panelled walls, the glass-fronted bookcases, the polished wooden floor and the rather ancient patterned rug that sat in front of his antique desk.

Nothing was antique about Jeremy, however. He was all modern style, dressed in a dark blue suit, blue and white striped shirt and a flashy red tie.

'Alice is here,' Madge said on walking in.

'Excellent,' he replied, and rose immediately from behind his desk. 'So glad you could make it.'

He didn't look her over as he had the other night, Alice noted with a contrary degree of dismay, his eyes not on her at all as he placed a couple of straight-backed chairs right in front of his desk then returned to sit in his own black leather office chair.

'Sit down, ladies, and we'll get right to it.'

Alice and Madge sat down whilst Jeremy picked up a sheet of paper that had been lying on top of his desk.

'I've been giving the matter of further fund-raising some considerable thought,' he said, his eyes on the paper. 'I've jotted down a few ideas, which I'd like to run by you.'

Finally, he looked up, and their eyes met. No sparkling this time. No smiles. He was dead serious.

'Go on,' Alice said, despising herself for feeling so disappointed.

'First, we need to set up a website plus a social media page telling people about our aims and where they can send their donations. We can't just target the wealthy. Ordinary people making small donations are the mainstay of charities. Maybe you could see to that, Madge. You're good at that sort of thing.'

'Yes, I can set those up, no trouble.'

'Of course, after the success of the dinner and auction last Wednesday,' he went on, 'it's only sensible that we have another night like that. But not too soon. I thought perhaps in early December. It could have a Christmassy theme. What do you think, Alice?'

Alice had to force herself to focus. 'I think that's a marvellous idea,' she said with false brightness. 'We could decorate the ballroom and all the tables. And have a big Christmas tree on stage, with all the prizes under the tree in pretty boxes.'

'Sounds good. You'd better get onto booking that same hotel a.s.a.p. Christmas is a busy time. And I'll be paying for the decorations. You shouldn't have to pay for a thing, Alice. Professional fund-raisers always have expense accounts.'

'But I'm not a professional fund-raiser!' she protested.

'Maybe not, but you still shouldn't be out of pocket.'

Her laugh was dry. 'I'm not.'

'Thought that would be the case. Now *I'll* see to rustling up the prizes. I have lots of contacts and there's lots of time. Though feel free, either of you, to help in that regard. Now, Madge, if you don't mind, could you get me some coffee and biscuits? I missed out on having lunch today and I need some sustenance and a caffeine hit. What about you, Alice? Feel like some coffee? Or tea, if you prefer? Madge has everything in the kitchen.'

'Some coffee would be nice. White with two sugars.'

'That's a lot of sugar for someone so slim,' he remarked after Madge left. 'How do you manage it?'

Alice shrugged, having resigned herself to Jeremy's apparent loss of interest. 'I go for an hour's run every morning before breakfast.'

'I do so admire people who can do that. I have to confess I'm not a morning person. I hit the gym a few times a week in the evening but I'm not a dedicated exerciser. But you should still try to give up sugar, Alice. It's bad for you.'

She sighed. 'I know. I've tried but it's a habit I can't seem to break. When I was at boarding school they made great pots of tea with the milk and sugar already in it. After I left and started drinking coffee I found it way too bitter without the sugar.'

For the first time that afternoon his eyes showed some interest. 'You went to boarding school?'

'Yes.'

'For how long?'

'Seven years.'

'And did you like it?'

'I didn't mind it,' she said. Anything was better than being at home.

His blue eyes suddenly became bleak. 'I was sent to boarding school when I was eight, and I loathed it.'

Though her curiosity was sparked, Alice decided not to pry.

'Were you able to contact those rich friends of yours?' she asked instead. 'The ones who donate a lot to charities.'

'I sent both Alex and Sergio emails,' he told her. 'They might take a while to get to it, especially Alex. His wife's due to have a baby any minute now. He lives in Sydney. And Sergio lives in Italy.'

'Goodness. How did you get to be friends in the first place?'

'We all went to Oxford together.'

'I see,' she said thoughtfully. Not just handsome and rich and charming, but super intelligent too.

'You must have gone to university,' he said.

'No. I went to a college. At night. I studied psychology. I worked as a model during the day. Not a runway model. I wasn't tall enough for that. A photographic model, doing fashion shoots for brochures and magazines.'

'Well, you're certainly good-looking enough.'

The compliment was said so matter-of-factly that she took no pleasure in it.

'Did you like being a model?'

'It was okay. It paid the rent. But it wasn't what I wanted to do.'

'Did you always want to become a counsellor?'

'Yes, actually. I did.'

Jeremy wanted to question her some more but decided that might show too much interest. He'd decided to use reverse psychology today in an attempt to spark *her* interest. It was a tactic he'd seen other men use when in pursuit of a woman. He'd personally never had to go that far, but Alice was proving to be an elusive prey. Just take the way she looked today. Okay, the red blouse was marginally sexy, but mostly covered by a black jacket, as were her jeans. Her lack of make-up plus that girlish ponytail did not shout, *I want you to look at me, Jeremy. And I want you to want me.*

But for all that he did want her. More than ever. Wanted to tear through that cool façade of hers to the woman beneath. He'd seen glimpses of that woman and she was hot.

Jeremy winced as his thoughts sent messages south of the border, relieved when Madge came back into the room at that moment with a tray full of refreshments.

Alice wondered what had precipitated that odd look of distaste that had flashed across Jeremy's face. She suspected it had something to do with her. Maybe, on seeing her again, un-dolled-up this time, he'd lost interest in her. Maybe he now found her boring. Maybe his male ego was regretting going to all this trouble. Alice certainly regretted buying new clothes in some ridiculous need to look attractive for him. She'd planned on wearing some red lipstick to match the red blouse, and to leave her jacket off and her hair down as well; but, of course, her courage had failed her in the end.

Though maybe it wasn't a matter of courage failing her but common sense rising up to quell this ongoing urge she had to throw caution to the winds and do whatever he asked her. Which was insanity, pure and simple. She should be thankful that he'd lost interest, not depressed.

It took an effort of will to put aside her conflicted feelings for Jeremy and focus on what Madge was doing.

'What lovely mugs,' she said as she watched the woman pour coffee from an elegant silver coffee pot into three blue and white mugs.

'They're Spode,' Madge said. 'They were my mother's. The coffee pot was hers, too. She liked nice things. Two sugars, did you say?'

'Yes, please.'

Madge used some elegant silver tongs to drop two cubes into one of the mugs, then added some milk before stirring, then handing that mug over to Alice.

'Thank you,' she murmured politely.

'I'll leave the plate of biscuits on the tray,' Madge said. 'Feel free to help yourself.' And she went about pouring coffee into the two remaining mugs.

When Alice leant forward to select one of the cream biscuits, she glanced over at Jeremy, who wasn't looking at her face, but down at the rather deep V of her red blouse, definite hunger burning in his hot gaze. The startling realisation that he still desired her brought an instant heat to Alice's neck, her nipples tightening the way they had the other night. Her hand trembled, Alice having to take a firm grip of herself before she spilled hot coffee into her lap. Holding the handle tightly, she lifted it to her suddenly dry lips and took a small sip. Jeremy's eyes lifted at the same time, meeting hers over the rim of the mug. He didn't smile. Didn't blink. Just stared. And in that instant she knew, as surely as she knew white was white and black was black, that she wasn't going to be able to resist this man.

A dark stab of triumph rocketed through Jeremy when he saw the telling colour creep up from her chest to her throat, her very delicious throat, which was normally pale not pink, all her skin fair and clear and unlined. She was more innocent than his usual choice of woman. But maybe that was what entranced him. Maybe he'd grown tired of sleeping with women who'd been around the block too many times. He didn't doubt Alice had had lovers. No girl who'd been a model and been to college would have stayed untouched, despite that touch-me-not air she liked to adopt at times. But he suspected she hadn't had too many boy-friends. And he was sure that at least one of them—possibly the last one—had treated her badly. It was the only thing he could think of to explain her wariness where he was concerned.

But he could see that that wariness was lifting. Still, he would not rush things. Or her. There was something strangely exciting about taking his time to get to know Alice before he got to know her in the biblical sense. Not that he didn't think about that moment when she surrendered herself to him. Hell, he thought about it all the time. He was thinking about it now as he drank his coffee and tried to pretend he didn't have an erection as impressive as the Eiffel Tower.

The sound of someone knocking at his office door startled all of them, Madge jumping up from her chair.

'Go see who it is, Madge,' Jeremy told her.

It was Kenneth Jacobs, his ruddy face beaming at Madge, then at Jeremy as he was ushered into the office.

'Sorry to interrupt, Jeremy,' he said, his voice still a bit nasal from his cold. 'But I was passing by this way and just had to drop in and tell you how grateful I was for you stepping into my shoes the other night. It was very good of you. I hated letting that nice Alice down. I also wanted to say how pleased I am with what you've been doing with my books. Those new covers are perfectly splendid. I love them. And my sales speak for themselves. If you don't watch it, I'm going to be a rich man. Now I won't keep you. I can see you're having a meeting of some sort,' he added, throwing Alice a warm smile.

'Don't go,' Jeremy said, and Madge immediately got an extra chair. 'Stay and have coffee with us. And you can meet that nice Alice in person.' He waved a hand directly towards Alice.

Kenneth, despite being portly and almost bald and the wrong side of sixty, proved to be an incorrigible flirt, raining compliments on both Alice and Madge too, Jeremy noted—and insisting they call him Ken. He refused coffee. Instead he sat down and asked endless questions about the auction, pulling out a pen and notebook from his slightly crumpled cream linen jacket and jotting down George and Mandy's names, promising to give them major roles in his next book.

'I might make George the murderer,' he said with ghoulish glee, 'and his wife the victim.'

'Oh, no, don't do that,' Alice said straight away. 'Mandy will want to be in your book all the way through. Make Mandy the killer and George the victim. She could be a serial killer of husbands. A black widow.'

'I like the way you think, girl. That's a wonderful idea. Makes for a nice twist on the husband always murdering the wife.'

'I would imagine that quite a few wives might want to murder their husbands,' Alice said drily, and Ken laughed.

Jeremy didn't, however, the bitter undertone in Alice's words sounding personal, making him wonder which actual husband she was referring to. It came to him out of the blue that maybe she'd been married before. Briefly, but unhappily. That would explain a lot.

'Now when I was walking around Mayfair today,' Ken was saying. 'If you must know I didn't pass your establishment by accident, Jeremy. I was actually doing a bit of research for my latest book. Anyway, during my perambulatory travels, I came by this trendy little wine bar tucked away down the end of a cobblestone alley. It's called Pizza and Vino. There was something about it which called to me.'

Jeremy chuckled. 'Probably the irresistible smell that wafts from the place. They make the best pizza outside Italy. And the wine's not too bad, either.'

'I gather you've been there before, then?' Ken said.

'Yes. Once or twice.' Sergio had given him a taste for all things Italian. Plus he liked discreet little wine bars that had a relaxing ambience and were off the beaten track.

'I planned on returning later,' Ken said. 'Look, what say you call it a day, folks? Then we four could trot down there together for a few glasses of wine and some of that delicious pizza. Unless you have other plans, of course,' he added, shooting Jeremy and then Alice a rather intuitive glance.

Jeremy realised few people would be able to put much past Ken. Possibly, being a writer, he'd become a keen observer of life, and body language, and all sort of unspoken things.

Jeremy smiled, not worried a whit if his interest in Alice had been noted. Now that he was confident she returned his interest, his heart felt light, his mood very affable.

'No, no plans,' he said. 'Have you got plans, Madge?'

'None at all,' Madge returned, looking very pleased with the invitation.

'What about you, Alice?'

Her expression showed a degree of surprise, but no displeasure. 'No. No plans.'

'That's all settled, then.'

'I'll need to go to the ladies' room first,' Madge said, and stood up.

'Me too,' Alice said, and stood up also.

Ken chuckled. 'Women,' he said after they were alone. 'They do love going to the powder room in pairs. I wonder what it is they discuss in there.'

'Best we don't know, Ken. It's secret women's business.'

Jeremy had difficulty controlling his excitement when Alice finally returned with some glossy red lipstick on and her gorgeous blonde hair lying loose and wavy around her shoulders. Nothing could have pleased him more. Or aroused him more. Jeremy was glad that his suit jacket wasn't too short or too fitted, covering a good deal of his lower half. Whilst he no longer felt he had to hide his interest in Alice, he didn't want to frighten her off with the evidence of his lust. But already he was thinking she might agree to come back to his place tonight…

CHAPTER TEN

ALICE COULDN'T BELIEVE how much she liked just walking along the street with Jeremy. The pavement wasn't wide enough for the four of them to walk together so they'd broken off into pairs, Ken and a beaming Madge leading the way, she and Jeremy a few strides behind. He didn't make any attempt to hold her hand, for which Alice was grateful. She was already shaking inside. But with excitement, not fear. No, no, that wasn't entirely true. There was some fear mixed with the adrenaline racing through her veins, the same kind of fear which she imagined took possession of a first-time skydiver before he jumped out of a plane. Jeremy couldn't realise how new she was at this. Why, she hadn't been on a date since that last appalling time. Not that this was a proper date, she reminded herself. It had all come about by accident, not design, which was why she'd agreed. Because they wouldn't be alone.

Fiona would still be disgusted with her, of course. A part of Alice was disgusted with herself. What did she thinking she was playing at, encouraging Jeremy by wearing her hair down and putting on lipstick? Red lipstick, no less! Next thing she knew he'd be asking her out for real again. And next time, she just might not be able to say no.

He's a playboy, she kept telling herself. *An infamous playboy. And you're a virgin. You're not equipped to have an affair with a man like Jeremy. He'll eat you alive, then spit you out.* Because that was what playboys did. They took what they wanted, then they moved on.

She turned her head to glance over at him for the umpteenth time, thinking how utterly gorgeous he was. But, oh, so dangerous.

He turned his head towards her at the same time. 'What is it?' he asked, frowning.

Alice searched her mind for something sensible to say. 'I forgot to tell you something back at the office,' she said.

'What?'

'The house next door to the refuge I was working at today is for sale.'

'What's the price?'

'I don't know. I never envisaged we'd have the money to buy it.'

'Where exactly is this refuge?'

'In Hammersmith.'

'I see. And how big is this house?'

'Quite big, actually. Needs some work but I would say it has four bedrooms at least. And a big garden.'

'Then you probably don't have enough to buy it. Yet. But there's no harm in looking at it. Are you working to-morrow?'

'I always work on Saturdays. Friday nights invariably bring us a new client or two, looking for shelter from their drunken partners. By Saturday they're looking for an ex-cuse to go back to them and it's my job to talk them out of it.'

'Do you have much success?'

'Not enough. But I try.'

'I'm sure you're very good at what you do. You have a compassionate heart, Alice, nothing like the other girls I've known from privileged backgrounds.'

His comment startled her. 'What do you know about my background?'

'Nothing much. But I knew before you told me you went to boarding school that you came from an upper-crust fam-ily. Your voice gave you away, Alice.'

She sighed. 'I've tried to get rid of my posh accent, but it won't go away.'

'Don't try to change, lovely Alice. You're perfect as you are.'

She stopped and stared at him. 'Please don't say things like that.'

'Why?'

'Because you don't really mean it.' He was just saying it to get into her pants!

'Ah, but I do mean it, Alice.'

How sincere he sounded. How flatteringly, seductively sincere. He was a wicked devil, all right. But, oh, so charming, and disarming.

Alice had to laugh. It was the only way to defuse her tension and survive the evening.

'My answer is still no,' she said. And almost meant it.

Jeremy grinned then took her hand, giving it a light squeeze.

'You don't mean that,' he said. 'You're just playing hard to get.'

'I'm not playing at anything. *You're* the player, not me.'

'That old chestnut again? Now come along and stop being difficult. Besides, has it escaped your notice that I haven't asked you out again yet? So your no is premature. Or was that no referring to something else?'

Alice expelled an exasperated breath. 'You're incorrigible.'

'Too big a word. Almost as bad as perambulatory.'

Alice couldn't help it. She burst out laughing. Madge and Ken turned round to look at them.

'You two sound like you're having fun,' Ken said.

'We are,' Alice said in surprise.

Surprised that she was having fun with him? Jeremy wondered. Or that she was having fun, full stop!

Jeremy suspected both, the thought making him resolve to do everything in his power to make sure she had fun this evening. Maybe then she would stop saying no to his invitation to a dinner date. Just then Ken turned down the alley that led to the wine bar, Jeremy tightening his hold on Alice's hand as they followed.

'Watch your step,' he told her. 'Easy to trip on these old cobblestones.'

Pizza and Vino was a hit. Alice loved the look of the wine bar, which had subtle lighting, murals of Italian scenes on the walls and comfy semi-circular booths along the back walls. It wasn't all that busy yet, with pizzas not being served for another half-hour. They'd only just fired up the oven. Jeremy didn't mind that at all, ordering a couple of bottles of a superb Italian wine—one white and one red—hoping that that covered everyone's taste. Ken was happy to bow to his judgment, admitting that his knowledge of wine was limited.

'I'm normally a beer and Guinness man,' he said. 'Rather like my detective in my books. But I don't mind expanding my horizons,' he added, throwing Madge a rather flirtatious glance.

The next hour was extremely productive in Jeremy's quest to find out more about Alice, a couple of glasses of wine loosening up Alice's tongue, allowing him to probe a little without seeming obvious. It also helped that Ken was busy chatting up Madge. Jeremy soon discovered that the flat she was living in was owned by a girl called Fiona, an old school chum of hers and the younger sister of Melody, one of Jeremy's exes, Alice pointed out again. Though Lord knew he could hardly remember her. He vaguely recalled a Melody who was the daughter of Neville Drinkwater, one of England's richest stockbrokers. But he'd only taken her out once or twice. Spoiled society princesses never lasted long with him. Apparently her sister was nicer, having kindly given Alice a room for free when she'd first come to London after leaving school. This statement had led to some more questioning, Alice finally confessing that she didn't get along with her mother and didn't want to turn out like her.

'My mother cares for nothing but money,' she said as he refilled her glass a third time. 'She hasn't done an honest day's work in her life!'

Jeremy didn't admit that he already knew that she'd been born the daughter of an earl. No need to tell her that. Someone as naturally reserved as Alice wouldn't like to think he'd been prying into her background. He'd have to mention to Madge not to say anything. He glanced across their table at his PA. Dear Madge… She was having a wonderful time, talking books to Kenneth Jacobs. Unlike himself, she'd read every one of Ken's thrillers and was able to talk about each one in depth, much to the author's obvious pleasure. Jeremy couldn't say that those particular books were to his taste. Too grizzly. Too repetitive.

The waitress finally arrived with the pizzas they'd ordered, along with their mouth-watering smell. There was such an amazing array on the menu that in the end they'd opted for the house special, which had a little bit of everything.

'You were right, Ken,' Madge said. 'This looks delicious.'

'I agree,' Alice said. 'Thanks, Ken.'

Jealousy jabbed at Jeremy till Alice turned her lovely eyes his way and said sweetly, 'And thank you too, Jeremy. For the lovely wine. I know those bottles weren't cheap. And for everything else you're doing for my charity. You really are a nice man.'

It wasn't jealousy that stabbed at Jeremy then. It was guilt. Because none of today had been him being nice. It had been him being a ruthless bastard. Everything he'd done had had one purpose. To win Alice over and get her into his bed. And whilst he would be good to her—very good—just how long did he think their affair would last?

Not all that long, he conceded. He didn't do long. Or broken hearts, remember? Maybe he should just forget about Alice. She seemed the vulnerable type and he didn't want to hurt her.

If only she hadn't leant over at that moment and kissed him lightly on the cheek. He stared deep into her eyes and saw that they were glazed. Alice was obviously tipsy, every ounce of her usual wariness gone. In its place was a dreamy softness, plus the promise of what she would be like when she was naked and wide-eyed beneath him. It sealed her fate, that image. No way could he give up his pursuit of her. His need for her sharpened, a wry smile curving his mouth as he gave in to his dark side.

'I like your way of saying no,' he said, then leant over and kissed her back.

But not on her cheek. On her mouth.

Oh, Lord, Alice thought dazedly as his lips brushed over hers. Her heart started hammering behind her ribs, her stomach tightening, her head whirling.

His mouth abandoned hers way too soon, only then Alice becoming aware of Ken's chuckling, plus Madge's astonished stare.

'Yes, I fancy her,' Jeremy said with a smile in his voice. 'All right, Madge?'

Madge smiled. 'Quite all right with me, boss, if it's all right with her.'

'Is it all right with you, Alice?' Jeremy asked with that wicked sparkle in his eyes.

Embarrassment sent a hot blush to her cheeks, but somehow she found a cool voice. 'I will blame the wine for my lack of decorum, and Jeremy's male ego for his. I told him the other night that I wouldn't go out with him, but he simply won't take no for an answer. Now I think we should eat our pizzas before they get cold.'

It was a struggle to keep her composure from that moment on, her mind invariably returning to that moment when his lips had met hers. How could such a brief kiss give rise to such a storm of desire? She was awash with longing. And need. It underlined to Alice how dangerous it would be to go out with Jeremy, alone. She hoped and prayed that he wouldn't ask her again, and strangely, *annoyingly*, he didn't. Though after they'd finished their meal with coffee, he did suggest they share a taxi home. She agreed, assuming that all four of them would be in the taxi together, till Ken said that he and Madge were going in the opposite direction, to a jazz club Ken liked. To refuse Jeremy's offer at that point would have been silly. Besides, Alice didn't like catching the Tube at night, especially a Friday night.

The ride back to Kensington was just as short and as silent as their taxi ride the other night. It wasn't all that late. Only eight-thirty. She half expected him to ask her back to his place for a nightcap. But he didn't. He did, however, climb out of the cab when it stopped at her address, Jeremy telling the cabbie to wait for him. He walked her up the steps to her front door, turning her to face him before she could escape. Alice confessed privately that she wanted him to kiss her goodnight. In truth, she wanted so much more. Such wanting brought tension, and fear. She was out of her depth here with this man, sinking into waters that she wasn't equipped to handle.

'What are you afraid of, Alice?' he asked, frowning as his eyes searched hers.

'Maybe I'm afraid of myself,' she replied.

'You think too much. Time to just feel, Alice, and to have fun.'

'Fun?' she echoed. When had she ever had fun with a man?

He smiled. 'Clearly fun is a concept you're unfamiliar with. Let me teach you, Alice. I'm an expert at the art of fun.'

'I don't doubt it.'

'You're going to come to dinner with me tomorrow night, aren't you?'

Somehow, the word no simply would not come.

'Yes,' she said, sick of arguing with herself over this.

'Good. I'll ring you tomorrow and we'll make definite plans.' With that, he turned and left her, flushed and frustrated, on the doorstep. She watched him walk away and get into the cab without a backward glance. He did look at her through the taxi window but he didn't wave or smile. She thought he looked oddly grim, but maybe it was just her imagination. Why should he look unhappy over her agreeing to do what he'd been wanting her to do since Wednesday night? Which was say yes to him. Yes, to dinner and whatever else he had in mind for afterwards.

A shaken Alice let herself in the front door, glad that Fiona always stayed out late on a Friday night. She walked slowly along the hall and into her bedroom where she stripped off and dragged on one of her slightly prissy nighties. None of the outrageously sexy nightwear that Fiona always wore filled Alice's wardrobe. After a trip to the bathroom, she climbed into bed where she lay awake for hours, thinking about Jeremy, and tomorrow night, and fun.

By fun he obviously meant sex. Casual sex. Maybe even kinky sex.

Alice shuddered at this last thought. No way could she ever entertain the thought of doing anything remotely kinky. It was as much as she could handle thinking about having normal sex with him. Even whilst she wanted to, the idea of actually doing it at long last was overwhelmingly nerve-racking. How would he react when he found out she was a virgin?

Maybe he won't find out, Alice, came the comforting thought. *You've gone horse riding for years. And used tampons. You're not likely to bleed. Or feel excessive pain.*

Oh, Lord, she thought and buried her face in her pillow. *What have I done?*

* * *

Alice was still awake when Fiona got home just after one. Thankfully, her flatmate would still be asleep when she got up for work in the morning. Alice couldn't bear the recriminations over her spending the evening in Jeremy's company, then agreeing to have dinner with him. Fiona would be all dire warnings and doomsday forecasts. Silly, really. Alice knew full well there was no future with Jeremy. She wasn't a total fool. Not that she wanted a future with him, anyway. To entrust any man with her happiness forever was never going to happen. But she couldn't seem to stop herself from going out with him. He'd bewitched her—that was what he'd done.

As she lay there, Alice wondered if he was still awake, if he was thinking about her the way she was thinking about him. Hardly, she decided cynically. Playboys didn't lose sleep over members of the opposite sex. She suspected that if a woman gave Jeremy cause for trouble, he simply shrugged her off and moved on. Clearly, that was what he'd done with Melody. Sex was a game to him. Women were rest and recreation. He didn't have relationships. He had fun. Girlfriends weren't permanent fixtures in his life. They were never proper girlfriends at all. They were just dates. Any woman foolish enough to go out with him had to accept that. Alice had already accepted it because, quite frankly, his way of life suited her. That didn't mean dating him didn't frighten the life out of her. It did. But there was no going back now. She was well past the point of no return...

Jeremy threw back the duvet, jumped out of bed and stalked, naked, from his bedroom along the hallway and down the stairs into his den. A typical man cave, it had everything he needed to entertain himself at home. A billiard table, a huge TV on the wall, games console, a large comfy sofa, an armchair near a bookcase full of complex spy thrillers, plus a well-stocked bar. Whilst Jeremy was a wine buff, when he was attacked by insomnia his mainstay was whisky. Pouring himself a hefty slug, he sipped it straight as he sank into the sofa and picked up the remote. But then he dropped it again. He didn't want to watch TV. He wanted to be in bed with Alice.

Damn the woman. She'd really got under his skin, hadn't she?

He knew why. Because she was different from the women he usually dated. Underneath that cool façade she hid behind, she was sweeter. Nicer. And sexier in a weirdly innocent way.

The look on her face when he'd left her on the doorstep, unkissed, had made him feel rotten. But he'd done it, anyway. Because he'd wanted her to go to bed wanting him.

Jeremy laughed, aware that his cold-blooded plan had backfired on him. He was the one left doing the wanting. Hell, he wanted her so badly that he couldn't sleep. She, no doubt, was already racking up zeds, whilst he was here, with a painful hard-on, drinking himself into oblivion. He took comfort from the fact that tomorrow would come. And so would tomorrow night. He wouldn't be leaving her unkissed tomorrow night, he vowed. There wouldn't be an inch of her delicious body unkissed.

Jeremy smiled a dark smile as he gulped back some more Scotch.

Just you wait, Alice. Just you wait.

CHAPTER ELEVEN

LUCKILY ENOUGH, NO new clients had arrived at the shelter on the Friday night, which meant that Alice's lack of concentration that Saturday wasn't obvious. She spent the morning talking to a few of the women who'd been there a while, encouraging one of them to go home to her parents, who had agreed to help. But she was too afraid of her ex showing up and making trouble. She had no confidence in the restraining order she'd taken out against him. No confidence in the police doing anything but smacking him on the wrist.

By the time Alice stopped to make some coffee to go with her sandwich for lunch, she felt decidedly weary. Not enough sleep, of course. On top of that, Jeremy hadn't rung. She wished he would put her out of her misery and just ring.

As if she had conjured him up by sheer wish power, her phone rang, and it was him, just the sound of his voice instantly dispelling her tiredness, in its place a fizz of excitement, and anticipation.

'How's my girl today?' he said.

'You are a terrible flirt,' she replied, but with a smile on her face. 'But you know that, don't you?'

'It's been mentioned once or twice. So would it be all right if I came over and we had a look at the house next door together some time this afternoon?'

'Oh. Oh, yes, I suppose so,' she said, thinking she didn't look as smart as she had yesterday. The jeans were the same but her top was a simple and rather cheap white T-shirt. The weather had turned warm, so a jacket was out of the question. She wondered if she'd have time to dash down the road and buy something new.

'What time were you thinking of coming?'

'Have no idea. When would you suggest?'

'Not for a couple of hours. I've got appointments,' she lied.

'Tell you what. If you give me the name of the estate agent handling the sale, I'll give them a call and arrange a proper inspection. How about three?'

'But what if he can't organise things that quickly? That's not much notice.'

Jeremy laughed. 'Trust me, Alice, the agent will drop everything to show me that house at three. Money speaks all languages, but especially that of greed. Now go get me a name. And you'd also better tell me your work address. I only know Hammersmith.'

After she told him everything he needed to know, she added that it would be better if she met him at the house rather than the refuge.

'Why's that?' he asked in a puzzled tone.

'There are lots of nervous women here, Jeremy,' she informed him. 'And you're a strange man. Sorry. No offence intended.'

'None taken,' he replied. 'Okay, we'll meet outside the house for sale at three.'

'Fine,' Alice agreed. 'Ring me if you can't make it. Bye.' And she hung up. Alice bypassed the coffee, stuffing the sandwich down her throat before telling Jane she was off up the road to do some shopping. One hour later she was the proud owner of a very nice floral blouse—floral was in this spring—along with an off-white shirt dress, which was simple yet stylish enough to take her to whatever restaurant he took her to tonight. Alice loved the way it gave her a very feminine shape, being cinched in at the waist with a wide self-covered belt. The buttons—which ran all the way from the V neckline to the hem—were gold, but small and dainty. She also splurged on a pair of nude high-heeled sandals. This was followed by a matching clutch purse, bringing the bill to more than she'd spent on clothes in years. Her final purchase before returning to work was a coral lipstick, bought on impulse as she walked past a shop that sold make-up.

Alice knew she was acting unwisely—everything she'd done since meeting Jeremy had been unwise—but there was no stopping now. But underneath her surface excitement, she was anxious.

As the clock ticked closer to three she started constantly popping her head out of the front door, checking to see if Jeremy had arrived. He'd be late for sure. Maybe he wouldn't come at all. She half expected her phone to ring, calling his visit off. By the time a silver Aston Martin pulled into the small off-street parking area in front of the house, Alice was in a right old state. She swallowed as she watched a dashingly attired Jeremy climb out from behind the wheel. God, but he was gorgeous, that pale grey suit he was wearing decidedly yummy. He was yummy all over, she conceded breathlessly as she quickly closed the door lest he see her ogling him again.

'Just popping out for a short while,' she called out to Jane, after which she took several deep breaths and tried to gain control of her silly self. Pride demanded she not let Jeremy know how much he was affecting her. Pride and common sense. If he suspected how crazy she was about him, he'd go in for the kill. Tonight. Alice needed more time before going to bed with him. She wasn't remotely as unconcerned about doing such a thing as she'd intimated to Fiona that other morning. Jeremy might think of sex as just fun, but for Alice to trust a man with her body was a huge leap of faith for her. A huge decision, and not one she aimed to make lightly.

'Hi there,' she said as she walked with feigned serenity towards him. 'You're very punctual,' she added.

Oh, the irony of that remark, Jeremy thought as he looked Alice up and down. If there was one thing he'd never been in his life, it was punctual. He'd improved a bit after buying his own business, but since meeting Alice he was in danger of becoming an obsessive clock-watcher. Waiting till lunchtime before ringing her today had been agony. He'd been tempted to come early this afternoon as well, but in the end had practised patience, instinctively knowing that rushing Alice in any way, shape or form would not work. At the same time, he hadn't expected to be greeted by cool blue eyes, showing him that *she* hadn't been on tenterhooks waiting for him to arrive.

Never had he known a girl run so hot and cold all the time! The thought that her co-operative behaviour last night had been due to her being drunk did not sit well with Jeremy. He much preferred to think that she'd finally fallen victim to the same uncontrollable desires that were currently gripping him. It was one step forwards and two steps backwards with her, he conceded.

Damn it, but she was lovely. He found more features to admire every time he looked at her. Her small shell-like ears. Her daintily pointed chin. Her clear, almost translucent skin. But always at the centre of his attention was that luscious mouth.

The temptation to grab her and kiss her senseless was acute, and most uncharacteristic of him. Jeremy never made love to a woman like some caveman. He never grabbed. He caressed. He never insisted. He persuaded.

'The owners are away in Spain so the place is empty. The chap handling the sale said we could inspect it at our leisure.'

The house proved to be in surprisingly good condition for a building as old as it was. The kitchen and two bathrooms had been renovated at some stage, and the walls freshly painted, though a lot of the Victorian features had been maintained, with the two reception rooms still having their original fireplaces and lovely ornate ceilings. There were four bedrooms, plus another small room, which was being used as a study. Of course the price was prohibitive, the million they'd raised not enough to purchase it. When Alice mentioned this, Jeremy turned to her.

'If you like I'll buy it and gift it to your charity.'

A shocked Alice blinked in amazement. 'That's too much, Jeremy. I can't let you do that.'

'Why not?'

'You know why not.'

He shook his head at her. 'My dear, cynical Alice, you're quite wrong. I would never go that far just to get a girl to go to bed with me. I genuinely want to help. I was touched by your speech the night of the auction. And I found the reason why I shouldn't just rock up at the refuge door quite heartbreaking. I feel genuinely sorry for all those poor women. I admit my offering to get more involved in your charity wasn't entirely altruistic at first,' he went on, that bewitching sparkle lighting up his eyes. 'Yes, I confess I wanted to see more of you and I thought you wouldn't give me the chance. But last night changed my game plan. You agreed to go to dinner with me tonight so you see I don't need to do this. I *want* to do it, Alice. I can easily afford it.'

Alice just stared at him, his words revolving in her head, especially his confession of having a 'game plan'. She'd suspected from the beginning that his offer to become a patron of her charity had been a ploy. Fiona had warned her that he was a devil when it came to women.

'Just how rich are you?' she threw at him in an effort to remind herself just who she was tangling with here. An infamous playboy. A man who thought of sex as a game. His needing a *game plan* in his pursuit of her had been very telling. She wished she didn't also find that thought secretly exciting, and perversely flattering.

He laughed. 'I don't usually tell women the extent of my wealth. But in the interest of putting your mind at rest I have a couple of billion at my disposal.'

Alice gasped. 'A couple of *billion*?'

'Yes.'

'Good Lord.'

'I have been lucky.'

'Lucky how?' she quizzed, shocked. He didn't seem old enough to have accrued so much money. He didn't look any older than thirty.

His shrug was nonchalant. 'I did inherit some of it. But the rest I earned myself. Plus an investment I made in my early twenties, which paid off big time last year.'

'What kind of investment?' She was both curious and intrigued.

'I'll tell you about it over dinner tonight. Right now there's something else I'd rather do…'

Alice knew he was going to kiss her well before he drew her into his arms and lowered his mouth to hers. She could have said no. Could have made some silly futile protest. But it wouldn't have been honest. She wanted him to kiss her. And not the light brushing of lips he'd given her last night. She wanted a more passionate display of his desire.

Be careful of what you wish for, Alice…

His kiss was soft at first. Almost gentle, his arms around her not threatening in any way. He teased her lips open, slowly, seductively. But once he gained entrance to her mouth, the tenor of his kiss changed. His arms tightened around her, his tongue delving deep, making her gasp as white-hot lights exploded in her brain. She couldn't get enough of him, her own arms sliding under his suit jacket to wind around him, clinging wildly to his firm, hard body. She moaned as fire flooded her own body, burning her up with a longing that was as powerful as it was wonderful.

When his phone rang, she groaned with dismay. He ignored it for a couple of rings, but then his head lifted, his eyes looking oddly stunned.

'Wow, Alice. What happened to my Ice Princess? Sorry, but I need to answer this.'

CHAPTER TWELVE

JEREMY KNEW HE didn't need to do any such thing. He wasn't expecting a call. He could have just ignored it. It would have gone to his voicemail eventually. The truth was he'd been close to losing control. Not a good idea when you were without a condom. He usually kept a couple in his wallet, but had run out recently. He'd bought a new box the other day, then forgot to open it. Which showed how crazy Alice had been making him.

He wouldn't be forgetting them tonight, he vowed darkly as he checked the identity of his caller. It was Sergio, possibly getting back to him over the email he'd sent concerning Alice's charity.

'Sergio,' he answered, throwing a flushed Alice an apologetic smile. Lord, but she looked even lovelier when she was hot and bothered. Now that he knew she wouldn't knock him back, tonight could not come soon enough. 'What are you up to, dear friend? I presume you got my email?'

'Email?' Sergio echoed, sounding confused for a second. 'Oh, yes, about the charity. I've already wired off a donation. Was half a mil enough?'

'Perfect.'

'That's not why I'm calling.'

'Oh? What's up?'

'The premiere of *An Angel in New York* is on in a fortnight's time. It's in New York, of course. I thought since you were one of the executive producers that you might like to come. Sorry I didn't invite you sooner but things have been up in the air with the release date for some time. Last-minute editing and all that. Anyway, I invited Alex as well, since he also put money into the movie, but with Harriet due any day now he refuses to travel.'

'Fair enough. But I'd love to come.'

'You can stay with us at Bella's New York apartment.'

'No, I wouldn't want to impose. Besides, I'll be bringing someone with me, if that's all right.'

'Of course. Who is she? Someone new?'

'Yes. Her name's Alice,' he said, glancing over at Alice, who was looking a little less flustered. 'She's the girl who started up the charity. She's a counsellor. Works for the women's refuges.'

'Sounds intriguing. And not your usual type.'

'Right on both counts.'

'Dare we hope you've fallen in love at long last?'

The question startled Jeremy, then annoyed him. Surely Sergio knew him well enough by now to know that was never going to happen. 'Don't be ridiculous.'

Sergio sighed. 'I don't think falling in love is ridiculous.'

'You're entitled to your opinion. But then, you're biased.' No doubt Sergio believed he was genuinely in love with Bella. Romantic love was an illusion, in Jeremy's opinion. A mirage. Get close enough and it disappeared. Liking and lust, however, were very real and more stable emotions. He liked Alice and he lusted after her. He had not, however, fallen in love with her. Jeremy knew from experience that love made men do seriously stupid things, like get engaged and vow eternal devotion. He didn't want to propose marriage to Alice. He just wanted her to go out with him, and go to bed with him.

'I didn't ring you to argue about love, Jeremy,' Sergio said, his stiff tone making Jeremy feel ashamed of himself. He had no right to spoil what was no doubt a happy time for Sergio. He should let him enjoy his marriage and his wife, whilst the gloss lasted.

'Sorry,' he said. 'I'm an old cynic, I know. Look, I'm a

bit busy right now. Could you send me the details of the premiere and I'll book a hotel?'

'Will do. We'll talk again soon. Keep well.'

'One of your old friends from Oxford?' Alice said after he put his phone away.

'Yes. Sergio's one of the main reasons I'm a billionaire. Plus why I'm addicted to Italian food. He and my Australian friend, Alex, were the instigators of the investment which reaped in all the money. They did most of the work. I was just the behind-the-scene money man.' He considered telling her more about the WOW bar franchise, then decided Alice didn't need to know the ins and outs of his past life. He'd found that telling a woman too much about himself gave her the impression you wanted more from her than what he was capable of giving. He was already in danger of giving Alice the wrong impression by becoming involved in her charity. Still, he did like talking to her. A lot. Hell, but he was damned if he did and damned if he didn't!

'From what George said the other night,' she said thoughtfully, 'you're a very clever man with money.'

Jeremy shrugged off his momentary emotional dilemma, determined not to go getting too serious here. Life was meant to be enjoyed, not fretted over. 'That I am,' he said.

'And with women,' she added pointedly.

'I do have talents in that area also.'

'You *are* incorrigible.'

'And you're a very good kisser.'

Alice had to laugh. If only he knew…

'What was that all about you bringing me along somewhere?'

'Sergio's wife has made a movie which is premiering in New York in a fortnight's time. It's called *An Angel in New York*. As one of the executive producers, I've been invited. I thought you might like to come with me.'

Her eyes widened. 'To New York?'

'Yes. What do you think?'

'I think you're very presumptuous,' she said. 'Is Sergio's wife a famous actress?'

'Bella? No, not really. She's a Broadway star.'

Alice gaped. 'What? You're talking about Bella? *The* Bella?'

'The one and only.'

'Oh, dear. Oh, you wicked man!'

'Why?'

'I saw her once, on stage, in London. She's simply brilliant and so beautiful. I would kill to be at the premiere of that movie.'

'Well, you don't have to kill anyone, Alice. Just buy yourself a nice new dress and come along with me.'

'Like I said, you're a wicked man.'

His smile made her melt inside, but she maintained her droll expression. 'I don't have money to burn, Jeremy. I am saving to buy my own flat. If I come with you—and I haven't said yes yet—I will wear the same outfit I wore to the charity auction the other night.'

'Fine,' he agreed equably. 'You looked great in that.'

'Now I have to get back to work,' she said before he could kiss her again.

'Fine,' he repeated, though through gritted teeth.

'What time are you going to pick me up tonight?' she asked him as they made their way outside.

'How about seven-thirty?' he suggested after locking up.

'Could we make it eight-thirty? Fiona will have gone out by then.'

He frowned. 'What's going on here, Alice? Why the cloak and dagger stuff? Are you ashamed of going out with me?'

'I'm not going out with you. I'm just going to dinner with you.'

'I see,' he bit out. 'In that case, we'll stick to seven-thirty. I don't like to eat late. But I'm disappointed in you,

Alice. I thought you were a girl who knew her own mind. And who didn't let other people influence you. You don't have to answer to your flatmate. You're a grown woman, without a husband, fiancé or boyfriend. You don't have to answer to anyone.'

Alice swallowed. He was right. She didn't. But there were times when she needed a shoulder to cry on, or some advice from others. It was hard not having a mother you could rely upon, or a big sister with any sense. Fiona might not be the sharpest tool in the box but she had Alice's best interests at heart, unlike the man standing in front of her. He didn't have her best interests at heart at all.

'Seven-thirty it is, then,' she said somewhat coldly.

'Oh, Alice, Alice,' he said, shaking his head at her. 'Whatever am I going to do with you?'

'You're going to take me to a very nice restaurant tonight,' she retorted with defiance in her eyes. 'And you're going to tell me how you came to be a billionaire.'

He stared at her for a long moment, then smiled. He was still smiling as he climbed behind the wheel of the sleek silver Aston Martin, which had playboy written all over it.

Alice watched him reverse out into the street, then roar off, her stomach tight with tension over the night ahead.

'Oh, Alice, Alice,' she muttered to herself as she turned and walked slowly back to work. 'Whatever *is* he going to do to you?'

CHAPTER THIRTEEN

As LUCK WOULD have it, Fiona wasn't there when Alice arrived home from work around six. She'd left a note propped up on the hall table, informing Alice that she'd gone to Alistair's place, and wouldn't be home till late. Relieved, Alice dashed to her bedroom, dropping her things on the bed before hurrying into the bathroom and turning on the taps of the claw-footed bath. She only had an hour and a half before Jeremy picked her up and there was so much to do…

Jeremy pulled in to the kerb outside Alice's flat right on seven twenty-nine, taking his time as he alighted the car, locked it then walked slowly up the steps to the front door. Scooping in a deep breath—Lord, anyone would think he was nervous!—he pressed the buzzer and waited impatiently for someone to answer, all the while wondering which Alice he was going to be taking out tonight. The hot babe who'd kissed him back so passionately this afternoon, or the Ice Princess whom he'd first met and who bobbed up with regular monotony. She was a mystery all right. Irritating and intriguing yet downright irresistible. He hadn't been this excited over a date in years.

The door opened and there she stood, the Ice Princess, in a prissy cream dress and her hair all scraped back into that bun thing. Not that she didn't still look beautiful. She did. But truly!

'You're early,' were her first words, served cold in that cut-glass voice of hers.

Jeremy didn't wear a watch, so he pulled out his phone and showed her the time.

'Oh,' she said. 'I must have lost track of time. I'll just get my bag.'

When she whirled round and walked back into the hall-way, the softly falling skirt of her dress flared out slightly. Jeremy's gaze dropped down to her shapely calves, and then down to her very sexy shoes. It came to him, when she walked back towards him with her bag tucked under her arm and keys in her hand, that the dress wasn't quite as prissy as he'd originally thought. He liked the way the buttons went from the neckline to the hem, his mind already anticipating the ease with which he could undress her.

'You look lovely,' he complimented as she locked up. 'I like that dress.'

'Do you?' She sounded uncertain. 'I liked it when I first bought it but when I put it on tonight I wondered if it was a bit old-fashioned.'

'It suits you,' he said.

'Thank you,' she replied stiffly before heading down the steps ahead of him, her shoulders squared as if she were going to face the firing squad.

Jeremy suppressed a sigh, saying nothing whilst he opened the passenger door for her, waiting till she was buckled up before he closed the door and made his way round to the driver's side.

'Is there anything wrong, Alice?' he asked her once he was behind the wheel. 'Did your flatmate make some more derogatory comments about me? What was her name again?'

'Fiona. And, no, she didn't say a single word about you. She wasn't at home. She'd gone over to her fiancé's place.'

'Then what's bothering you?'

Alice winced before turning to throw him a small, apologetic smile. 'To coin an old cliché, Jeremy: it's not you. It's me.'

'Want to talk about it?'

'No. No. Not yet. I'll sort myself out. Let's just have a nice night out.'

'That won't happen unless you relax, Alice.'

Her smile turned rueful. 'Perhaps after a couple of glasses of wine, I'll do just that.'

Jeremy frowned. He didn't want her drunk. He wanted her well aware of who was making love to her later tonight. Which would be him, Jeremy Barker-Whittle. More than ever before, he suspected that some man in her past had done her wrong. And he was suffering for it.

'Do you mind if I ask you one question before we go?'

'What?'

'Have you ever been married?'

The look on her face gave him his answer.

'No. Right. My mistake. Just thought it might explain why you're so wary of men. A bad marriage can be very damaging. I know. My family's littered with bad marriages. The number of divorces they've accrued between them must be some sort of record.'

Alice heard the bitterness in Jeremy's voice, a most unusual occurrence. He was usually so easy-going, so carefree in his attitude to life.

'Like...how many divorces?' she asked.

Jeremy laughed as he gunned the engine. 'Let's see now... Dear old Dad's on his fourth marriage. Mother's got three divorces behind her. Fortunately, she hasn't married her current partner, which is a bonus since I hear that's already on the rocks. My oldest brother, Winston, is about to enter his third marriage whilst my other brother, Sebastian, is really letting the side down. He's only on his second marriage.'

'Goodness. That is a lot of divorcing.'

'Tell me about it,' he said as he drove off. 'And they wonder why I've chosen a different path in life. I decided a long time ago to remain a bachelor.'

'Understandable,' she said. And she *did* understand. 'We are all products of what happens in our families,' she went on, thinking of her father's suicide plus her mother's blind materialism. Alice blamed her entirely for Marigold sticking with her abusive husband, just because he was rich. 'It's impossible to remain unaffected by our parents' mistakes. In an ideal world, they should be role models. But real life doesn't always work out that way.'

Jeremy flashed her a surprised glance. 'I keep forgetting that you studied psychology. But let's not talk about such matters tonight. At the risk of disappointing you by eating Italian two nights in a row, I'm taking you to my favourite Italian restaurant where we're going to eat some seriously good food, washed down with some seriously good wine.'

'And afterwards?' Alice asked before she could think better of it.

His shrug seemed nonchalant. 'Afterwards will be up to you. I can either take you straight home, or you can come back to my place for a while.'

'Where we would do what, exactly?'

He smiled over at her. 'Have some seriously good sex.'

A highly charged shiver ran down Alice's spine. Oh, Lord, she'd walked right into that one, hadn't she?

'Do you always have sex at the end of a dinner date?' she asked with feigned calm.

'Pretty well. Don't you?'

'I haven't had many dinner dates lately.'

'Or any dates at all, I'm beginning to suspect.'

'No…'

'Why not?'

Alice wasn't ready to tell him the total truth. She'd already decided to go to bed with him tonight. It was time. And he was ideal, a handsome, experienced lover with an irresistible sex appeal. On top of that, she *trusted* him. A perfect first lover for her, in every way.

'Why not, Alice?' he persisted.

She could see that she had to tell him something.

'I had a bad experience with a date a little while back.' To say five years would have sounded neurotic. Which she was, of course. Alice understood her own emotional baggage very well. But understanding did not always bring change. Her decision to go to bed with Jeremy tonight was a huge change for her. A huge decision. It was also the reason for the crippling tension that had gripped her when she'd met him at the house earlier, making her freeze up when she saw him standing there; a real man, not some fantasy figure.

Jeremy was shaking his head. 'My God, Alice, are we talking date rape here?'

Alice swallowed. 'Close to.'

The shock—and the sympathy—on Jeremy's face was strangely soothing.

'That's terrible, Alice. Simply terrible. You must have been horribly upset. Did he hurt you?'

'Not physically. I managed to get away before he could actually do the deed.'

Maybe not physically, Jeremy thought. But the emotional damage had been enormous. It explained a lot about Alice. Her distrust of men. Her wariness with him. He'd bet London to a brick on that her assaulter had been rich, and arrogant, and not used to taking no for an answer.

A bit like you, Jeremy, that annoying voice piped up.

I'm nothing like that, he argued back. *Not even remotely.*

Still, he realised he would have to take things carefully with Alice.

'I thought something bad must have happened to you to make you so wary of the opposite sex,' he said gently. 'But you can't let one man taint your view of all of us, Alice. I would never force myself on any woman. I respect them too much for that. My mother might be a fool when it comes to relationships but she's a lady who taught me how to treat a lady. If there's one thing I'm grateful to her for it's that she brought me up to have manners.'

But no morals, Alice almost said, just biting her tongue in time.

'I can see that you're a gentleman, Jeremy,' she said instead. 'Otherwise I wouldn't be here with you.'

'Good. Glad we got that straight. We're here,' he announced, pulling his car off the road and driving down a narrow side street into a small back car park, which was almost full.

The restaurant was nothing like she expected. Not very Italian in decor, it had a distinctly Bohemian atmosphere, its maître d' a redhead of around forty who eyed her up and down with the kind of look Alice imagined an ex-girlfriend would employ. Very droll, as though wondering what on earth Jeremy saw in her.

Her smiles were all for Jeremy as she escorted them upstairs to a table tucked away in a very private corner.

'Our special tonight is mussels,' she informed them once they were seated, 'cooked in a delicious white wine sauce and served with our magnificent home-made pasta. Or salad, if the lady is looking after her weight.' This, with a smirk towards Alice.

'No salad for me,' Alice said crisply. 'But the mussels sound lovely.'

'You don't want a starter?' Jeremy asked.

'No. But some bread would be nice.'

Jeremy ordered herb bread to begin with, and a bottle of white wine. A Chablis.

'A marvellous wine,' the redhead complimented. 'But then, you do know your wine, don't you, darling?'

She swanned off, leaving Alice exasperated and Jeremy blithely unconcerned.

'You've slept with her, haven't you?' Alice said.

Jeremy seemed startled by her accusatory tone.

'Only the once.'

Alice rolled her eyes at him in total exasperation.

'She was very upset one night,' he elaborated. 'It was a couple of years ago now. Her husband had just left her for another woman.'

'So you stayed and comforted her,' Alice said drily.

Jeremy smiled. 'I like you jealous.'

Alice pressed her lips tightly together lest she said something very unwise.

'No need to be jealous,' he went on. 'I don't really fancy Sophia, you see. I was just being kind.'

Alice had to laugh. She was still laughing when Sophia returned with a plate of bread. This time, she threw Alice a warm smile.

'That's better,' the older woman said. 'For a minute there I thought Jeremy had lost his mind, going out with someone so serious. He likes to have fun, my Jeremy, don't you, darling?' And she bent to give him a hug around his shoulders.

'I'm teaching Alice to have fun,' he said with a mischievous smile her way.

Alice stiffened when it looked as if Sophia was going to hug her as well. But she just leant close and whispered, 'Lucky girl,' in her ear before straightening and hurrying off again.

'What did she say to you?' Jeremy asked.

Alice gave him one of her cool looks. 'That's private.'

'I hope she didn't say anything uncomplimentary.'

'Not at all.'

'Good.'

A rather elderly Italian waiter brought the wine and a portable ice bucket, explaining as he opened it up then poured a taste-testing amount into Jeremy's glass that Sophia was busy with another customer and he'd be looking after their table for the rest of the evening. Alice hated feeling relieved at this news. Hated her jealousy as well. She didn't want to become emotionally involved with Jeremy. She just wanted to sleep with him. Which brought her to another matter that had begun bothering her.

'I don't think I can go to New York with you,' she said after the waiter had left and she'd indulged in a relaxing gulp of what was a truly delicious wine. A one-night stand with Jeremy was one thing. She could survive that. To spend a glamorous weekend with him in New York would be to risk becoming emotionally involved. She was already more emotionally involved with him than was wise.

Jeremy's blue eyes narrowed over the rim of his glass. 'Why not?'

'I can't really take the time off work.'

'That's just an excuse, Alice. Come on, don't start back-pedalling again.'

'Back-pedalling? What do you mean?'

'You know what I mean. That brute you dated has made you afraid of men. And nervous. You've no need to be nervous with me, Alice. Now no more nonsense, you're coming with me and that's that. I've already booked our hotel. It's a great hotel, and reasonably close to the theatre.'

'That was quick.'

'Had to be. With the premiere on that weekend all the hotels near the theatre involved have been heavily booked. To be honest, I couldn't get a normal room or even a normal suite, so I booked the honeymoon suite. Some lucky bastard had just cancelled.'

Alice bit her lip in an effort not to laugh. He really was a terrible cynic where marriage was concerned. But perversely funny at the same time.

'That was extravagant of you. And yes, before you say it, I know you can afford it.'

'I can. And speaking of money, once Alex sends his donation—Sergio's already sent his—you could well have enough to buy that house yourself, with some left over. That way, you won't have to feel beholden to me.'

'How did you know I didn't want that?'

'Alice, for pity's sake, it's obvious.'

Their meal arrived at that point, and Alice was left to mull over Jeremy's comment. She supposed she did have a heightened sense of independence, having vowed as a young girl never to rely on a man for anything. But she had good reasons for that, the same way Jeremy had good reasons for being anti-marriage.

'Time to eat, Alice,' he said. 'No more of that thinking.'

She glanced over at him and smiled. 'You're right.'

The food was delicious, the wine superb and the company highly entertaining. Alice almost forgot what was going to happen after they left the restaurant. But not quite. Jeremy insisted on dessert, claiming he had a sweet tooth. She wasn't sure exactly what he ordered, but when it came it looked decadent and very fattening, a large pastry case full of chocolate and custard, with more chocolate on the side. It proved to be as delicious as it looked. When the waiter asked if they wanted to order coffee, Jeremy glanced at her for her wishes and she shook her head, knowing that she couldn't sit there much longer thinking about *afterwards* back at his place. When he asked for the bill, she excused herself and dashed for the nearby powder room, not sure if her shaky legs and suddenly spinning head were due to the amount of wine she'd drunk or the imminence of what she was about to do. She was amazed that the small mirror above the wash basin didn't betray her inner feelings. Her bladder could certainly have just given testimony to her tension. But her face looked quite calm. Maybe she'd practised composure for so long that it was automatic. Still, it was better than looking as if she was about to fall apart with nerves.

When she presented herself back at the table, Jeremy was standing, waiting for her.

'Ready to go?' he asked her.

She was never going to be ready, Alice accepted. If she could have run away right now, she would have. But to do so would have been the ultimate in cowardice. Instead, she tightened her fluttering stomach and steeled her spine.

'Yes,' she said coolly.

CHAPTER FOURTEEN

JEREMY CONTAINED HIS frustration with difficulty as he escorted her from the restaurant. A few short minutes she'd been in that powder room, but in that brief time the warm, witty companion he'd been enjoying dinner with had disappeared, and in her place was the Ice Princess.

At least she was true to form, but did she have to revert to type just before he was about to enjoy what he'd been hoping to enjoy with her all damned week? Jeremy sympathised with what had happened to her but he refused to let her use it as an excuse not to live life to the full. Which was what he believed in. Living life to the full, which included a normal sex life.

'Are you all right to drive?' she asked pointedly once they were both back in his car.

'Perfectly,' he replied, turning on the engine and backing slowly out of his parking bay. 'I only had two glasses. You drank the rest.'

'Yes, I suppose I did. I was trying to relax, if you recall.'

'Something tells me you could do with another glass or two when you get to my place,' he said as he headed for home. 'You've gone all buttoned up on me again.'

Her sigh was long, and heavy. 'Sorry. Bit nervous.'

His irritation melted at her admission. 'I can understand that,' he said gently. 'It's your first time since that creep assaulted you. I promise not to rush things, Alice. And you can always say no at any stage. I'll stop straight away.'

The smile she slanted his way was heartbreakingly sweet. 'I can't imagine many girls saying no to you at any stage.'

'You have. Repeatedly.'

'True. Thank you for that reassurance, Jeremy. I needed to hear that.'

'My pleasure.'

After a few moments of a rather awkward silence, she said, 'You never did tell me how you came to be a billionaire.'

'You didn't ask.'

'I forgot. But I'm asking now.'

He gave her a potted history of how Sergio and Alex had found a rundown wine bar for sale near the university, which they'd thought had potential, and how he'd bankrolled them, via an inheritance he'd received from his grandmother. Then he went on to explain how they'd gradually acquired more wine bars all over England till it had become too much for them to manage, so they'd formed the WOW franchise. He was amazed that Alice hadn't heard of them—clearly she wasn't into wine bars—and had to explain that WOW meant Wild Over Wine. Finally, he told her that they'd sold the franchise last year to an American firm for a few billion.

'You must have been over the moon,' she said.

'I was. In a way. But not in another. Selling the franchise also meant a severing of our business relationship, so we don't see much of each other any more. Sergio went back to work in his family business in Milan and Alex returned to Australia to concentrate on property development back there. I miss them terribly. I can't wait to go to New York and see Sergio again. You'll like him, Alice. He's a great guy.'

'He must be if Bella married him. She wasn't exactly known for commitment, was she?'

'You can say that again. Hopefully, their marriage will work but who knows? I haven't much faith in marriage.'

'I'm a little of the same mind.'

This surprised him. Most girls he knew had romantic ideas about marriage.

'You don't want to get married?' he asked.

'Never in a million years.'

Jeremy should have been super pleased with this news. So why wasn't he?

Not that he was *dis*pleased. At least now he wouldn't have to worry about Alice wanting more from him than he could give.

'You're a most unusual girl,' he remarked. 'But who am I to judge? I believe marriage is the kiss of death when it comes to relationships.'

'Well, you don't have to worry about that,' she said with laughter in her voice. 'You don't *have* relationships. Women, for you, are just ships passing in the night.'

'Oh, come now. That's a bit harsh. I'll have you know that one of my girlfriends lasted for several weeks.'

'Really? What happened? Were you laid up with a broken leg or something?'

He laughed. 'Actually, I was. Skiing accident.'

Now she laughed. 'Thought as much.'

'Feeling a bit more relaxed now?' he asked hopefully as he turned down the cobbled street that led to his mews house.

'Much. Is this where you live?' she asked when he pulled up in front of his garage, lights automatically coming on when he pressed the remote for the door to roll up.

'Yes. This is home.'

'It's lovely.'

It *was* lovely. Two-storeyed, but with three entrances. One at the top of the ivy-clad iron-railed steps that led up to the first floor. One near the garage door on the bottom floor, and an internal door that led from the garage into the ground floor hallway. Not a large house by any means, but it suited Jeremy's bachelor lifestyle perfectly. He led her out of the garage and up the steps to the top floor, unlocking the heavy wooden door that led into the upstairs hallway, steering her into the main living room, which served as both lounge and dining areas. Depositing her on one of the large cream leather sofas that faced each other in front of the stone fireplace, he immediately went over to the drinks cabinet where he asked her what she wanted whilst he poured himself a rather stiff Scotch.

Alice was beyond wanting anything, except for him to start making love to her. But she smiled and said that perhaps she should stick to white wine. She knew from experience that mixing drinks did not sit well with her.

He nodded. 'There's a bottle of dry white in the fridge. I'll just get you a glass.'

When he disappeared through a doorway to his right, she allowed herself a deep sigh, then a long look around. The inside of his place was pretty much what she'd expected. Not quite a bachelor pad, but slick and modern, all polished wooden floors and leather furniture, with just enough wooden furniture to stop it from becoming too cold. All the tables were wood. And the lighting was nicely subtle, a small chandelier hanging over the dining table and standing lamps in the corners. She personally hated recessed lighting, though of course it was practical when you had low ceilings. Jeremy's ceilings weren't low, they were very high, telling of the Edwardian era in which this place had been originally built.

Jeremy returned with her glass of wine. Alice was proud of her hand for not shaking when she took it from him. He sat down close to her, having added ice to his own drink. They both sipped for a few seconds, then looked at each other and smiled, she nervously and he confidently. Jeremy soon took her glass and placed it along with his drink on the low coffee table before slowly, oh, so slowly, taking her into his arms. He didn't kiss her straight away, just looked deep into her eyes.

'Did I tell you tonight how beautiful I think you are?' he murmured.

* * *

Jeremy's phone ringing at that precise moment brought an uncharacteristic swear word to his lips. 'I meant to turn that damned thing off. It's Alex. The timing of that man! Do you mind, Alice? I won't be long.'

'Go ahead,' she told him.

He reached to give her back her glass of wine and put the phone to his ear.

'What's up, bro?'

'I've just become a father, mate. Would you believe that? *Me.* A father!'

'That's wonderful, Alex. Congratulations. How's Harriet?'

'Marvellous. God, but women are brave.'

'And the baby. How is he?'

'A right little corker. Big, like me. And smart as a whip. Do you know, he smiled at me within a minute of being born?'

'I think that might be gas, Alex.'

'Rubbish. Jeremy's going to be a genius.'

Jeremy's heart caught. 'You named him after me...'

'Too right. I always liked your name. It has class. His full name is Jeremy Sergio Kotana. Sounds good, doesn't it? And I promise I won't call him Jerry. Look, I can't stay and chat. I have to ring Sergio and then I'm going to help the nurse give my son his first bath. I'll send pictures.'

He hung up before Jeremy could say another word.

'That was Alex,' he said on picking up his own drink again. 'His wife's just had their baby. A boy. They named him Jeremy.'

Alice could see how touched Jeremy was, which touched her.

'He already thinks the boy's a genius. Ah, the optimism of new parents. But enough of that. Now where were we?'

'Have you turned your phone off?' Alice asked as he swooped on her drink again.

'Hell no. I'll do it as soon as I get rid of these glasses.'

Once empty-handed, he switched off his phone then returned to take her into his arms again, not quite so slowly this time. His head descended in a rush for which she was grateful. She didn't want any more time to think, or to worry.

His mouth was still gentle at first, his kiss seductive in its subtle demands. His nipping softly at her bottom lip eventually brought a low moan to her throat, her lips falling apart in open invitation. His tongue slid inside, entwining with hers in a highly erotic fashion before withdrawing. Her own tongue blindly followed his, seeking more. His lips clamped around the tip, sucking it ravenously. Again she moaned, twisting in his arms till somehow they were lying together on the sofa, face to face, mouths fused, their bodies jammed up against each other, his against the back of the sofa.

She felt his hand on her left leg. She wasn't wearing stockings, having shaved and moisturised her legs in anticipation of just such a moment. Her breath caught underneath his kiss as his hand travelled up under her skirt, getting closer and closer to where she was already burning for him. When it stopped mid-thigh, she almost cried out. Instead, she just kissed him harder. She even sucked on *his* tongue.

His hand moved again, but not to touch her more intimately. He caressed her thigh for a while before lifting his hand away. She wasn't aware of his undoing the buttons on her dress till her skirt fell open and she felt his hand on her belt. Wrenching her mouth away in surprise, she stared up into his face. But he wasn't looking at her. He was looking at what he was doing. The belt was quickly dispatched, and the remaining buttons flicked open. When he pushed her dress back off her shoulders, she lifted her body to help him. He tossed her dress across the coffee table, then returned his attention to her body.

Her white satin bra surrendered to his fingers in no time, leaving her with nothing on but her matching bikini briefs and her nude sandals. When he laid her back on the sofa, she went, her eyes dazed upon him. When he stood up, she thought he was about to undress. But he didn't. He just shrugged out of his suit jacket and took off his tie, throwing them next to her other clothes, startling her when he knelt down on the rug next to the sofa. As his head started to descend towards her bared breasts with their eager rock-like nipples, Alice squeezed her eyes tightly shut.

Oh, Lord, she thought shakily.

No man had ever *seen* her breasts naked before, let alone done what he was doing. In her teenage fantasies she'd imagined a man kissing her nipples, but hadn't anticipated how it would actually feel. It felt incredible, her back arching as he tugged on one nipple with his teeth whilst he kneaded her other breast. Not roughly. Gently. Playfully. Yet they soon became oversensitive. When she moaned her discomfort, he stopped, licking the burning nipples over and over till she sighed with pleasure. At the same time one of his hands drifted down over her stomach, which immediately tightened. Alice held her breath when he finally pushed her legs apart, her left leg dropping off the edge of the sofa, her right leg moving restlessly, till it was bent at the knee, her shoe digging into the sofa. He took them off, oh, so slowly, caressing each foot as he went, her eyes finally flinging open when his fingers brushed over her ticklish toes.

'Don't!' she cried. 'I can't stand being tickled there.'

He just smiled. 'My apologies. Still, perhaps it's time to adjourn to the bedroom.'

She gasped when he scooped her up into his arms as if she were a feather. But as he carried her from the room, a memory hit of another time when a man had carried her into his bedroom, carried her there and dumped her onto his bed. He hadn't bothered to undress her, just ripped off her knickers. Hadn't bothered to undress himself, just undid his zipper and fell on top of her.

Jeremy didn't dump her onto his bed. He laid her down quite gently. And he did undress, quickly stripping down to his underpants.

Alice tried to recapture her earlier desire as she looked at his beautiful male body. But it was no use. The moment had gone, spoiled by that brute back at college, spoiled by her own irrational reaction. For Jeremy was nothing like that other man. She hated herself for saying no at this last stage but it had to be done before he became embarrassingly naked.

'Jeremy,' she said sharply with a tidal wave of regret.

'What?' he asked, his expression freezing.

'I'm sorry,' she choked out. 'I… I can't.'

'Can't what?'

'I can't do this. I'm saying no.'

Disbelief ripped through Jeremy. Disbelief and frustration. Surely she couldn't expect him to stop at this late stage. Surely not!

But one look at her anguished eyes told him that she did.

He couldn't help it. He swore.

'I'm so sorry,' she blurted out. 'I didn't mean for this to happen. I'm not a tease. Honestly. I… Oh, God…' With a sob, she covered her face with her hands, rolled over and burst into tears.

Jeremy's frustration disappeared in the face of her distress. And so did his erection. Sitting down on the bed behind her, he reached out to pat her shaking shoulder with a gentle hand. 'Please don't cry, Alice. It's all right. Truly, it is.'

'No, it's not,' she blubbered into her hands. 'I've ruined everything, me and my crazy screwed-up mind.'

Clearly, this all went back to that date rape. Or near date rape. Jeremy wondered just how far the creep had got before she was able to stop him. 'Is there anything I can say to help?'

She rolled back over, her face all red and tear-streaked. 'Like what? Look, don't waste any more time on me, Jeremy. It's useless. I'm useless. If I can't be a normal woman with someone like you then there's no hope for me.'

Jeremy heard a compliment in there somewhere.

Before he could think of what to say next she was up off the bed and striding from the room, her shoulders squared in an attitude of fierce determination.

'Would you please call me a taxi?' she threw over her shoulder as she made her way across the hall and back into the living room. By the time he dragged on his trousers and caught up with her, she was already dressing.

'There's no need for a taxi,' he said. 'I'll drive you home.'

'Absolutely not! You just had a whisky. You'll be over the limit.'

'I didn't drink all of it.'

'You drank enough. For pity's sake, Jeremy, stop playing the gentleman,' she snapped, doing up her last button with angry fingers. 'And just call me a taxi.'

He called her a taxi.

'I'll ring you tomorrow,' he said whilst they waited for the taxi to arrive.

'Please don't.' Her voice was as cold as her face.

'Why not?'

The look she gave him said it all. 'Because I don't want you to. Move on to someone else. Someone who'll give you what you want, because it's painfully obvious that I can't.'

'What if I said I don't want anyone else? I just want you.'

'You don't. Not really. I was just the girl who dared to say no. I was a challenge, Jeremy, one which you went to great lengths to meet. Which reminds me. Please don't feel obliged to continue pretending interest in my charity. You and I both know that was just a ploy to see me again. Underneath, I knew that all along.'

He didn't deny it. How could he? It was true. But only in the beginning. Still, she wouldn't believe him if he told her that he'd come to truly care about what she was doing for those poor women. That it had made him feel good, helping them. He couldn't win, no matter what he said.

He had to let her go. For now, that was. But he had no intention of giving up on her.

He wanted her. And she wanted him. He just had to find a way past the mental blockage that was haunting her. She couldn't go her whole life being afraid of men, and sex. It wasn't healthy.

'What about the house I was going to help you buy?'

'Forget that. If you're right about your rich friends coming through with their donations then the charity will be able to afford to buy the house.'

'I'm still going to call you.'

She sighed and picked up her bag. 'Do what you like. You will, anyway. But I won't be going out with you again, Jeremy. Trust me on that.'

'We'll see,' he bit out.

'No. *You'll* see.'

A horn honking outside signalled that the taxi had arrived. Suddenly her eyes softened on him, her face full of regret.

'I'm not angry with you. Truly. I'm angry with myself. You have been a gentleman through and through, for which I am profoundly grateful. Goodbye, Jeremy.' At the last moment she came forward and kissed him gently on the cheek. And then she was gone, bolting out of the room, and his home.

Jeremy stood there, frozen to the spot, as he listened to the banging of a car door and the sound of the taxi moving off. Finally his hand lifted to touch the moist spot where her lips had met his skin.

'It's not over, Alice,' he muttered as his chest squeezed tight. 'Not by a long shot.'

CHAPTER FIFTEEN

'COME IN, MADGE,' Jeremy said when his PA knocked. It was just before five the following Friday afternoon, Jeremy's mood not matching his new sales figures, which were great. Ken's e-Books were going from strength to strength.

Madge came in, looking very well groomed, he finally noticed, and wearing a dress he hadn't seen before. Jeremy wondered if dear old Kenneth had something to do with that as well.

'I just had a rather surprising call from Alice,' she said straight away.

'Surprising in what way?' he replied, taken aback that she'd called his office at all.

'She thanked me for the work I'd done setting up the website, then said she would take it from there. When I asked if she wanted to speak to you, she said "no, thank you very much." Then hung up.'

'I see,' he said, sighing. He'd refrained from ringing her all week, hoping that time would be on his side. Clearly, not.

'Things didn't work out between you and Alice last weekend, then?' Madge asked gently.

'How did…?' Jeremy stopped, remembering their behaviour in that wine bar last Friday night. Anyone would have seen how taken they were with each other. But it hadn't been enough to overcome her fears.

'No,' he said simply. 'Things didn't work out.' Finally, he was beginning to accept that it was over before it had even begun. Never before had he felt so down. Or so alone.

'What a shame. I thought she was perfect for you.'

Jeremy shook his head at Madge, not sure how she came to that conclusion. So he asked.

Madge shrugged. 'Hard to put my finger on it. She just was.'

'Thank you for your insight, Madge,' he said drily. But he knew what she was getting at. Alice's appeal was as mysterious as she was.

'Why don't you try again?' she asked. 'You know the old adage. If at first you don't succeed…'

'Maybe I will,' he said, not very convincingly.

'Maybes won't cut the mustard, boss. Where there's a will there's a way.'

Jeremy had to laugh. 'Enough of the sayings, Madge. All right. I'll ring her. Tonight.'

'Good idea. By the way, thought you might like to know that Ken and I have become an item.'

'I thought there had to be a reason behind the new dress. Going anywhere special tonight?'

'To a concert. A rock concert. Ken said we had to widen our horizons further. Then tomorrow we're going up in a hot-air balloon.'

'Good for you. Have fun, then.'

'I will.'

She sashayed out, humming happily to herself. Amazing what a fun relationship could do for one's attitude to life. He'd wanted to show Alice how to have fun. But he doubted that would happen now. Still, he did have to try again, or he'd never be able to live with himself. Yet by a quarter to eight that night, he still hadn't rung Alice. No man liked constant rejection, and Jeremy wasn't different from any other man.

'Ring the girl, you coward,' he lectured himself after the clock ticked over to eight.

Snatching up his phone from where it was sitting on a side table, he brought up her number and pressed.

'Alice Waterhouse,' she answered on the third ring.

'Alice. It's Jeremy. Please don't hang up,' he added, his heart racing in his chest.

Her sigh wafted down the line. 'All right,' she said. 'What do you want?'

'Just to talk to you. Maybe take you for coffee somewhere. Are you home or at work?'

'I'm still at work. One of the case workers went home sick so I have to stay late.'

'How late?'

'Not sure. Ten. Maybe eleven.'

'You will take a taxi home, won't you? Not the Tube.'

'I will take whatever I want to take, Jeremy,' she said coolly.

The thought of her walking to the station, alone, at that time on a Friday night worried him sick.

'Call me when you're finished and I'll come and drive you home.'

She didn't answer him for a few seconds. 'That won't be necessary. I'll take a taxi.'

He didn't believe her. 'Promise?'

'Jeremy, might I remind you that you are not my boyfriend.'

'I know that. But I am your friend. And I miss you.'

He heard her sharply sucked-in breath.

'Will you go somewhere for coffee with me tomorrow?' he asked. 'Just coffee.'

There was resignation in her sigh. 'Why won't you give up?'

'I like you too much for that, Alice.'

Another heart-stopping silence.

'Ring me tomorrow,' she said at long last. 'Now I really must go. A new client has just arrived.'

Alice had lied. There was no new client. They were having another blessedly quiet Friday night. But she simply hadn't been able to talk to Jeremy any longer. This last week had seen her besieged with regret and remorse. She really had treated him very poorly. He'd been so nice to her. He was still being nice.

She'd missed him too. Way too much. He filled her mind every moment of every day. She'd found it difficult to concentrate on her counselling all week. She despised herself for not being able to go through with things last Saturday night. She was sure it would have been a memorable experience, if only she could have overcome her silly fears. His lovemaking on that sofa had been amazing. He'd be a fantastic lover. Unfortunately, she couldn't say the same for herself. She would never be a fantastic lover. She'd always be waiting for one of those hideous memories to hit, dampening her desire as if she'd had a bucket of iced water thrown over her. Far better that she continue with her dateless, celibate lifestyle. It wasn't as though she wanted to get married. She did crave being normal, however. And she craved Jeremy. Crazy, really.

She should never have agreed to have coffee with him. Well, she hadn't really agreed yet. When he rang her tomorrow she could say no again. The trouble was that saying no to Jeremy was always very, very hard...

By ten o'clock, Alice started to yawn. It had been a long day. And a long week. Finally, she stood up from behind her desk and went to find Jane, telling her that she was going home. She momentarily considered calling a taxi but she didn't have all that much money with her. Saving for her flat had now become more important to her than ever before. Slipping on her black jacket, she looped her carryall over her left shoulder and headed for the door.

It was cold outside, and pitch-black, clouds blanketing the sky. The street lights weren't all that great, either. And did not work very often. Feeling unusually nervous—Jeremy had put bad thoughts into her mind—Alice put her head down and started to hurry along the street. She'd only gone a couple of blocks when two young men in hoodies stepped out in front of her from a darkened alley, forcing her to stop. They were probably just teenagers, but well grown, and tough-looking.

'Goin' somewhere in a hurry, love?' the taller one said, his voice slurred.

Whilst fear had Alice's heart slamming against her ribs, she tried not to look scared to death.

'Get out of my way,' she snapped, reaching for the rape alarm that she always kept in her bag. 'Or I'll call the police.'

'Not wiffou' your phone, darlin',' the other boy said, wrenching the bag off her shoulder.

A scream came to Alice's throat but never made it past her lips. The first man was behind her in an instant, one arm snaked around her waist, the other clamped over her mouth.

'Be nice to me, sweetheart,' he whispered in her ear as he pushed her towards the alley, 'and you won't get hurt. All we want is what yuh give the boyfriend every night. He won't miss it. Honest.'

Alice was already crying inside when, suddenly, she was free, a familiar voice echoing in the night air. 'Are you all right, Alice?' Jeremy asked.

A shaking Alice stared up at him. 'I... I think so...'

'Well, well, if it isn't the boyfriend,' the leader said smarmily, despite having been yanked aside with relative ease. 'A fancy man to go with little Miss Fancy Pants. You fink you can take the two of us, matey?'

Alice couldn't believe the smile of satisfaction that crossed Jeremy's handsome face. 'Won't be a sec, Alice.'

She watched, stunned, whilst Jeremy had both of her assailants flat on their backs in no time, using his feet and his hands in a display of martial arts that was as unexpected as it was impressive. They weren't unconscious but they were moaning and groaning, one clutching his groin whilst the other writhed on the ground in pain.

Jeremy returned to put a comforting arm around her

still-trembling body as he whipped out his phone and rang the police.

She only half listened as he relayed what had happened and where they were, her mind distracted with horrible thoughts. What if Jeremy hadn't rescued her? What if…?

'Let's go, Alice,' Jeremy said, taking her arm and steering her across the street to where his car was parked by the kerb.

'But shouldn't we wait for the police?' she asked, still shaking with shock.

'We are. I just think you need to sit down. You're in shock.'

'Oh.'

He'd just seen her safely seated in the passenger seat when the police arrived.

'Stay right where you are, Alice,' Jeremy told her. 'I'll handle this.'

The police locked the still-stunned offenders in the back of their van before talking to Jeremy for a few minutes, taking notes. Meanwhile the female police officer came over to talk to Alice, gently leading her through what had happened before getting her to sign a witness statement. In less than ten minutes the police were gone.

Alice's head was still reeling when Jeremy got back into the car, carrying her dropped handbag with him.

'You okay?' he asked with a worried look her way.

'I will be,' she reassured him.

'You'll be pleased to know that the police recognised those two. They're on parole for various offences so they'll be going straight back to jail.'

Alice sighed a shaky sigh. 'That's a relief. I wasn't looking forward to having to give evidence in court. Though I would have, if I had to. I can't stop thinking what might have happened if you hadn't come along.'

'No point in thinking like that, Alice,' he said sternly.

'I did come along and nothing happened. Now let's get you home.'

As he drove off, Alice stared over at him, still amazed at the ease with which he'd dispensed with those two thugs. 'You've done that kind of thing before, haven't you?'

'Only once,' he said. 'In my second last year at school. A young boy was being bullied, the way I'd been bullied. Till I grew tall and took up Kung Fu, karate and kick-boxing, that is. When I came across a couple of big boys humiliating this poor defenceless little kid, old tapes went off and I decided to put all those martial arts lessons I'd taken to good use.' A self-satisfied smile pulled at Jeremy's mouth. 'Trust me when I say those two never bullied another boy. Not whilst I was there, anyway.'

'You became a hero,' she said, awe in her voice.

His smile turned wry. 'Not according to the headmaster. I was almost expelled.'

'Well, I think you're a hero. You were my hero tonight.'

'Glad to be of service.'

'Of course, I'm not sure what you were doing there in the first place. You weren't stalking me, were you?'

'Absolutely not. I simply didn't trust you not to take the Tube, so I was on my way to drive you home when I passed you in the street. You'd left earlier than you said, you naughty girl.'

'I should have called a taxi, like *you* said.'

'Yes, you should have.'

'I will, in the future.' Lord, yes. No way would she risk having what happened tonight happening ever again. Another deep shudder ran through her. What if Jeremy *hadn't* saved her...?

'You're still in shock,' Jeremy pronounced. 'You need someone to be with you tonight, Alice. Is your flatmate home? Can I safely leave you in her hands to look after you, or do you want me to stay with you?'

As Jeremy pulled up outside her flat, Alice decided that

another white lie was called for. She needed to be alone to de-stress, and to think, *without* Jeremy's disturbing presence.

'Yes, Fiona's home. See?' she said, pointing to the light in the front room. That's her bedroom.' It was a habit they'd got into when they went out, to fool the baddies. How naive could they be?

'At least let me walk you to the door,' Jeremy insisted.

When they got there, he drew her into his arms and hugged her tightly.

'God, Alice. I nearly died when I saw that man with his filthy hands on you.'

Alice's heart turned over at the depth of emotion in Jeremy's voice. He cared about her. He really did.

'My hero,' she murmured, and hugged him back.

'I wouldn't go that far.'

'I would.'

'Look, I don't like leaving you.'

'I'll be all right. Truly,' she reassured him.

'I'll be ringing you tomorrow.'

She nodded. 'I'd like that. But not too early.'

'You won't change your mind in the morning?'

'No,' she said, a plan already forming in her surprisingly clear mind. 'I won't.'

CHAPTER SIXTEEN

JEREMY WOKE AROUND NINE, astonished at how good a night's sleep he'd had. Possibly because Alice had agreed to at least talk to him. He hoped she'd slept okay, hoped that flatmate of hers had given her the comfort and support she'd obviously needed. Being grabbed like that after her other earlier assault must have been terrifying. It didn't bear thinking about what they would have done to Alice, if he hadn't come along. He needed to get through to her today to never take such a risk again.

Though perhaps she already knew that. Alice was a sensible young woman. She was also, however, incredibly stubborn.

Rising, Jeremy showered and shaved before pulling on some casual clothes. Dark blue jeans. A pale blue polo. No shoes. He padded, barefooted, into the kitchen where he poured himself some muesli and orange juice. After breakfast, he went down to his den where he spent some time answering emails on his computer—Alex had sent more photos of his baby boy and Sergio wanted details of his booking arrangements for the weekend in New York. He told Sergio he was definitely bringing someone with him, hoping against hope that Alice would agree to come. But he wasn't supremely confident. He was never supremely confident where Alice was concerned. Damn, but he hated that.

By noon, Jeremy was itching to call her. He was about to reach for his phone when it rang. When the screen showed it was Alice calling, his stomach tightened with a sudden jab of fear. As he put the phone to his ear, he told himself not to be such a fool. She wouldn't be mean to him after last night. Surely not.

'Hello, Alice?' he answered. 'I was just about to call you.'

'That's nice,' she said coolly. Too coolly for his liking. 'I was wondering,' she added, 'if you would like to come over to my place tonight and I'll cook you dinner. As a way of thanking you for what you did last night. But also to talk. Fiona's gone to Paris with her fiancé for the weekend so we'll be alone.'

For a split second Jeremy didn't know what to think. Was she suggesting what he thought she was suggesting? Why mention that her flatmate had gone away if she didn't want him to stay the night? Surely she would know exactly what her invitation was implying.

How brave she was to try again so soon, he thought. How wonderfully, incredibly brave. That was why she was trying to sound so cool. He'd figured out a while back that her Ice Princess act was just a façade. Underneath, she was all warm woman. With hang-ups, admittedly. And quite a lot of emotional baggage. But he knew what to expect now. He could work out in advance what to do, and what not to do.

'I'd like that,' he said. Which was the understatement of the year. He'd wanted to make love to Alice from the first moment he'd seen her, his desire for her the strongest he'd ever experienced. He'd been suppressing that desire this past week, because he'd thought it was futile. But it had always been there, flickering away like a fire down to its last ashes. It had only taken one small gust of hope to make the dying flames flare up again into a fire that would burn bright all day.

'What time would you like me to be there?' he said, thinking he'd race over there now if she'd like.

'Would seven o'clock be too early?'

'Not at all. Should I bring wine?'

'Absolutely not. No wine. I will provide the wine. And no flowers. Or chocolates. This is my treat.'

'You should never tell a man not to bring chocolates and flowers.'

'Perhaps, but that's what I want. Just bring yourself.'

'Just myself,' he echoed. And lots of condoms...

The thought set his desire into overdrive. Lord, but he'd have to do something to dampen *that* down before tonight. He couldn't imagine anything worse than showing up at Alice's place with an obvious hard-on. As much as she might want him to stay the night, he would have to be careful not to frighten her, or to rush anything.

'Casual dress?' he asked her.

'That would be perfect.'

'I'll look forward to it. Now before you go, did you sleep okay? Did Fiona take care of you last night?'

Another of her telling silences.

Jeremy sighed. 'She wasn't there, was she? You were all alone.'

'Yes, I was alone, but I was fine,' she said crisply. 'It saved me having to explain what happened. There's no point in going on and on about it, is there? A miss is as good as a mile.'

'True.' Jeremy empathised with Alice's pragmatism, but he wasn't convinced she wasn't still somewhat traumatised by last night's events. He decided then and there to talk to her at length tonight before attempting any lovemaking. It would kill him, but it was the right thing to do.

'I should go, Jeremy, I have lots to do to get ready for tonight.'

'Shall I hope for *cordon bleu* cooking?'

She laughed. It was a lovely sound. 'You can hope but you won't get. I'm a competent enough cook, but not a chef.'

'I will still look forward to it.'

Which was his second understatement of the year.

'That's good,' she said cheerily, and hung up, leaving Jeremy fizzing with a frustrating mixture of excitement and anticipation. How he was going to get through this day was anyone's guess!

Seven saw him outside Alice's place, having walked there, not wanting to have to watch what he drank. He suspected he might need a glass or three to settle his own nerves. Amazing for him to feel nervous over making love to a woman but there it was. In two short weeks Alice had managed to totally turn him inside out. He'd even dithered over what to wear, finally settling on beige trousers and a mustard-yellow polo that he hadn't worn in ages, but which Sergio had once said suited him. With the evening promising to be cool with the forecast of drizzle, he'd thrown on a brown suede jacket, which had cost him a mint at an exclusive menswear store in Milan and which he'd rarely worn. If truth be told, he had way too many clothes, a symptom he'd read somewhere of loneliness. At the time he'd dismissed such a notion as laughable. Now he wasn't so sure.

Jeremy took a deep breath then rang the bell.

After a short delay, Alice opened the door looking delicious in white trousers and that pretty floral blouse she'd been wearing last week. Her fair hair was down, curling softly around her shoulders. Her make-up was minimal, her lipstick a delicate coral colour. Her feet were shod in flat white sandals, her toenails painted a bright red. Not her fingernails, however, which were unpainted but shiny.

'Where's your car?' were her first words.

Dismay sent Jeremy's stomach plummeting, but he didn't let it show. He supposed it had been optimistic of him to think Alice would want him to make love to her after what had happened to her last night. Clearly, this dinner invite was a gesture of gratitude, not a desire to try again.

He hoped his shrug looked suitably nonchalant. 'It's a nice night. I thought I'd walk.'

'But it's supposed to rain later.'

'Is it? I'm sure I can borrow an umbrella, if need be.'

She gave him a frowning look. 'I suppose so. Come in.

Let me take your jacket. It's quite warm inside. I've had the oven on for hours.'

She hung his jacket on a coat stand near the door, then led him down the hallway into a kitchen that wasn't overly large but which had been renovated at some stage to make use of every inch. The cupboards were white, the counter tops and small breakfast bar made of black granite, and the two stools white with stainless-steel bases. All the appliances were stainless steel, including the oven from which wafted the mouth-watering aroma of roast lamb.

'Smells good,' he said, sliding up onto one of the stools whilst she picked up an oven mitt and had a quick peek.

'Bronwyn once told me that men liked roast dinners more than anything, so I decided to give it a whirl. To be honest, this is my first roast dinner and I'm beginning to wish I'd made stir-fry.'

'I'm sure it'll be great. And who's Bronwyn?'

'She was the cook at home when I was growing up.'

'And home is…where?' he prompted. Though of course he already knew.

'In Dorset,' was her curt reply.

'No kidding. My family home is in Cornwall. We could almost be neighbours.'

'Not quite. There's a whole county between us. Would you mind opening the wine?' she asked, putting two bottles of red onto the breakfast bar along with a bottle opener. 'It's not the kind that unscrews. I meant to open a bottle earlier and let it breathe but I've been flat out with setting the table and the dinner as well as trying to look presentable.'

'You look lovely,' he said as he picked up the first bottle and glanced at the label. 'Good Lord, Alice, this is very expensive wine. It must have cost you heaps, especially if you bought it at the local bottle shop.'

'I didn't have to buy it,' she confessed. 'Fiona had a birthday party a little while back and these were left over. Some rich friend of her father's sent over a case. Red wine isn't to Fiona's personal taste and she said I could have it, if and when I needed a drink. I don't think she knew how good a wine it is.'

'But *you* knew.'

'Oh, yes. My father gave me a first-class education in wine, especially red wine. He had a marvellous cellar, full of the best wines from all over the world. Or he did, till he got into debt and had to sell everything off. It upset him so much that he went down in the empty cellar one day and shot himself.'

'Good grief,' Jeremy said, amazed at how calmly she'd relayed this news; amazed too that she was telling him such a personal detail. Why? he wondered.

'It was a terrible shock at first,' she went on, getting two wineglasses down from a cupboard and placing them on the breakfast bar. 'I was only ten. But not as big a shock as when my older sister, Marigold, married one short year later, her husband proving to be one of those abusive partners whose wives I try to counsel.'

Jeremy didn't know what to say, so he didn't. He just opened the wine and poured. Alice picked up one of the glasses and drank a decent mouthful.

'When I told my mother that Rupert was hitting Marigold behind closed doors, she refused to believe me. When I made a right old fuss, she packed me off to boarding school. Which Rupert paid for, of course. He was very rich, you see, and had repaid all of Daddy's debts as well as bankrolled the lifestyle which Mother had grown used to.'

Jeremy was beginning to get a good picture of what had fashioned Alice's character. No wonder she didn't trust men. The surprise was that he was here at all! Once again, he wondered why. Something was going on here that he wasn't privy to. Yet.

'As you can imagine, I didn't cry when Rupert was killed in a motorcycle accident last year. Couldn't have happened to a nicer man,' she added, lifting her glass in a mock toast.

'Did they have children?' Jeremy asked.

Alice's face softened. 'Yes, a dear little boy. Dickie. He'll be four soon. His father doted on him, of course. It was just the mother he loathed. And loved, according to Marigold.' Alice shook her head in exasperation. 'She has no idea what true love is.'

'Do *you*, Alice?'

'I know what it isn't.'

'Why are you telling me all this?'

She looked at him long and hard. 'Because I want you to know why I am as I am. Because I'm going to give you a truly difficult job to do. Because I think you're the only man who could do it even remotely right.'

Jeremy didn't have a clue what she was getting at. 'Might I ask what this difficult job entails?'

She took another huge gulp of wine. 'I wasn't going to ask you at the beginning of the evening. I was going to feed you and get you a bit tipsy. And me a lot tipsy. And when I thought the time was right, after I'd explained everything I just explained, *then* I was going to ask you. But nerves are playing havoc with my plans and now I'm just going to say it.'

'Say what?' he demanded impatiently.

Her eyes were suddenly full of fear. But then she scooped in a deep breath, lifted her chin up and said, 'I want you to take my virginity.'

There! She'd said it!

He just stared at her, his beautiful blue eyes wide, his whole body stilled with shock. His wineglass was mid-air, his hand frozen.

After what seemed like an eternity he put down his glass and stood up.

'No, Alice,' he said, his voice even deeper than usual. 'No. I don't do love or marriage or broken hearts. So I definitely don't do virgins.'

'But I don't want your love!' she protested. 'And I certainly don't want marriage,' she insisted. 'So my heart won't be broken. All I want is your kindness. And your expertise.'

'My...expertise,' he repeated, clearly taken aback. Possibly even offended. Which was the last thing she wanted.

'Yes. I already know first-hand about your lovemaking skills. Before I went bonkers the other night, I was having a wonderful time. Honestly. You were great. I can't think of any man I've ever met who's made me want to have sex with him more than you.'

'Obviously,' he said in droll tones. 'Since you haven't had sex with any man at all!'

She tried not to blush but it was futile.

'Which brings us to the question of why that is, Alice. You're...how old?' he asked as he slowly sat back down.

'Twenty-five.'

'Twenty-five,' he echoed, amazement in his voice.

She supposed it *was* pretty amazing in this day and age.

Jeremy shook his head from side to side in an attitude of disbelief. 'I could understand you being turned off men and sex after your near date rape, but that didn't happen all that long ago, so...'

'Five years,' she broke in. 'It happened five years ago.'

'Still no excuse,' he refuted bluntly. 'What about before that, when you were working as a model? And what about during all your teenage years when your hormones were going wild? Or are you saying you didn't fancy anyone enough then as well? I mean, you did come home from school on holidays, didn't you? I know I did. I made good damn use of them with the opposite sex. I lost *my* virginity at fourteen.'

'Well, bully for you!' Alice snapped, frustration finally getting the better of her. 'But we're not all like you, Jeremy, where sex is just fun and games. Some of us—teenage females especially—like to think they're in love to have sex.

And that just wasn't going to happen to me after what I'd seen Marigold's husband do to her. So if you don't mind, try to have a little sensitivity where my lack of sexual experience is concerned.'

'You're not in love with *me*, are you?' he asked, looking horrified.

'Certainly not.'

'That's a relief.'

She threw him a caustic glare. 'I've finally grown up enough to know that one's libido is not necessarily connected with love. To use your own words, Jeremy, I fancy you.'

'That's good. I can handle being fancied. I can't handle being loved. That's a deal breaker for me, Alice. I'm not into love.'

'Tell me something I don't already know,' she bit out whilst her heart squeezed out a small warning.

'The dinner's in danger of burning,' he said with a wry smile.

'Oh, Lord!' she exclaimed, whirling to open the oven. 'Oh, thank heavens, it's not really burnt. Just a bit singed around the edges. But I hope you like crispy potatoes,' she added as she grabbed two oven mitts and lifted the baking dish out of the oven, placing it on the draining tray next to the sink.

'I *love* crispy potatoes,' he assured her.

'Well, at least he loves something,' she muttered under her breath.

'What was that?'

'Nothing. Why don't you go into the dining room and light the candles? There's a box of matches on the table. And take the wine and glasses with you. I shouldn't be too long. I've already made the gravy. You do like gravy, don't you?'

'I love gravy.'

Alice almost laughed.

* * *

Jeremy was touched by how much trouble she'd gone to with the table, the elegant setting reminding him that Alice was, after all, the daughter of an earl. She would have been brought up with fine things, and to do things the right way. But as he lit the candles his mind wasn't on her aristocratic heritage, but on the 'job' she wanted him to do for her.

Never in his wildest dreams had he imagined Alice was a virgin. She was far too beautiful and far too sexy, once she let her guard down. The way she'd kissed him had shown a highly passionate nature. It had just been her wretched background, and that other unfortunate happening, he decided, that had forced her into adopting a manner that kept men at bay. Fear—and a lack of trust—had been the overriding factors that resulted in her being a virgin at twenty-five. Now that he thought about it more deeply, Alice was right. It had been insensitive of him to act so shocked, and to question her like that.

Jeremy vowed to do better in the future. Refilling their glasses with wine, he sat down and started giving the situation some serious thought. Clearly, she'd been going to go to bed with him last Saturday night, but at the last second she'd gone into a meltdown. He recalled this had happened shortly after he'd carried her into the bedroom. He couldn't be sure but he suspected that other creep might have done something similar.

Right, Jeremy thought. No carrying. No playing macho man. Nothing like that. His approach would have to be very different.

When Alice came into the room with their meals, looking pleased with herself, the thought popped into Jeremy's head that Alice liked being in control. Which gave him an idea...

CHAPTER SEVENTEEN

'I MIGHT TRY another roast some day,' Alice said after they'd both polished off their meals in double-quick time. 'I was worried for a minute there that I'd spoiled everything.'

She placed her knife and turned-over fork down in the middle of the plate before glancing up at Jeremy, her nerves still strung tight. 'I haven't, have I, Jeremy? Spoiled everything?'

They hadn't talked much whilst they ate, their only conversation about the food and the wine, and the rain outside.

His warm smile set her heart fluttering.

'Not in the slightest,' he said. 'I was just startled there, for a minute or two.'

'You understand why I'm still a virgin, then? You don't mind any more?'

His smile turned rueful. 'Of course I mind. It goes against my principles to deflower virgins. But there are exceptions to every rule and you, sweet Alice, are undoubtedly the exception.'

'Oh…' He was just so nice. She knew she was right to do this. If only she could stop her hands from shaking. And her insides.

'I have been giving the matter some further thought, however,' he went on, his voice serious, 'and I have decided not to make love to you tonight.'

Her dismay was as great as her frustration.

'I want *you* to make love to *me*,' he added with a wickedly sexy sparkle in his eyes.

Was she shocked? Relieved? Or simply terrified?

'But I can't!' she blurted out. 'I mean… I wouldn't know what to do!'

'Come now, Alice, you're a well-educated girl,' he said as he sat back and took another sip of wine. 'You've read lots of books and seen lots of movies. On top of that, you have a highly passionate nature. You'll work it out.'

All the air left Alice's lungs in a rush. 'Oh, Lord...'

'No need for prayers. Just do what comes naturally.'

'But...but...'

He put his glass down and stood up, holding his hand out to her. She stood up somewhat shakily and put her hand in his.

'Before we do this, Alice,' he said, his beautiful blue eyes softly caressing, 'I want you to know how much I admire you. And desire you. I've wanted you since the first moment I set eyes on you.'

His romantic words thrilled her and soothed her at the same time. Never had her decision to go to bed with Jeremy seemed so right. She suddenly felt like the most desirable woman in the world. And totally, wonderfully safe.

His eyes suddenly changed from soft to very sexy. 'Now lead me to your bedroom, Alice, where I want you to have your wicked way with me. But be gentle. It's been a while...'

She couldn't help it. She laughed, and in doing so released the rest of her tension. At the same time, her excitement level soared. She could hardly wait to have her wicked way with him. And she did know what to do, really. She'd been doing it in her head from the first moment she'd set eyes on him...

When Alice led him across the hallway into her stylishly furnished bedroom with its thankfully queen-sized bed, Jeremy wished he weren't quite so aroused, worried that the extent and size of his erection might frighten her. Not that she seemed overly frightened. He'd been right to give her control of tonight. It was what she needed this first time. To be in control.

'Do you want me to undress you, mistress?' he asked on a teasing note once they were standing by her bed with its delicate floral duvet and mountain of decorative pillows. 'Or would you rather I undress first?'

Her eyes widened at this last suggestion.

'I am yours to command,' he added, and waited avidly for her reaction.

She stared at him for a long moment before sucking in a deep breath then letting it out slowly. Her chin lifted slightly. 'That sounds like an excellent idea,' she said coolly as she tossed some of the excess pillows onto an antique armchair in the corner of the room. 'Once you're naked I want you to lie down on top of the bed.'

Good God, he thought as his loins leapt. She didn't take much encouragement, did she?

She sat on the end of the bed whilst he undressed slowly, her eyes glued to him all the while. It was shockingly exciting. And something Jeremy had never done before. Her big blue eyes definitely rounded when he finally divested himself of his underpants and stood there in front of her in all his naked glory. He was dying for her to touch him, or to stand up and kiss him. But she did neither, and he didn't dare make a move towards her. Instead, he did as ordered and lay down on the bed, crossing his ankles as he linked his hands up behind his head in a casual, non-threatening attitude. He didn't say a word, just waited for her to make the next move.

Two emotions swept through Alice as she got to her feet. Disbelief that she was actually doing this. And that Jeremy seemed to like it. Though, of course, he'd suggested the idea in the first place. Amazing, that. But her overriding emotion was a desire so fierce and so strong that it was rattling her brains. What it was doing to her body was equally powerful. She could actually feel the heat between her thighs. Her heart was hammering away, her stomach as tight as a drum. And her nipples… Oh, God, she didn't want to know what they would look like once she took off her bra. Which was what she was about to do. Not just her bra but all of her clothes. Every last stitch.

Why weren't her hands shaking, she wondered, as she undid the buttons of her blouse?

Because they weren't. They were quite steady, focusing on what they were doing instead of what was going on in her head. After she'd taken off her blouse she took off her trousers, kicking off her sandals as she did so. Her eyes went to his when she bent her arms around to unhook her bra. He wasn't ogling her, but he was definitely watching closely. After a brief hesitation, she did the deed, exposing her hard-tipped breasts to his gaze, her own eyes looking down as she took off her knickers, afraid suddenly that he wouldn't like the way she'd shaven her whole pubic area that day. She'd read somewhere that some men liked that look, but maybe he didn't. She needn't have worried, his admiring expression told her when she finally looked up again.

'Beautiful Alice,' he complimented in that incredible voice of his. 'And so, so sexy.'

She did feel sexy. Extremely sexy.

Climbing onto the bed was not easy, her nerves returning as she stretched out on her side next to him. She tried not to look directly at his erection but it was difficult.

'You don't have much body hair,' she said as she ran her fingers through the small smattering of light brown curls in the centre of his chest.

'No. I did have my chest waxed once but it hurt like hell, so I let it grow again.'

'Should I kiss you first?' she asked, her confidence taking another dive.

'You should do whatever you want to do, Alice. I'm easy.'

But when she slid down his body and did what she

wanted to do—what she'd been thinking of doing all day—
his hips jerked up, his ankles unhooked and his arms shot
out from behind his head.

'Hell, Alice,' he protested when she stared up at him,
her face all flushed and hot.

'Was I doing it wrong?' she asked breathlessly.

'Hardly. I just wasn't ready for that. I mean... I'm just a
tad excited, woman, in case you hadn't noticed. I've been
trying to relax, but that striptease of yours undid me entirely.'

Alice liked the sound of that. She smiled a rather naughty
smile.

'I didn't realise you were so...'

'So what?' he growled.

'So into me,' she said cheekily.

His laugh was dry. 'I'm not into you yet, Alice. But I'm
hoping I will be soon.'

Jeremy was mightily relieved when she crawled back up
onto his chest and kissed him, on the mouth this time.
He wound his arms round her without thinking, his heart
lurching as he held her naked body tightly against his.
How brave she was, he thought. And how sexy. He could
not get enough of her.

When she sat up and straddled him across his thighs, he
sighed in relief. But when she reached over and opened a
bedside drawer, extracting a box of condoms, it struck him
just how prepared she'd been for tonight's outcome. Maybe
not for the being-on-top part, but for having sex with him.
Perversely, Jeremy found himself feeling slightly offended.
A crazy reaction, given the circumstances. But it was no
use. He hated the idea that he might be just the means to
an end for Alice. Yes, she fancied him. That much was obvious. But what would happen afterwards? Would she roll
off him and say, *Thank you very much, Jeremy dear, but
you can go now. Your job is done*?

'I'm sorry,' she said suddenly after tearing open one of the foil packets. 'I don't think I can manage. I mean…it looks so small and you're so big.'

'My size is average,' he said more sharply than he intended. 'Erections tend to be large when the man is as turned on as I am. Here! Give it to me.'

He rolled the condom over himself with the speed afforded by lots of practice.

'Heavens,' she said. 'That was impressively quick.'

Jeremy prayed for patience. 'Could we possibly move on, please?' he bit out through gritted teeth.

The heartbreakingly hesitant look she gave him quashed his anger. But did little to quell his rampant desire for her.

'I'm n-not sure what to do next,' she said.

'Go up on your knees,' he told her. 'Take me in your hands and push me inside a little, then hold it firmly at the root as you lower yourself gently onto me.'

She did as he said, the concentration on her face broken by a sudden gasp. Whether it was pain or pleasure he wasn't sure. On his part he thought she felt fantastic. Tight and wet and delicious.

'Are you all right?' he asked whilst he clenched his jaw in an attempt to gain control of his flesh. Lord, but he was already close to disaster.

'Yes,' she replied somewhat shakily. 'Fine. It feels fine. No, it feels more than fine. Oh, God, it feels fantastic.'

I'm not an it, he wanted to throw at her. *I'm a him. A person. A man.*

She began rocking to and fro, then rising up and down, riding him, killing him. He groaned, aware of hot blood rushing through his veins. Hell, he was only seconds from coming. Fortunately, she came first, throwing her head back as her mouth gaped open and a keening cry erupted from her lips. His release followed instantly, their bodies shuddering as one, Jeremy having not felt an orgasm like that in his life, his physical satisfaction overlaid by a most uncharacteristic emotional response.

Jeremy almost panicked—falling in love with Alice was *not* on his agenda—but he finally realised that his feeling of intense satisfaction was connected with being Alice's first lover, plus happiness over the fact she'd found the experience so pleasurable. He doubted many girls had screaming orgasms during their initiation into sex. Not that he could take too much credit for that. His male ego was suffering from an underlying irritation that he hadn't exactly done much to achieve that. Just lain there and let her use his body.

Next time, he vowed, it was not going to be like that.

'Absolutely not,' he muttered under his breath when she collapsed across him, his arms encircling her still-panting body with a fierce possessiveness. He definitely would not be letting her dismiss him afterwards, either, as if he were just a convenient piece of meat. He would not rest till she agreed to a lot more than this one time.

Alice lay across Jeremy's chest, wallowing in the security of his arms whilst trying to come to terms with what had just happened. She'd always suspected she would enjoy sex, if she could learn to trust a man enough. And now that she'd experienced the real thing, she wanted to experience more of it. But not with other men. With Jeremy. He was the one she wanted. He was the one she…

Alice caught herself up short before she even thought that dreaded word. She didn't love Jeremy. *Could* not love him. He didn't want her to. And really, she didn't want to, either. He was a playboy, a confirmed bachelor who changed women as often as he changed his clothes. Which was pretty often. She hadn't seen him in the same outfit or suit since they'd met.

'Everything okay?' he murmured into her hair.

'Yes. Yes, I'm good.'

'You might be a little sore tomorrow.'

Her head lifted and she smiled down at him. 'How would you know? You don't do virgins. Till tonight, that is.'

He gave a narrow-eyed glance. 'I have had many female friends over the years. Women like to talk. The things I know about the opposite sex would surprise you.'

'Nothing you know about the opposite sex would surprise me, Jeremy,' she said as she dropped her head back down on his chest.

'That didn't sound like a compliment.'

'It wasn't a criticism, either. Just a fact.'

'So where do we go from here, Alice?' he asked her.

Her head lifted again. 'What do you mean?'

'I sincerely hope you're not going to tell me that this is it—that my job is done and it's *hasta la vista*, baby. Whilst I might have had the odd one-night stand in the past, that's not what I want with you, Alice.'

'What do you want, then?'

'I want you to be my girlfriend.'

Alice swallowed. This was dangerous territory here. 'For how long?'

'Who knows? For as long as it lasts, I guess.'

'As what lasts?'

'Our lust for each other.'

'You think that's all it is between us? Lust?'

'Not on my part. I like you as well. I don't just want to take you to bed, Alice. I want to take you out. To show you how to have fun. I think you need that. But I'm going to be brutally honest. In my experience, once the lust begins to fade—and it always does eventually—then the liking soon follows.'

'I see. Well, I wouldn't know about that. I've never been in lust before. So how often would you be wanting to take me out?'

'I would imagine every weekend. And perhaps at least

once during the week. I'd certainly like to see you again fairly soon. I want to make love to *you* next time, Alice.'

Alice's mouth dried at the thought. She could hardly wait. But feminine instinct warned her that to be too eager would be the kiss of death with Jeremy. It might be the kiss of death with her, too. She suspected that if the next time was as marvellous as this first time, it wouldn't be long before she fell in love with this man. She didn't want that. It would be the height of foolishness. If truth be told, she should finish things right here and now. But she simply could not. At the same time, she vowed to keep some control over their relationship.

'I don't know about becoming your girlfriend, Jeremy. Could we just be friends and lovers? Neither of us are interested in marriage, or commitment for that matter, so I think it's best we don't pretend differently.'

His frown showed some displeasure with her counter suggestion.

'I would not want you dating anyone else whilst you're dating me,' he said.

She tried not to look as thrilled as she felt. 'The same goes for me.'

'Good. So when will I see you next? Tomorrow night?'

As much as she wanted to, she feared that having Jeremy make love to her so soon might see her getting way too emotionally involved way too quickly. Fortunately, she had a legitimate reason to delay things. 'Sorry, but I'll have to say no. Like you said, I might be sore tomorrow. On top of that, my period is due in the afternoon and I'm as regular as clockwork.'

Jeremy sighed. 'I see. So how long does your period last?'

'I should be right by Thursday.'

'Damn. I have to go to Paris on Thursday. I'm trying to set up an office there but the woman I wanted to head the place has taken a job elsewhere. I have to interview some new applicants for the job.'

'You speak French?'

'Passably.'

Alice lowered her head back to his chest. 'I'm hopeless with languages.'

'You'll still come to New York with me next weekend?' he asked, one hand trailing tenderly up and down her spine.

She sighed with a mixture of pleasure and resignation. 'Yes, of course. I can't wait.'

'Me too. Look, the rain's stopped so I think I'd better go.'

She sat up abruptly and pushed back her messy hair with both hands. 'But why? You haven't had dessert yet and I made a peach pie.'

He laughed. 'If I stay, *you're* the one who'll be my dessert, sore or not. Now don't look at me like that. I've done the job you asked me to do. Time for me to go.'

Guilt saw her flushing. 'I never meant it to sound like that. I was just trying to be pragmatic about everything. I thought you would prefer it that way. I knew you wouldn't want hearts and flowers.'

'You're the one who didn't want flowers,' he pointed out. 'I'm not averse to a little romance occasionally.'

'Sorry. I've been a bit screwed up.'

'And you're not screwed up now?'

Only in so far as I might already *be falling in love with you*...

'I think I'm going to be a normal girl from now on,' she pronounced.

His blue eyes narrowed. 'Normal how? You won't start wanting a ring on your finger, will you?'

'Not in the near future,' she said. 'And not with you, Jeremy. You've made your position quite clear.'

'Good. Now I'll be off. I'll ring you tomorrow. If we can't have sex, we can at least talk.'

She stayed naked whilst he dressed, shamelessly ogling

him as he did so. What a gorgeous body he had. Broad shoulders. Flat stomach. Slim hips. Great skin. And a penis to die for. He was wrong about his size. He wasn't obscenely huge but he *was* above average. Of course, Jeremy was above average in every department. He was smarter and kinder, and he could kick butt like Alice could hardly believe. She would always feel safe around him. She *did* feel safe. And strangely loved. She knew he didn't actually love her but he liked her enormously. And he cared about her. That was obvious.

Once he was dressed he bent to give her a long lingering kiss. 'Talk to you tomorrow,' he said when his head finally lifted.

'Jeremy...'

'Yes?'

'Thank you.'

His smile had an odd edge to it. 'My pleasure.'

Alice wondered afterwards what it had meant. That smile. In the end she decided she didn't want to know. She would enjoy whatever time she had with Jeremy, without regrets. She would be wretched when he moved on, but she would survive. Somehow. Tonight, he'd given her the tools to survive. He'd made her feel normal.

CHAPTER EIGHTEEN

NEW YORK. IN a few minutes she'd be in New York. With Jeremy.

Alice's stomach tightened with pleasurable anticipation. She wasn't sure what excited her the most. Going to the red-carpet premiere of *An Angel in New York*, or spending a whole night with Jeremy. In a five-star honeymoon suite no less!

Having to wait a week before they could make love again had increased her desire for him to fever pitch, all his long chatty, caring phone calls making her fall for him with a dizzying depth that could not be denied any longer. Silly to keep denying it, at least to herself. Given Jeremy's playboy history, it would have been better if she'd been the type of girl who could enjoy a strictly sexual fling without emotional involvement. But she hadn't been made that way, had she?

Still, she wouldn't worry about that right now, turning her head and smiling over at him.

God, but he was gorgeous. Dressed in another suit, this one charcoal-grey, combined with a grey and white striped shirt and a bright gold tie. A rather bold choice but she loved it, as she loved him. And desired him. Tonight could not come soon enough.

Maybe you won't have to wait till tonight, came the heart-stopping thought. *It's only lunchtime. The premiere doesn't start till this evening.* They could spend the afternoon making love.

'What on earth are you thinking?' Jeremy suddenly asked.

'What? Oh, nothing important. Just working out how I'm going to do my hair for tonight.'

'You little liar,' he chided laughingly. 'You were thinking about sex, weren't you?'

Alice's heart sank, perhaps because he'd used the word sex and not making love. Was that all their being together meant to him? Sex?

She suppressed a sigh. Being in love could be self-destructive, she decided, forcing a smile back to her lips.

'Well, of course I'm thinking about sex,' she said. 'Having discovered the joys of the flesh, I'm keen for some further education under your expert hands.'

For some reason her breezy answer didn't please him, his eyes darkening with a definite cloud of annoyance. 'Really?' he said in mocking tones. 'Well, I would hate to disappoint you. I've never coveted the role of sexual tutor. But there's a first time for everything, I guess.'

Alice frowned, his cutting tone having put a dampener on her excitement.

You bastard, Jeremy thought as he saw the light go out in her eyes. *Why do that to her, just because of your own crazy mixed-up feelings? Of course she wants more sex, her naturally high libido having being released after all those years of enforced celibacy. Don't be such a louse. Give her what she wants. And do it well. She deserves it.*

And she deserves a man a whole lot better than you!

Leaning over, he kissed her on the cheek. 'It will be my pleasure, beautiful,' he murmured in a slightly husky voice. 'We'll make love all afternoon, if that's what you want.' He lifted his head to smile down at her. 'It's certainly what *I* want. This past week has been sheer torture with missing you.'

'I missed you, too,' Alice said, his sweet words restoring her happiness in a flash.

Getting through Customs took a while, but Alice didn't care as long as Jeremy was holding her hand—which he was—and giving her those smouldering, desire-filled glances. He might not love her but he certainly wanted her. That would have to do for now.

When they finally emerged into the terminal, wheeling their luggage, Sergio was waiting for them with a big grin on his handsome Italian face. Alice knew it was Sergio because he called Jeremy's name out before striding over and drawing his friend into a big bear hug, slapping him on the back whilst giving her a raised-eyebrow glance over Jeremy's shoulder.

'*Dio*, but I have missed you!' Sergio boomed.

Jeremy's expression was classic Jeremy. 'Good God, you've gone all Italian again.'

Sergio laughed. 'But I *am* Italian, my friend.'

'You weren't all those years you lived in London. You could have been taken for British.'

'Never. You are the British boy. And still a swanky dresser, I see. But something is different, I have noticed.' And he directed his eyes at Alice.

Jeremy whirled, looking sheepish. 'Sorry, Alice. I wasn't deliberately ignoring you.'

'It's perfectly all right, Jeremy,' she said with a warm smile. She had enjoyed seeing the two friends together, had found comfort in Jeremy's affection for his friend. He was capable of loving a person, then. 'So this is Sergio?' she said, coming forward and holding out her hand. 'I've heard a lot about you and your days at Oxford together.'

Sergio bypassed her outstretched hand and hugged her too. 'And I have not heard nearly enough about you,' he returned. 'But I am impressed, Jeremy. Alice is the kind of lady I always thought would be the perfect partner for you.'

Jeremy groaned. 'Watch it, Alice. He'll have us married off before you know it. Sergio used to be as committed a bachelor as myself but after he turned thirty-five the rot set in.'

'I don't think Bella would like being described as rot,'

Sergio retorted. 'Besides, you knew full well that I intended on marrying when I returned to Italy. I told you that my days as a member of the Bachelor Club were well and truly over.'

'What's the Bachelor Club?' Alice asked.

Sergio gave Jeremy a reproving look. 'You haven't told her about the Bachelor Club?'

Jeremy shrugged. 'It didn't seem necessary. After both you and Alex left, our little club was no more.'

'But you're still a member?' Sergio asked, casting another long glance at Alice.

'I am, despite being thirty-five.'

'What has thirty-five got to do with anything?' Alice asked, her curiosity piqued.

'It was the age we vowed to remain bachelors till,' Jeremy informed her. 'Perhaps we should go get a cab, Sergio. Alice is tired after the flight and needs to have a little lie-down before tonight.'

Alice sucked in a sharp breath. Still as wicked as ever, she conceded. And annoyingly enigmatic at times.

The ride from the airport into the city was slow and tedious, New York traffic on a par with London's. Thank heavens the taxi drivers were just as chatty as London cabbies. Theirs kept showing them points of interest, taking them for tourists. They didn't tell him otherwise. Finally, they arrived at their hotel, porters taking care of their luggage, Jeremy handling their check-in whilst Sergio stayed with Alice.

'How long have you known Jeremy?' he asked straight away.

Alice had to think for a moment. 'About three weeks,' she said, astonished that it was so short a time. It felt as if she'd known him for much longer than that.

'How did you first meet?' came his next question.

She told him the truth, about the charity auction, her fund-raising, her job, et cetera, believing that truth was always the best policy. Of course, she did omit some facts. Sergio didn't have to know the circumstances behind their becoming an item, letting him fill in the blanks, probably wrongly. Like Jeremy, he would never imagine she'd been a virgin till recently, or that Jeremy was her first lover.

'Jeremy's a good man,' Sergio said. 'But he's been damaged by that appalling family of his.'

'Yes, I know,' she said softly. 'But no more about that. He's coming back.'

'So he is. Glad to have met you, Alice. And to have this opportunity to talk to you. It's going to be busy tonight so I might not get another chance.'

'Chance to do what?' Jeremy asked as he joined them.

'To chat,' Sergio said. 'Have to go, I'm afraid. Hell, I almost forgot. I've hired a limousine to pick you up tonight at seven.'

'How very Hollywood of you,' Jeremy said laughingly.

'It's what you have to do. The media can make or break a movie and we all have money in the damned thing, you included.'

'Not as much as you, I'll warrant,' Jeremy said. 'Is it a good movie?'

'Haven't seen it yet. But Charlie says it's great.'

'He's Bella's agent, isn't he? You can't believe him.'

'Don't say things like that. I'm stressed enough as it is, keeping Bella calm and confident. Now I do have to go. See you tonight. Your seats are next to ours, but we have to be there before you. Photos and interviews. Ciao.'

'They won't take photos of us, will they?' Alice asked a bit anxiously after Sergio left.

'Possibly. But why the frown? You'll look beautiful as always.'

'I should have bought a new dress.'

'Rubbish. That black number is gorgeous. And not in any way cheap. It has designer label written all over it. I know my fashion, Alice.'

'It was Fiona's dress. She gave it to me.'

'Who cares? It will do perfectly.'

'I won't hold a candle to Bella.'

'You'll outshine her in my eyes.'

'Oh…' Alice's heart went to mush. 'You say the nicest things.'

'You make me a better man,' he quipped, then grinned. 'Come on. Let's go upstairs to our room.'

Of course, it wasn't just a room. It was the honeymoon suite. Five star and fabulous.

'This must be costing you a small fortune,' she said as she walked through the enormous sitting room then glanced into the opulent bathroom with its corner spa bath and shower built for three.

'I'm using the money I saved from not having to buy you an original ten-thousand-dollar gown to wear tonight, plus a diamond necklace to go with it. No, whoops. I lied about the necklace part.'

Alice's eyes almost popped out of her head when he whipped a black velvet case out of his jacket pocket and held it out to her.

'You are kidding me,' she said when she opened it and saw the most exquisite diamond necklace. A sinfully expensive choker, with three rows of diamonds whose sparkle was reflected in her suddenly bright eyes. 'They can't be real,' she added as she drew it out of the box with reverent fingers.

'They'd better be,' he said drily.

'You shouldn't buy me expensive gifts like this, Jeremy,' she chided.

'Why not?'

'I'm your friend, not your mistress.'

'Can't a man buy a friend gifts?'

'Not ones that cost as much as this. And if you say you can afford it, I'm going to hit you.'

'Not with that lethal weapon in your hands, I hope.'

Alice stared down at the gorgeous necklace some more, unable to hold on to the tinge of dismay which had accompanied his giving it to her.

'When did you buy it? In Paris?'

'No. I was too damn busy in Paris to go shopping.'

'Please don't tell me you had Madge buy it for you.'

'Lord no,' he said laughingly. 'She would have had us married off even quicker than Sergio. No, I have many connections, Alice, from my financial consultancy days. One of them is a jeweller. He showed me this online, let me have it wholesale and couriered it over to me yesterday evening. So you do like it?'

'Do I like it? I love it,' she said, clasping it close to her heart. *And I love you*, she added silently.

'I could have bought matching earrings but I thought the necklace was enough. Too much glitz would detract from your classy look. And your beauty.'

Tears pricked at her eyes, which alarmed him.

'You're not going to cry, are you?'

'Sorry.' She quickly blinked them away. 'It's been a long time since I've been given something so fabulous. Thank you, Jeremy.' And she came forward to peck him on the lips.

'Surely you can thank me better than that.'

She feigned confusion. 'What would you suggest?'

'A shower first, I think, then a little lie-down together when you can show me just how grateful you are.'

Very grateful, Jeremy was to think ruefully when they were in the shower together.

Her kisses were wildly passionate, her tongue as avid as his own. She didn't take much encouragement to go down on her knees before him. He tried to recapture his earlier resentment over his body being used by her, but it would not come. All he could think about was how incredible her lips felt, how much he wanted her to keep doing what she was doing.

And she did, shocking him with her quite wanton passion, forcing him to use every ounce of willpower he owned to stop her before she went all the way. For that was not what he wanted on this occasion. He wanted to make love to *her*, not the other way around. He wanted to make her desperate for him. Wanted to watch her come and come. Wanted to show her that she couldn't possibly have so many orgasms with any other man, that only he, Jeremy, could do that for her.

And when he couldn't stand it any more, he would allow the beast in him to take her in a way where she couldn't see his eyes, couldn't glimpse the depth of his feelings, feelings that scared the life out of him.

Alice lay back on the bed, her legs stretched wide, her eyes squeezed tightly shut as Jeremy did to her what she'd often fantasised about but never hoped to enjoy. How delicious it felt to be made love to that way. Totally decadently delicious.

'Eyes open, Alice,' he ordered thickly, and she did so. 'Now keep them open.'

Frustration brought a moan to her lips. He dropped his head again and soon she was twisting her own head from side to side, her mouth gasping wide, frantic hands clutching at the sheets. Her climax made her cry out, twisting at her insides, which felt oddly empty. Almost bereft. She thought he would stop then but he didn't. He kept going, licking, sucking, exploring, and soon that awful tension was gripping her once more. Awful this time because it was no longer what she wanted. But she felt powerless to stop her body from responding, unable to say no. She came again, her pleasure not nearly as sharp, or as satisfying.

When he continued, she simply could not bear it. 'No, Jeremy, no,' she begged. 'Enough.'

He slid back up her body and kissed her, making her taste herself on his lips. She could not believe how exciting she found that, how much she loved his tongue in her mouth. She moaned in dismay when he abandoned it to concentrate on her breasts, which felt swollen and heavy and, yes, eager for attention. He gave them that, and more, till her nipples were burning and she was once again pleading with him to stop. He shocked her then by turning her over and kissing her all the way down her spine to the cleft between her buttocks.

Panic churned her stomach at the thought that he might do something she didn't want him to do. But he didn't. After reaching for a condom, he pulled her up onto her hands and knees and entered her from behind, bringing a sigh of relief, and, yes, the most exquisite pleasure. How ready she was for him to do this, she thought as he moved inside her. How madly, marvellously ready. Her bottom pressed back hard against him, her breathing going haywire, her blown-away mind on nothing but the feel of his flesh filling hers.

'Oh, yes,' she cried out when he started rocking back and forth. 'Yes...'

His hands finding her aching breasts and plucking at her needy nipples tipped her immediately over the edge, a violent orgasm ripping right through her. He came too, roaring his release, his hands squeezing her breasts as his body shuddered into her own shuddering flesh. Alice collapsed onto the bed in a crumpled heap, Jeremy falling on top of her. And there they lay, chests heaving, hot breaths panting from their lungs till slowly, finally, the air stilled around them and the room fell quiet.

Alice surrendered to sleep first, Jeremy lying sprawled across her unconscious form for a long while before slowly withdrawing and heading for the bathroom.

CHAPTER NINETEEN

THE MOVIE WAS GOOD, Jeremy thought even before the credits started to roll. No, it was more than good. It was great. A winner. All total fantasy, Jeremy accepted, but enjoyable in a strictly escapist fashion, a feel-good movie in every way. The music was great too, the lyrics emotional and uplifting. Bella had sung most of the songs and she'd been incredibly good. Jeremy had heard her sing once before—at a royal gala performance in London—but she had outdone herself this time. His investment in the movie was safe. Not that he cared about that for himself. He hadn't put that much money in it. But he was glad for Sergio.

The audience stood up and started clapping at the end. When Jeremy turned to Alice, she had tears in her eyes. Women! Such emotional creatures. But if truth be told, he'd been touched himself by the story.

'Wasn't Bella wonderful?' she said as they made their way slowly down the aisle. 'And this theatre is amazing!'

The premiere had been held at the Paris theatre, the last remaining single auditorium theatre in New York and patron of independent movies. Built post war, it was not as opulent as other theatres of that era, but it still retained that air of old-fashioned elegance and glamour, with a magnificent velvet curtain covering the large curved screen and almost six hundred surprisingly comfortable leather seats.

Jeremy tapped Bella on her shoulder. She and Sergio were just in front of them.

'Alice said you were wonderful,' he told her. 'And you were. So was the movie.'

Bella stopped and turned, giving them both a warm smile. 'Thank you, Jeremy darling. And you, too, Alice. I know we haven't had the opportunity for girl talk yet but Sergio said you were just what the doctor ordered for Jeremy.'

Jeremy rolled his eyes. 'Enough of the matchmaking, Sergio. Alice and I are just good friends. Let's leave it at that for now.'

Bella gave him one of her intuitive looks. 'If you say so. You are coming to the after party, aren't you?'

'Wouldn't miss it for the world.'

The after party was held at Bella and Sergio's New York apartment, a splendid place, spacious and tastefully furnished. And a stone's throw from Broadway. Alice wasn't overawed—she'd been brought up around moneyed people—but she was amused by the antics of Bella's agents, Charlie and Josh. They were so over the top, and given to extravagant compliments. Within minutes of being introduced, they tried to sign Alice up, saying she was a wonderful cross between Grace Kelly and Audrey Hepburn—perhaps it was because she'd worn her hair up. Such a style plus Fiona's designer dress and Jeremy's fabulous necklace did give her a coolly sophisticated look. When she'd informed them she wasn't an aspiring actress but a counsellor, working with victims of domestic violence, they hadn't missed a beat, saying it would give her acting more depth to have had such tough life experiences. Unfortunately, at the time Jeremy was engaged talking to Sergio. Alice was relieved when Bella came to the rescue.

'Sorry, my darlings,' she said to her eager agents, 'but I need Alice here for a sec. Secret women's business,' she added before steering her away from the living room into a nearby bedroom, shutting the door firmly behind them.

'They can be a bit much, can't they?' Bella said.

'They mean well.'

Bella laughed. 'They are both greedy opportunists. And never to be trusted. But I can't blame them for pouncing on you. You are so lovely, and like a breath of fresh air after all the plastic wannabes which abound in our industry.'

'Well, *you're* nothing like that,' Alice said, thinking how exquisitely beautiful Bella looked in that one-shouldered white chiffon gown. Princess line, it was, with a long flowing skirt that brushed the floor. Her lovely face was made up perfectly, her long white-blonde hair cascading in gentle waves over her shoulders.

Her smile was a little wry. 'My looks have been a great asset but I hope my voice is what I am remembered for. But enough of that, I wanted to talk to you about Jeremy, and that silly Bachelor Club of theirs. Sergio tells me you didn't know anything about it.'

'No. Should I? I already know Jeremy is a confirmed bachelor.'

A frown formed on Bella's high forehead. 'And you're okay with that?'

Something unhappy must have shown on Alice's face.

'I didn't think you would be,' Bella said drily. 'You're in love with him, aren't you?'

'How…how can you tell?'

Bella shrugged. 'Most women fall in love with Jeremy. Fortunately, when I met him I was already besotted with Sergio, otherwise I might have surrendered to the spell of his wicked charm.'

Alice sighed. 'He does have a way about him.'

'But he won't marry you, Alice. Don't delude yourself into thinking he will.'

'I won't. Don't worry.' Though the horrid hope had briefly crossed her mind. 'Tell me about this Bachelor Club.'

'Look, it's just some silly club the three of them formed at Oxford. It had a whole lot of ridiculous rules. Mainly, they vowed to become billionaires by the time they turned thirty-five, and not to marry before then, either. They trundled along for years, making heaps of money and playing musical beds. It wasn't till they actually reached thirty-five and had achieved their financial goal that Sergio and Alex saw that it was crazy to block themselves off from the joy of true love. Sergio came looking for me and Alex found Harriet. But Jeremy seems trapped in his inability to open his heart to any woman. Sergio believes he's afraid of falling in love. Do you know about his family and all their divorces?'

'Yes, I do.'

'Well that's obviously the reason behind his playboy lifestyle. Maybe one day he'll realise that we all forge our own destinies in life—that we're not programmed to follow our parents' poor example. But I'm worried that before that happens, you are going to be very hurt.'

Her words moved Alice, as did her kindly concern. What a sweet woman she was.

Alice reached out and took Bella's hands in hers.

'It's all right, Bella,' she said. 'I'll be all right. I'm a survivor.' She'd had to be.

Bella shook her head. 'Then you're a lot tougher than I am. I don't know what I would have done if Sergio hadn't loved me back.'

How could he not have loved her back? She was so sweet and so lovable.

'Maybe Jeremy cares about me more than he knows,' Alice said with a sudden burst of optimism. 'He bought me this necklace. And he offered to buy me a house. Well, not for me personally. It was for the charity I started up to help abused women.'

Bella's eyes rounded. 'He did that for you?'

'Indeed he did.'

'Goodness. I'll have to tell Sergio. I'm sure he doesn't know. Maybe Jeremy is already changing. Love changes people, you know. Now we'd better get back before they send out a search party.'

'So where did you and Bella disappear to for a while?'

Jeremy asked in the taxi ride back to their hotel. It was very late, everyone having waited till the reviews came out on the movie. All had been positively glowing.

'Oh, she was having trouble with the zipper on her dress,' Alice invented. 'It took some time to fix.'

Jeremy nodded. 'That's because she's pregnant.'

Alice's head whipped round in surprise. 'She *is*?'

'Yes. Four and a half months. She didn't tell you?'

'No. Why would she? I'm not a relative, or a special friend. But that's great. She must be very happy.'

'Sergio's over the moon. It's a boy, according to the ultrasound.'

'I can't imagine a man like Sergio caring whether it's a boy or a girl, provided the baby is healthy.'

'True. He's one in a million, Sergio. The best friend a man could have.' Jeremy sighed. 'I just wish that he didn't live in Italy. Though speaking of Italy, he's invited us to visit them one weekend at his villa on Lake Como. Would you like that?'

'I'd love it,' she said, her heart dancing with happiness.

'Good. Then we'll go in July. Lake Como in the middle of summer is perfect.'

July was two months away, Alice thought. Which meant Jeremy didn't anticipate their relationship ending before then. Maybe it would never end. Maybe one day he'd confess he'd fallen in love with her and ask her to marry him.

And maybe pigs would start falling out of the sky.

But as she lay in his arms later that night, her body sated from more wonderful lovemaking, Alice's mind kept plaguing her with the romantic fantasy of their being married, and having a baby of their own. Astonishing thoughts, really, given the people involved. Jeremy hadn't been the only one who'd spent their life up till now not wanting marriage. Alice had always believed she'd never trust a man enough with her body to contemplate such a union. The fact that she trusted Jeremy enough to consider putting her happiness in his hands was truly amazing. Was it the blindness of her own love that inspired such optimism?

Possibly.

Probably.

As she finally drifted off to sleep she kept thinking of what Bella had said. How she was afraid that one day Jeremy was going to hurt her. Terribly.

CHAPTER TWENTY

'I CAN'T BELIEVE you and Jeremy are still seeing each other,' Fiona said over breakfast that Monday morning. 'I mean, it's been over a month now, hasn't it?'

'Six weeks actually,' Alice said. May had given way to June, summer having arrived in London, along with the humidity and the tourists.

Fiona shook her head. 'Amazing. It's not like him at all. And not like you either, sweetie. Of course, he *is* pretty irresistible. Even I can see that. But do try not to get too carried away. Or start thinking he'll marry you because he won't. And speaking of marriage, I'll be sending out my wedding invitations this week and I wondered what I should put on yours. Perhaps Alice Waterhouse and partner would be best, don't you think? After all, you and Jeremy might not be together by late August.'

Alice had a faint suspicion that Fiona was slightly jealous of her relationship with Jeremy, and was looking forward to the moment it failed. Her own fiancé wasn't nearly as handsome as Jeremy, or as nice. If truth be told Alistair was a right royal snob and so were his parents. Alice didn't envy Fiona one bit.

'Alice and partner would be fine,' Alice replied. 'Oh, and, Fiona, I'll be moving out soon.'

'You're not going to move in with Jeremy, are you?'

'No.' Though she practically lived at his place, spending every weekend and several nights during the week there. 'I've saved the deposit for a flat of my own and I found one I rather liked yesterday.'

'Really? Where is it?'

'In Chelsea.'

'Chelsea! Can you afford a flat in Chelsea?'

'Yes. It only has one bedroom, but it's on the ground floor and has a nice little courtyard.' She didn't add that Jeremy's father's bank was footing the mortgage with her paying only the smallest interest. Fiona seemed put out as it was.

'But I was going to ask you to take over this place when I got married,' Fiona said snippily. 'I wouldn't have charged you too much. And you could have had a flatmate to share the cost.'

'I'm sorry, Fiona. I'm grateful for all you've done for me, but it's time I had a place of my own.'

Fiona sighed. 'I'm going to miss you, sweetie.'

But not too much or for too long, Alice accepted. She'd imagined they were close friends, but not close enough, apparently, for Fiona to ask her to be a bridesmaid. Yet she was having six.

Alice's phone ringing stopped this increasingly irritating conversation in its tracks. She imagined it was Jeremy. They were constantly on the phone with each other.

But it wasn't Jeremy. It was her mother.

'Hello, Mother,' an astonished Alice answered, standing up and heading to her bedroom for some privacy. She hadn't seen or spoken to her mother since last Christmas, their relationship still strained, despite the departure of Marigold's husband. Alice had only gone home at Christmas because it was the done thing. Plus, she'd wanted to see her nephew. Her sister, she'd long lost patience with. The sight of Marigold weeping over her husband's grave last year had turned her stomach. 'What's happened?' she asked, instant worry in her voice. 'Is Dickie all right?'

Her mother's sigh was audible down the line. 'Dickie is fine. I've rung to tell you that your sister has become engaged and wants you to meet her fiancé. We're having a small family celebration this Saturday night. Not a party.

Jarod didn't want that. Just dinner and a cake. So can you come? *Will* you come?' she amended.

Alice took a few moments to assemble her thoughts, shock at this news having rendered her temporarily speechless.

'Who's this Jarod?' were her first words. 'Where on earth did Marigold meet him?'

'He's one of the gardeners she employed to landscape the grounds.'

A gardener. Alice could not believe it. First, Marigold married an abusive billionaire. Then, when she should have been old enough to know better, she got herself seduced by a possible gold-digger.

'Now don't jump to conclusions, Alice. You have a habit of doing that. Jarod's not after her money. He really loves her. And she loves him.'

I'll be the judge of that, she thought angrily.

'So will you come?' her mother asked somewhat tentatively.

'Wild horses wouldn't keep me away,' Alice bit out.

'Excellent. I'll see you Saturday, then. Let me know what train you'll be on and I'll have someone meet you at the station.'

Alice hesitated for a moment, then said, 'I won't be coming by train. I'll be driving down.'

'You've bought a car?'

'No. I... I've got myself a boyfriend.' Oh, Lord. Jeremy would hate being called her boyfriend. He'd probably hate taking her to a family function as well. Hopefully, he'd do it for her, if she asked nicely, because the thought of going alone was horrendous.

'A boyfriend!' her mother exclaimed. 'At last! Oh, Alice, I'm so pleased. Who is he?'

'His name is Jeremy Barker-Whittle.'

'Not one of *the* Barker-Whittles, is he? The banking dynasty?'

Trust her mother to know the names of every family in Britain with money. 'His family is in banking, yes. But Jeremy is in books. He's a publisher.'

'A publisher. How exciting! I love books.'

'Then you'll have plenty to talk about. It is all right that I bring him, then?'

'Of course. I'll put you both in the blue room.'

'Really, Mother? And if I asked for separate bedrooms?'

'Are you?'

'No.'

'Good. That pleases me even more.'

Alice just shook her head. She would never understand her mother.

'See you Saturday,' she said, and hung up, thankful that she didn't have to explain that conversation to Fiona. But she rang Jeremy immediately, unable to keep such news to herself. She caught him just before he left for work.

'I have some appalling news to tell you,' she said straight away.

'You're pregnant.'

'Don't be ridiculous. Of course not. I'm on the pill and you've been using condoms. Though you can throw them away now. The unsafe month is up.'

'And you call that appalling news?' he said laughingly.

'That's not it. Marigold is getting married. To a gardener, no less.'

'At the risk of calling you a snob, Alice love, what's so terrible about that?'

'Nothing. And I'm not a snob. But I just know he's after her money.'

'Ah. That old lack of trust in men raises its ugly head again.'

'Her husband's only been dead a year!' she protested.

'A husband she couldn't have loved,' Jeremy pointed out.

'She cried over his coffin.'

'They were probably tears of relief.'

'I thought you would understand,' Alice wailed.

'I do understand, my darling,' he said gently. 'You have every right to be wary for your sister. You love her. Look, I'll have a background check done on him. See if he has a criminal history. And I'll check out his financial status. Would that make you feel better?'

'Oh, yes, it definitely would. And, Jeremy...'

'Yes?'

'They're having a small celebratory dinner at home next Saturday night. Unfortunately, I opened my big mouth and asked if I could bring my new boyfriend with me. Sorry.'

'I see,' he said, not sounding too put out. 'Am I to presume you meant me?'

'Who else? So would you take me? *Please?*'

'Of course,' he agreed in that wonderfully easy-going way that she adored.

'You are so good to me,' she said with a soft sigh.

'It's easy to be good to someone like you, Alice.'

She almost told him then that she loved him. But she didn't, knowing instinctively that Jeremy didn't want to hear words of love. But she had no doubt in her heart that he knew she loved him, and that possibly he almost loved her back. He showed it all the time. Actions could be louder than words. Alice hugged that positive thought to herself.

CHAPTER TWENTY-ONE

When Jeremy picked up Alice the following Saturday afternoon, the weather was humid, but drizzly. Alice, he saw straight away, looked beautiful but tense.

As soon as she was buckled up in the passenger seat, he handed her an A4-sized envelope.

'When you read that,' he said, 'you might feel better. It's the background check on Marigold's fiancé, as promised.'

'You were able to get it done in time!' she said with a relieved smile. 'You said it might be hard, given you didn't know this Jarod's surname.' Only because she'd refused to ring and ask.

'I called in a favour,' he replied, thinking of how small the world was. It turned out that the security firm he'd contacted to do the investigation was being managed by the very boy he'd saved from being bullied at school. Once Graham had found out his saviour was his new client, he had pulled out all stops to get the information Jeremy had wanted by this morning. But it had cost him a packet. Jeremy had refused Graham's offer of no fee, not wanting to take advantage of the man's gratitude.

Alice shook her head at him, though her expression was admiring. 'You are such a clever man.' Without further ado she ripped open the envelope.

Jeremy concentrated on getting out of London whilst Alice read the report, her occasional murmur of surprise pleasing him no end. He'd read the report himself, of course, and had been relieved to find out that Jarod Adams—that was his surname—was not some fortune-hunter. He actually owned more than three landscaping businesses and several nurseries. A self-made man, he had many millions in his bank, and many properties in his business portfolio, including a town house in Richmond and a seaside apartment in Brighton. Whilst having been born poor, he'd worked long and hard to get where he was today. He had no criminal convictions against his name, and his reputation was spotless. His employees couldn't speak highly enough of him. He was thirty-seven years old, six feet tall and very fit, according to the gym where he worked out. He had never been married. His parents had passed on, and his only sister lived in Australia.

'Not quite what you were imagining,' Jeremy said when her head finally lifted from her lap.

'No. He seems the real deal. Lucky Marigold. She deserves to be happy at long last.'

'Yes, she does, from what you've told me. So let's act happy for her when we arrive and not in any way suspicious. And try to be nice to your mother. I know your relationship is strained. I'm not stupid. But nothing's to be gained by letting your feelings show.'

Alice dragged in a deep breath before letting it out slowly. It was all very well for Jeremy to say that, but the hurts ran deep.

'I wonder if you'd be so nonchalant if you had to go to another of *your* family's weddings,' she said.

'God, the mind boggles at such a thought.'

'See? You wouldn't be so pragmatic if that happened.'

'True. But it won't. I think even they've had enough of the divorce court.'

'Not every marriage ends in divorce, Jeremy,' she said, hating herself for even bringing up the subject. But it was impossible not to hope that one day Jeremy might get over his aversion to commitment. He loved her. She was surer now than ever that he did. He just refused to admit it. 'Your two best friends seem very happy in their marriages,' she pointed out quietly.

He slanted her an incisive glance. 'I hope you haven't changed your mind, Alice. You told me you weren't interested in marriage.'

Alice saw immediately that she'd backed herself into a corner. What to say? How to handle this?

Her shrug was brilliantly nonchalant. 'All I am saying is that not every marriage ends in the divorce court.'

'It does, if there's a Barker-Whittle involved. Just be happy with what we have, Alice. Don't spoil things by wishing for the moon. Our relationship works because we have our feet firmly on the ground. Marriage changes things. So does living together. Speaking of living arrangements, when are you going to move into your new flat? It will be good not to have Fiona hovering behind you every time I come to pick you up.'

Alice dared not look over at him, lest her dismay show in her eyes. She'd been half hoping that Jeremy might ask her to move in with him at some stage. If he'd loved her he would have. Clearly, his feelings didn't run that deep.

Her heart sank as she accepted that her foolish optimism where he was concerned was just that. Foolish. She'd known what he was when she became involved with him. She'd been well warned. It was a minor miracle that things had lasted this long.

'Should be in by the end of the month,' she said, striking what she hoped was the right common-sense tone. 'I'm really looking forward to it. I like my own space at times. Having my own place will be a dream come true.'

She was one independent woman, Jeremy thought irritably. He was glad now that he hadn't given in to that insane temptation this last week to ask her to rent out her flat and move in with him. After all, she would have only said no. Yes was not a word Alice was overly comfortable with. She did say yes quickly enough when she was turned on, but other than that she could be extremely difficult. In the end, she hadn't even let him contribute to the purchase of that house next door to the refuge, buying it instead with funds raised, the website Madge had designed bringing in lots of donations for her charity.

She did finally agree to let him pick her up at work when she stayed back late, but she still took the Tube during the day. Neither would she let him lavish her with designer clothes, choosing instead to scour the markets for once-expensive vintage dresses to wear when he took her out to the kind of society do he was always getting invited to. Not that she didn't always look beautiful. She did. But he liked buying her things. Liked spoiling her.

The possibility that he was falling in love with Alice continued to haunt him at times. But none more so than at this very moment. Jeremy had always known that his family was flawed when it came to love. They often fell hard and fast, made stupid decisions, then fell out again just as quickly, leading to shattered marriages and shattered children.

I will not be a party to that stupidity, he vowed. *Not even for Alice*. Not that she would want him to. Clearly, she wasn't in love with him. Women in love couldn't wait to tell you and she'd never mentioned that particular four-letter word. This realisation should have made him feel better but it didn't. Damn it, but he had to pull himself together here.

'Surprisingly little traffic,' he said once they were safely on the M3. 'The rain, no doubt,' he added, the earlier drizzle having become much heavier.

'I don't mind the rain,' Alice said. 'I like to lie in bed and listen to the rain.'

'I like to lie in bed with you,' he said. 'Will we be in the same bedroom tonight?'

'Yes. But be warned. As soon as my mother heard that you were a member of the Barker-Whittle banking dynasty, she whipped us into the best guest room together.'

Jeremy laughed. 'I could grow to like your mother.'

'Huh. You are going to behave yourself, I hope. No flirting with Marigold or trying to seduce my mother.'

'Spoilsport. How old is she?'

'Marigold is thirty-three.'

'I meant your mother.'

'She turned fifty-nine last month.'

'Still a spring chicken.'

'Jeremy, you are incorrigible.'

'And you are delightful when you're jealous. But you don't have any cause for worry, my darling. Since I met you, I haven't even looked at another woman.'

'I don't believe that for a minute.'

'Would I lie to you?'

'Yes,' she pronounced firmly.

The trip took almost three hours, with their stopping once for coffee on the way, Alice's tension over the night ahead returning as they drove up the long driveway to the home she'd never been happy living in after her father died. A Georgian mansion built eons ago, it sat on the top of a hill overlooking the coast, though the sea could only be glimpsed from the two upper floors. The outer walls were fawn, the windows white, the roof and chimneys terracotta. Inside, not counting the servants' quarters downstairs, there were eight bedrooms, five bathrooms, a huge ballroom, spacious receptions and dining rooms, and a magnificent oak staircase. Most of the furniture were genuine antiques, the massive amount of artwork having been collected over the centuries by every earl to inhabit Hilltop Manor.

The original estate had had many acres and farms, but a lot of land had been sold off to pay her father's debts. The furniture and artwork might have gone too, if Marigold hadn't found herself a rich husband, a self-made mobile phone magnate. As it turned out, Rupert had coveted the grandeur of the house with its aristocratic history and opulent decor, but he hadn't been much interested in the gardens, so the grounds had been badly neglected for years.

Not so now, Alice thought with wonder as the extent of work done since Christmas became obvious. An impressive circular gravel driveway now greeted guests as they arrived, along with a lovely fountain, which sparkled in the sunshine, the rain being left behind as they'd travelled further south. Red roses lined the rather plain front of the house, their blooms full and rich. To the right and left she could see that there'd been groups of trees planted, which, though still young, would one day provide wonderful shade, and a pleasant place to sit.

'Sergio's villa on Lake Como has a fountain,' Jeremy said as his car crunched to a halt next to the elegant front portico, which was framed by Corinthian pillars made from creamy white marble. 'But it's a little more…shall we say… provocative?'

'What do you mean? Provocative?'

His smile carried amusement. 'Difficult to describe. You will see for yourself when we go visit there soon. Sergio suggested next weekend. Would that suit you?'

'Yes, I suppose so.' She couldn't think about next weekend, with her mind totally on this weekend. On the here and now. Her breath caught when the heavy front doors were thrown open, and her sister emerged on the arm of a well-built, pleasant-faced man with thick brown hair and broad shoulders. Both were smiling, then laughing when little Dickie dashed between their legs and ran over to the passenger door.

'Auntie Allie's here, Auntie Allie's here!' he chorused, jumping up and down with childish glee.

'Wow,' Jeremy murmured. 'Wish I was as popular with Auntie Allie.'

'Don't be silly,' she threw at him. 'You know I'm crazy about you.' And she climbed out of the car to embrace her eager nephew.

* * *

I'm crazier about you, Jeremy thought as he too alighted. *Too crazy for my peace of mind.*

'Jeremy. Come and meet my sister and her fiancé,' Alice insisted, little Dickie already in her arms.

Marigold was not overly like Alice, either in looks or personality. She was pretty, yes, but a good few inches shorter, with curly strawberry-blonde hair, an ordinary mouth and blue-grey eyes. Her figure was very hourglass, with wide hips and a lush bosom. She was also a follower, he could see, forever glancing over at her beloved and looking to him for approval. He gave it, in spades, the man obviously in love. Jeremy wished them the best with warm words, but privately he was no less cynical than usual when it came to believing they were set for their happiness.

After introductions, the two men carried their luggage upstairs, the two sisters already chatting happily away behind them. Their mother, Marigold had informed Alice, was lying down with a migraine and wouldn't be joining the family till dinner, news that had inspired an eye-roll from Alice. Jeremy suspected that dinner could be tricky, resolving to use all his social skills to avert a possible disaster. They were here to celebrate Marigold's engagement, not settle old scores.

'Nanna's put you in the blue room,' an excited Dickie told Jeremy as they ascended the staircase. 'It's the biggest and bestest bedroom in the house.'

'I *am* privileged,' he replied with a warm smile. The child really was delightful. Almost made you want one for yourself. Jeremy immediately thought of his two friends' sons, a pang of uncharacteristic envy twisting his heart.

'What does privileged mean, Auntie Allie?' Dickie asked Alice.

'It means lucky,' she replied. 'Jeremy's a lucky man and you're a lucky boy.'

'Very lucky,' Jeremy murmured an hour later when they

were lying, replete, in each other's arms on top of the four-poster bed with its blue satin quilt and mountain of matching pillows. They'd begged off coming down for afternoon tea, both claiming weariness after the drive and the need for a shower and a nap before dinner this evening. Marigold had given them a surprisingly knowing look, making Jeremy revise his opinion of Alice's sister. Maybe she was smarter than she seemed.

'So what did you think of him?' Alice asked.

'I think Dickie is delightful,' he replied, tongue in cheek.

Alice punched him on the arm. 'You know who I mean.'

'I think Jarod's very much in love with your sister, and vice versa.'

'I do too. Gosh, but it's a relief. I was so worried. You know, Jeremy, it wasn't till I arrived here today that I realised just how much I do love my sister. When I saw her looking so happy, I just melted inside.'

'Mmm, yes, you do seem somewhat melted,' Jeremy said, his hands wandering into nicely moist places.

'Will you just stop that and let me talk for a while?'

'I'm not stopping you from talking. Please continue.'

Her sigh carried resignation to what he was doing. 'I can't think when you're doing that.'

'Then don't, Alice.'

She didn't.

CHAPTER TWENTY-TWO

ALICE SHOULD HAVE known that Jeremy would be a hit with her mother. But did he have to sit next to her at dinner, dragging his chair even closer so that Alice couldn't overhear what they were talking about? With only five of them seated at a huge dining table, which could be extended to seat twenty, there was already a decent space between chairs. Dickie, of course, had long been put to bed. Alice chatted away with Marigold whilst her ears strained to catch what Jeremy was saying. With a voice like his, one would think that would be easy, but he could talk softly when he wanted to. It wasn't till the main course was whisked away and their glasses of wine were being replenished that Alice's mother spoke to her directly.

'Jeremy tells me that Kenneth Jacobs is one of his authors. He said that you'd met him, is that right?'

'Yes, we all had drinks and dinner together one night not long ago.'

'Oh, I do envy you both. I think he's an incredible author. I'd love to meet him some day.'

'No reason why you can't,' Jeremy said. 'Do you ever come to London?'

'Not very often.'

'Then you should. This is a lovely home but it must get lonely living here at times.'

'Yes, it does,' she said with a sigh.

'Let me know when you want to come and you can stay at my place.'

'Oh!' Her mother actually blushed. 'How kind of you. I might just do that.'

* * *

'What in God's name were you doing asking my mother to stay at your place?' Alice snapped after she banged the door of the blue room shut around midnight, her temper finally getting the better of her. Or was it jealousy?

'Why shouldn't I ask your mother to stay?' he said in that annoyingly innocent way he could adopt at times. 'I was just trying to be nice.'

Her hands found her hips. 'Well, if you keep being that nice, she'll be booking us a church and reception place in no time. Is that what you want?'

'Hardly,' he replied. 'Look, I just felt sorry for the woman. Did you know how poor she was as a child?'

'Rubbish! She wasn't poor. Her family was old money.'

'Money which had dissipated over the years, due to death duties and poor investments. After the great depression there was nothing left but their warped pride. Then the war came, making matters even worse. In the end, her family was living in a crumbling old ruin, which had no electricity and very little furniture. Her mother became an alcoholic and her father succumbed to early dementia. *Your* mother had to leave school and get work in a local pub so they could eat.'

Alice stared at him in shock and disbelief. This was the first she'd heard of such things. 'How on earth do you know all this?' she demanded to know.

He shrugged. 'Women feel they can talk to me. They tell me things. Did you know Lily was working as a waitress when she caught your father's eye?'

So it was Lily already. Lord, but he was a fast worker. At the beginning of dinner he'd been addressing her as Lady Waterhouse. 'That's not true,' she countered sharply. 'Mother met my father at a New Year's Eve party, right here in this house.'

'She did. But she wasn't a guest. She was serving drinks.'

'If that's true, then why didn't she tell me? Why pretend she was part of the hoi polloi that night? I wouldn't have judged.'

'I don't know the answer to that. But I suspect Marigold knows. They seem very close.'

'They are,' Alice said with a sigh before falling silent for a full minute, her thoughts in a whirl. 'You know, Marigold told me tonight that Rupert wasn't nearly as bad as I'd imagined. She claimed he suffered from depression after his upbringing as a foster child and was prone to fits of uncontrollable anger. That was when he yelled at her and hit her. She assured me that after she fell pregnant with Dickie, he changed. He finally went to a doctor, got diagnosed as bipolar and started taking medication. Of course, by then I'd left home permanently so I didn't witness any such improvement. When I visited every Christmas I thought he was just pretending to be a good husband. Marigold claimed he'd really loved her and she loved him back. She said she knew his behaviour was unacceptable at times but she couldn't leave him because she'd been terrified he'd kill himself like our father did. When I asked her if she'd told Mother all this, she said she had, eventually, but she'd hidden the truth from her at first. When I'd made my fuss over his hitting her, Mother had actually come to Marigold for an explanation, Marigold saying I'd just overheard a lovers' spat and that it had been she who'd slapped Rupert, not the other way around. She said she was very convincing. So maybe Mother wasn't the monster I always thought.'

'She still shouldn't have sent you away to school.'

'Maybe she thought I needed to get away after Daddy's death,' Alice said with more insight into the situation. 'I was very much a Daddy's girl,' she went on rather wistfully. 'We would go riding together almost every day. He even took me to the races. I didn't know then that he was addicted to gambling. I thought it was all great fun and I loved him to death. When he killed himself I was beside

myself with grief. It…it was a terrible time.' Guilt claimed
Alice as she recalled blaming her mother for her father's
death, screaming at her that it was all her fault; that she
spent too much money on clothes and silly things like perfume and jewellery.

'I was pretty awful to my mother at the time,' Alice said
sadly. 'It's no wonder she doesn't like me.'

'Don't be silly,' Jeremy said as he drew her into his arm
and stroked her hair. 'Your mother loves you very much.
She told me so. Reading between the lines, I think she's
also very guilty over not believing you where Marigold's
husband was concerned. Still, perhaps now you can understand why she was tempted to turn a blind eye. She must
have been in a panic after your father died, bankrupt and in
debt. To suddenly be poor again would have been her worst
nightmare. Then along comes a white knight to seemingly
rescue everyone, so she didn't want to hear what you had to
say. Not that that makes it right. It wasn't right. She should
have listened to you. But I think she's sorry. She said how
happy she was to see you so happy. She's also very lonely,
Alice. Maybe she'll meet someone if she comes to London
and gets out and about.'

Alice pulled out of Jeremy's arms to stare up at him.
'You're not going to try to fix her up with Ken, are you?'

'Good God no, he's already fixed up with Madge.'

'He is?'

'Didn't I tell you?' he said as he wandered over to pick
up his phone, which he'd left behind on a bedside table.

'No, you didn't.'

'Well, I'm telling you now,' he said as he checked his
messages. 'I… Oh, no!' he groaned. 'I don't believe it. Hell,
are they insane?'

CHAPTER TWENTY-THREE

'YOU DIDN'T HAVE to come with me,' Jeremy growled as he drove away from Hilltop Manor after breakfast the next morning. 'I could have picked you up on my way back. It's not as though I'll be staying there very long.'

Alice shot him a worried look. She'd never seen him like this, simmering away with a barely held fury, which she feared was about to explode. She didn't trust him to drive properly if she wasn't with him. And she certainly didn't trust him not to say unforgivable things to his parents.

Clearly, the news last night that they were back together again—with the full intention of remarrying once their respective divorces were finalised—did not sit well with Jeremy. After reading the message from his father, he'd thrown the phone down and begun pacing the room, enlightening Alice as to the situation in a painfully caustic tone, deriding both his parents as romantic fools if they thought this marriage would work any better than it had the first time round. Alice had been unable to make him calm down. Or to make him see sense.

'You can't control other people's lives,' she'd said to him at one stage. 'And who knows? Maybe it *will* work this time. Maybe they've always loved each other, underneath, but lost their way, as people do sometimes.'

He'd ground to an angry halt before spearing her with a savage look. 'If you honestly think that then you're as big a romantic fool as they are.'

That had hurt. It still hurt. But there was no use telling Jeremy that. He was hurting too, old tapes having risen to distress him to a degree that had shocked her. She hadn't realised till then just how badly his parents' initial divorce

had affected him. Silly of her when she'd studied abandonment issues and the emotional damage associated with
them. It confirmed her earlier opinion that Jeremy's becoming a playboy was a direct result of the misery he'd felt all
those years ago, his life motto being better not to love at
all if it didn't ever last.

Maybe she *was* a romantic fool for thinking that he
might have finally fallen in love. With her. But she did.
Alice glanced over at the bleak set of his face and wished
with all her heart that she could tell him that she loved him;
that she would never not love him.

But she didn't dare. Not right at this fraught moment.

'I want you to stay in the car when we get there,' came
his harsh edict. 'Like I said, I won't be long. Ten, fifteen
minutes max. Just long enough to tell them what I think
of this marriage. And of them. It's way past time that they
heard the unvarnished truth. Winston and Sebastian won't
dare in case they get cut out of the will. I don't give a damn
about Father's money. Frankly, I couldn't care less if I never
set eyes on either of them from this day forth.'

'That's the biggest load of old rubbish I've ever heard,'
Alice said with deceptive calm. As a counsellor she'd per-
fected sounding calm when sometimes she was anything
but.

'What?' he said, his head whipping round so he could
glower at her.

'You heard me, Jeremy. The reason you're so upset with
them is *because* you love them.'

'*Love* them?' he spat as he headed for an exit off the
main road. 'I don't love them. I *despise* them. Why, they'd
have to be the most selfish, shallow, superficial human
beings I have ever come across. They have no concept of
true caring, or commitment. They only had children as a
reflection of their own egos. At least they can't do that this
second time round. They're too damn old!'

With that pronouncement, he stopped the car briefly at

a Give Way sign before turning left and speeding down a narrow curving road. Alice held her breath as the tyres screeched on the first corner. Fortunately, this did make Jeremy slow down a little.

'If you despise them so much,' she said, still in that same calm tone, 'then why have you chosen to emulate them?'

'What in hell are you talking about, woman? I'm as different from them as I could possibly be.'

'Really? Before I met you, Jeremy, I was warned that you were selfish and shallow and superficial, with no concept of true caring and commitment.'

He stared over at her. And it was whilst he was staring over at her that a lorry pulled out of a hidden driveway on their left. Alice screamed out, Jeremy swearing and slamming his foot on the brake. The car went into a side slew, clipping the front of the lorry with a force that sent it catapulting into the air, his door ricocheting off the trunk of a tree before landing on its passenger side, in a ditch.

Thank God for airbags, Jeremy thought dazedly, then glanced over at Alice.

She was still and silent. *Too* still and silent, her pale face pressed against an airbag.

'Oh, God, *Alice*!' he cried out. 'Are you all right? Speak to me, Alice!'

She didn't speak. But she did make a slight moaning sound. Not dead, came the gut-wrenching realisation. Dear heaven, if she'd been dead he would not have wanted to live. But what if she still died? What if...?

Suddenly, someone was knocking on his broken window.

'Are you all right, mate?' the man shouted.

'Yes. But my girlfriend's unconscious. Call an ambulance, will you?'

'Will do.'

Jeremy tried to get out but his door was jammed. He

could do nothing but wait till the emergency services arrived. He tried not to think of what Alice had said to him just before the accident, but how could he not think about her final words? Because they were true. So true. Till he met her, that was. Meeting Alice changed him. Made him nicer, kinder, less selfish and shallow. He'd even started secretly wanting what Alex and Sergio had. True love. And marriage. Even children. Yes, children. Children he would cherish and never send away to damned boarding school.

But none of that would happen if Alice died.

Why in God's name hadn't he told her he loved her before this; that he wanted more than their just being friends and lovers? Anyone could see that she probably loved him. She hadn't said so because he'd told her that he didn't want her love.

Jeremy groaned as despair filled his soul.

In the end, he closed his eyes and prayed.

CHAPTER TWENTY-FOUR

'CAN I GET you something, Jeremy?' the middle-aged nurse asked kindly. 'Coffee perhaps?'

'What? Oh, no. No, thanks. I had some earlier.' He hadn't, but he didn't want to have to leave Alice's side to go to the bathroom. Not now when she might wake up at any moment. He'd allowed Madge to drag him away on other nights after the doctors told him that they were putting Alice in an induced coma for a few days after her surgery to alleviate the swelling in her brain. She'd hit her head on the roof of the car during the accident, causing a depressed fracture of her skull, fluid forming to protect the brain. Too much fluid, unfortunately.

She'd never been on the critical list, but no one could convince Jeremy she wasn't in imminent danger of dying. The thought that he might still lose her—and that it was all his own stupid fault—tortured his mind whenever he was away from her bedside. So he was always back first thing the next morning, sitting with Alice all day, the kindly staff bringing his drinks and food. He still lost weight, his eyes sinking into his head. For the first time in his life, Jeremy looked every day of his thirty-five years, and more.

He wasn't aware of how worried everyone was about him. His parents had been aghast at his appearance. So were his brothers. Marigold and her mother had been equally shocked when they'd visited each day, having driven to London and booked into a hotel close to the hospital. Madge, of course, had acted with her usual common sense, taking him in hand and insisting that he go home every night where she made him some hot chocolate before putting him to bed. She even laid out fresh clothes for him in the bathroom, having discovered that he'd lost interest in clothes and would have worn the same ones the next day if she'd left them there on the floor where he dropped them. Most days, he didn't even shave.

When she'd tried to take him home tonight, however, Jeremy had been firm in refusing, because this afternoon they'd stopped doing whatever it was they were doing to keep Alice asleep, informing Jeremy that she should start coming out of her coma within the next twenty-four hours.

'Why don't you go home and have a sleep?' the nurse continued. 'The doctor said Alice won't wake up till tomorrow morning at least.'

Jeremy glanced at the wall clock. It was five past twelve. 'Well, it *is* tomorrow morning,' he pointed out with a small smile. 'So I'll stay here, if you don't mind.'

Here was a green vinyl armchair in which he'd sat every day for the past six days, watching Alice lying there with tubes entering and exiting her body.

'I have to go do my rounds,' the nurse said gently. 'Just press the buzzer if you need anything or you notice any change.'

Jeremy nodded, glad to be left alone with Alice. He wanted to talk to her out loud, tell her things that he hoped she might hear. He'd read where people in comas could hear more than people realised. Drawing the armchair closer to the bed, he picked up her left hand and held it gently within both of his.

'You're going to wake up soon, Alice,' he murmured. 'And you're going to be all right.' He gulped at the memory of the doctors saying they didn't anticipate any brain damage. God help them if they were wrong. 'First of all I want to say how sorry I am for the way I acted that day. If I hadn't been so damn irrational and childish then none of this would have happened. But in a weird kind of way, maybe good can come out of something bad. I still wish this had never happened, but it made me realise, my dar-

ling, just how much I love you. I tried to convince myself
that I didn't, but it has been there for ages, in the back of
my mind. You're in love with Alice, that voice kept telling
me. You want to marry her. Can you imagine how Jeremy,
the perennial playboy, reacted to that? It was untenable.
Unthinkable! I took comfort in the fact that you said you
didn't want marriage either. I thought I was safe. But you
know what? I don't want to be safe any more. I would risk
anything and everything to be with you, Alice. To live
with you. Not as a lover but as your husband. I even want
to have children with you. Is that amazing or what? Alex
and Sergio are never going to believe it.'

The joy that dream evoked was quickly replaced by
worry. 'But none of that is going to happen if I'm wrong
and you don't love me back...'

Tears pricked at Jeremy's eyes at this most horrible
thought. For what if she *didn't* love him back? What if
he'd ruined everything with his stupidity and his insensi-
tivity, his selfishness and, yes, his shallow attitude to life
and love. He didn't deserve someone as wonderful as Alice;
didn't deserve her love. Why *would* she love him? He was
worse than his stupid parents. At least they were willing
to give their love a second chance, whereas he'd just run
away from it, like some coward.

Her fingers twitching against his sent Jeremy's eyes flying to her face. Was that a smile forming on her lips? Yes,
yes, it was a definite smile. Her eyelashes fluttered, then
slowly lifted, her gaze a little unfocused.

''Course I love you,' she croaked out before her eyelids
closed again.

Jeremy dropped her hand and jumped up, forgetting all
about the buzzer he was supposed to press and racing out
into the corridor like some kind of demented idiot.

'She's awake!' he shouted out to the empty corridor.
'She's awake and she loves me!'

No one answered him, or heard him, so he bolted back

into Alice's room, found the buzzer in the bed and pressed it. The nurse came quickly, frowning when she saw the patient was sound asleep.

'Yes, what is it?' she asked in slightly harried tones.

'She woke up,' Jeremy told her. 'She spoke to me.'

The nurse sighed. 'Well, she's gone back to sleep now. Look, I suggest you go home and do the same. Nothing is to be achieved by this all-night vigil, you know. Don't you want to be all rested when your fiancée wakes up properly later today?'

'My fiancée?' he repeated, having forgotten that that was what he'd said to gain unlimited access to Alice's room.

'Yes, your fiancée,' the nurse said, not unkindly but knowingly. 'Perhaps a shave would be in order as well.'

Jeremy rubbed his hand across his three-day growth. 'A shave. Yes. You're right. Can't let Alice see me looking like this.'

'Good man. Now off you go. The hospital will let you know if there's any sudden change.'

Jeremy hurried off, resolving to do everything right this time. He'd been given a second chance with Alice and he wasn't about to waste it. Or waste time. He didn't go home straight away. Instead, after making a very important phone call, he drove into the city where a somewhat bemused jeweller showed up eventually to open up his store in the dead of night.

'Are you sure that's the one you want?' the man asked after Jeremy had paid for his selection. 'We have rings with bigger diamonds.'

'Alice wouldn't want anything too big, or too showy.' Not that the ring was cheap. The diamond was flawless, which meant it was expensive.

'Well, you know her better than I do. So are congratulations in order, Jeremy? This is an engagement ring you've just bought, after all.'

'I certainly hope so,' he said. 'But Alice has been known to say no to me.'

'I doubt she'll say no to this. Now, I will expect an invitation to the wedding,' the jeweller said as he locked up the shop.

Jeremy raced home with his precious purchase in his pocket. An hour later, he was back in the green vinyl chair, showered, shaved and dressed in his favourite grey suit. The nurse lifted her eyebrows at him when she came in around five to check Alice's vital signs.

'Well, you look a lot better,' she said. 'Nice bright tie. But I suspect you haven't had any sleep.'

'I dozed in this chair for a while.'

'Not enough. Still, I guess I'd do the same if I were in your shoes. You love Alice a lot, don't you?'

'More than I can say.'

'How romantic. So when are you going to ask her to marry you for real?'

'The second she wakes up.'

The nurse nodded, smiled, then left the room.

An hour later, Alice stirred. Jeremy didn't ring the buzzer, just held Alice's hand and waited, struggling all the while to contain his emotions.

I must not cry, he told himself. *I must not cry.*

Very slowly, her eyes opened, and this time her gaze was clear.

'Jeremy,' she said, smiling a sweet smile at him.

Jeremy swallowed. *I must not cry*, he repeated valiantly.

'How long have I been asleep?' she asked him.

'Six days,' he told her. And six long nights.

'That long. Where am I exactly?'

'In London. They flew you to this hospital when it became obvious you needed specialist care.'

'I see...and am I all right?' she asked, fear clouding her eyes.

'You banged your head in the accident. Cracked your skull. But yes, you're going to be fine.'

'That's good.'

'Do you want me to call for the nurse? Or the doctor?'

'No. Not yet. You know, I have this hazy memory of you talking to me and my saying something to you. Was I dreaming or did I talk to you during the night?'

'You did say something,' he admitted.

'What did I say?'

'You said you loved me.'

'Ooh. Oh, I see. Sorry. I know you don't want to hear things like that.'

'Don't be sorry. And I *do* want to hear it. Because I love *you*, Alice. I love you so much.' Knowing that actions always spoke more loudly than words, he reached into his jacket pocket and pulled out the ring box. 'I love you and I want to marry you.' He fell to his knees beside the bed and opened the box, placing it on the bed next to her. 'Will you marry me, Alice?'

She stared at the ring, then at him, stunned.

'You really mean that, Jeremy? This isn't some guilty reaction from the accident?'

Jeremy's expression turned from desperate to wry. He'd told her before that he kept forgetting she'd studied psychology. 'No, my darling Alice, it's nothing like that. I admit the accident opened my eyes. The thought of losing you that day nearly killed me. But I was already wildly in love with you before then.'

'You were?'

'I was just too damned scared to face it. But I'm much more scared of living my life without you. So will you marry me, my darling?'

Alice tried not to cry. She didn't think Jeremy would want her to cry. She stared down at the lovely ring he'd chosen. It was exactly what she would have chosen herself.

'Of course I'll marry you,' she choked out, picking up the ring and slipping it onto her finger. It fitted perfectly. 'Thank you, Jeremy. You've made me so happy. I... I...' Alice broke off as the dam of emotion she'd been trying to control suddenly burst, tears flooding her eyes.

'Oh, my darling!' Jeremy exclaimed as he leapt up and hugged her, and in doing so accidentally pressed the buzzer. They were both still hugging each other when the nurse hurried back in.

'Well, I see I'll have to go get the doctor,' she said happily. 'Then I'll see if I can find some champagne!'

EPILOGUE

St Paul's Cathedral. Twelve months later.

IT WAS SATURDAY AFTERNOON, just after four p.m. The weather was warm, but not hot. No rain in sight. All the wedding guests were seated. The bridegroom and his two best men were waiting somewhat impatiently at the head of the aisle for the bride to arrive.

'Alex said to tell you that he's brought the gun,' Sergio whispered to Jeremy.

Jeremy's head jerked back as he turned and stared at his two best men. 'What in God's name are you talking about?'

'You said if you ever fell in love,' Alex elaborated, 'that I was to shoot you.'

Jeremy had to laugh, which brought a mock glare from Sergio. 'Have some decorum. You're about to be married. Marriage is serious business and not to be joked over.'

'You can say that again,' Jeremy returned. 'I'm a bundle of nerves.'

'Not having any second thoughts?' Alex asked cheekily.

'Hell, no. Frankly, I've never looked forward to something so much in all my life. If I'd had my way I would have been married months ago, but Alice wouldn't have a bar of it. She said she wanted to be a June bride, with all the trimmings. She wouldn't even agree to move in with me, said I had to wait till she was Mrs Jeremy Barker-Whittle for that privilege.'

'She's one strong-minded woman,' Sergio said. 'But then that's exactly what you needed, Jeremy. You were way too used to getting your own way with women.'

'That's what Alice always says. And Madge.'

'Who the hell is Madge?'

'My PA.'

Alex nodded. 'Well, we all have to keep an eye on you,' he said. 'Women seem to fall in love with you even when you don't do a damned thing. I was down at the back of the church a little while ago and there was a row of attractive young ladies sitting there, chattering away, the subject of their conversation being what did the bride have that they didn't have. All exes of yours, I gathered.'

Jeremy smiled. 'I could have told them.'

'Then tell us,' Sergio suggested. 'We have to talk about something, given how late the bride is.'

Jeremy thought for a long moment, then sighed. 'It's actually quite difficult to put into words. Alice is an enigma. A contradiction in terms. Not contrary. But she has two sides to her personality, both of which I love. She's fire and ice. Light and dark. She's not perfect by any means, but then who is? But she's perfect to me. I love her stubbornness and her fierce independence. I love her compassion, and her passion. But most of all I love the way she fell in love with me, despite knowing what I was. She looked past the shallow life that I'd been living and saw the decent man that I could become.'

'The man you *have* become, my friend,' Sergio said admiringly. 'Alex and I are very proud of you.'

'Amen to that,' Alex agreed. 'Hey, I think your paragon has finally arrived.'

Whatever else they might have said was drowned out by the sounds of Wagner's 'Bridal Chorus' bursting forth from the pipes of the massive grand organ St Paul's Cathedral was famous for. All the guests—and there were over two hundred of them—rose as one to watch the procession down the aisle.

Once the music started up, all of Alice's nerves fled. The moment had come. Soon she would become Mrs Jeremy

Barker-Whittle. He would be her husband for life. Oh, how she loved that man, never more so than when she told him last month that something must have gone wrong with her mini pill—its failure possibly due to a gastric attack—and she'd fallen pregnant. He hadn't been annoyed or disappointed or put out in any way. He'd been thrilled, reassuring her that he hadn't wanted to wait long to have a baby anyway. They hadn't said anything to anyone yet. It was still early days, but the test had been positive. Alice herself was over the moon. She hadn't wanted to wait, either. And it wasn't as though she'd be fat for her wedding. If anything her pregnancy had made her strapless bridal gown fit her even better, her breasts already larger, filling out the boned bodice in a rather provocative fashion. In fact, she thought she looked quite sexy.

Harriet and Bella looked sexy too, in their own strapless blue gowns, made in the palest blue chiffon and draped to suit their shapely figures. Both of them had their hair up, their stylish buns decorated with the same tiny white flowers that filled the posies they held. Alice's hair was up too, enhanced with an exquisite diamond tiara that had once belonged to Jeremy's gran and which he'd inherited many years before but had forgotten about. Alice's bridal veil was a froth of tulle that reached down her hips. She had opted not to have a face veil. She didn't like that idea much.

Alice watched as her two matrons of honour preceded her elegantly down the aisle, smiling at the memory of the wonderful holidays the six friends had already spent together. She and Jeremy along with Sergio and Bella had joined Alex and Harriet in Australia last Christmas, along with their two little boys. Jeremy's namesake was by then nine months old, with Bella's son, Alberto, a few months younger. They'd also spent Easter together at Sergio's villa on Lake Como. What a lovely stay that was. They'd promised each other not to let a year go by that they wouldn't meet up somewhere, preferably somewhere warm and relaxing. The thought pleased Alice that next time she'd have her own baby with her to be admired and photographed.

'Time for us to go, Alice,' her mother said as she hooked her arm through Alice's. Her mother was giving her away, since she didn't have a father to do the honours. 'But before we do, let me say how very beautiful you look today.'

'You too,' Alice replied. Her mother was wearing a slimming ice-green coat dress with a matching hat. 'Jeremy said the other night that you were a dish, and that it wouldn't be long before some lucky man whisked you off to the altar.'

'Oh, that man!' she said, but she was blushing just the same.

Mother and daughter began the slow walk down the very long aisle, the glorious music echoing in the vaulted ceiling above them. Alice smiled at all her wonderful guests, who were many and varied. Along with relatives she never knew she had, there were all of Jeremy's rather large family, people from work, plus lots of women whom she had helped. Finally, she saw Fiona and Alistair, who both beamed at her, Fiona patting her small baby bump to indicate that she was expecting. Marigold and Jarod were expecting as well—next month, actually—which was the main reason Marigold had chosen not to be in the bridal party. She was huge! Dickie called out loudly to Auntie Allie whilst he jumped up and down on the seat, till Jarod swept him up into his big strong arms and told him to hush.

Alice hugged her own good news to herself, thinking how happy everyone would be when she finally told them. At last, Harriet and Bella reached the end of the aisle and turned left to clear the way for Alice. It was then that she spied Jeremy, looking his usual resplendent self in the black dinner suit he'd worn the night she'd first seen him. Alice had refused to let him buy a new suit, saying he couldn't look any better to her than he had in that suit.

He did look a little nervous, the poor darling, she thought as she drew closer.

There's nothing to be nervous about, she telegraphed to him with her mind as her smile widened and her eyes sparkled.

Jeremy should not have been surprised at how beautiful Alice looked. She was already beautiful. But seeing her dressed as a bride, in that divine ivory dress with its tight satin bodice and *Gone with the Wind* skirt just blew him away. She seemed to glide down the aisle, her smile the smile of sheer happiness. Emotion welled up threateningly within him, but he controlled it. No way would Alice want him weeping at their wedding. She needed her man to be her rock, not some wishy-washy waterworks.

So he pasted a smile on his face and prayed for composure. But his hand still trembled when he took her hand in his.

'You're nervous,' Alice whispered.

'Terrified,' Jeremy agreed quietly.

'Don't worry, my darling. I'll look after you.'

The archbishop cleared his throat and the organ music immediately died down.

'We are gathered here today,' he began in a voice to rival Jeremy's, 'to join this man and this woman in holy matrimony...'

Madge wept silently in her pew. Ken put his arm around her shoulder. 'Would you like to get married, love?' he asked her gently.

Madge stared up at him, then nodded, her eyes awash.

'Good,' he said. 'So would I.'

Alice's baby was a girl. In keeping with the tradition of floral names for girls they called her Jasmine Rose. She was the apple of her daddy's eye, exquisitely beautiful and totally charming.

Jeremy knew that from the time she turned twelve he would not have another moment's peace.

* * * * *

THE ULTIMATE
PLAYBOY

MAYA BLAKE

To David and Peter. Life would be so much duller without you two!

CHAPTER ONE

New York

NARCISO VALENTINO STARED at the box that had been delivered to him. It was large, made with the finest expensive leather, trimmed with velvet rope, with a horseshoe-shaped clasp made of solid twenty-four-carat gold.

Normally, the sight of it brought anticipation and pleasure.

But the ennui that had invited itself for a long-term stay in his life since he'd turned thirty last month leached excitement from him as the stock market leaked money after a juicy disaster.

Lucia had accused him of turning into a boring old man right before her diva exit out of his life two weeks ago.

He allowed himself a little grin of relief. He'd celebrated her departure with a boys' weekend ski trip to Aspen where he'd treated himself to a little palate cleanser in the form of a very enthusiastic Norwegian ski instructor.

But much too quickly, the jaded hollowness had returned.

Rising from his desk, he strode to the window of his seventieth-floor Wall Street office and stared at the New York skyline. Satisfaction eased through him at the thought that he owned a huge chunk of this city.

Money was sexy. Money was power. And The Warlock of Wall Street—as the newspapers had taken to calling him—never denied himself the pull of power and sex.

The opportunity to experience two of his favourite things lay within the package on his desk.

Yet it'd remained unopened for the last hour...

Shrugging off the lethargy, he returned briskly to his desk and flipped the clasp.

The half mask staring up at him from a bed of black satin was exquisite. Pure silver edged with black onyx and Swarovski crystals, its intricate design and flawless detail announced the care and attention that had gone into creating it. Narciso appreciated care and attention. It was what had made him a millionaire by eighteen and a multibillionaire by twenty-five.

His vast wealth was also what had gained him admission into *Q Virtus,* the world's most exclusive gentlemen's club, whose quarterly caucus invitation was the reason for the mask. Two four-inch-long diamond-tipped pins held the mask in place. Pulling them out, he flipped it over to examine the soft, velvet underside, which held the security microchip, his moniker—The Warlock—and the venue, *Q Virtus,* Macau. He ran his thumb over the smooth surface, hoping to summon a little enthusiasm. Failing miserably, he set the mask down and glanced at the second item in the box.

The List.

Zeus, the anonymous head of *Q Virtus,* always provided club members with a discreet list of business interests who would be attending the caucuses. Narciso had chosen not to attend the last two because he'd already dealt with those lists' major players.

His gaze skimmed the heavily embossed paper and his breath caught. Excitement of a different, dangerous kind sizzled through him as the fourth name jumped out at him.

Giacomo Valentino—*Daddy dearest.*

He perused the other names to see if anyone else on the list would make his attendance worthwhile.

His lips twisted. Who the hell was he kidding?

One name and one name only had become *the* deciding factor. There were one or two business interests worth cultivating during the two-day event, but Giacomo was who he intended to interact with.

Although perhaps *interact* was the wrong word.

Setting the list down, he fired up his computer. Entering the security codes, he pulled up the file he kept on his father.

The report his private investigator updated on a regular basis showed that the old man had rallied a little from the blow Narciso had dealt him three months ago.

Rallied but not fully recovered. Within minutes, Narciso was fully up to speed on his father's latest business dealings.

He didn't fool himself into thinking it gave him any sort of upper hand. He knew his father kept a similar file on him. But the game wouldn't have been this interesting if advantages had been one-sided. Nevertheless Narciso gained a lot of satisfaction from knowing he'd won three of their last four skirmishes.

He was contemplating the latest approach to his annihilation campaign when his phone buzzed.

Allowing the distraction, he thumbed the interactive surface and read the message from Nicandro Carvalho, the closest thing he had to a best friend.

Still caught in premature midlife-crisis mode, or are you ready to shake off that clinging BOM image?

Boring old man. A corner of his mouth lifted as his gaze slid to the list and his father's name. Suddenly energised, he whipped back a response.

BOM has left the building. Care to get your ass whopped at poker?

Nicandro's response—Dream on but bring it on—made him laugh for the first time in weeks.

Powering down his laptop, he slammed it shut. His gaze once again fell on the mask. Picking it up, he stashed it in his safe and shrugged into his suit jacket.

Zeus would receive his RSVP in the morning, once he'd devised exactly how he was going to take his father down once and for all.

The internet was a scary place. But it was an invaluable tool if you wanted to hunt down a slippery son of a bitch.

Ruby Trevelli sat cross-legged on her sofa and stared at the blinking cursor awaiting her command. That she was reduced to online trawling for a solution to her problem spiked equal measures of irritation and frustration through her.

She'd made it a point to avoid anything to do with social media. The one time she'd foolishly typed her name into a search engine, the sheer volume of false information she'd discovered had scared her into never trying again.

Of course, she'd also found enough about her parents to have scarred her for life if she hadn't already been scarred.

Tonight, she had no choice. Because despite thousands of pages featuring Narciso Media Corporation, every effort to speak to someone who could help her had been met with a solid stone wall. She'd already wasted a solid hour discovering that a thirty-year-old billionaire named Narciso Valentino owned NMC.

She snorted under her breath. Who on earth named their child *Narciso* anyway? That was like inviting bullies and snark-mongers to feast on the poor child. On the flip side, his unique name had eased her search.

Sucking in a breath, she typed in her next request: *Narciso's New York hangouts.* There were over two million entries. Awesome.

Either there were millions of men out there named Narciso or the man she sought was indecently popular.

Offering up a Hail Mary, she clicked the first link. And nearly gagged at the graphic burlesque images that popped up.

Hell no!

She closed it and sat back, fighting the rising nausea.

Desperate was fast becoming her middle name but Ruby

refused to accept that the answers to her woeful financial predicament would be found in a skin den.

Biting her inside lip, she exhaled and typed again: *Where's Narciso Valentino tonight?*

Her breath caught as the search engine fired back a quick response. The first linked the domain of a popular tabloid newspaper—one she'd become rudely acquainted with when she'd received her first laptop at ten, logged on and seen her parents splashed over the home page. In the fourteen years since then, she'd avoided the tabloid, just as she avoided her parents nowadays.

Ignoring the ache in her chest, she clicked on the next link that connected to a location app.

For several seconds, she couldn't believe how easily she'd found him. She read the extensive list of celebrities who'd announced their whereabouts freely, including one attending a movie premiere right now in Times Square.

Grabbing the remote, she flipped the TV channel to the entertainment news station, and, sure enough, the movie star was flashing a million-dollar smile at his adoring fans.

She glanced back at the location next to Narciso Valentino's name.

Riga—a Cuban-Mexican nightclub in the Flatiron District in Manhattan.

Glancing at the clock above the TV, she made a quick calculation. If she hurried, she could be there in under an hour. Her heart hammered as she contemplated what she was about to do.

She despised confrontation almost as much as her parents thrived on it. But after weeks of trying to find a solution, she'd reached the end of her tether.

She'd won the NMC reality TV show and scraped together every last cent to come up with her half of the hundred-thousand-dollar capital needed to get her restaurant—Dolce Italia—up and running.

Any help she could've expected from Simon Whittaker, her

ex-business partner and owner of twenty-five per cent of Dolce Italia, was now a thing of the past.

She clenched her fist as she recalled their last confrontation.

Finding out that the man she'd developed feelings for was married with a baby on the way had been shock enough. Simon trying to talk her into sleeping with him despite his marital status had killed any emotion she'd ever had for him.

He'd sneered at her wounded reaction to his intended infidelity. But having witnessed it up close with gut-wrenching frequency in her parents' marriage, she was well versed in its consequences.

Cutting Simon out of her life once she'd seen his true colours had been a painful but necessary decision.

Of course, without his business acumen she'd had to take full financial responsibility of Dolce Italia. Hence her search for Narciso Valentino. She needed him to stand by his company's promise. A contract was a contract....

A gleaming black limo was pulling up as she rounded the corner of the block that housed the nightclub. The journey had taken an extra half-hour because of a late-running train. Wincing at the pinch of her high heels on the uneven pavestones, she hurried towards Riga's red-bricked façade.

She was navigating her way around puddles left by the recent April shower, when deep male laughter snagged her attention.

A burly bouncer held open the velvet rope cordon as two men, both over six feet tall, exited the VIP entrance in the company of two strikingly beautiful women. The first man was arresting enough to warrant a second look but it was the other man who commanded Ruby's interest.

Jet-black hair had been styled to slant over the right side of his forehead in a silky wave that flowed back to curl over his collar.

Her steps faltered as the power of his presence slammed into her, and knocked air out of her lungs. His aura sent a challenge to the world, dared it to do its worst.

Dazed, she documented his profile—winged eyebrow, beautifully sculpted cheekbone, a straight patrician nose and a curved mouth that promised decadent pleasure—or what she imagined decadent pleasure looked like. But his mouth promised it and, well, this guy looked as if he could deliver on whatever sensual promises he made.

'Hey, miss. You coming in any time this century?'

The bouncer's voice distracted her, but not for long enough to completely pull her attention away. When she looked back, the man was turning away but it wasn't before Ruby caught another quick glimpse of his breathtaking profile.

Her gaze dropped lower. His dark grey shirt worn under a clearly bespoke jacket was open at the collar, allowing a glimpse of a bronzed throat and mouth-watering upper chest.

Ruby inhaled sharply and pulled her coat tighter around her as if that could stem the heat rushing like a breached dam through her.

The drop-dead gorgeous blonde smiled his way. His hand dropped from her waist to her bottom, drifted over one cheek to cup it in a bold squeeze before he helped her into the car. The first man shouted a query, and the group turned away from Ruby. Just like that, the strangely intimate and disturbing link was broken.

Her insides sagged and she realised how tight a grip she'd held on herself.

Even after the limo swung into traffic, Ruby couldn't move, nor could she stem the tingling suspicion that she'd arrived too late.

The bouncer cleared his throat conspicuously. She turned. 'Can you tell me who that second guy was who just got into that limo?' she asked.

He raised one *are-you-serious?* eyebrow.

Ruby shook her still-dazed head and smiled at the bouncer. 'Of course you can't tell me. Bouncer-billionaire confidentiality, right?'

His slow grin gentled his intimidating stature. 'Got it in one. Now, you coming in or you just jaywalking?'

'I'm coming in.' Although the strong suspicion that she'd missed Narciso Valentino grew by the second.

'Great. Here you go.' The bouncer placed a Mayan-mask-shaped stamp on her wrist, glanced up at her, then added another stamp. 'Show it at the bar. It'll get you your first drink on the house.' He winked.

She smiled in relief as she entered the smoky interior. If her guess had been wrong and she hadn't just missed Narciso Valentino, she could nurse an expensive drink while searching him out.

She'd worked in clubs like these all through college and knew how expensive even the cheapest drinks were. Which was why she clutched an almost warm virgin Tiffany Blue an hour later as she accepted that Narciso Valentino *was* the man she'd seen outside.

Resigned to her fruitless journey, she downed the last of her drink and was looking for a place to set the glass down when the voices caught her attention.

'Are you sure?'

'Of course I am. Narciso will be there.'

Ruby froze, then glanced into one of the many roped-off VIP areas. Two women dripping in expensive jewellery and designer dresses that would cost her a full year's salary sat sipping champagne.

Unease at her shameless eavesdropping almost forced her away but desperation held her in place.

'How do you know? He didn't attend the last two events.' The blonde looked decidedly pouty at that outcome.

'I told you, I overheard the guy he was with this evening talking about it. They're both going this time. If I can get a job as a *Petit Q* hostess, this could be my chance,' her red-headed friend replied.

'What? To dress in a clown costume in the hope of catching his eye?'

'Stranger things have happened.'

'Well, hell will freeze over before I do that to hook a guy,' the blonde huffed.

Statuesque Redhead's lips pursed. 'Don't knock it till you try it. It pays extremely well. And if Narciso Valentino falls in my lap, well, let's just say I won't let that life-changing opportunity pass me by.'

'Okay, you have my attention. Give me the name of the website. And where the hell is Macau anyway?' the blonde asked.

'Umm…Europe, I think?'

Ruby barely suppressed a snort. Heart thumping, she took her phone from her tiny clutch and keyed in the website address.

An hour and a half later, she sent another Hail Mary and pressed send on the online forms she'd filled out on her return home.

It might come to nothing. She could fail whatever test or interview she had to pass to get this gig. Heck, after discovering that she was applying to hostess for *Q Virtus,* one of the world's most exclusive and secretive private clubs, she wondered if she didn't need her head examined. She could be wasting money and precious time chasing an elusive man. But she had to try. Each day she waited was another day her goal slipped from her fingers.

The alternative—bowing to the pressure from her mother to join the family business—was unthinkable. At best she would once again become the pawn her parents used to antagonise each other. At worst, they would try and drag her down into their celebrity-hungry lifestyle.

They'd made her childhood a living hell. And she only had to pass a billboard in New York City to see they were still making each other's lives just as miserable but taking pleasure in documenting the whole thing for the world to feast on.

The Ricardo & Paloma Trevelli Show was prime-time viewing. The fly-on-the-wall documentary had been running for as long as Ruby could remember.

When she was growing up, her daily routine had included

at least two sets of camera crews documenting her every move along with her parents'.

TV crews had become extended family members. For a very short time when it'd made her the most popular girl at school, she'd told herself she was okay with it.

Until her father's affairs began. His very public admission of infidelity when she was nine years old had made ratings soar. Her mother publicly admitting her heartbreak had made worldwide news. Almost overnight, the TV show had been syndicated worldwide and brought her parents even more notoriety.

The subsequent reunion and vow renewal had thrilled the world.

After her father's second admission of infidelity, millions of viewers had been given the opportunity to weigh in on the outcome of Ruby's life.

Strangers had accosted her on the street, alternatively pitying and shaming her for being a Trevelli.

Escaping to college at the opposite end of the country had been a blessing. But even then she hadn't been able to avoid her roots.

It'd quickly become apparent that she had no other talent than cooking.

The realisation that the Trevelli gene was truly stamped into her DNA was a deep fear she secretly harboured. It was the reason she'd cut Simon out of her life without a backward glance. It was also the reason she'd vowed never to let her parents influence her life.

Which was why she needed a ten-minute conversation with Narciso Valentino. A tingle of awareness shot through her as she replayed the scene outside Riga.

With a spiky foreboding, she recalled the dark, dangerously sensual waves vibrating off him; those bronzed, sure fingers drifting over the blonde's bottom, causing unwelcome heat to drag through Ruby's belly.

God, what was she doing lying in bed thinking of some stranger's hand on his girlfriend's ass?

She punched her pillow into shape and flipped off her bed-side lamp. She couldn't control the future but she could control the choice between mooning over elegant hands that looked as if they could bring a woman great pleasure or getting a good night's sleep.

She was almost asleep when her phone pinged an incoming message.

Exhaling in frustration, she grabbed the phone.

The brightness in the dark room hurt her eyes, but, even half blinded, Ruby could see the words clearly. Her CV had impressed the powers that be.

She'd been granted an interview to become a *Petit Q*.

CHAPTER TWO

Macau, China, One Week Later

THE RED FLOOR-LENGTH gown sat a little too snugly against Ruby's skin, and the off-the-shoulder design exposed more cleavage and general flesh than she was comfortable with. But after two gruelling interviews, one of which she'd almost blown by turning up late due to another delayed train, the last thing she could complain about was the expensive designer outfit that spelt her out as a *Petit Q*.

She was careful now to avoid it getting snagged on her heels as she walked across the marble floor of her hotel towards the meeting place, from where they'd be chauffeured to their final destination. In her small case were two carefully folded, equally expensive outfits the management had provided.

An examination had shown that they, too, like the dress she wore, would be tight...everywhere. It was clear that someone, somewhere in the management food chain had got her measurements very wrong.

She'd already attracted the attention of an aging rock star in the lift on the way to the ground floor of her Macau hotel. It didn't matter that he'd seemed half blind when he'd leered at her; attracting *any* attention at all made her stomach knot with acid anxiety.

She'd let her guard down with Simon, had believed his interest to be pure and genuine, only to discover he wanted nothing more than a bit on the side. The idea that he'd assumed because she was a Trevelli she would condone his indecent proposal, just as her mother continued to accept her father's, had shredded the self-esteem she'd fought so hard to attain when she'd removed herself from her parents' sphere.

She wasn't a coward, but the fear that she might never be able to judge another man's true character sent a cold shiver through her.

Pushing the thought away, she straightened her shoulders, but another troubling thought immediately took its place.

What if she'd made a huge mistake in coming here?

What if Narciso didn't show? What if he showed and she missed him again?

No, she had to find him. Especially in light of the phone call she'd received the morning after she'd signed on to be a *Petit Q*.

The voice had been calm but menacing. Simon had sold his twenty-five-per-cent share of her business to a third party. 'We will be in touch shortly about interest and payment terms,' the accented voice had warned.

'I won't be able to discuss any payment terms until the business is up and running,' she'd replied, her hands growing clammy as anxiety dredged her stomach.

'Then it is in your interest to make that happen sooner rather than later, Miss Trevelli.'

The line had gone dead before she could say anything more. For a moment, she'd believed she'd dreamt the whole thing, but she'd lived in New York long enough to know loan sharks were a real and credible threat. And Simon had sold his share in her business to one of them.

Panicked and angry with Simon, she'd been halfway across the Indian Ocean before she'd read her *Petit Q* guidelines and experienced a bolt of shock.

No doubt to protect its ultra-urban-legend status, the *Q Virtus* Macau caucus was to be a masked event at a secret location in Macau.

Masked, as in *incognito.* Where the chances of picking out Narciso Valentino would be hugely diminished.

The memory of broad shoulders and elegant fingers flashed across her mind. Yeah, sure, as if she were an expert in male shoulders enough to distinguish one from the other.

Her fingers clenched around her tiny red clutch. She'd come all this way. She refused to admit defeat.

The redhead from Riga turned towards her and Ruby fought not to grit her teeth as the other woman dismissed her instantly.

As the door to the Humvee limo slid shut behind them another jagged stab of warning pierced her. Every cell in her body screamed at her to abandon this line of pursuit and hightail it back home.

She could use the app to find out when Narciso returned to New York. She could confront him on home turf where she was more at ease, not here in this sultry, exotic part of the world where the very air held a touch of opulent magic.

But what if this was her last chance? A man who would fly thousands of miles for a highly secretive event could disappear just as easily given half a chance. She'd been lucky to be in the right place to find out where he'd be at this point in time.

Fate had handed her the opportunity. She wasn't going to blow it.

The limo hit a bump, bringing her back to reality.

Despite the glitzy lights and Vegas-style atmosphere, the tiny island of Macau held a charisma and steeped-in-history feel that had spilled over from mainland China. She held her breath as they crossed over the Lotus Bridge into Cotai, their final destination.

Bicycles raced alongside sports cars and nineteen-fifties buses in a spectacular blend of ancient and modern.

Less than ten minutes later, they rolled to a stop. Exiting, she looked around and her trepidation escalated. The underground car park was well lit enough to showcase top-of-the-line luxury sports cars and blinged-out four-by-fours next to stretch limos.

The net worth in the car park alone was enough to fund the annual gross domestic product of a small country.

The buzz of excitement in her group fractured her thoughts and she hurried forward into waiting lifts. Like her, the other nineteen hostesses were dressed in red gowns for the first evening, and the ten male hosts dressed in red jackets.

Six bodyguards accompanied them into the lifts and Ruby stemmed the urge to bolt as the doors started to close. Five seconds later it was too late.

The doors opened to gleaming parquet floors with red and gold welcoming carpet running through the middle of the vast, suspended foyer.

On the walls, exquisite tapestries of dragons flirting with maidens were embellished with multihued glass beads. Red and gold Chinese-silk cloth hung in swathes from the tapered ceiling to the floor, discreetly blacking out the outside world.

Two winged staircases led to the floor below where a sunken section in the middle had been divided into twelve gaming tables, each with its own private bar and seating area.

All around her, masked men in bespoke tuxedos mingled with exquisitely clad women dripping with stunning jewellery that complemented their breathtaking masks. Granted, the number of women was marginally less than men, but from the way they carried themselves Ruby suspected these women wielded more than enough power to hold their own against their male counterparts.

A tall, masked, jet-haired woman wearing a sophisticated-looking earpiece glided forward and introduced herself as Head Hostess. In succinct tones, she briefed them on their roles.

Ruby tried to calm her jangling nerves as she descended the stairs and headed for the bar of the fourth poker table.

A bar she could handle.

Nevertheless, she held her breath as the first group of men took their places at the table. They all wore masks in varying degrees of camouflage and design. As she mixed her first round of drinks and delivered it to the table, Ruby tried to glean if any of them resembled her quarry.

One by one, she dismissed them. Eventually, they drifted off and another group took their place.

A grey-haired man—the oldest in her group—immediately drew her attention. He carried himself with command and control, but he was too old to be Narciso Valentino and his frame was slightly stooped with age.

He snapped his fingers and threw out an order for a glass of Sicilian red. Ruby pursed her lips and admonished herself not to react to the rudeness. Five men took their places around the table, leaving only one other space to be filled.

Safely behind the bar after delivering their drinks order, she watched their bets grow larger and bolder.

Music pumped from discreet loud speakers, and through a set of double doors guests took to the dance floor. It wasn't deafening by any means but Ruby felt the pulse of the provocative music through the soles of her feet.

She swallowed down the mingled distaste and latent fear as she noticed things were beginning to get hot and heavy as guests began to loosen their inhibitions.

She could do this. Just because she was a Trevelli didn't mean she would lose sight of her goals. Decadence and excess were her parents' thing. They needn't be hers…

The lights overhead dimmed.

A door to one side of the lift labelled The Black Room swung open and two men stepped onto the gangway.

One wore a gold half-mask that covered him from forehead to nose. The aura of power that radiated from him raised the very temperature of the room.

But the moment Ruby's eyes encountered the second man, her belly clenched.

The head hostess drifted towards him but he raised a hand and waved her away. At the sight of those slim fingers, recognition slammed into her. She watched, dry-mouthed, as he sauntered down the steps and headed for her side of the room.

He stopped in front of her bar.

Silver eyes bore into hers, drilling down hard as if he wanted to know her every last secret. The smile slowly left his face as he continued to stare at her, one eyebrow gradually lifting in silent query.

His silver and black onyx mask was artistically and visually stunning. It revealed his forehead and the lower part of his face and against its brilliance his olive skin glowed in a way that made her want to touch that chiselled jaw.

Piercing eyes drifted over her in a lazy sweep, pausing for a long second at her breasts. Her breath hitched in her throat as her body reacted to his probing gaze.

Narciso Valentino. If she'd had two dollars to rub together she'd have bet on it.

Her mouth dried as she looked into his eyes and lost every last sensible thought in her head.

'Serve me, *cara mia*. I'm dying of thirst.' His voice was raw, unadulterated sin, oozing what Ruby could only conclude was sex appeal.

At least she thought so because the sound of it had transmitted a tingling to parts of her body she hadn't known could tingle just from hearing a man's voice. And why on earth had her hands grown so clammy?

When his brow arched higher at her inactivity, she scrambled to think straight. 'W-what would you like?'

His eyes moved down again, paused at her throat, where her pulse jumped like a frenzied rabbit.

'Surprise me.'

He turned abruptly and all signs of mirth leached from his face.

Across the small space between the bar and the poker table, he speared the silver-haired man with an unforgiving gaze.

The man stared back, the part of his face visible beneath his mask taut despite his whole body bristling with disdain.

Animosity arced through the air, snapping coils of dangerous electricity that made Ruby's pulse leap higher. Her gaze slid back to the younger man as if drawn by magnets. She told herself she was trying to decipher what sort of drink to make him but, encountering those broad shoulders again, her mind drifted into impure territory, as it had outside the nightclub in New York.

Focus!

The older man had requested a Sicilian red but instinctively she didn't think the man she'd concluded was Narciso would go for wine.

Casting her gaze over the bottles of spirits and liqueurs, she quickly measured the required shots, mixed a cocktail and placed it on a tray.

Willing her fingers not to shake, she approached the poker table and placed his drink at his elbow.

He dragged his gaze from the older man long enough to glance from the pale golden drink to her face. 'What is this?' he asked.

'It's a...*Macau Bombshell*,' she blurted out the name she'd come up with seconds ago.

One smooth brow spiked as he leaned back in his seat. 'Bombshell?' Once again, his gaze drifted over her, lingered at the place where her dress parted mid-thigh in a long slit. 'Would you place yourself in that category, too? Because you certainly have the potential.'

Right, so really he was one of those. A Playboy with a capital *P*.

A man who saw something he coveted and went for it, regardless of who got hurt. The clear image of his hand on another woman made her spine stiffen in negative reaction, even as a tiny part of her acknowledged her disappointment.

Irritated with herself, she pushed the feeling away.

Now she knew what sort of man she was dealing with, things would proceed much smoother.

'No, I wouldn't,' she said briskly. 'It's all about the drink.'

'I've never heard such a name.'

'It's my own creation.'

'Ah.' He sipped the champagne, falernum, lemon and pineapple mix. Then he slowly tasted the cocktail without taking his eyes off her. 'I like it. Bring me one every half-hour on the button until I say otherwise.'

The implication that she could be here for hours caused her teeth to grind. She looked from the dealer to the other players at the table, wondered if she could ask to speak to Narciso privately now.

'Is there a problem?' he queried.

She cleared her throat. 'Well, yes. There are no clocks in this place and I don't have a watch, so...'

The silver-haired man swore under his breath and moved his shoulders in a blatantly aggressive move.

'Hold out your hand,' Narciso said.

Ruby's eyes widened. 'Excuse me?'

'Give me your hand,' he commanded.

She found herself obeying before she could think not to. He removed an extremely expensive and high-tech-looking watch from his wrist and placed it on her right wrist. The chain link was too large for her but it didn't mask the warmth from his skin and something jagged and electric sliced through her belly.

When his hand drifted along the inside of her wrist, she bit back a gasp, and snatched her hand back.

'Now you know when I'll next need you.'

'By all means, keep me waiting as you try out your tired pick-up lines,' the older man snapped with an accent she vaguely recognised.

Silver Eyes shifted his gaze to him. And although he continued to sip his cocktail, the air once again snapped with dark animosity.

'Ready for another lesson, old man?'

'If it involves teaching you to respect your betters, then I'm all for it.'

The resulting low laugh from the man next to her sent a shiver dancing over her skin. On decidedly wobbly legs, she retreated behind the bar and forced herself to regulate her breathing.

Whatever she'd experienced when those mesmerising eyes had locked into hers and those long fingers had stroked her was a false reaction. She refused to trust any emotion that could lead her astray.

Focus!

She glanced down at the watch. The timepiece was truly exquisite, a brand she'd heard of and knew was worth a fortune.

Unable to stop herself, she skated her fingers over it, her pulse thundering all over again when she remembered how he'd looked at her before slipping the watch on her wrist. She shifted as heat dragged through her and arrowed straight between her legs.

No!

She wasn't a slave to her emotions like her parents. And she wasn't the gullible fool Simon had accused her of being.

She had a goal and a purpose. One she intended to stick to.

Exactly half an hour later, she approached, willing her gaze not to trace those magnificent shoulders. Up close they were even broader, more imposing. When he shifted in his seat, they moved with a mesmerising fluidity that made her want to stop and gawp.

Keeping her gaze fixed on the red velvet table, she quickly deposited his drink on the designated coaster and picked up his almost-empty one. He flicked a glance at her.

'Grazie.'

The sound of her mother tongue on his lips flipped her stomach with unwanted excitement. She told herself it was because she was one step further to confirming his identity but Ruby suspected it was the sheer sexiness of his voice that was the bigger factor here.

'Prego,' she responded automatically before she could stop herself. She bit her lip and watched him follow the movement. A deeply predatory gleam entered his eyes.

'I want the next one in fifteen minutes.' His gaze returned

to his opponent, who looked a little paler since the last round of drinks. 'I have a feeling I'll be done by then. Unless you want to quit while you're behind?' he asked, sensual lips parted in a frightening imitation of a smile.

The older man let out a pithy response that Ruby didn't quite catch. Two players quickly folded their cards and left.

The two men eyeballed each other, pure hatred blazing as they psychologically circled one another.

Narciso laid down his cards in a slow, unhurried flourish. His opponent followed suit with a move that was eerily similar and made Ruby frown. The connection between the two men was unmistakable but she couldn't quite pin down why.

When the older man laughed, Ruby glanced down at his cards. She didn't know the rules of poker, but even she guessed his cards were significant.

She held her breath. Not with so much as a twitch did Narciso indicate he'd just lost millions of dollars.

'Give it up, old man.'

'Mai!' Never.

Ten minutes later, Narciso calmly laid down another set of cards that won him the next game. Hearing Giacomo's grunt of disbelief was extremely satisfactory. But it was the indrawn breath of surprise from the woman next to him that drew his attention.

He didn't let himself glance at her yet. She'd proven a seriously delicious distraction already. He had plans for her but those plans would have to wait a while longer.

For now, he revelled in Giacomo's defeat and watched a trickle of sweat drip down his temple.

They were barely an hour in and he'd already divested him of several million dollars. As usual, Giacomo had been lured in by the promise of trouncing his son, enabling Narciso to lay the bait he knew wouldn't be resisted.

The last game had won him a midsize radio station in Anaheim, California.

It would be a superb addition to his already sizeable news

and social media portfolio. Or he could shut it down and declare it a loss.

It didn't matter either way.

What mattered was that he had Giacomo's financial demise within his grasp. How very fitting that he should be in the perfect place to celebrate once he'd hammered the last nail into the coffin.

His gaze flickered to the stunning woman in red who regarded him with a touch of wariness and a whole lot of undisguised interest.

The silky cognac-coloured hair begged to be messed with, as did that sinful, pouting mouth she insisted on mauling every time he won a hand.

But her body, *Dio!* Her dress was a little too tight, sure, but even the fact that it made her assets a little too in your face didn't detract from the fact that she was a magnificent creature.

A magnificent creature he would possess tonight. She would be the cherry on his cake, one he would take the utmost pleasure in savouring before he devoured.

But first…

'Do you yield?' he asked silkily, already anticipating the response. In some ways they were so very similar. Which wasn't surprising considering they were father and son.

Although a father and son who detested the very ground each other walked on put an interesting twist on their *relationship*.

'Over my dead body.' Giacomo snapped his fingers at the dealer and threw his last five-million-dollar platinum chip in the middle of the table.

Beside him, his hostess's mouth dropped open. The sight of her pink tongue sent a spike of excitement through his groin.

*Sì…*he would celebrate well tonight. For a while there, he'd begun to suspect that beating Giacomo would be his only source of entertainment in Macau. Which was why he'd sought the old man out instead of leaving him to squirm a little longer. He'd wanted to be done and out of here as soon as possible.

The other deals he'd come to negotiate had taken the necessary leap forward and he'd believed there was nothing left.

But now…

His groin hardened as he watched her mouth slowly press shut and her eyes dart to his with the same anticipated excitement that flowed within him.

He let his interest show, let her see the promise of what was to come.

Heat flared up her delicate neck and flawless skin into a surprisingly innocent face that could've graced a priceless painting.

Dio, she was truly entrancing. And yet she was in a place like this, where the likelihood of being hit on, or more, was very real.

He gave a mental shrug. He'd stopped trying to reason why people took the actions they took well before he'd grown out of long socks.

Otherwise he'd have driven himself mad from trying to decipher why the father whose DNA flowed through his veins seemed to hate every single breath he took.

Or why Maria's betrayal still had the power to burn an acid path in his gut—

No.

That train had long left the station. Giving it thinking room was a waste of time and his time was extremely precious.

Keeping his eyes on his hostess, he downed his drink and held out his empty glass.

'I'm thirsty again, *amante.*'

With a nod, she sashayed away in her too-tight dress and returned minutes later with his drink.

When she started to move away, he snagged a hand around her waist. The touch of warm, silk-covered flesh beneath his fingers short-circuited his brain for a few moments. Then he realised she was trying to get away from him.

'Stay. You bring me luck when you're near.'

'Shame you need a woman to win,' Giacomo sneered.

Narciso ignored him and nodded to the dealer. He wanted this game to be over so he could pull this magical being tighter into his arms, feel her melt against him, his prize for emerging triumphant.

Giacomo threw his chip defiantly into the fray. Narciso's chest tightened with the anger that never quite went away. For as long as he remembered, his father had treated him like that chip—inconsequential, easily cast aside. Underneath all the anger and bitterness, a wound he'd thought healed cracked open.

Ignoring it, he calmly plucked his cards from the table.

'Let's up the stakes.'

Eyes that had once been similar to his own but had grown dimmer with age snapped at him. 'You think you have something I want?'

'I *know* I do. That tech company you lost to me last month? If I lose this hand, I'll return it to you, along with all of this.' He nodded to the pile of chips in front of him, easily totalling over thirty million dollars.

'And if I lose?' His voice held a false confidence Narciso almost smiled at. *Almost*.

'You hand over the other five-million chip I know is in your pocket and I'll let you keep your latest Silicon Valley start up.'

Giacomo sneered but Narciso could see him weighing up the odds. Thirty million against ten.

He waited, let the seductive scent of his hostess's perfume wash over him. Unable to resist, he slid his hand lower. The faintest sensation of a thong made his groin tighten. Again, she tried to move away. He pulled her back towards him and heard her breath catch.

'My offer expires in ten seconds,' he pressed.

Giacomo reached into his tuxedo pocket and tossed the second chip onto the table. Then he laid out cards in a flourish.

Four of a kind.

Narciso didn't need to glance down at his own cards to know *he'd* won.

And yet…the triumph he should've experienced was oddly missing. Instead, hollowness throbbed dully in his chest.

'Come on, then, you coward. It's your turn to answer this—do you yield?'

Narciso breathed in deep and fought the tight vice crushing his chest. Slowly, the hollowness receded and anger rushed into its place. 'Yes, I yield.'

His father's bark of victorious laughter drew attention from other tables but Narciso didn't care.

His hand was tightening over her waist, anticipation of a different sort firing his body. He was about to turn towards her when Giacomo reached for the cards Narciso had discarded.

A straight flush. A winning hand more powerful than his father's.

The evidence that he'd been toyed with registered in Giacomo's shocked eyes. *'Il diavolo!'* He lunged across the table, his whole body vibrating with fury.

Narciso stood, his eyes devoid of expression. '*Sì*, I am the devil *you* spawned. You'll do well to remember that next time we meet.'

CHAPTER THREE

I AM THE devil you *spawned.*

Had he meant that literally?

Ruby glanced at the man who had her imprisoned against his side as he steered her towards...

'Where are you taking me?' she demanded in a rush as electrifying fingers pressed more firmly into her skin. Who knew silk was an excellent conductor of heat?

She burned from head to toe and he wasn't even touching her bare skin.

'First to the dance floor. And then...who knows?'

'But my duties...behind the bar—'

'Are over,' he stated imperiously.

Despite the alien emotions swirling through her, she frowned. 'Can you do that?'

'You'll find that I can pretty much do anything I want.'

'You deliberately lost thirty million dollars two minutes ago. I think doing what you want is pretty obvious. What I'm asking is, am I risking my job by deserting my post?'

He ushered her into the lift, took hold of her wrist and held the smartwatch against the panel. When it lit up, he pressed the key for the floor below. 'You're here to serve the members of this club. I require your services on the dance floor. There, does that ease your anxiety?' He asked the question with a thread of cynicism that made her glance closely at him.

The tic throbbing at his temple and tense shoulders indicated that he hadn't shrugged off his encounter at the poker table.

'Who was that man you were playing with?' she asked.

Silver eyes hardened a touch before they cleared and he smiled. Ruby forced herself not to gulp at the pulse-destroying transformation his smile achieved.

'No one important. But you—' he faced her fully as the lift stopped and the doors glided open '—are much more fascinating.'

One hand brushed her wrist and slid up her arm. The shiver when he'd first touched her returned a hundredfold, sending soul-deep tremors through her.

What on earth was going on? She'd believed herself in love with Simon, enough to come within a whisper of making a fool of herself, and yet he'd not triggered an iota of what she was feeling now.

Chemistry.

The word fired alarm bells so loud in her head she jerked backwards. Her back hit the lift wall and panic flared high as he stepped closer. Heat waves bounced off his hard-packed, unapologetically male body straight into hers.

'I'm not fascinating. Not in the least,' she said hurriedly.

He laughed, a deep, husky sound that sent warning tingling all over her body.

Was this how helpless prey felt within the clutches of a merciless predator? She was nobody's prey; nonetheless she couldn't deny this man's seriously overwhelming presence.

'You're refreshingly naïve, too.' His gaze probed, then his smile slowly faded. Although the hunger didn't. 'Unless *that's* the ploy?' he queried in the same silky tone he'd used at the poker table.

Ruby's breath caught as the unmistakable sense of danger washed over her again. 'There's no ploy. And I'm not naïve.'

His fingers had reached her shoulder. They skated along her collarbone, perilously close to the pulse jumping at her throat.

The doors started to slide shut. His fingers stopped just shy of touching her pulse, then returned to grasp her wrist. With a tap on the smartwatch the doors parted again.

'Come and dance with me. You can tell me how un-naïve and un-fascinating you are.'

He led her to the middle of a dance floor much larger than the one upstairs. Over a dozen guests graced the large space, moving to the beat of the sultry blend of Far Eastern music and western jazz.

They could've danced apart. In fact Ruby was counting on the brief reprieve from close contact. But he had other ideas.

He caught her close, one arm around her waist and the other catching her hand and imprisoning it against his chest as he began to sway. The fluidity with which he moved, his innate sensuality, told her that this man knew a lot about sex and sexuality. Would know how to take a woman and leave her utterly replete but desperate for more.

'I'm waiting for you to enlighten me.'

For a second she couldn't get her brain to work. Sensations she'd never felt before crashed through her as his hard thighs brushed hers.

'About what?'

'About why you think you're not fascinating. Those impure thoughts running through your head we'll leave for later.'

She sucked in a shocked breath. 'How…? I wasn't…'

'You blush when you're flustered. As endearing as that is, you'd make a lousy poker player.'

'I don't gamble. And I don't know why I'm having this conversation with you.'

'We're performing the requisite mating dance before we… mate.'

She stopped dead. 'In your dreams! I'm not here to be your, or anyone's, appetiser.'

'Don't sell yourself short, sweetheart. I'd place you more as a deliciously forbidden dessert than an appetiser. But one I intend to devour nonetheless.'

She was on a dance floor thousands of miles away from home, immersed in a debate about which food course she was.

Surreal didn't even begin to cover the emotions coursing through her as she glanced up at him and encountered that blatantly masculine square jaw and those hypnotic eyes.

'Look, Mr...?'

He raised a brow. 'You're at a masked event, shrouded in secrecy, embroiled in intrigue and mystery, and you want to know my name?' he asked cynically.

Damn, how could she have forgotten? 'Why do I get the feeling that all this bores you rigid?'

His eyes gleamed. 'How very intuitive of you. You're right— it does. Or it did, until I saw you.'

Her heart gave a little kick. One she determinedly ignored. 'You were fully engaged when you played your game. And *that* had nothing to do with me.'

Again that reminder hardened his eyes. 'Ah, but I lost thirty million dollars so I could make what's happening between us happen sooner.'

'There's nothing happening—'

'If you believe *that* then you really are naïve.'

Another couple danced closer. The flash of red hair distracted Ruby enough to make her look. *Redhead* was in the arms of another man but her hungry eyes were fixed squarely on Narciso.

Irrational irritation jerked up Ruby's spine.

Pursing her lips, she tilted her chin at the redhead. 'Why don't you help yourself to her? She definitely wants you.'

He didn't bother to glance where Ruby indicated. He merely smiled and shrugged. 'Every woman wants me.'

'Wow, you're not the shy type at all, are you?' she snapped.

He leaned forward, and a swathe of luxurious black hair fell over his forehead to curl over the top of his mask. 'Are those the types that turn you on?' he whispered.

The image of shy, self-effacing...*duplicitous* Simon fleeted across her mind. She stiffened. 'We're not discussing my tastes here.'

'I've clearly hit a nerve. But if you don't tell me what your tastes are, how will I know how to please you?' His mouth was a hair's breadth from her ear.

Ruby fought to breathe. Her chest was a mere inch from his but her lower body was plastered against his in a way that made his body's response blatant and unmistakable.

He was aroused. And he meant her to know it.

Her abdomen clenched so forcefully, she lost her footing and stumbled.

Strong hands righted her and began to pull her back into his arms but Ruby quickly stepped back.

'You can start by buying me a drink.'

He reluctantly dropped his hand from her waist. Expecting overwhelming relief, Ruby frowned when it didn't arrive.

A white-jacketed waiter hovered nearby. 'Champagne?'

She shook her head. 'No. Something else.'

Something that would take several minutes to make and give her time to get her perplexing emotions under control.

'State what you wish,' he said.

She almost blurted her reason for being in Macau there and then. But this wasn't the right time. She needed to get him alone in a place where he couldn't blow her off as easily as his employees had these past weeks.

Casting her gaze around, she pointed to the far side of the room. 'There.'

'The ice-vodka lounge? Is this a delaying tactic?'

'Of course not. I really want a drink.'

He watched her for several seconds, then he nodded.

This time her relief was tangible. But the reprieve didn't last long. His arm slid possessively around her waist as he led her off the dance floor.

She was suppressing the rising tide of that damned *chemistry* when he leaned in close. 'You're only trying to delay the inevitable, *tesoro*.'

'I have no idea what you mean.'

His laughter drew gazes and turned heads. Ruby had a feeling everything this man did compelled attention. And not just of the female variety.

Powerful men stepped aside as he steered her towards the vodka lounge. A faux-fur coat appeared as if by magic and he draped it over her shoulders before they entered the sub-zero room. She headed for an empty slot at the bar, near an ice sculpture carved in the shape of a Chinese dragon.

The bartender glanced at her unmasked face with a frown.

'I'd like a *Big Apple Avalanche*, please. Heavy on the apple.' She needed a clear head if she intended to stay toe to toe with Narciso Valentino.

The bartender didn't move. 'I don't think you're allowed—'

'Is there a problem?' The hard rasp came from over her shoulder.

The bartender snapped to attention. 'Not at all, sir.' He grabbed the apple mixer and the canister of top-range vodka.

'I'll take it from here.' Narciso took the drinks from him and waved him away.

Despite the warmth of her coat, she shivered when he turned to her.

'Ready?'

God, this wasn't going well at all. Far from feeling under control, she felt her thoughts scatter to the wind every time he looked into her eyes.

'Yes,' she said as she inserted the specialised drinking spout into the ice outlet and brought her lips to it.

Her eyes met molten silver ones and fiery heat rushed into her belly. He slowly tipped the canister and icy vodka and apple pooled into her mouth.

Cold and heat simultaneously soothed and burned their way down her throat but the power of the decadent drink came nowhere close to the potent gleam in his eyes.

Before discovering Simon's duplicity, sex had been something she'd imagined in abstract terms; something she'd accepted would eventually happen between them, once the trust and affection she'd thought was growing between them was solid enough to lean on.

Sex just for the sake of it, or used as a weapon the way she'd watched her parents use it, had made being a virgin at twenty-four an easy choice.

But looking into Narciso's eyes, she slowly began to understand why sex was a big deal for some women. Why they dwelled on it with such single-minded ferocity.

Never had she wanted to drown in a man's eyes. Never had she wanted to kiss sensually masculine lips the way she wanted to kiss him right now. She wanted to feel those arms around her again, holding her prisoner the way they'd held her on the dance floor. She wanted to spear her fingers through his luxurious hair, scrape her nails over his scalp and find out if it brought him pleasure.

'Have another one,' he commanded huskily. He raised the sterling silver mixer, his gaze riveted on her mouth.

He wanted to kiss her badly. The same way she wanted to kiss him. Or would have if she didn't know from painful experience how treacherous and volatile sexual attraction could be.

'No, thanks. It's getting late. I need to go.'

One beautifully winged brow rose. 'You need to go.'

'Yes.'

'And where *exactly* do you intend to go?'

She frowned. 'Back to my hotel, of course.'

He slowly lowered his arm. 'I thought you understood your role here,' he murmured coolly.

Icy foreboding shivered down her spine. 'What's that supposed to mean?'

'It means, the moment the last guest arrived, the whole building went into lock down. You're stuck here with me until tomorrow at six.' He discarded the canister and stepped closer. 'And I have the perfect idea of how we can pass the time.'

* * *

Narciso watched a myriad expressions dart over her face.

Excitement. Anxiety. Suspicion.

Two of those three weren't what he expected from a woman when he announced they were effectively locked in together. Most women would be salivating at the thought and making themselves available before he changed his mind.

Not this one.

Even the hint of excitement was fading. Now she just looked downright frightened.

He frowned. 'I expected a more enthusiastic response.'

Her gaze went to the watch—his watch—then back to his face. Narciso decided not to think about why the sight of his large watch on her delicate wrist pleased him so much.

He would gift it to her. She could keep it on during sex. Once he'd dispelled that unacceptable look from her face.

'You just told me I can't leave. And you expect me to be excited?'

'You have some of the world's richest and most influential men gathered in one place. Everyone who attends these events has the same agenda—network hard and party harder, especially the *Petit Qs*. You, on the other hand, are acting as if you've received a prison sentence. Why?'

Her eyelids lowered and she grabbed the lapels of her coat.

Faint alarm bells rang at the back of his mind. Going against a habit of a lifetime, he forced himself to ignore it as she raised those delicate lids to lock gazes with him.

Her sapphire-blue eyes held a combination of boldness and shyness that hugely intrigued him. She wanted something but wasn't quite sure how to get it.

He had every intention of showing her how to get exactly what she wanted once he got her to his suite upstairs. He might even tempt her into using the velvet ropes that held back his emperor-size bed's drapes...

Desire slammed into him with a force he hadn't experienced

in years…if ever. The strength of it struck him dumb for a few seconds before he realised she was speaking.

'…knew about the club, of course, and that my hostessing gig was for two days. I didn't know I'd be staying here for the duration.'

'Ah, one small piece of advice. Always read the small print.'

Her delicious mouth pursed. He had the sudden, clamouring urge to find out if it tasted as succulent as it looked. Her narrowed-eyed glare stopped him. Barely.

'I always do. I can't say the same for other people though. Especially people who have the small print pointed out to them and still wilfully ignore it.'

The alarm bells grew louder. 'That's decidedly…pointed. Care to elaborate?'

She opened her mouth, then shut it again. 'I'm cold. Can we leave?'

'That's an excellent idea.' He walked her to the door of the ice bar and helped her out of her coat.

The sight of her hardened nipples—an effect of the sub-zero temperature—fried a few million brain cells. That clawing hunger gutted him further, making him fight to remember whether he was coming or going.

Going. Definitely. Up to his allocated suite with this woman who sparked a reaction within him that left him reeling, and wanting more. He hadn't wanted anything this badly for a long time. Not since his eleventh birthday…

He shut off his thoughts and walked her to the lift, absurdly pleased when she didn't protest. Perhaps she'd accepted the inevitable.

They were meant to be together. Here in this place where the events of earlier this evening with Giacomo had nearly soured his experience.

She would take away the bitterness for a while. Take away his unsettling hollowness when he'd held the old man's financial demise in his grasp but hadn't taken it.

All would be better in the morning.

For tonight, he intended to seek the most delicious oblivion.

'Should I bother to ask where you're taking me now?'

His smile felt tight and his body on edge. 'No. Don't bother. What you should ask is how many ways will I make you like what's coming next.' He activated the electronic panel. When the chrome panel slid back to reveal the row of buttons he selected the fiftieth floor for his penthouse suite.

'If you're planning to throw a few more millions away, then I'd rather not watch.' Again there was that censorious note in her voice that strummed his instincts.

From experience he knew women always had hidden agendas, be it the urge to make themselves indispensable in his life the moment he so much as smiled their way or to take advantage of his power and influence—as well as his body—for as long as possible.

But the woman in front of him was exhibiting none of those traits. And yet there was something... Narciso didn't like the mixed signals he was receiving from her.

'Have we met before?' he demanded abruptly, although he was sure he would have remembered. She had an unforgettable body, and that mouth... He was absolutely certain he would have remembered that mouth.

'Met? No, of course not. Besides, I don't know who you are, remember?'

'If you don't know who I am then how do you know we haven't met before?'

Her eyes shifted away from his. 'I...don't know. I just think a man like you...I'd have remembered...that's all.'

He smiled at her flustered response, deciding he definitely liked her flustered. 'I like that you think I'm unforgettable. I aim to make that thought a permanent reality for you.'

'Trust me, you already have,' she quipped.

Narciso got the distinct impression it wasn't a compliment.

He stepped forward. She stepped back. Her eyes widened when she realised she was trapped against the wall of the lift.

His pulse thundered when her gaze darted to his mouth and then back to his eyes.

'Somewhere along the line, I seem to have made a bad impression on you. Normally I wouldn't care but...' He stepped closer, until the warmth of her agitated exhalations rushed over his chin. Her scent hit his nostrils and he nearly moaned at the seductive allure of it.

'But...?' she demanded huskily.

'But I find myself wanting to alter that impression.'

'You want me to think you're a good guy?'

Laughing, he slid his hand around her trim waist. 'No. *Good* is taking things a touch too far, *amante*. I haven't been *good* since...' he blunted that knife of memory again '...for ever.'

Her darkened eyes dropped to his mouth again and Narciso barely stopped himself from groaning. But he couldn't stop his hands from tightening on her waist. In contrast to her lush hips, her waist was so tiny, his hands spanned it easily.

'Then what do you want from me?'

Before he could succinctly elaborate, the lift doors slid open. The double doors leading into his suite beckoned. Beyond that the bedroom where he intended to make her his.

He grasped her wrist and tugged her after him. Using the smartwatch to activate the smaller panel, he pressed his thumb against the infrared scanner and pushed the doors open. He didn't bother to shut it because the doors were automatic. Security was exemplary at all *Q Virtus* events, especially the private suites. He had the whole floor to himself and no one would disturb them unless he wanted them to.

And he had no desire for any interruptions—

He noticed she'd stopped dead and turned to find her staring at him.

'You've brought me to your suite,' she blurted.

The pulse pounding at her throat could've been excitement. Or more likely it was the trepidation he'd seen earlier.

'Very observant of you.'

'Know this now—I won't be indulging in anything…illicit with you.'

'Since we haven't established exactly what it is we'll be doing I think we're getting a little ahead of ourselves.'

'I wish you'd stop toying with me.'

His shoulders moved with the restlessness that vibrated through his whole being. He couldn't remember the last time he'd had to work this hard to get a woman to acknowledge her interest in him. 'Fine. Do you deny that there's something powerful and undeniable happening between us?'

'I don't want—'

'If you really don't want to be here, say the word and I'll let you leave.' That wasn't strictly true. First he'd use his infinite skills to convince her to stay. Arrogance didn't come into his awareness that he was attractive to most women, and, despite her mixed signals, this woman was as attracted to him as he was to her.

She might need a little more work than usual—and the thought wasn't unpleasing—but he was more than up to the task.

He watched her debate with herself for an endless minute. Then she turned towards the window.

Narciso forced himself to remain still, despite his every cell screeching at him to grab her. Picking up a control device, he pushed the button that allowed the glass windows to turn from opaque to transparent.

Macau City lay spread before them in a cascade of lights, glittering water and awe-inspiring ancient Portuguese, Chinese and modern architecture.

Since he'd started doing business here, his fascination with the city had grown along with his bank balance.

But right now his fascination with her was much more paramount.

'Tell me you'll stay.' His voice emerged rougher than normal.

The thought that he wanted her badly, alarm bells or no alarm bells, made him frown. He'd trained himself not to want anything he absolutely could not have. It was why he calculated his every decision with scalpel-like precision.

That way he avoided disappointment. Avoided…heartache…

She turned from the window, arms crossed at that tiny waist. Her response took a minute, two at a stretch, but they were the longest minutes of Narciso's life.

'I'll stay…for a little while.'

He swallowed and nodded. Suddenly, his fingers itched to remove the pins in her hair, to see its silky dark gold abundance cascade over her shoulders.

'Take your hair down,' he instructed. The time for playing was over.

Her eyes widened. 'Why?'

'Because I want to see it. And because you're staying.'

Her fingers touched the knot at the back of her head. Anticipation spiked through him only to be doused in disappointment when she lowered her hand.

'I prefer to keep it up.'

'If you're trying to keep me hyped up with interest, trust me, it's working.'

'I'm not, I mean… My hair is no big deal.'

'It is to me. I have a weakness for long hair.'

Her head tilted to one side, exposing a creamy neck he longed to explore. 'If I take my hair down, will you take your mask off?'

As much as he wanted to rip his mask off, something told him to delay the urge. 'No,' he replied. 'My house, my rules.'

'That's not fair, is it?'

'If life was fair you'd be naked and underneath me by now.'

A blush splashed up her exquisite throat and stung her cheeks. Molten lust rushed into his groin and spread through his body. Feeling restricted and seriously on edge, he shrugged off his tuxedo jacket and flung it over the long sofa. Next came the bow tie. He left that dangling to tackle the top buttons of his shirt and looked up to find her gaze riveted on him.

Good, he was not alone in this. Sexual desire pulsed from

her in drenching waves. Which made the reticence in her eyes all the more intriguing.

Enough!

In three strides, he stood in front of her. She made a high, surprised noise as he tugged her close. Without giving her a chance to protest further, he swooped down and took her lips with his.

She tasted glorious. Like a shot of premium tequila on a sultry night. Like warm sunshine and decadent, sticky desserts. Like jumping off the highest peak of an icy mountain with nothing beneath him but air and infinite possibilities.

Narciso's lids slid shut against the drugging sensation of her lips.

Madre di Dio! He was hard. Harder than he'd ever been. And he'd only been kissing her a few seconds.

She made another sound in her throat and her lips parted. Her tongue darted out to meet his and he plunged in, desperate for more, desperate to discover her every secret.

He deepened the kiss and groaned as her hands slid up his biceps to entwine around his shoulders. In a curiously innocent move, she tentatively caressed his nape before boldly spiking her fingers into his hair.

The scrape of her fingers against his scalp made him shudder with escalating arousal. Raising his head, he gazed down into eyes darkened with desire. *'Amante,* you already know what pleases me.'

Shock clouded her expression, as if what she'd achieved had stunned her.

Without giving her a chance to speak, he took her luscious mouth again. The highly potent sound of their kisses echoed in the room as they devoured each other.

Pulling her even closer, he finally touched the pulse that had taunted him all evening. It sang beneath his touch, racing with her excitement.

She inhaled deeply, and her breasts smashed against his

chest. He cupped one, glorying in the weight and perfect fit of it as his thumb brushed across one rigid nub.

She jerked and her teeth sank into her bottom lip. With a rough sound, she pulled away.

Narciso continued to play with her nipple as they stared at each other. Her mouth, wet and slightly swollen, parted as she sucked in panicked breaths.

'You like the way I make you feel?' He brought his other hand up from her waist and cupped her other breast, attending to the equally stiff and aching peak. 'I promise I will make you feel even better. Now take your hair down and show me how gorgeous you really are.'

The words pulled Ruby from the drugged stupor she was drowning in. Reality didn't rush in, it trickled in slowly.

Blinking eyelids heavy with desire, she tried to focus on something other than his arrestingly gorgeous face—the part not covered by his mask.

First, she noticed the stunning chandelier. Then a repeat of that bold dragon motif from downstairs on the wall behind his shoulder. Reality rushed in faster. Stunningly designed black velvet sofas, including an authentic French chaise longue perfect for reclining in...

Then her focus drew in closer. She glanced down at the powerful hands cupping her breasts.

The sight was so erotically intoxicating it nearly knocked her off her feet.

Sensation shot between her thighs, stinging so painfully, she wanted to place her hand there, seek some sort of relief.

'Take your hair down for me,' he insisted again.

She came plunging back down to earth. 'No!'

Telling herself she didn't care about the jaw that tightened in displeasure, she took several steps away from his hot, tempting body.

Focus, Ruby!

The last time she'd mixed business with pleasure, she'd almost ended up becoming the one thing she despised above all else—a participant in infidelity. It didn't matter that she hadn't known Simon was married. The very thought of what could've happened made shame lodge in her belly.

She was here to get Narciso Valentino to honour his deal with her, not to get pulled into the same dangerous vortex of emotions that led to nothing but pain and heartache.

Her father's inability to limit his sexual urges to his marital bed and her mother's indecision whether to fight or turn a blind eye had made her childhood a living hell. It'd been the reason why she'd slept most nights with her headphones on and music blaring in her ears. Even then she'd been unable to block out the blistering rows or her mother's heart-wrenching sobs.

And after her experience with Simon, there was no way would she allow herself to jump on that unpredictable roller coaster.

She took another step back, despite the magnetic pull of desire dragging her to Narciso. Despite the soul-deep notion that sex with him would be pulse-poundingly breathtaking. Despite—

Despite nothing!

Her treacherous genetic make-up didn't mean she would allow herself to fall into the same trap as her mother just because an unrepentant, unscrupulous playboy like Narciso Valentino crooked his wicked finger.

But she couldn't risk alienating him before she got what she'd come here for. Licking tingling lips, she forced her brain to track.

She cast her gaze around the large, luxuriously appointed suite. Seeing the extensive, well-stocked bar on the far side of the room, she made a beeline for it. 'Here, let me get you another drink.'

'You don't need to get me drunk to have your way with me, *amante*.'

She flushed and stopped, whirling to find him directly behind her. The sheer size of him, the arousal stamped so clearly in his eyes, made her breath fracture. 'Stop calling me that.'

A small smile played around his exquisite mouth. 'You know what it means.'

She nodded. 'Yes, I'm Italian.'

'And I'm Sicilian. Big difference, but we will speak your language for now.'

'Whatever language we speak, I don't want you referring to me as a…as your…'

'Lover?'

'Yes. I don't like it.'

'What do you want me to call you?'

'Just call me Ruby.' She didn't mind telling him her name. In order to explain her presence here, she would have to disclose who she was.

So no harm done.

'Ruby.'

Definitely lots and lots of harm done. The way he said her name—wrapped his mouth and tongue around it in a slow caress—made her pulse leap crazily.

'Ruby. It suits you perfectly,' he murmured.

Against her will, his response drew her interest. 'How do you mean?'

'Your name matches the shade of your mouth after I've thoroughly kissed it. I imagine the same would apply to other parts of your body by the time we're done.'

Her flush deepened. *'Seriously?'*

He laughed but the hunger in his eyes didn't abate. 'Too much?'

'*Much* too much.'

He shrugged and nodded to the bar. 'I'll give you the reprieve you seek. But only for a little while.'

She dived behind the bar and gathered the first bottles that came to hand. Almost on automatic she replicated one of her favourite creations and slid it across the shiny surface.

He picked it up and sipped without taking his eyes off her.

He rolled the drink in his mouth before his eyes slowly widened. 'You're very talented.'

Pleasure rushed through her. 'Thank you.'

'Prego.' He threw back the rest of the drink and set the glass down with a decisive click. 'But enough with the foreplay, Ruby. Come here.'

Heart pounding, with nowhere to hide, she approached him.

'Give me what I want. Now.'

She debated for a tense few seconds. Then, figuring she had nothing to lose, she complied.

Her hair was thick, long and often times unmanageable. She'd spent almost an hour wrestling it into place tonight and in the end had chosen to wear it up. Her effort to straighten it would've worn out by now, and she couldn't help but fidget when his gaze raked over the golden-brown tresses once, twice and over again.

'You're exquisite,' he breathed after an endless moment during which her stomach churned with alien emotion. 'Your skin is flawless and I want to drown in your eyes, watch them light up with pleasure when I take you.'

Ruby couldn't believe mere words could create such heat inside her. Hell, everything about him made her hot and edgy.

She needed to nip this insanity in the bud before it went any further. 'I'm sorry if I gave you the impression that something more was going to happen between us. You won't be… taking me.'

'Will I not?' he asked silkily, his finger drifting down her cheek to settle beneath her chin. 'And what makes you say that?'

'Because you don't really want me.'

His laugh was rich, deep and incredibly seductive.

'Every nerve in my body disagrees with that statement. But if you need proof…' He bent low, scooped her up and threw her over his shoulder.

His laughter increased at her outraged squeal. 'Put me down!'

The hallway passed in a blur as he took her deeper into the

suite. Her hair entangled with his long legs as he strode with unwavering purpose.

'I don't know what the hell you think you're doing but I demand you put me down right—' Her breath whooshed out of her lungs as she was dumped on a bed. A very large emperor-size bed with slate-coloured sheets and over a dozen pillows.

'You were saying?'

She brushed her hair out of her eyes and saw him tugging off his shoes. When he unhooked his belt, she scrambled off the bed.

He caught her easily and placed her back in the centre. 'Are you going to be a good girl and wait for me?' Silver eyes speared her.

'Wait for... Hell, no!'

He stepped forward and caught her chin in his hand. When his head started to descend, she jerked away. 'What the hell do you think you're doing?'

'Capturing your attention for a moment. You don't need to be frightened, *dolce mia*. Nothing will happen in this room without your consent.'

Oddly, she believed him. 'You don't need to kiss me to capture my attention.'

Slowly he straightened and dropped his hand. 'Shame. Let me remind you of some ground rules before we proceed. We're not supposed to reveal ourselves to each other. However, since you've done me the honour of revealing your name to me, I'll grant you the courtesy of removing my mask. But you'll give me your word that it will stay between us, *si?*' He started unbuttoning his shirt, revealing mouth-watering inches of golden skin.

Heat slammed into her chest and she sucked in a gulping breath.

Crunch time. Time to get this dangerously bizarre situation over and done with.

'There's no need. I already know who you are. You're Narciso Valentino. You're the reason I'm here in Macau.'

CHAPTER FOUR

HE FROZE AT her announcement. A second later, he drew the mask over his head, and Ruby got her first full glimpse of Narciso Valentino.

He was breathtakingly gorgeous. With a definite edge of danger that sent her already thundering pulse straight into bungee-jump mode.

She watched his face grow taut. Watchful…condemning.

'You know who I am.' His words were icily precise, the warmth in his tone completely gone.

Licking dry lips, she nodded. His other hand dropped from his belt, leaving her curiously disappointed.

'You're American.'

'Yes, I live in New York, same as you. That's where I came from.'

'And you followed me all the way to Macau. Why?' The clipped demand came with eyes narrowed into cold slits.

A mixture of anger and trepidation rushed through her, propelling her from the bed.

He caught her easily. 'Move again and I'll be forced to restrain you.'

Panic flared through her. Tugging at his hands, she fought to free herself. Before she could fathom his intentions, her wrists were bound to the bedpost with velvet rope he'd pulled from the side of the bed.

She looked from her wrists to his face, unable to believe what was happening. He tossed his mask on the bed, whipped the unbound tie from his neck and flung it across the room, barely suppressed fury in the movement. 'Okay, fine, you've made your point. But you can't keep me prisoner for ever.'

'Watch me.'

'I could scream, you know.'

Nice, Ruby. Nice.

'You could. And I can turn you over to the management and let them deal with what can only be regarded as a security breach. Trust me, breaches aren't taken lightly.'

She tugged at her bound wrists. 'I can't believe you tied me up.'

'You left me no choice. Now start talking before I call security.'

Her breath caught as images tumbled through her head of being stuck in a foreign prison. Aside from her roommate, Annie, no one knew her whereabouts. And even if Annie tracked her down to Macau, she wouldn't have the first clue where to find her.

'Tell me what you want to know,' she offered in a rush.

'Is Ruby really your name?' he asked, his gaze dropping to her lips.

Remembering what he'd said about her mouth, she felt heat spike through her belly again.

'Yes.'

'And your earlier assurance that we hadn't met before?'

'Is true. Although we almost did…last week.'

One sleek brow shot upward. 'How?'

'I tried to find you at a nightclub—Riga—but you were leaving when I arrived.'

He prowled closer to the bed, and a fresh load of anxiety coursed through her system. Hands poised on lean hips, he stared down at her.

'I've had women do…unexpected things to get my attention but I don't think I've had the privilege of a full-blown crazy stalker before.' His eyes raked her from head to toe. 'Perhaps I should've made it happen sooner.'

'I'm not a crazy stalker!' She yanked at the restraints and only succeeded in tightening them.

'Of course not. Because those ones readily admit to their charges.'

'Look, I can explain. Just…untie me.'

He ignored her and leaned down, placing his palms flat on the bed so his face was level with hers. 'We could've had so much fun, *amante*. Why did you have to spoil it?' There was genuine regret in his tone, but bitterness had crept in with the iciness.

'I have a genuine reason for being here.'

'For your own sake, I hope so. I don't take lightly to being manipulated.'

Her mind flashed to earlier in the evening. Watching him toy with his opponent had shown her just how dangerous this man was. Despite the outward charm and spellbinding magnetism, he could become lethal on the turn of a dime.

He turned and prowled to the window. With jerky movements, he tore off his expensive shirt, sending cufflinks she was almost certain were made with black diamonds pinging across the room.

Tossing the shirt the way his bow tie had gone, he shoved his hands into his pockets.

The movement contracted his bronzed, strongly muscled back. Among the electrons firing crazily in her brain came the thought that this was the first time she'd come this close to a semi-naked man worth looking at.

He turned and the sight of his naked torso was almost too much to bear. A light smattering of hair grew outward from the middle of his sculpted chest and arrowed down to disappear into his waistband.

Heat intensified as her gaze landed on his flat brown nipples. A decadent shudder coursed through her. She grasped the sturdy, intricately carved bedpost made of highly polished Chinese cedarwood, pulled herself closer to the edge of the bed and peered closer at the intricate knots that bound her.

'Where do you think you're going?' he rasped.

'I can't stay trussed up like a Thanksgiving turkey all night long.'

'Answer my questions and I'll consider freeing you.'

'You'll *consider* it?'

'Have you forgotten already that I hold all the cards here?' He sauntered back and stopped in front of her.

Suddenly, Ruby wished she'd stayed put in the middle of the bed. *This* close the heat emanating from his satin-like skin blanketed her. The urge to move her fingers just that little bit and touch the skin covering his ribcage was immense.

'Go ahead,' he invited softly. Silkily.

Flames leapt through her bloodstream. 'Excuse me?'

'You want to touch me. Go ahead. We can pick up this conversation in a moment once you've satisfied your craving.'

'I… You're wrong. I don't want to touch you. There's no craving. What I want is to be set free—'

Her words froze when he placed large hands on her hips and pulled her into his body.

'Well, despite you ruining my evening, I *still* have a craving for you.'

He smothered her protests by capturing her mouth again. It was as potent as before but this time there was a rough demand in his kiss that spoke of his fury beneath all that outward calm.

But rough didn't mean less pleasurable. Her lips parted, welcoming the jagged thrust of his tongue and the domineering pressure of his kiss.

She moaned before she could stop herself, flexing fingers that wouldn't obey their order to stay put, and touching the velvety smoothness of his neck and collarbone.

By the time he lifted his head, they were both panting. He slowly licked his lips, savouring her taste. The sight of his wet tongue sent liquid fire straight to that raging hunger between her thighs.

Ruby shut her eyes in shuddering despair and opened them to find him sliding off her shoes.

'God, will you please stop doing things like that?' she snapped.

'I'm into kinky when the occasion calls for it, but I don't generally risk puncturing a lung with stiletto heels unless the payback is worth it.' He flung her shoes away. 'Do you need help with your dress?'

'No! Why on earth would I want that?' She edged away from him, the fear that her emotions wouldn't be as easy to control around this man spiking through her.

'It's nearly two a.m. And we're yet to have our little tête-à-tête. But if you want to keep cutting off your circulation in that restricting dress, suit yourself. Tell me why you're here,' he bit out, as if he wanted to be done with the conversation.

'Release me first,' she insisted.

'I released you three minutes ago.'

Shocked, Ruby glanced down at her wrists. Sure enough, the velvet rope was loose enough to free herself. She'd been too spellbound by his kiss to notice.

She met his hard, mocking gaze. Rubbing her right wrist, she encountered his watch. She pulled it off and held it out to him.

He didn't take it. 'I'm waiting for an answer.'

'My name is Ruby Trevelli.'

He continued to stare at her. 'Should that mean anything to me?'

Despite knowing how self-absorbed he was, that flippant question hurt. She flung his watch on the bed. He calmly retrieved it, took hold of her wrist, slipped it back on, and returned to his predator-like position.

'What—?'

'Answer me. Should your name mean anything to me?'

'Yes. I was recently voted Élite Chef.'

His lips twisted. 'My apologies. I don't keep up with pop culture,' he said.

'Well, you should. Your TV company sponsored the show.'

He frowned. 'I have over sixty media companies scattered

all over the world. It would be impossible to keep up with every progamme that's aired through my networks. So you're here to collect some sort of prize—is that it?' The disappointment she'd heard earlier was back, accompanied this time by a flash of weariness that disappeared as quickly as it'd arrived.

'You make it sound like a whimsical endeavour. I assure you, it's not.'

'Enlighten me, then, Miss Contest Winner. Why have you flown thousands of miles to accost me?'

Put like that it *did* sound whimsical. Except this was her life and livelihood they were talking about, the independent life she'd worked hard for so she wouldn't be pulled into her parents' damaging orbit. The life that was being threatened by a loan shark.

'I want your company to honour its agreement and pay me what I'm owed.'

His face hardened into a taut, formidable mask of disdain. 'You came after me because of *money?*' His sneer had thickened.

Ruby couldn't really dwell on that. She needed to state her purpose and leave this room, this suite. He was close, so tantalisingly close, the warmth of his skin and the spicy scent of his aftershave made stringing words together an increasingly difficult task. He smelled like heaven. And she wanted to drown in it.

'Prize money, yes.'

His eyes narrowed. 'But why come after me? Why not go after the man I've put in place to head NMC?'

'You think I haven't tried? No one would take my calls.'

'Really? No one in a company with over a thousand employees?'

'No. Trust me, I have the phone bill to prove it.'

'Well, clearly, I need to hire better staff.'

'I don't like your tone,' Ruby snapped. She sidled towards the edge of the bed.

He caught her and placed her back in front of him, keeping her captive with one large hand on her waist.

'What tone do you mean?' Silver eyes gleamed with cynical amusement.

With every breath she took, the imprint of his hand seared her skin. 'You obviously don't believe me. Why would I travel thousands of miles unless it was because I'd hit a brick wall?'

'Or you'd hoped an extra tight dress and body that won't quit would get you an even better deal?'

The image his words conjured up made blood leach from her face. It was one she'd vowed never to portray. 'I understand you don't know me, Mr Valentino, but I've never used sex or my sexuality to further my career. You can be as offensive and as delusional as you want. The simple fact is Nigel Stone never took my call in the two dozen times I tried to reach him.'

His eyes narrowed at her furious words but he kept silent.

'We can resolve this very quickly. Call him now, get him to talk to me. Then I'll get out of your hair.'

'It's Saturday morning back in the States. I make it a point never to disturb my employees during the weekend.'

Anger stiffened her spine. 'Yeah, right.'

His cynical smile widened. 'You don't believe me?'

'I believe you do exactly what you want when you want. If it suited you, you'd be on the phone right now.'

His shrug outlined sleek muscle beneath his skin. He moved with an innate grace that made Ruby's pulse race shamefully. 'Fine. I admit I ride my employees hard when I have to. But I also recognise their need for down time the same way I recognise the need for mine.'

'You're telling me you need your beauty sleep to function?' she snapped.

'Down time doesn't necessarily mean sleep, *amante*. Tonight, I was counting on wild, unfettered sex,' he delivered smoothly.

She flung herself away from him, from the temptation his words dredged up inside her, before that Trevelli gene she so feared could be fully activated.

Far too often since she'd clapped eyes on him, she'd found herself imagining what sex would be like. Her roommate had referred to the best sex as sheet-clawing, toe-curling. At the time Ruby had silently scoffed at how anything besides the best, decadently prepared dessert would feel that great.

Now she couldn't stop herself from wondering…

Disgust at herself propelled her off the bed. She refused to sink into the quagmire of rampant promiscuity.

Her feet hit the luxurious carpet, bringing a much-needed return to reality. She darted out of the door and hurried along the long hallway towards the main suite doors.

With relief, she grasped the door handle and yanked it down. Nothing happened. She pulled harder.

Glancing around wildly, she spotted the electronic panel and pressed the most obvious-looking button.

Nothing.

'You can't get out unless I allow you out.'

She whirled. He casually leaned one shoulder against the hallway wall. The sight of him standing there, looking sexily tousled and half naked, made panic flare anew inside her.

'Then let me out.'

'I could. But once I do, any hope of a discussion about why you're here ends. My company, if it's liable as you say, owes you nothing the minute you walk out of here.'

'That's preposterous! I signed a contract. *You* signed a contract. You can't just back out on a whim.'

'Think about it, Ruby. You've travelled thousands of miles to get my attention. I intend to give you that attention. Do you think it prudent to walk out now, when you could be so close?'

'I…' She sucked in a breath as overwhelming feelings swamped her. 'Why can't we discuss it now?'

'Because I don't like to discuss business without a clear head. And since you've plied me with exquisite cocktails all evening, I'd be making those decisions under severe influence.' He tilted his head again in that alarmingly endearing way and a lock of hair fell over his eyes.

Dear God. This man was truly lethal. He oozed sex and sensuality without so much as lifting a finger.

'You didn't ply me with all those drinks in order to take advantage of me, did you? Because that would be horrifyingly disappointing.'

Outraged, she gasped. 'I most certainly did not.'

Slowly, he extended a hand to her. 'In that case, Ruby Trevelli, there's no earthly reason not to stay. Is there?'

Narciso was doing his best to stop his fury from showing. The same way he was doing his best to keep from kicking himself for ignoring the alarm bells.

Usually he could spot chancers and gold-diggers a mile away, be they tuxedo-clad or dressed in designer gowns that looked too small for them.

For a moment he wished she'd kept her mouth shut until after he'd slept with her to make her avarice known. He would've been a lot more generous than he was feeling now.

He would also have felt used.

Fury mounted and his frustrated erection threatened to cut him in half as she stayed out of his reach. Out of his arms.

Recalling her responsiveness, the gut-clenching potency of her kiss, he nearly growled.

She kissed as if she were born for it. Narciso wondered how many men she'd kissed like that in the past and felt a red haze wash over his fury.

Dio, what was wrong with him? He should find the nearest phone and report her to management.

Zeus, his host and owner of the club, had so far excelled in keeping people like Ruby away from *Q Virtus* guests. Sure, most *Petit Qs* would accept a generous gift from a guest, but blatant stalking wasn't tolerated.

Except, his stalker seemed eager to get *away* from him, her catlike blue eyes apprehensive as she glanced at his outstretched hand.

'Come here,' he commanded.

She swayed towards him, then abruptly halted her forward momentum. 'If you're too drunk to talk, what other reason is there for me to stay? And don't mention wild sex. Because that's not going to happen.'

Contrary to what he'd said, his mind was as clear and as sharp as a fillet knife. And it sensed a curious dichotomy in her words and actions. The dress, make-up and screw-me stilettos said one thing. Her words indicated another.

He intended to burrow until he found the truth.

Nice choice of words, Narciso, he thought as arousal spiked higher in his blood. Lowering his hand, he turned abruptly.

'I'm returning to the bedroom. If you're not there within the next minute, I'll take it that our business is concluded,' he said over his shoulder.

'Wait! You can't do that…'

Narciso smiled with satisfaction at her frustration. Whether she followed him or not, there was no way he was letting her out of his suite tonight. Not until he'd had her checked out thoroughly and satisfied himself what sort of threat she posed.

He recalled the circumstances of their meeting. Of all the tables she could've been hostessing, she'd been at Giacomo's table.

This time he didn't ignore the churning in his gut. Giacomo had played that game before…

He turned and found her two steps behind him but any satisfaction was marred by the new set of questions clamouring for answers.

'Why are you really here, Ruby? Did the old man send you?'

Fresh trepidation flared in her eyes at his harsh tone. 'Who… Oh, that guy you were playing with? No, I have no idea who he is and I'd never met him before tonight.'

He tried to read her. Surely, even seasoned liars couldn't look him straight in the eye as she was without flinching?

'Be warned, if I find that to be untrue, there'll be hell to pay.'

'I'm telling you, I don't know him.' Her fingers meshed together and she began to fidget. But not once did her stare waver from his.

Narciso decided to be satisfied. For now. He entered the bedroom and crossed to the en suite.

'So I'm here. Now what?' she asked.

'I'm going to take a shower. You do whatever you want. As long as you don't leave this room.'

'God, this is nuts,' he heard her mutter as he entered the bathroom. Despite the volatile emotions churning through him, he smiled. From the corner of his eye, he watched her head once more to the stunning view of Macau City.

Silhouetted against the view, her body was so perfectly stunning, his mouth dried. Disappointment welled in his chest but he suppressed it as he undressed.

The cold shower was bracing enough to calm his arousal but not enough to wash away the bitterness as he replayed his evening.

Giacomo was bent on trying to take Narciso down.

Well, that suited Narciso fine. Although Narciso could've destroyed him with that last move, the notion of leaving him dangling a little bit longer had been irresistible.

The opportunity would present itself again soon enough. Giacomo was predictable in his hatred for him, if for nothing else.

And at thirty, exactly ten years after his father's most cutting betrayal, the need for vengeance burned just as brightly in Narciso's veins.

For as long as he'd been old enough to retain his memories, Narciso had known that Giacomo bore him a deep, abiding hatred. As a child he'd been bewildered as to why nothing he did pleased or satisfied the man he once called Papa.

On his eleventh birthday, a whisky-soaked Giacomo had finally revealed to him the reason he detested the sight of his son. At first, even reeling from the shock of the discovery, Narciso had stupidly believed he could turn things around, make his father, if not love him, at least learn to cohabit peacefully with him. He'd made sure his grades were perfect, that he was quiet and obedient and exemplary in all things.

Narciso's mouth twisted. That had lasted all of a year before he'd accepted he was flogging a dead horse. When his thirteenth birthday had come and gone without so much as a single lit candle on a store-bought birthday cake, he'd finally admitted that war was the only way forward.

He'd suppressed whatever heartache had threatened to catch him unawares in the dead of night and used animosity to feed his ambitions to succeed. He'd won scholarships to the best colleges in the world. His head for figures had seen him attain his first million by eighteen. By twenty he'd been a multi-millionaire.

Twenty…also the age he'd met Maria, the unexpected tool his father had used against him. The wound gaped another inch.

With a sharp curse, he shut off the shower. Snapping up a towel, he tied it around his waist.

Maria was dead to him, but, in a way, he was pleased for her transient presence in his life ten years ago. She'd reinforced his belief that lowering his guard, even for a moment, was foolhardy. That even fake love came at a steep price.

Money and sex were the two things he thrived on now. Emotions…connections, hell, *love,* were a complete waste of his time.

He entered the bedroom and found Ruby reclining on the bed, legs crossed, one bare foot tapping in agitation. She shot upright at his entry. After that one quick look, Narciso barely glanced in her direction as he walked to the connecting dressing room.

The whole evening was screwed up. His thwarted efforts to bed her, and now his unexplained trip down memory lane had left him in an edgy mood. Snatching at his fast-dwindling control, he reached for the rarely used silk pajama bottoms and dropped his towel.

The choking sound made him glance over his shoulder through the open door. She sat frozen on the bed, her eyes wide with astonishment.

'Something wrong?' he asked as he stabbed one leg into the garment. At her silence, he started to turn.

She shut her eyes and jerked away from him. He pulled the bottoms on and entered the bedroom. 'Open your eyes. It's safe to look now.'

She opened her eyes but kept her gaze averted.

'Come on, now, the way you're acting you'd think I was the first naked male you'd ever seen.'

That gurgling sound came again and Narciso shook his head. 'I have very little interest in virgins, *amante*. If you hope to snag my attention, I suggest you drop that particular act.'

She inhaled sharply. 'It's not an—' She bit off the rest of her answer as he drew back the sheets.

Four of the six pillows he threw to the floor before he got in. The sight of her sitting so stiffly made his jaw tighten. Reaching across, he pulled her into the middle and pulled the sheet over them.

'You were saying?'

She shook her head. 'Nothing. Are you really going to sleep?'

'Yes. I suggest you get some sleep too even though I fear for your circulation in that dress you're wearing.'

'I'm fine.'

'If you say so.' He relaxed against the pillows. Sleep would be elusive with her so close. For a moment he wondered why he was torturing himself like this.

Keep your friends close and your stalkers closer?

He suppressed a grim smile, grabbed the remote and doused the light in the bedroom. But with one sensory factor taken away, her erratic breathing became amplified.

Good. If he was to be tortured with images of what sex between them would be like, it was only fair she experienced the same fate.

'What happens tomorrow?' she asked quietly.

'Tomorrow we talk. And by talk I mean you come clean, completely, as to why you're here. Because if you hold anything back from me, I won't hesitate to throw you to the wolves.'

CHAPTER FIVE

RUBY WOKE WITH the distinct feeling that something had changed. It took a millisecond to realise what that *something* was.

'You took my clothes off?' she screeched, her fingers flying to the hem of the black T-shirt that had miraculously appeared on her body.

The man who lay so languidly beside her, his head propped up on his hand, nodded.

'I feared you'd suffocate in your sleep in that dress. Despite your dubious reasons for being here, even I would find it difficult to explain death by designer gown to the authorities. You were quite co-operative. I think it was the only time you've been co-operative since we reached my suite, which tells me you were as uncomfortable as I suspected.'

She licked her lips and struggled not to squirm under his scrutiny. At least her bra and panties were intact. But the fact was she didn't recall what had happened. And there was only one worrying explanation for that. 'I was tired,' she bluffed.

'Right.' Silver eyes bore into her until she felt like a fly hooked on a pin.

His gaze dropped to her twisting fingers, and she abruptly stilled the movement. 'Tell me what happened. *Exactly.*'

One brow rose at her firm directive but Ruby was desperate to know what had happened during the night. She'd tossed and turned in agitation until sheer exhaustion had finally pulled her under some time before dawn.

'You tried to escape a few times. I brought you back to bed.'
God. No. It'd happened again...
Definitely time to leave. She tried to move, and felt a snag on her foot. Shoving aside tangled sheets, she stared in horror at the rope tied around her ankle.

'You tied me up again! Do you have a thing for bondage?'

His eyes gleamed. 'Until last night, I'd never needed to tie a woman to keep her with me.'

'Oh, well, lucky me. Did you tie me before or after you took off my dress?'

'After the second time you tried to take the door off its hinges to make your escape, we came back here and I relieved you of your suicidal gown and put the T-shirt on—' A deep frown slashed his face. 'Are you saying you don't remember any of this?'

She sucked in a slow breath and looked away.

He caught her chin in his hand and forced her to look at him, his steady gaze demanding an answer. '*Dio,* you really don't remember?'

Ruby had no choice but to come clean. 'No. sometimes I… sleepwalk.'

His brows hit his hairline. 'You *sleepwalk?* How often is sometimes?'

'Not for a while, to my knowledge. It only happens when I'm…distressed.'

His frown intensified. 'You found last night distressing?'

'Being tied up and kept prisoner? No, that was a picnic in the park.' She tugged at her ankle restraint. 'And now I'm tied up again.'

'It was for your own good. After I put the restraint on, you stopped making a run for it. I think secretly you liked it.' His fingers caressed along her jaw, his eyes lowering to her lips.

Instantly the mood changed, thickened with sensual promise. 'I'm *not* into bondage.' Or sex with playboys, or anyone for that matter!

'How do you know? Have you ever tried it?'

'No. But I've never jumped off a cliff either, and I'm certain I wouldn't enjoy that experience.'

'Fair point. For the record, I have. With the right equipment, all experiences can be extremely enjoyable. Exhilarating even.'

She watched, terrified and mesmerised, as his head started to lower. 'What are you doing?'

'I'm kissing you *bon giornu, bedda*. Relax.'

That was easier said than done when every nerve in her body was strained in anticipation of the touch of his mouth on hers. She told herself she was sluggish because she was sleep deprived. But it was a lie.

As much as she yearned to deny it, she wanted the pressure of his demanding kiss and the heady racing of her blood through her veins.

His moan as he deepened the kiss echoed the piercing need inside her.

One hand clamped on her hip, drew her sideways into him. At the sensation of his sleep-warmed body against hers, she moaned. The fact that she was clothed from neck to hip and he was clothed from hip to ankle didn't alter the stormy sensation of their bodies meshing together.

Nipples, stung to life at the touch of his mouth on hers, peaked and ached as they brushed his chest.

When his hand moved under the T-shirt and skimmed over her panties, Ruby jerked at the vicious punch of desire that threatened to flatten her.

She was drowning. And she didn't want to be rescued.

'*Dio mio,* you're addictive, *bedda*,' he murmured against her mouth before plunging back in. His tongue shot between her lips to slide against hers. He staked his claim on her until she couldn't think straight. Even when his mouth left hers to nibble along her jaw, she strained closer, her hand sliding up his chest in a bold caress that shocked and thrilled her at the same time.

When her nail grazed his nipple, he hissed. Stunned at the surge of power that action gave her, she flicked her nail again.

'Careful, *amante,* or I might have to repay the kindness.'

Lost in a swirl of desire, she barely heeded the warning. Bringing up her other hand between them, she flicked both flat nipples at once.

'Maledizione!' He pushed her back onto the bed and yanked up her T-shirt.

Danger shrieked in her head a second before his mouth closed over her nipple. Tonguing, licking, he pulled the willing flesh deep into his mouth.

Sensation as she'd never felt before tore through her. Between her legs where her need burned fiercest, liquid heat fuelled her raging desire.

Her fingers curled up and spiked into his hair as he transferred his attention to her other nipple. A little rougher than before, he used his teeth this time.

Her tiny scream echoed through the bedroom as her head slammed back against the pillow.

Feeling his thick arousal against her thigh, she moved her leg, eager to rub closer against the potent evidence of his need.

The snap of the ankle rope broke through her haze. The reality of what she was doing hit Ruby with the force of a two-by-four.

'No!' She pushed at his shoulders until he lifted his head. The sight of her nipples, reddened and wet from his ministrations, made dismay slither through her in equal measures. She was nothing like her parents. Nothing—

'What's wrong, *bedda?*' he grated huskily.

'What's wrong? Everything!'

'Everything is a huge undertaking. Narrow it down for me a little. I'll take care of it.'

She pushed harder. 'For a start. Get. Off. Me.'

His nostrils flared with displeasure and his fingers bit into her hip. 'You were moaning your willingness a moment ago.'

'Thankfully, I've come to my senses. Get off me and take off that…shackle you've placed on my ankle.'

He slowly levered himself off her but not before she got

another sensation of his thick arousal. Flames rushed up her cheeks.

Back in his previous position, he dropped his gaze from hers to her breasts. Realising she was still exposed, she yanked her bra cups into place and tugged down the T-shirt. A T-shirt that bore his unique scent, which chose that moment to wash over her again. As if she weren't suffering enough.

'I don't like women who blow hot and cold, *tesoro*.'

'Where I come from a woman still has the right to say no.'

'A stance I fully respect. Except your actions and your words are at direct variance with each other. You crave me almost as much as I crave you. I can only conclude that this is a ploy to string me along until I'm too whipped to put up much protest against your demands.'

Again his description of her behaviour struck painfully close to the bone, pushing all her fears to the fore. Struggling to hide it, she raised an eyebrow.

'Wow, you really have a low opinion of yourself, don't you? Or is that a high opinion on my sexual prowess?'

'Unlike you, I'm not afraid to admit my desire for you. It's almost enough to tempt me to tell you to name your price so we can be done with this…*aperitivo* and get to the main course.' There was a hard bite to his voice that instinctively warned her to do that would be a mistake.

'I only want you to hear me out. You said we'd talk this morning.'

He got up from the bed in a sleek, graceful move that brought to mind a jungle creature.

The unmistakable evidence of his arousal when he faced her made her swallow. He showed no embarrassment in his blatant display of manhood. Even in thwarted desire, Narciso Valentino wore his male confidence with envy-inducing ease. Whereas she remained cowering beneath the sheets, afraid of the sensual waves threatening to drown her.

'And so we will. Come through to the kitchen. Caffeine is a

poor substitute for sex but it'll have to do.' With that pithy pronouncement, he walked out of the bedroom.

She lay there, floundering in a sea of panic and confusion. If anyone had told her she'd be in Narciso Valentino's bed mere hours after meeting him, she'd have laughed herself hoarse. Particularly since she'd vowed never to mix business with pleasure after what had happened with Simon.

But what Narciso had roused in her just now had frightened and excited her. Kissing him had been holding a live, dangerous firework in the palm of her hand. She hadn't been sure whether she would experience the most spectacular show of lights or blow herself to smithereens with it.

And yet she'd been almost desolate when the kiss ended. Which showed how badly things could get out of hand.

Squeezing her eyes shut, she counted to ten. The earlier she finished her business with Narciso and got on the plane back to New York, the better.

Throwing off the sheet, she glanced at the velvet rope around her ankle. Twisting her body into the appropriate position, she tugged on the double knot, surprised when it came loose easily.

Again, the realisation that she could've freed herself at any time made her view of him alter a little. Her fingers lingered on the rope warmed from her body.

Bondage sex. Until now, the scenario had never even crossed her mind. But suddenly, the thought of being tied down while Narciso laid her inhibitions to waste took up centre stage in her mind.

Heat flaming her whole body, she jumped from the bed. Upright, his T-shirt reached well past her knees, and covered her arms to her elbows.

She glanced at her gown, laid carefully over the arm of the chaise longue, and made up her mind. She would dress after they'd had their talk. She couldn't bear being restrained in the too-tight dress just yet. Ditto for her heels.

Stilettos and a T-shirt in the presence of a dangerously sexual man like Narciso Valentino evoked an image she didn't want to tempt into life now, or ever.

For some reason, her body turned him on. She wasn't stupid enough to bait the lion more than he was already baited.

Barefoot, she left the bedroom and went in search of the kitchen.

He stood at a centre island in a kitchen that made the chef in her want to weep with envy. State-of-the-art equipment lined the surfaces and walls and through a short alcove a floor-to-ceiling wine rack displayed exquisite vintages.

'You get all this for a two-day stay?'

He jerked at her question. Before he could cover his emotions, Ruby glimpsed a painfully bleak look in his eyes.

A second later, the look was gone as he shrugged. 'It suits my needs.'

'Your needs… I'd kill for a kitchen like this in my restaurant.'

'You own a restaurant?' he asked.

She concluded her survey of the appliances and faced him. 'Not yet. I would've been on my way to opening Dolce Italia by now if NMC had honoured its commitments.'

'Ah, the sins of imaginary corporate sharks.'

The coffee machine finished going through its wake-up motions. He pressed a button and the beans started to churn.

'Not imaginary.' Ruby stepped forward when she realised what he was doing. 'Wait, you're doing it wrong. We're in a warm climate. The coffee beans expand in warm weather so you need to grind them looser to extract the maximum taste. Here let me do it.' Even though stepping closer would bring her dangerously close to his sleek frame, she seized the opportunity to make herself useful and not just stare at his broad, naked back. A back she could suddenly picture herself clawing in the heat of desire.

Just as she tried not to stare when he leaned his hip against the counter and crossed his arms over his bare chest.

'How are you at multitasking?' he asked.

'It's essential in my line of business.' Content with the setting, she pressed the button to resume the grinding and went to the fridge. She grabbed the creamer, and forced herself not to gape at the mouth-watering ingredients in there.

'Good, then you can talk while you prepare the coffee. Tell me everything I need to know.' His brisk tone was all business.

Quickly, she summarised the events of the past two months.

'So you entered this competition as a chef?' he asked.

'Yes, I have a degree in hospitality management and a diploma in gourmet cuisine and I'm an approved board-certified mixologist.'

He grinned. 'You have to go to college to mix drinks?'

'You have to go to school to wash dishes right these days or someone will sue your ass.' She started to grin, then stopped herself. 'I mean…if you don't want to be sued for accidentally poisoning someone. Besides, I plan to make my cocktail bar accessible to allergy-sufferers, too, so I need to know what I'm doing.'

'Which of your drinks is your favourite?' he fired back.

The question threw her for a second. Then she shrugged. 'They're all my favourite.'

'Describe the taste of your signature drink,' he pressed.

She went in search of coffee cups, opening several cabinets before she located them. She had to reach up to grab them and the cool air that passed over the backs of her legs reminded her how exposed she was.

'Umm, I don't actually like cocktails that much,' she blurted to distract herself from her state of undress.

'You're a mixologist who doesn't like her own creations? How do you know you're not poisoning the general population?'

'Because nobody's died yet sampling my drinks. And as to how I know my drinks rock? I try them out on my roommate.'

'You want me to invest…how much does my company owe you?'

'Two hundred thousand dollars to help towards construction and advertising costs for Dolce Italia.'

'Right, two hundred thousand dollars, based on your room-mate's assessment of your talent?'

She poured and passed him a cup, forcing herself not to react to the spark of electricity when their fingers brushed. 'You threw away thirty million last night without blinking but you're grilling me over two hundred thousand?'

He stiffened. 'That was different.' His voice held icy warning.

She heeded it. *'Anyway,'* she hurried on, 'thousands of people voted for me to win *your* show based on three of my best dishes and cocktails.'

His gaze drifted over her, lingered at her breasts then down her legs before he came back to her face. 'Are you sure that's the only reason they voted?'

The sudden tremble in her fingers made her set the cup down. 'You're an ass for making that inference.' Again, much too close to home. Too many times her mother had been ridiculed for using her sexuality to boost ratings, a fact Ruby had burned with humiliation for every single time.

'What inference?' he asked with a sly grin.

'The stupid sexist one you're making. Are you saying they voted for me because I have boobs?' Her rough accusation finally got his attention. The smile slid from his face but not the stark hunger in his eyes.

'Very nice ones.'

Despite her annoyance, heat rushed through her. 'Yeah, well, two of the other contestants had boobs, too.'

'I have no interest in theirs,' he returned blandly.

She picked up her cup and started to blow on her coffee, noticed his intense gaze on her mouth and thought better of it. 'Are you really that shallow?'

'*Sì*, I am.'

'No, you're not.'

'You wound me.'

'You wound yourself. You're clearly intelligent—'

'*Grazie*—'

'Or you wouldn't be worth billions. I fail to see why you feel the need to add this to the equation.'

'Tell me, sweet Ruby, why is it sexist to state that I appreciate an attractive body when I see it?'

Her mouth tightened. 'It's sexist when you imply I got where I am by flaunting it when you couldn't be more wrong.'

'Point taken.' He said nothing further.

'Is that supposed to be an apology?'

'Yes, I apologise unreservedly for making observations about your body.'

'That's almost as bad as saying "I apologise if your feelings are hurt" instead of "I'm sorry for hurting your feelings".'

'Let's not dwell on the pedantic. You have my unreserved apologies.' His gaze was steady and clear.

Ruby chose to believe he meant it. 'Thank you.'

'Good. I tried to reach Stone. I've been informed he's on vacation and can't be reached.'

She took a huge gulp of coffee and nearly groaned at the superb taste. Then his words broke through. 'Right. I wasn't born yesterday, you know.'

The seriously gorgeous grin returned. 'I know, and I'm very grateful for that.'

'Get to the point, *please*.'

'Stone is trekking in the Amazon for the next three weeks.'

Alarm skated through her. 'I can't wait another three weeks. I'll lose everything I've poured into getting the restaurant off the ground so far.'

'Which is what exactly?'

'Simon secured the rent but I put up my own money for the conversion of the space and the catering equipment.'

He froze. 'Who is Simon?' he asked in a silky tone threaded with steel.

'My ex-business partner.'

'Enlighten me why he's your ex,' he said in that abrupt, imperious way she'd come to expect.

The ache from Simon's betrayal flared anew. 'We didn't see eye to eye so we parted ways.'

Narciso's eyes narrowed. 'Was he your lover?'

She hesitated. 'Almost,' she finally admitted. 'We met in college, but lost touch for a while. A year ago we met again in New York. I told him about opening my restaurant and he offered to become my partner. We got close…'

He tensed. 'But?'

'But he neglected to tell me he had a pregnant wife at home and…I almost slept with him. He almost made me an accomplice in his infidelity.' The thought sent cold anger through her.

'How did you find out?'

Her hand tightened around her coffee cup. 'We were on our way to Connecticut for a romantic getaway when his wife called to say she'd gone into labour. I trusted him, and he turned out to be no better than…' She shook her head angrily and jumped when his fingers touched hers. Looking up, her eyes connected with his surprisingly gentle ones.

'I think you'll agree he takes the douche-bag crown, no?'

She swallowed the lump in her throat. 'Yes.'

He remained silent for several minutes, then he drained his cup. 'So my company's contribution is to help finish your restaurant?'

'That and the advertising costs for the first six months.'

'Do you have any paperwork?'

'Not with me, no. I couldn't exactly bring a briefcase to the job last night. But Nigel can prove it…'

'I'm taking over from Nigel,' he said abruptly.

'Excuse me?'

He set his cup down. 'As of now, I've relieved him of his duty to you. You'll now deal with me and me alone.'

That felt a little too…sudden… Ruby assured herself it was the reason why her heartbeat had suddenly escalated. She refused to let hope rise until she'd read the small print in his words. 'So…you'll sign over what NMC promised me?'

His eyes gleamed as he regarded her. 'Eventually,' he said lazily.

'Ah, there it is. The big, fat catch. What does *eventually* mean?' she demanded.

'I need proof that you're as good as you say you are. I don't endorse mediocre ventures.'

'Wow, are you always this insulting in the morning?'

'Sexual frustration doesn't sit well with any man, *amante*, least of all me.'

'And you think bringing your sexual frustration into a business discussion is appropriate?'

Silver eyes impaled her where she stood. 'You followed me thousands of miles and inveigled yourself into my company under false pretenses. You wish to discuss who holds the monopoly on what's appropriate right now?'

'What other choice did I have? I couldn't lose everything I've worked for because your employee is chasing orangutans in the Amazon.'

'I may be way off the mark but I don't think there are any orangutans in the Amazon. Borneo, on the other hand—'

'I didn't mean it literally. I meant...' She sighed. 'Bottom line is, NMC agreed to help me launch my business and it's reneging on the deal.'

'And I'm giving you a chance to get things back on track.'

'By making me jump through even more hoops?'

'I employ the best people. There must be a reason why Stone delayed in honouring the agreement.'

'And you think the fault is mine?' Irritation bristled under her skin. He stood there, arrogant and nonchalant as she flailed against the emotional and professional sands shifting under her feet.

'I'm trying to meet you in the middle.'

'All you have to do is review the show's footage. There were world-renowned food critics who judged my cuisine and cocktails the best. I won fair and square.'

'So you keep saying. And yet I'm wondering if there's something else going on here. If everything was above board, why didn't you use lawyers to hold my company to account? Why the very personal touch?'

'I don't have the kind of money it takes to involve lawyers. Besides, I was hoping you'd be reasonable.'

He moved towards her, his gaze pinned on her face. Danger blazed from his eyes. Along with hunger, passion and a need to win at all costs.

Her heart hammered as she forced herself to return his stare.

'You lied in order to get close to me. And you continued to lie until we were alone together. Having caught a glimpse of who I am, Ruby, how reasonable do you think I am?' His tone was silky soft, but she wasn't fooled. Underneath the lethally thrilling charm and the man who'd shown a surprising gentle side moments ago lay a ruthless mogul who ate amateurs for breakfast.

During her internet trawl she'd come across his moniker— The Warlock of Wall Street.

It took a special kind of genius to reach multibillionaire status by twenty-five and even more to attain the kind of wealth and influence Narciso Valentino wielded by his thirtieth birthday. If she didn't tread carefully, she'd leave Macau the same way she'd arrived—with nothing.

'I'm not unwilling to renegotiate our terms, Mr Valentino...' she ventured.

'I've had my mouth on parts of your body that I believe have earned me the right to hear you say my first name.'

Her blush was fierce and horrifyingly embarrassing. 'Fine. You can have thirty per cent,' she blurted.

His eyebrows shot up. 'Thirty per cent of your body?'

'What are you talking about? God, you think I'm renegotiating with my *body*?' She gasped in shocked horror. 'I'll have you know that I'd rather *die* than do something like that!'

His discomfiture was evident as he slowly straightened and spiked a hand through his hair. 'I'm...sorry,' he murmured.

A touch of warmth dispelled the ice. 'Apology accepted.'

'*Per favore,* enlighten me as to what you meant.'

'Part of the deal for winning was that you'd help with the cash prize and advertising and I'd give you a twenty-five-percent share in my business for the first three years. After that I'd have the option to buy it back from you. I'm willing to go up to thirty per cent.'

His shook his head. 'I have a new proposal for you. Agree to it and you can keep your extra five per cent.'

'Do I have a choice?'

'There's always a choice, *cara.*'

'Okay, let's hear it.'

'Convince me of your talent. If you're good enough, I'll hire you to cater my upcoming VIP party. If you're better than good, I'll recommend you to a few people. Now, the only thing you need to decide is if it's a choice you wish for yourself.'

'But I've already proved I deserve this by winning the show.'

'Then this should be a doozy.' He raised an eyebrow. 'Do you agree to my terms?'

The sense of injustice burned within her, the need to stand her ground and demand her due strong.

But from what she'd seen of him so far he could destroy her just as easily as he'd offered to help her. He'd rightly pointed out that she'd sought him out under false pretences. She should be thanking her lucky stars he hadn't turned her over to the security guards.

The small print in her *Petit Q* contract had warned of serious repercussions if she breached confidentiality or behaved inappropriately towards a *Q Virtus* member.

So far she'd breached several of those guidelines. It was therefore in her interest to stay on the right side of Narciso Valentino.

If he could throw away thirty million dollars with the careless flick of those elegant fingers, surely it was worth her while to endure this small sacrifice to prove herself to Narciso. Getting her restaurant opening back on track would also send her parents the message once and for all that she had no intention of bowing to their pressure to join the family business.

She sucked in a breath, which hopelessly stalled when his eyes darkened. 'Yes, I agree to your terms.'

He didn't move. He just stood there staring at her. Ruby had the weird sensation he was weighing her up, judging her...

Unable to stand his stare, she started to turn away. His eyes dropped to her bare legs, heat flaring in his gaze. The power of it was so forceful she took a step back. Then another.

'Stop,' he rasped.

'Why?'

'I need you.'

Her heart hammered. 'What?'

His nostrils flared as he reached and captured her arm. Strong fingers slid down her elbow to her wrist. Ruby's pulse raced harder under the pressure of his fingers as he raised her right arm.

The electronic beep as he activated the smartwatch on her wrist knocked her out of her lust haze. Biting the inside of her cheek to bring her down to reality worked for a few seconds, until he started to speak.

Sicilian wasn't in any way similar to the language she'd learnt growing up, but she managed to pick up a few words that had her frowning.

'You're not returning to New York?'

'Not yet. My plan was to take a long-needed vacation after Macau.'

Her heart sank. 'So I still have to wait until you come to New York to finalise this agreement.'

'Not at all, Ruby. I leave for Belize tonight. And you're coming with me.'

The sight of her open-mouthed was almost amusing. Almost. Had he not been caught up in the maelstrom of severely thwarted desire, Narciso would've laughed at her expression.

As it was, he couldn't see beyond the need to experience again the sensational taste of those lips.

Pure sin. Wrapped in sweet, angelic deliciousness.

He'd never kissed lips like hers. Or tasted nipples like hers. In fact, so far Ruby Trevelli was proving disconcertingly unique in all aspects. Even the confession of her bastard of an ex's betrayal had touched him in a way he most definitely did not desire.

The flash of pain he'd seen had made his insides clench with an alien emotion that had set even more alarm bells clanging.

He hadn't intended to go to Belize till after the party he'd planned for when his Russian deal was completed.

But he was nothing if not adaptable.

'Belize?' Astonishment blazed from her stunning blue eyes.

'Yes. I have a yacht moored there. We'll sail around along the coast, dive in the Blue Hole. And in between, you'll stun me with your culinary delights. But be warned, nothing short of perfection will satisfy me.'

'I've never provided anything short of that. But...' She hesitated, again displaying that reticence he'd sensed in her earlier. If she wanted to play hard to get, she was going about it the right way. He wanted her...hard. But he was no pushover.

'But what?'

'We need to agree on one thing.' Her pulse throbbed under his thumb. He wanted to stop himself from caressing the silky, delicate skin but he couldn't help himself.

'*Sì?*'

'From now on things remain strictly business between us. The next time we have a discussion, I'd rather do it without the need for ropes.'

The hard tug of arousal the image brought almost made him groan out loud. 'I guarantee you, *amante,* the next time I tie you up, it'll be because you beg me to.'

She snatched her wrist from his grasp.

'Okay. And Superman rides on a unicorn, right?'

'I have no idea about that. Ropes, on the other hand—'

'Will play no part in our interaction for the duration I'm to prove myself to you. Unless, of course, you're bringing your girlfriend along. In which case, what you get up to with her is your business.'

Irritation fizzed inside him. Having the attraction he knew she reciprocated dismissed so casually stuck like a barb under his skin. 'I'm currently unattached. But I don't think I'll stay that way for much longer,' he said.

Her eyes widened but her lips pursed. Again arousal bit deep.

Suddenly, he wanted to leave Macau. Wanted to be alone with her so he could probe her deeper. The double entendre brought a grim smile.

Veering away from her, he stalked out of the kitchen.

The case he'd asked his personal butler to fetch was standing by the sofa in the living room. She spotted it the same time he did.

'You had my things removed from my room?' The incredulity in her voice amused and irritated him at once.

'I don't believe in wasting time when my mind is made up.'

'And what about *my* mind? You didn't know what choice I would make!'

'That's where you're wrong. I did. I'm very familiar with the concept of supply and demand. You want something only I can provide. You wanted it enough to hop on a plane on the strength of an eavesdropped conversation between complete strangers. I wagered on you being ambitious enough to agree to my demands.'

'You make me sound so mercenary.'

'On the contrary. I like a woman who states what she wants upfront. Subterfuge and false coyness are traits I actively despise.'

'Somehow I don't believe that.'

'You think I like liars?'

Her gaze slid away. 'I didn't say that.'

He forced himself to turn away, resume his path towards his bathroom and another cold shower. *Maledizione!*

'As for your case, I had it brought here to avoid any awkwardness. Or would you rather have answered questions as to why you've been absent from your duties for the last several hours?'

She groaned. 'Oh, God! What will they think?'

'They'll think the obvious. But you're with me, so no one will question you about it.'

'I…I…'

'The words you're looking for are *thank you*. You can use the second bedroom suite to get ready. I have a brunch meeting in the Dragon Room in half an hour.'

'And you want me to come with you?'

'Of course. From here on in, you serve no one but me.' His words echoed in his head and his fists clenched.

For the second time in less than ten minutes another unwanted emotion sideswiped him. *Possessiveness.*

Just as he'd trained himself not to trust, he'd trained himself not to become attached. Possessiveness suggested an attachment to something…*someone.*

Narciso didn't *do* attachment. And yet—

'What happens after your meeting?'

He forced nonchalance into his voice. 'We return here to indulge in…whatever we please. Tomorrow when the lock down is lifted, we leave.'

CHAPTER SIX

THE REST OF the morning turned out to be a study in how the very rich and influential operated. Having grown up in relative wealth and seen the lengths to which people went to keep what they had, Ruby had imagined she knew how power and influence were wielded.

Watching Narciso Valentino command a room just by walking into it took her education to a whole different level. People's attitude transformed just by him entering their presence, despite his mask now being back firmly in place.

Although dressed more casually than he'd been last night, he exuded the same authority and attention as he moved from room to room, chatting with other well-heeled guests. The brief time he left her to attend his meeting, Ruby was left with a floundering feeling in her stomach that irritated and shocked her at the same time.

She was finishing her buttered brioche and café Americano when she sensed a gaze on her. Anticipating another of the speculative looks she'd been on the receiving end of since she came downstairs with Narciso, she stemmed her apprehension and raised her head.

The man who'd played against Narciso last night and won thirty million dollars was watching her with stormy grey eyes.

He moved forward and pulled out a chair. 'May I join you?' He sat down before she could stop him.

'Sure. It's a free country, I think.'

His smile didn't quite reach his eyes. He steepled his fingers together and stared at her. 'Where's my… Where's your companion?'

'At a meeting…' She paused and stared down at his wrist. 'I thought those smartwatches could tell you where each guest is. Why are you asking me?'

'Perhaps I just wanted a conversation opener.'

'Needing an opener would mean you have something specific to discuss with me. I don't see what that could be.' Her discomfort grew underneath that unwavering, hostile stare. She started to put her flatware down, thought better of it and hung on to the knife.

His gaze went to it and swung back to hers. 'You won't be needing that.'

'I'll be the judge of that. Now, can I help you with something?' As she'd thought last night, there was something vaguely familiar about him. But like every single guest present, his mask was back on and nothing of the rest of his features was enough to pinpoint where she might have seen him before, and she was not going to commit another faux pas by asking him his name.

'I merely came to offer you a warning. Stay away from The Warlock.'

'Considering you won over thirty million dollars from him last night, I'd have thought you'd be in a better frame of mind, perhaps even celebrating your huge windfall, not wasting your time casting aspersions on someone you defeated.'

'He thinks he has bested me but he'll soon learn the error of his ways.'

'Right. Okay…was that all?' she asked, but his eyes had taken on a faraway look, as if he were somewhere else entirely.

'He's been poison ever since…' His mouth tightened and his eyes grew colder. 'For as long as I've had to deal with him, he's been nothing but trouble. He was given his name for a reason.'

'The Warlock?'

His hand fluttered in a dismissive gesture. 'No, I meant his real name. Take my advice and remember that once he tells you who he really is.'

'I'm not supposed to know who he is, so what you're saying means less than nothing to me.'

'Or you could understand perfectly what I mean.' His upper lips twisted. 'Unless spreading your legs for him has robbed you of all common sense.'

The barb struck too close to home. 'How dare you?' She jerked back at the sheer hatred pouring from him. Ice-cold sensation drenched her veins at the same time as warm hands cupped her shoulders.

'Ruby?' Narciso clipped out her name. 'What's going on here?' The question was quite rhetorical because she was sure he'd caught part of the exchange.

Certainly, his flint-hard gaze and tense jaw made her think of her earlier assessment of just how dangerous an opponent he could be.

For whatever reason, the man sitting across from her spewing vitriol had wronged Narciso Valentino on a very deep level. The skin around his mouth was white and the hands curved over her shoulders were a little less than gentle.

Ruby carefully set her knife down and took a deep breath. 'Nothing. He was just leaving. Weren't you?'

The older man smiled and took his time to rise. His eyes locked on Narciso's and for a moment Ruby thought she understood the connection, then dismissed it. What she was imagining couldn't be possible.

Pure visceral hate existed between these two men. It coloured the air and crawled over her skin.

In her darkest days before she'd actively distanced herself from her parents, her father's behaviour had permeated every single corner of her existence and she'd imagined she hated him. She could never accept the way Ricardo Trevelli lived his life or the careless way he treated her mother. But she'd never encountered hate this strong. It was a potent, living thing.

She shivered. Narciso felt it and glanced down at her before refocusing on her unwanted guest.

'Do I need to teach you another lesson, old man?'

'Keep your money, hotshot. I understand the need to brag in front of your woman. Shame it had to cost you so much last night.'

'It was worth it to see your face. If you need a refresher on how to win, I can accommodate you.'

The old man sneered. 'The time is coming when I'll wipe that smug look off your face once and for all.'

Narciso's smile was arctic. 'Do it quickly, then. I'm growing tired of your empty promises.'

Ruby sucked in a shocked breath at the blatant taunt. With a thick swear word that would singe the ears off a Sicilian donkey, the old man swivelled on his heel and walked away.

Narciso pulled back her chair, caught her up and swung her around to face him. 'What did he say to you?' he demanded, his nostrils pinched hard with the anger he was holding back.

'Oh, he was educating me on the real meaning of your name, albeit very cryptically. Who is he anyway?'

He looked after the departing man and visibly inhaled.

'I told you—he's no one important. But I want you to stay away from him.'

'That would be difficult since I don't even know who he is.'

Tucking her arm through the crook of his elbow, he led her out of the dining area styled with large, exquisitely scrolled Chinese screens. She'd heard one of the guests comment that the stands holding up the scrolls were made of solid gold. *Q Virtus,* its mysterious owner, Zeus…in fact this whole place was insane with its surrealistic extravagance, secrecy and decadence.

'You're an intelligent woman, hopefully equipped with enough of that intuition you women are so proud of. Use it and stay clear of him.'

'Funny, he said the same thing about you. And why does that sound suspiciously like a threat?'

He led her into another express lift and used his thumbprint and her smartwatch to activate the panel before pressing the button for the sub-basement.

'Because it is one.'

'So we've graduated from ropes to threats?' Her attempt at humour fell flat when his face tightened further.

'Don't tempt me. I'm this close to breaking point.' He held two fingers together for emphasis.

She froze when the arm imprisoning hers drew her closer to his warm body. 'Did something go wrong with your meeting? A deal fall through or something?'

'What makes you ask that?'

'Aside from the confrontation just now, you seem to be in a foul mood. Did something happen?'

'No, sweet Ruby. The "network hard" part of my day is ticking along nicely. It's the "play harder" part that has failed miserably.'

So she was partly to blame for his disagreeable mood.

Time for a subject change.

'Where to now?'

'The champagne mixer in the Blue Dungeon. Then we're leaving,' he clipped out.

'I thought we couldn't leave until the lock down was lifted tonight?'

'I've asked for a special dispensation from Zeus,' he said, his gaze on the downward-moving arrow. They were sinking deeper into the bowels of the building. Ruby felt as if she were disappearing into Alice's Wonderland. 'The dispensation should be coming through on your smartwatch any minute now. Let me know when it does.'

'The owner's name really *is* Zeus. Seriously?'

'You don't find my moniker incredulous.'

'That's because…' She paused, unwilling to voice the thought rattling through her head.

'Because?'

She shrugged. 'The Warlock suits you, somehow.'

He faced her fully, his gaze raking her face in that intensely raw way that made her feel vulnerable, exposed.

'In what way does it suit me?' he asked silkily.

Because you mesmerise me with very little effort. Ruby cleared her throat.

'You're obviously a genius at what you do.'

'And you think my success stems from sorcery?'

She shrugged. 'Not in the chicken bones and goat sacrificing sense but in other ways.'

One hand rose, trailed down her jaw to rest on the pulse pounding at her throat. 'And will I be able to sway you into my bed with this potent magic of mine?'

'No.'

His smile this time was genuine. And devastating to her senses. 'You sound so very sure.'

'Because I am. I told you, I don't mix business and pleasure.'

His smile dimmed. 'Would this have anything to do with your ex-almost-lover?'

'I believe it's a sound work ethic,' she answered.

Once Narciso had left her on her own, she'd replayed the events of last night and this morning. Shame at her behaviour had charged through her, forcing her to quickly reinforce her crumbling self-control.

Letting her feelings run wild and free was not an option. Heartache and devastation could be the only result if she didn't get herself back under control.

'So you intend to let him win?' Narciso queried softly.

'This is *my* choice.'

'If you say so.'

She had no chance to respond before the doors opened and they entered the most surreal room Ruby had ever seen. Blue lights had been placed strategically on the floors, walls and ceilings of a huge cavern. And bottles of champagne hung on wires, their labels combined with the words *QV Macau*.

'What does *Q Virtus* mean?' she asked.

His smile was mysterious. 'I could tell you but I'd have to—'

'Oh, never mind.' She turned as an excited murmur went through the crowd.

Six acrobats clad in LED-lit costumes swung from tension cables from one end of the room to the other.

She couldn't help her gasp of wonder at their movement. 'Oh, my God.'

'So *that's* what it'll sound like.' The wicked rasp was for her ears alone. His warm breath tickled her ear, sending a tingle right to her toes.

'What *what* will sound like?'

'Your gasp of wonder when I'm deep inside you.' His lips touched her lobe and she jerked at the electric sensation.

'Since that's never going to happen, you'll just have to keep guessing,' she replied.

He merely laughed and plucked two glasses off a sterling-silver tray that dropped down from the ceiling as if by magic. 'Champagne?' He passed her a glass.

She took it simply for something to do besides staring at his gorgeous face, which had transformed dramatically from his earlier formidable demeanour. He clinked glasses with her and raised his in a toast. 'To the thrill of the challenge.'

'I won't participate.'

'Too late. You threw the gauntlet. I accepted. Drink your champagne. That's a five-thousand-dollar glass you're holding.'

She stared down into the golden liquid before answering. 'I don't really drink that much.'

'I guessed as much. Another souvenir from the ex?'

The pain of the memory scythed through her before she could guard herself against it. She shook her head.

'Why don't you drink, Ruby?' His voice was hypnotic, pulling on a cord deep inside that made her want to reveal everything to him.

'I don't like the loss of control it gives me.'

Silver eyes narrowed. 'Something happened to you?'

'You could say that.'

'Something bad?'

'Depends on your definition of bad. Someone upset me. I thought getting drunk would solve the problem. It didn't. It made it worse.'

'Who was it?'

'My father—' She stopped as she realised how much she was revealing to him.

'Ah, *sì*. Fathers. It's such a shame they're necessary for evolution, isn't it?' Although his words were light, his eyes had taken on that haunted look she'd glimpsed this morning in his kitchen.

Out of nowhere came the overwhelming urge to take his pain away. 'I can't believe we're standing in one of the most spectacular rooms I've ever seen, discussing our daddy issues.'

'You're discussing *your* daddy issues. I have none.'

She frowned. 'But you just said—'

His mouth tightened. 'I merely expressed a view on evolution.' He took a large slug of his drink and set the glass aside. 'Come, the show's about to begin.'

He walked her deeper into the room, to an even larger space where a stage was brightly lit in hues of blue and green.

Several more acrobats struck different poses from their ropes but as the oriental-themed music filled the room they started to perform as one. Immediately she recognised the world-renowned group whose exclusivity was reserved to royalty and the crème de la crème of A-listers.

The fluidity of their movement and sheer talent taken to hone such an awe-inspiring performance kept Ruby mesmerised for several minutes, until she noticed Narciso's renewed tension. A glimpse at his profile showed a tense jaw and tightly pursed lips.

She debated for a second, then took a breath.

'It's okay if you don't want to admit to having daddy issues. I lived in denial myself for a long time,' she whispered, aware several guests stood close by.

'Excuse me?' he rasped.

'I could apologise but I thought we were…you know…sharing.'

'I don't *share,* Ruby. At least not in that way.'

'Listen—'

'You're missing the show,' he cut across her.

Forced to curb her reply, she resumed watching the show, aware that he grew tenser with every passing minute.

A particularly daring acrobat surged right over their heads. Narciso's hand tightened around hers. Thinking he was reacting to the spectacular display, she glanced at him, to find his gaze fixed across the stage, on the man who'd confronted her less than an hour ago.

In that instant, the resemblance between them struck her hard. Their similar heights, their silver eyes, the proud, arrogant way they viewed the world. How could she not have seen it until now?

'Oh, my God, he's your father.'

He stiffened and glanced down at her with cold, grim eyes. 'He's a man whose DNA I happen to share. Nothing more.'

Applause broke through the crowd as the show finished in a crescendo of dives and leaps choreographed so fabulously, she couldn't help but clap despite her shocking discovery.

They were father and son. And they hated each other with a passion that was almost a separate being every time they were within feet of each other.

She wanted to know what had placed such a wide divide between them but she held her tongue. She had no right to pry into anyone's life. Her own baggage was enough to be dealing with. After fighting for so long and so hard to get away from the noxious environment her parents chose to inhabit, the last thing she wanted was for someone like Narciso Valentino to dredge it all up.

The smartwatch on her wrist beeped twice.

Narciso glanced down at it. 'We're leaving.'

Her heart climbed into her throat, and she fought the snap of excitement fizzing through her. What on earth was wrong with her? She couldn't be secretly thrilled with the thought of being alone with this man.

Could she?

Within minutes their cases were being loaded into the trunk of the stretch limo that stood idling in the underground car park, with a smartly dressed driver poised at the door. She slid in and Narciso joined her.

The moment the door shut, she wanted to fling it open and dive out. She'd thought she was venturing into the unknown by coming to Macau.

By agreeing to go to Belize with The Warlock of Wall Street, she was really stepping into an abyss.

'I…don't think I can…' She stopped. What was she doing? She'd forced herself to endure a TV show after Simon had convinced her it was the only way she could fund Dolce Italia.

She'd plunged herself into the very environment she'd grown up in and actively detested just so she could establish her independence. Now she stood on the threshold of seeing it pay off.

'Having second thoughts?' he asked as the car rolled up a ramp and exited into bright mid-afternoon sunshine.

'No. I'm not,' she insisted more to herself than to him.

'Good.'

The smartwatch emitted several discreet beeps. 'What's it doing?'

'It's erasing the evidence of my activities here.'

'Wow, you're not part of the CIA, are you?'

'I could be if spies are your thing.' He gave another of those wicked smiles and her mouth dried.

'I'll pass, thanks. Although I'm curious what you have to do to belong to a club like that.' She took the watch off and examined its multifaceted detail.

'It involves a lot more than chicken bones and goat sacrifices, I can assure you.'

Against her will, a smile tugged at her mouth. Letting go, he laughed. He joined her, his perfectly even teeth flashing in the sunlight. The deep sound echoed in the enclosed space and wrapped itself around her.

Danger! Her senses screamed again. But it was a seductive

danger, akin to knowing that extra mouthful of rich, decadent mousse was deadly for you but being unable to resist the taste.

And she'd quickly discovered that if she let herself fall under his spell, he would completely bypass her hips and go straight to her heart.

'Here, take this back.' She held out his watch, stressing to herself that she didn't miss having something of his so close to her skin.

'Keep it. It's yours.'

'Are you serious?' she gasped. 'But what about its value—'

'I wasn't thinking of its monetary value when I offered it. And if you're thinking about pawning it, think twice.'

'I meant its sentimental value to you, of your visit here? And I'd never pawn a gift!'

'I'm happy to hear it. As for sentiments, I prefer mine to be warm-blooded.' He took off his mask and laid it on his knee. 'Luckily, I have you.'

The statement sent equal parts of apprehension and excitement through her. She slowly slid the watch back onto her wrist and watched as they approached the Pearl River. Luxury super yachts in all shapes and sizes lined the marina.

The limo drew to a stop beside a sleek speedboat and Narciso helped her out. The driver held out a leather case, its velvet inside carved in the exact shape of his mask. Narciso placed the mask inside, shut the case and handed it to the driver.

Seconds after their luggage was loaded, the pilot guided the boat towards the open river.

'I've spent a lot of time asking you where we're going but need to ask you one more time.'

'Don't you trust me?' he asked with a mockingly raised brow.

'No.'

He laughed again. And again, the sound tugged deep inside.

'We're heading to the airport. My private jet will fly us to Belize.'

Nodding, she watched the disappearing skyline of Macau City. It'd earned its name, Vegas of the East, but there was also soul in this place, and in other circumstances Ruby would've loved to explore a lot more.

She turned to find him watching her. The hunger was back in his eyes, coupled with a dangerous restlessness.

'What?' she demanded when she couldn't stand his intense scrutiny any longer.

'I came here for a purpose. You succeeded in swaying me from that purpose. I intend to find out why.'

'Was that purpose to destroy your father?' she asked before she thought better of it.

He immediately stiffened. The breeze rushing over the water ruffled his hair. He slowly scythed his fingers through it without taking his eyes off her.

'Among other things.'

'But you decided to spare him at the last minute.'

'A very puzzling notion indeed.'

Her heart hammered as his speculative gaze rested on her lips.

'I don't think it's puzzling at all. I think you knew exactly what you were doing.'

His eyes narrowed. 'And what would that be, O Wise One?'

'You were extending the thrill of the chase, delaying the gratification of the kill blow.'

'How very astute of you.'

'So what were the other things?'

'Perdono?'

'You said among other things.'

His gaze drifted down the neckline of her black tube dress, again a tighter fit than she would've preferred. 'What do you think?'

'According to online sources you have an IQ of a hundred and forty-eight.'

'It's closer to one-fifty but who's counting?'

Her mouth pursed. 'It also says you're a rampantly rabid playboy who thinks about nothing else but the next woman he intends to sleep with. It's a shame you've chosen to use *all* hundred and fifty to chase skirts.'

He grinned. 'No, I only use one hundred and forty-eight. I need the other two to walk and talk.'

She rolled her eyes even though the corners of her mouth curved. The boat pulled up to a jetty, beyond which she could see several planes parked on tarmac.

Narciso's plane was the same silver shade as his eyes, with a black trim that made it stand out among the other jets.

He lived a life of extreme luxury and decadence, while making people like her jump through hoops to claim what was rightfully theirs.

'What's wrong? You're frowning.'

'You're asking me to spend time and energy claiming something that should be already mine. I'm trying to see the fairness in that.'

'Something about going the extra mile? Doing whatever it takes?' he mocked, but his eyes held a flash of warning. 'Get on the plane, Ruby.'

'Or what?'

'Or you lose everything. Because I won't renegotiate and I despise being thwarted.'

Her feet remained leaden. Her instinct warned her she wouldn't emerge unscathed if she went with him.

'Is this how you do business? You strike a deal, you renegotiate, then you renege?' he demanded.

'Of course not. I'm only here because *your* company reneged on the deal it struck with me!'

'A fact I'm yet to verify. The quicker you get on the plane, the quicker this can be resolved.'

She had no argument against that. And the reality was she'd come too far to turn back. And there was the small problem of Simon's loan shark lurking in the background.

Taking a deep breath, she started to mount the steps. Recalling something he'd said, she twisted and nearly collided with his lean, muscular frame. The steadying hand he threw around her waist burned through to her skin. This close, without the hindrance of his mask, she could see how his envy-inducing cheekbones and long eyelashes framed his impossibly handsome face.

'What did you mean about being thwarted?'

'Sex, Ruby. I meant sex. We're going to have it together. It's going to be spectacular and, yes, I know you're going to protest. But it will happen. So prepare yourself for it.'

She was still reeling from the raw, brazen words hours later as she tried to doze in her fully reclined seat two rows from where he conducted a teleconference call.

She had no idea how long the flight to Belize would take. She had no idea what the temperature would be this time of year.

In fact, her mind was empty of everything but the words Narciso had uttered to her on the steps of his plane.

Punching her pillow, she silently cursed herself for dwelling on it. It was *never* going to happen. She'd have to be ten kinds of fool to repeat what she'd nearly gone through with Simon—

'If you punch that pillow one more time, it'll give up its secrets, I'm sure of it.'

She twisted around and found him standing beside her seat, one hand held out.

'Sleep is eluding you. Let's spend some time together.'

'No, thanks.'

He dropped his hand and shoved it into his pocket. Ruby tried not to stare at the way his shoulders flexed under the snow-white T-shirt he'd changed into. 'Please yourself. But if you end up serving me food that I find abhorrent because you haven't done your homework, you'll only have yourself to blame.'

The challenge had the desired effect. Pushing aside the cashmere throw the stewardess had provided, she went after him.

He smiled mockingly and waved her into the club chair opposite his.

Ruby smoothed her dishevelled hair down, and activated her tablet. 'Okay, shoot. What's your favourite food?'

'Life offers such vast richness. Having favourites is severely restricting.'

She sighed. 'This isn't going to be easy, is it?'

He shrugged. 'I take entertainment where I can get it.'

'Okay, next question. Any food allergies?'

'Peanuts and avocado.'

Her head snapped up. 'Seriously?'

'I don't joke with my health, *amante*.'

She noted it on her tablet. 'How do you feel about Sicilian food?'

'I'm completely indifferent.'

She looked up in surprise. 'Really? Most Sicilians are passionate about everything to do with their homeland.'

'Probably because they have a connection to be passionate about—' He stopped suddenly and his jaw clenched.

She watched him try to rein in his control and her chest tightened. 'And you don't?'

Tension gripped his frame. 'Not for a long time.'

Her tablet dimmed, but she didn't reactivate it. The flash of anguish in his eyes snagged her attention.

'Because of your father?' she pushed.

His eyes narrowed. 'Why does this interest you so much?'

The question took her aback, made her ask herself the same thing. 'I...I thought we were making conversation.'

'This is one subject I prefer to steer clear of. *Capisce?*'

'Because you find it upsetting.'

He cursed under his breath and raked back his hair as that stubborn lock fell over his forehead again. 'Not at all. The subject of my father fires up my blood. I just prefer not to discuss it with near strangers.'

Despite cautioning herself to stick to business, she found herself replying, 'Haven't you heard of the saying make love not war?'

'Why do I need to choose one when I can have both? I'll make love to you and I make war with Giacomo.'

'For how long?'

'How long can I make love to you? Is that another challenge to my manhood?'

'I meant your father, and you know it.'

'I intend to keep going until one of us is in the ground.'

She gasped. 'You don't really mean that, do you?'

Again that flash of pain, gone before it'd even formed. '*Sì*, I do.'

'You know, he called you poison.'

This time the anguish stayed for several seconds, shattered his expression. Her heart fractured at the pain she glimpsed before his face settled into neutral indifference. 'He's right. I am poison.'

His unflinching admission made her heart contract. 'What happened between you two?'

'I was born.'

Narciso watched her try to make sense of his reply. She frowned, then shook her head. 'I don't understand.'

He wanted to laugh but the vice gripping his chest every time he thought of Giacomo made that impossible. He rose and walked to the bar at the mid-section of his plane. Pouring two glasses of mineral water, he brought one to her and gulped down the other. 'That's because you're trying to decipher a hidden meaning. There is none. I was born. And Giacomo has hated that reality ever since.'

'He hates being a father?'

He paused before answering, unwilling to utter the words he hadn't said aloud for a very long time, not since he'd wailed it as a pathetic little boy to the housekeeper who'd been the closest thing he'd known to a mother.

'No. He hates me.'

Shock darkened Ruby's eyes.

He sat back down abruptly, and willed back the control he'd

felt slipping from him since he'd walked into the poker den in Macau last night. He glanced up and saw sympathy blazing from Ruby's face. The rawness abated a little but, no matter how much he tried, he couldn't shake off the unsettling emptiness inside him.

He swallowed his water and set the glass down.

'Enough about me. Tell me about *your* father.'

She stiffened. 'I'd rather not.'

'You were ready to *share* just a little while ago.' He settled deeper into his seat and watched her face. And it was a stunning face. The combination of innocence and defiance in her eyes kept him intrigued. She didn't hide her emotions very well. Right now, she was fighting pain and squirming with a desire to change the subject.

The sudden urge to help her, to offer the same sympathy she'd just exhibited, took him by surprise.

Dio, what was wrong with him?

This woman who'd flown thousands of miles after him was an enigma. An enigma with daddy issues. He should be staying well clear.

He leaned forward. 'Since you seem shocked by the depth of my…feelings towards Giacomo, I'm assuming your feelings towards your father are much less…volatile?'

Those full lips he wanted to taste again so badly pressed together for a moment. 'I don't hate my father, no. But I prefer to keep my distance from them.'

'*Them?*'

She fidgeted. 'You're going to find out anyway. My parents are Ricardo and Paloma Trevelli.'

Her stare held a little defiance and a whole load of vulnerability. 'Sorry, you lost me.'

A delicate frown marred her perfect skin. Again his fingers ached to touch. Soon, he promised himself.

'How come you own several media companies and yet have no clue what goes on in the world?'

'My line of work doesn't mean I compromise my privacy. So your parents are famous?'

Her eyelids swept down to cover her expression. 'You could say that. They're famous celebrity TV chefs.'

'And their fame disgusts you?' he deduced.

Blue eyes flicked to his. 'I didn't say that.'

'Your voice. Your eyes. Your body. They all give you away, Ruby Trevelli.' He loved the way her name sounded on his lips. He wanted to keep saying it… 'So you despise them for being famous and cashing in on it. Isn't that what you're doing?'

'No! I'd never whore myself the way—' She stopped and bit her lip.

'Do they know you have this view of them?' he asked.

She shrugged. 'They've chosen a lifestyle I prefer not to be a part of. It's that simple.'

'Ruby…' he waited until her eyes met his '…we both know it's not that simple.'

Shadows chased across her face and her mouth trembled before she firmed it again. Before he could think twice, he reached out and touched her hand.

She swallowed hard, then pulled her tablet towards her. 'How many people will I be catering for at your event?'

He told himself he wasn't disappointed by her withdrawal. 'Are we back to all business again?'

'Yes. I think it's safer, don't you?'

Narciso couldn't deny the veracity of that. Dredging up his past was the last thing he'd intended when he'd boarded his plane. And yet, he resented her switch to all-business mode.

'If you say so,' he replied. 'You think you can handle a VIP dinner?'

'I believe in my talent as much as you believe in your abilities as the Warlock of Wall Street. If I say I'll rock your socks off, I will.'

A reluctant smile tugged at his lips. 'A confident woman is such a turn-on.'

She glared at him. 'If you say so,' she replied sweetly. 'Is there a guest of honour that I should pay particular attention to?'

'Vladimir Rudenko. I'm in the last stages of ironing out a deal with him. He's the VIP guest.'

She started to make another note when her tablet pinged. He heard her sharp intake of breath before she paled.

'What is it?'

'It's nothing.'

The blatant lie set his teeth on edge. 'Don't lie to me.' He reached for the tablet but she snatched it off the table.

'It's a private thing, all right?'

'A private thing that's obviously upset you.' He watched her chest rise and fall in agitation and experienced that disconcerting urge to help again.

'Yes, but it's my problem and I'll deal with it.'

Before he could probe further, she jumped up. 'You said I could use the bedroom if I wanted. I'll go finish making my notes now and get some sleep, if that's okay?'

It wasn't okay with him. Nothing had been okay since he met Ruby Trevelli. But short of physically restraining her, an action sure to bring brimstone upon his head, he let her go.

'We won't be landing for another six hours. I'll wake you before we do.'

She nodded quickly. 'Thanks.'

He watched her walk away, her short, tight black dress framing her body so deliciously, his groin hardened. He couldn't suppress his frustrated growl as the bedroom door shut after her.

The image of her lying in his bed haunted him. But those images were soon replaced by other, more disturbing ones as his thoughts turned to their earlier conversation.

His father.

He shoved a hand through his hair. He'd come so close to revealing the old, bottled-up pain. Hell, he'd even contemplated spilling his guts about Maria.

Maria. The tool his father had used to hammer home how much he detested his son.

His laptop beeped with an incoming message. Casting another glance at the bedroom door, Narciso pursed his lips.

The next six hours would be devoted to clearing his schedule.

Because once they were in Belize, he would devote his time to deciphering the code that was Ruby Trevelli and why she had succeeded in getting under his skin.

CHAPTER SEVEN

SHE WAS WARM. And comfortable. The steady sound drumming in her ears soothed her, made her feel safe from the erratic dreams that still played in her mind.

But she wanted to get warmer still. Wanted to burrow in the solid strength surrounding her.

The heart beating underneath her cheek—

Ruby jerked awake.

'Easy now, tigress. You'll do yourself an injury.'

'What the hell…? What are you doing here?'

'Sharing the bed. As you can see, once again I managed to restrain myself. And this time we're both fully clothed. That means I win brownie points.'

'You win nothing for letting yourself into my bed uninvited.'

'Technically, this is my bed, Goldilocks. Besides, you were muttering in your sleep and tossing and turning when I looked in on you. I had to make sure you didn't sleepwalk yourself out of an emergency exit in your agitation.'

Ruby tried to pry herself away from the inviting length of his warm body, but the arm clamped around her waist refused to move. 'I wasn't that agitated.'

Silver eyes pinned hers. 'Yes, you were. Tell me what upset you.' His voice was cajoling, hypnotic.

She wanted to tell him about the undeniable threat in the email that had made a shaft of ice pierce her nape and shimmer down her spine. The loan shark had stepped up his threat level, implicating her mother.

Ironic that Narciso, the world-famous playboy and media mogul, had no idea who her mother was but some two-bit loan shark who inhabited the dregs of society knew who Paloma Trevelli was enough to threaten to break her legs if Ruby didn't reply with a timescale of payment.

Her reply had bought her a few more days but there was no way she intended to tell Narciso what was going on.

'I told you. It's my business to handle.'

'Not if it will potentially impede your ability to perform your job.'

'I can cook blindfolded.'

'That I would pay good money to see.' He pulled her closer, wedging his thigh more firmly between hers so she was trapped. Some time during sleep, she'd curled her hand over his chest. Now, firm muscles transmitted heat to her fingers, making them tingle.

Awareness jolted through her when his lips drifted up her cheek to her temple. 'If we weren't landing in less than thirty minutes, I'd take this a step further, use other means to find out what's going on.'

'You're operating under the assumption that I would've permitted it.'

He laughed, then sobered. 'It wasn't your father, was it?'

'No, it wasn't.'

He stared down at her for a long time, then nodded. 'I did some research while you were asleep. I know about your parents.'

'Oh?' She couldn't help the wave of anxiety that washed over her.

His eyes narrowed. 'Has it always been like that with them?'

That mingled thread of pain and humiliation when she thought of them tightened like a vice around her heart. 'You mean the crazy circus?'

He nodded.

'Until I went to college, yes. I didn't return home afterward. And I have minimal contact these days. Any more and it gets… unpleasant.'

'For whom?'

'For everyone. My father is a serial adulterer who doesn't understand why I won't condone his behaviour. My mother doesn't understand why I don't forgive my father every time he strays. They both want me to join the family business. The same business for which they shamelessly exploit their fame, their family, their friends—' She ground to a halt and tried to breathe around the pain in her chest.

His hand stroked down her cheek. 'You hate yourself for the way you feel.'

Feeling exposed, she tried to pull away. He held her firmer. '*Ruby mio,* I think you'll agree we went way past business when we spent the night together in my bed. Talk to me,' he coaxed.

She drew in a shaky breath and reassured herself that they were talking. Just talking. 'I hate that my family is broken and I can't see a way to fix it without being forced to live my life in a media circus.'

'And yet you chose that avenue to fund your business.'

'Believe me, it wasn't my first choice.'

'Then why did you do it?'

'We'd tried getting loans from the banks with no success. Simon heard about the show and convinced me to enter. Taking three weeks out of my life to be on the show felt like a worthy sacrifice.'

'So you returned to the thing you hate the most in order to achieve your goal.'

'Does that make me a fool?'

'No, it makes you brave.'

The unexpected compliment made her heart stutter. Silver eyes rested on her, assessing her so thoroughly, she squirmed. Of course the movement made her body rub dangerously against his.

He emitted a leonine growl and the arm around her waist

tightened. One hand caught her bent leg and hitched it higher between his legs. The bold imprint of his erection seared her thigh. Heat flared between them, raw and fervent.

'So you don't think it's wrong to do whatever it takes to achieve one's dreams?'

His eyes darkened. 'No. In fact, it's a trait I wholeheartedly admire.'

Her throat clogged at the sincerity in his voice. The barriers she'd tried so hard to shore up threatened to crumble again. A pithy, mocking Narciso was bad enough. A gentle, caring Narciso in whose eyes she saw nothing but admiration and praise was even more dangerous to her already fragile emotions.

Scrambling to regroup, she laughed. 'Dear God, am I dreaming? That's two compliments within—'

'Enough,' he snapped. Then he kissed her.

Ruby's heart soared at the ferocity of his kiss. Desire swept over her, burying the volatile memories under even more turbulent currents of passion as he mercilessly explored her mouth with a skill that left her reeling.

Narciso could kiss. She already had proof of that. But this time the sharper edge of hunger added another dimension that made her heart pump frantically, as she saw no let-up in the erotic torrents buffeting her.

When he sank back against the pillows and pulled her on top of him, she went willingly. Strong, demanding hands slid up her bare thighs to cup her bottom, press her against that solid evidence of his need.

Unfamiliar hunger shot through her belly to arrow between her legs. Desperate to ease it, she rocked her hips deeper into him.

His thick groan echoed between their fused lips. He surged up to meet her, thrusting against her in an undeniable move that made her blood pound harder.

With her damp centre plastered so firmly and fully against him, she moaned as the beginnings of a tingle seized her spine. Hunger tore through her as rough fingers bit into her hips, keeping her firmly in place as they found a superb synchronicity that needed no words.

The first wave of sensation hit her from nowhere. She cried out, her fingers spiking into his hair as she grasped stability in a world gone haywire.

'*Dio!* Let go, baby. Let go.'

The hot words, crooned in her ear from a voice she'd found mesmerising from the very first, were the final catalyst. With a jagged moan, Ruby gave into the bliss smashing through her. She melted on top of him, giving in to the hands petting down her back as her shudders eased.

'I don't know whether to celebrate for making you come while we're both fully dressed or spank you for your appalling timing.'

Slowly, the realisation of what she'd just done pierced her euphoria.

Beneath her cheek, his heart raced. She could feel his erection still raging, strong and vital.

She'd orgasmed on top of Narciso Valentino and he hadn't even needed to undress her.

'*Oh, God.*'

Narciso held himself very still. He had to, or risk tearing her clothes off and taking her with the force of a rutting bull.

'God isn't going to help you now, naughty Ruby. You have to deal with me.'

'I... That shouldn't have happened.'

He nodded grimly. 'I agree.'

Wide blue eyes locked on his. 'You do?'

He swallowed hard. 'It should've happened when I was inside you. Now I feel woefully deprived.' Unable to stop himself, he moved his hands up and down her back. He tensed as her breathing changed. Desire thickened the air once more. Sensing her about to bolt, he flipped her over and trapped her underneath him. 'But I have you now.'

She tried to wriggle away but all she did was exacerbate the flashflood of desire drowning them both.

'No, I can't… We can't do this.'

He stiffened. 'Why not?'

'It won't end well. Simon—'

His eyes narrowed into warning slits. 'Was a cheating low-life who didn't deserve you. You and I together…we're different. We deserve each other.'

Narciso speared his fingers into her soft hair. But instead of kissing her, he grazed his lips along her jaw and down her throat to the pulse racing crazily there. He drew down her sleeves, exposing her breasts to his mouth. His mind screamed at him to stop before it was too late, but he was already sliding his tongue over one nipple.

Dio! He'd never known a woman to smash so effortlessly through his defences.

Her nails raked his nape and he groaned in approval. By the time he turned his attention to her other nipple, her whimpers were adding fire to his raging arousal.

She tugged on his shirt and he gave in to her demand. With a ragged laugh, he helped her reef it over his head and divested her of her dress.

Stark hunger consumed him as he took a moment to feast his eyes on her exposed body. 'You're so beautiful.' He drifted a hand down her chest and over her stomach to the top of her panties.

That disconcerting throb of possessiveness rocked through him again. He didn't want to know who else she'd been with but, in that moment, Narciso was glad her ex-business partner had failed to make her his. He settled himself over her, taking her mouth in a scorching kiss that obliterated words and feelings he didn't want to examine too closely.

His hand slid over her panties, hungrily seeking the heart of her. Her breath caught as his fingers breached her dampness and flicked over her sensitive flesh.

She jerked and squeezed her eyes tightly shut.

'Open your eyes, *amante*,' he commanded. He wanted…no, *needed* to see her, to assure himself that she was sliding into insanity just as quickly as he was. When she refused to comply, he applied more pressure. 'Do it or I'll stop.'

Eyes full of arousal slowly opened. His breath fractured at the electrifying connection. His whole body tightened to breaking point and he mentally shook his head.

What the hell was happening here?

Her delicate shudder slowed his flailing thoughts. Absorbing her reaction, he inserted one finger inside her, drinking in her hitched cry as she shuddered again.

'*Dio,* you're so tight.' He waited until she'd adjusted, then pressed in another finger.

Narciso was unprepared for her wince.

Instantly alert, he asked, 'What's wrong?'

She shook her head but he could see the trepidation in her eyes.

Those now familiar alarm bells shrieked. 'Answer me, Ruby.'

Nervously, she licked her lips. 'I'm…a virgin.'

Shock doused him in ice. For several seconds he couldn't move. Then the realisation of how close he'd come to taking her, to staking a claim on what he had no right to, hit him like a ton of bricks.

He surged back from her, reefing a hand through his hair as he inhaled sharply.

'You're a virgin,' he repeated numbly.

Raising her chin, she stared back at him. 'Yes.'

Several puzzle pieces finally slotted into place—the touches of innocence he'd spotted, her bolshiness even as she seemed out of her depth.

Her trepidation.

What had he said a moment ago—they *deserved* each other? Not any more.

Regret bit deep as he forced himself off the bed. 'Then, *cara mia,* this is over.'

Ruby came out of the bathroom of her cabin and slowed to a stop. Glancing around her room, she tried again to grapple with the sheer opulence around her. The three-decked yacht, complete with helicopter landing pad, had made her jaw drop the first time she'd seen it two days ago.

But the inside of Narciso's yacht was even more luxurious.

Black with a silver trim on the outside, it was an exact reverse on the inside. Silver and platinum vied with Carrara marble mined from the exclusive quarries north of Tuscany.

Her suite, complete with queen-size bed, sunken Jacuzzi bath and expensive toiletries, was the last word in luxury.

But all the opulence couldn't stem the curious emptiness inside her.

Since her arrival in Belize, she'd barely seen Narciso. The only times she saw him was when she served the list of meals he'd approved the day they'd boarded *The Warlock*.

At first the studied consideration with which he'd treated her after she'd blurted her confession had surprised her. Who knew he was the sort of playboy who treated virgins as if they were sacred treasures?

But then she'd seen the look in his eyes. The regret. The banked pain. Her surprise had morphed into confusion.

She was still confused now as she tugged off her towel and headed for the drawer that held her meagre clothes. Only to stop dead at the sight of the monogrammed leather suitcase standing at the bottom of the bed.

She opened it. Silk sarongs, bikinis, sundresses, designer shoes and slippers fell out of the case as she dug through it, her stomach hollowing out with incredulity.

Dressing in the jeans and top she'd travelled to Macau in and taken to wearing since her arrival simply because the three evening gowns were totally out of the question, she went in search of the elusive Sicilian who seemed hell-bent on keeping her permanently off balance.

She found him on the middle deck, after getting lost twice. He wore white linen shorts and a dark blue polo shirt. The early evening sun slanted over jet-black hair, highlighting its vibrancy and making her recall how it had felt to run her hands through the strands.

The sight of his bare legs made her swallow before she reminded herself she wasn't going to be affected by his stunning physique any longer. He'd pointedly avoided her for two whole days. She was damned if she'd let him catch her drinking him in as if he were her last hope for sustenance.

She was here to do a job. Whatever closeness they'd shared on his plane was gone, a temporary aberration never to be repeated. Her focus now needed to be on what she'd come here to do. But before that…

'You bought me clothes?' she asked.

He turned around, casually shoving his hands into his pockets. When his eyes met hers, she couldn't read a single expression in the silver depths. The Narciso who'd alternately laughed, mocked and devoured her with his eyes was gone. In his place was a coolly remote stranger.

'The size of your suitcase suggested you'd packed for a short stay. This is a solution to a potential problem. Unless you plan on wearing those jeans every day for the next week?'

True, in the strong Belizean sun, they felt hot and sticky on her skin. Not to mention they were totally inappropriate for the job she was here to do. When she cooked, she preferred looser, comfortable clothes.

But still. 'I could've sorted my own wardrobe.'

'You're here on my schedule. Making time for you to go shopping doesn't feature on there.'

'I wouldn't have—'

'It was no big deal, Ruby. Let's move on. It's time to step up your game. I want to see how you fare with a three-course meal. Michel will assist you if you need it.' He glanced at his watch. 'I'd like to eat at seven, which gives you two hours.'

The arrogant dismissal made her hackles rise. The distance between them made her feel on edge, bereft.

She assured herself it was better this way. But deep down, an ache took root.

Michel, Narciso's chef, greeted her with an openly friendly smile when she entered the kitchen.

'What do you have in mind for today for *monsieur?*' the Frenchman asked. Deep blue eyes remained contemplative as he stared at her.

'He wants to eat at seven so I was thinking of making a special bruschetta to start and chicken parmigiana main if we have the ingredients?'

'Of course. I bought fresh supplies this morning from town.'

The mention of town made her wonder when Narciso had bought her clothes. Had he shopped for them himself or given instructions?

Shaking her head to dispel the useless wondering, she followed Michel into the pantry. 'Oh…heaven!' She fell on the plump tomatoes and aubergines and squealed when she saw the large heads of truffles carefully packed in a box.

Freshly sliced prosciutto hung from specially lined containers that kept it from drying out and Parma ham stayed cool in a nearby chiller.

Michel took out the deboned chicken breast in the fridge. 'Would you like me to cut it up for you?'

'Normally, I'd say yes, but I think it's best if I do everything myself.' She smiled to take the sting out of the refusal.

He shrugged. 'Shout if you need anything.' After helping himself to a bottle of water, he left her alone.

Ruby selected the best knife and began chopping garlic, onions and the fresh herbs Michel kept in the special potted containers in the pantry.

The sense of calm and pure joy in bringing the ingredients together finally soothed the unsettled feeling she'd experienced for the last forty-eight hours.

Time and anxiety suspended, and her thoughts floated away as she immersed herself in her one salvation—the joy of cooking.

She started on the caviar-topped bruschetta with ricotta and peppers while the parmigiana was in the last stages of cooking.

Setting it out on a sterling-silver tray, she headed upstairs to where the crew had set the table.

Her feet slowed when she saw the extra place setting, then she stopped completely at the intimacy created by the dim lighting and lit candles. Her stomach fluttered wildly as steel butterflies took flight inside her.

'Are you going to stand there all evening?' Narciso quipped from where he sat on a sofa that hugged the U-shape of the room.

'I...thought I was cooking for just you.'

'You thought wrong.' He stood, came over and pulled out her chair. 'Tonight we eat together.' His gaze took in her jeans. 'Right after you change.'

'I don't need to change.'

'One rule of business is to learn to let the little things slide. Standing on principle and antagonising your potential business partner doesn't make for a very good impression.'

'I really appreciate you helping me out but—'

'I would personally prefer not to eat with a dinner companion wearing clothes smeared with food.'

Ruby glanced down and, sure enough, a large oily streak had soiled her vest top.

He'd gone to the trouble of providing new clothes for her comfort. Would it hurt to show some appreciation? In a few days, she'd be back in New York, hopefully with a contract firmly in her pocket. He'd made it clear she was no longer attractive to him in the sexual sense, so she had nothing to fear there.

'I'll go and change,' she murmured around the disquiet spreading through her.

'*Grazie,*' he replied.

Returning to her suite, she quickly undressed and selected a soft peach, knee-length sundress with capped sleeves. Slipping her feet into three-inch wedged sandals, she tied her hair back and returned to the deck.

His gaze slid over her but his face remained neutral as he pulled out her chair.

'Sit, and tell me what you've made for us.'

The intimate *us* made her hand tremble. Taking a deep breath, she described the first course. He picked up a piece of bruschetta, slid it into his mouth and chewed.

The process of watching him eat something she'd made with her two hands was so strangely unsettling and erotic her fingers clenched on her napkin.

'Hmm, good enough.' He picked up another piece and popped it in his mouth.

When she found herself staring at his strong jaw and throat, she averted her gaze, picked up a piece and nibbled on the edge. 'Damned with faint praise.'

'The cracked pepper adds a zing. I like it.'

Heady pleasure flowed through her. 'Really?'

'I always mean what I say, Ruby.' His grave tone told her they weren't talking about just food.

'O...okay,' she answered. 'I have to check on the parmigiana in ten minutes.'

'That's more than enough time for a drink.'

Abandoning her half-eaten bruschetta, Ruby headed for the extensive bar, only to stop dead.

'We're no longer moored?' The bright lights of the marina had disappeared, leaving only the stunning dark orange of the setting sun as their backdrop.

'No, we're sailing along the coast. Tomorrow morning, I intend to dive the Blue Hole. Do you dive?' he asked.

She continued to the bar, her nerves jumpier than they had been a minute ago. 'I did, a long time ago.'

'Good. You'll join me.'

'Is that a request or a demand?'

He'd ignored her for the past two days. The idea that he now wanted to spend time with her jangled her fraying nerves. As she recalled what had happened on the plane heat and confusion spiked anew through her.

'It's a very civilised request.'

And yet...

Regardless of what Narciso was requesting, the last thing she needed to be doing was anticipating spending any time in his company. He made her lose control. She only had to look into his eyes to feel herself skating close to emotional meltdown.

The last thing she'd wanted when she met Narciso was to give in to the attraction she'd felt for him. But perversely, now he'd made it clear he intended to give her a wide berth, her mind kept conjuring up scenarios of how things could be between them.

She'd been wrong to compare Narciso to Simon, or even to her father. Despite the playboy exterior, she'd glimpsed a core of integrity in her potential new business partner that was markedly absent from the men she'd so far encountered.

Potential new business partner...

Therein lay her next problem. Whether active or passive, if she passed his test, Narciso would own a share in her business. They'd have a *business* relationship.

Which meant, nothing could be allowed to develop between them personally.

She worked almost absent-mindedly and only realised the drink she'd made after she opened the cocktail shaker. Aghast, she stared into the bold red drink.

'Are you going to serve...what is that anyway?'

Flames surged up her cheeks. 'Allow me to present the *Afrodisiaco.*'

One brow cocked; a touch of the irreverence she'd become used to darted over his features. 'Is there a message in there somewhere?'

That she'd produced one of the most suggestive cocktails on her list made her pulse jump as she poured it. 'It's just a name.'

He immediately shook his head. 'I've learned that nothing is ever what its face value suggests.' He sipped the cocktail, swirled it around in his mouth. 'Although now I've tasted this, I'm willing to alter that view.'

'Narciso...' The moment she uttered his name he froze. An-other crack forked through the severely compromised founda-tion of her resistance as she watched his eyes darken.

'No, Ruby *mio,* you don't get to say my name for the first time like that.'

She paused. 'I'm sorry, but you need to explain to me what the last two days have been about.'

'Basta...' His voice held stark warning.

'Non abbastanza! I didn't ask you to seduce me on your plane. In fact, I made it very clear I wanted to be left alone be-cause I knew— I wasn't... Look, whatever experiences you've had in the past are your own. But you told me you didn't like women who blew hot and cold. Well, guess what, that's exactly what you're doing!'

'Are you quite finished?' he grated out, his face a mask of taut control.

She gripped the counter until her knuckles whitened and she stared down at her dress. 'As a matter of fact, I'm not. Thank you for buying the clothes. If I appeared unappreciative before it was because I've learnt that nothing comes for free.'

'You're welcome,' he replied coolly. 'Now am I allowed to respond to that diatribe?'

'No. I have to check on the chicken parmagiana. The last thing I want to do is jeopardise my chances by serving you burnt food.' She rounded the bar and walked past him.

He grasped her wrist, easily imprisoning her.

Instantly, heat and electricity flooded through her. 'Let me go!'

'I haven't been blowing hot and cold.'

'You've certainly made avoiding me an art form.'

'I was trying to save us both from making a mistake, *tesoro.*'

The realisation that she didn't want that choice made for her sent a bolt of shock through her. Sheer self-preservation made her raise her chin. 'Well, you needn't have bothered. In fact you did me a favour back on your plane.'

His hand tightened. 'Really?'

'Yes. You reminded me that you're not my type.'

His nostrils flared. 'And how would you know what your type is considering your lack of experience?'

'I don't need experience to know playboys turn me off.'

His mouth flattened. 'You didn't seem turned off when you climaxed on top of me, then proceeded to writhe beneath me.'

The reminder made her pulse skitter. The hungry demand that hadn't abated since then made her pull harder. He set her free and she retreated fast. 'Maybe I wanted to see what the fuss was all about. Whatever. You helped me refocus on the reason I'm here on your boat. Now if you'll excuse me, I have to check on the main course.'

Narciso watched her go, furious that he'd allowed himself to be drawn into her orbit again.

The way he'd operated the last two days had been the best course.

So what if he'd climbed metaphoric walls while locked in his study? He'd sealed two deals and added to his billions, and he'd even managed to stop thinking about Ruby Trevelli for longer than five minutes.

But then his investigator had presented him with another opportunity to finish off Giacomo. And once again, Narciso had walked away, unable to halt the chain reaction inside that seemed to be scraping raw emotions he'd long ago suppressed; unable to stop his world hurtling towards a place he didn't recognise.

That his first thought had been to seek out Ruby and share his confusion had propelled him in the opposite direction.

His reaction to her continued to baffle him. In the last two days, he'd expended serious brainpower talking himself out of tracking down the woman who kissed like a seductress but whose innocence his conscience battled with him against tainting.

Dio, when the hell had he even *grown* a conscience?

With a growl, he grabbed the last of the canapés and munched on it. Delicate flavours exploded on his tongue.

The past two days had shown him how talented Ruby was in the kitchen and behind the bar. Her skill was faultless and she'd risen to his every challenge. In that time, while he'd locked himself in his study to resist temptation, he'd also reviewed the TV show footage and seen why she'd won the contest.

Her skittishness every time the camera had focused on her had also been made apparent.

She hated being under the spotlight. And yet she'd forced herself to do it, just so she could take control of her life.

His admiration for her had grown as he'd watched the footage even as he'd cursed at the knowledge that she was burrowing deeper under his skin.

He looked up as she entered, a silver-topped casserole dish in her hand. The flourish and expertise with which she set the dish down spoke of her pride in her work. He waited until she served them both before he took the first bite.

His hand tightened around his fork. 'Did you cook this for Simon?'

She visibly deflated. 'You don't like it.'

He didn't just like it. He loved it. So much so he was suddenly jealous of her sharing it with anyone else. 'I didn't say that. Did you cook it for him?'

Slowly, she shook her head.

Relief poured through him. 'Good.'

'So, you like it?' she asked again.

'*Sì*, very much,' he responded, his voice gruff.

The pleasure that lit up her face made his heart squeeze. He wanted to keep staring at her, bathe in her delight.

Dio, he was losing it.

He reached for the bottle to pour her a glass of chilled Chablis.

'No, thanks,' she said.

His hand tightened around the bottle. 'You have nothing to fear by drinking around me, Ruby.'

She raised her head and he saw a mixture of anguish and sadness displayed in her eyes. In that moment, Narciso wanted to hunt down the parents who'd done this to her and deliver unforgettable punishment.

'I know, but I'd like to keep a clear head, all the same.'

He set the wine aside and reached for the mineral water. 'Well, getting blind drunk on my own is no fun, so I guess we're teetotalling.'

She rolled her eyes and smiled, and his gut clenched hard.

'We haven't discussed wines yet. When we're done meet me at the upper deck. And wear a swimsuit. The sun may have gone down but you'll still boil out there in that dress.'

The tension in his body eased when she nodded.

After dinner, he made his way up to the deck. They could do this… They could have a conversation despite the spiked awareness of each other. Or the hunger that burned relentlessly through him—

Five minutes later, she mounted the stairs to the deck and his thoughts scattered.

Madre di Dio!

The body he could see beneath the sarong was spectacular. But he couldn't see enough of it. And he wanted to, despite the *off limits* signs he'd mentally slapped on her.

Seeing doesn't mean touching.

'Drop the sarong. You don't need it here.'

She fidgeted with the knot and his temperature rose higher. It loosened as she walked over to the lounger. She finally dropped it, sat down, and crossed her legs. Minutes ticked by. She recrossed her legs.

'Stop fidgeting.'

She blew out a sigh. 'I can't stand the tension.'

'Well, running away won't make it go away.'

'I wasn't planning to run,' she replied. 'You wanted to talk about wines, remember?'

He nodded, although he'd lost interest in that subject. Forcing himself to look away from the temptation of the small waist that flared into very feminine hips and long, shapely legs, he stared at the moon rising over the water.

'Or I could easily return to my cabin and we can continue to treat each other like strangers.'

He considered the idea for exactly two seconds before he tossed it.

'What the hell, Ruby *mio*, let's give civility a try.'

She exhaled, sat up and poured a glass of mineral water from the jug nearby. 'Okay, first, I have to ask—what the heck is up with your name, anyway?'

He smiled despite the poker-sharp pain in his gut. 'You don't like it?'

'It's…different.'

'It was Giacomo's idea of a joke. But I've grown into it, don't you think?' Despite his joviality, the pain in his chest grew. Her eyes stayed on him and he saw when she noticed it. For some reason, revealing himself in that way didn't disturb him as much as he'd thought it would. In fact, talking to her soothed him.

'You've never wanted to change it?'

'It's just a name. I'm sure a few people will agree I can be narcissistic on occasion. I have no problems in pleasing number one.'

Her eyes gleamed with speculative interest. 'It really doesn't bother you, does it?'

'It may have, once upon a time,' he confessed. 'But not any more.'

Sympathy filled her eyes. 'I'm sorry.'

He tried to speak but words locked in his throat. Two simple words. Powerful words that calmed his roiling emotions. *'Grazie,'* he murmured.

His eyes caught and held hers. Something shifted, settled between them. An acknowledgement that neither of them were whole or without a history of buried hurt.

'The email on the plane. What was that about?' he asked abruptly.

She slowly inhaled. 'Before I tell you, promise me it won't

affect the outcome of this test run.' Her imploring look almost made him reply in the affirmative.

He hardened his resolve when he realised she was doing it again. Getting under his skin. Making a nonsense of his common sense.

'Sorry, *amante,* I don't make blind promises when it comes to business.'

Her lips firmed. 'Simon sold his share of the business to a guy who doesn't see eye to eye with my business plan.' In low tones, she elaborated.

He jerked upright. 'You're being threatened by a loan shark?'

'Yes.'

'And you didn't think to inform me?' he demanded.

'Would you have believed me? Especially in light of how I approached you?'

'Perhaps not right then, but...' The idea that he was prepared to give her the benefit of the doubt gave him a moment's pause. 'What's his name?'

'I don't know—he refused to tell me. All he wants is his money.'

'So I own twenty-five per cent of your business and a loan shark whose name you don't know another twenty-five per cent?'

'Yes.'

He slowly relaxed on his lounger and stared at her. 'You do realise that our agreement is transforming into substantially more than a talent-contest-prize delivery, don't you?'

A flush warmed her skin. 'I'm not sure I know what you mean.'

'What I mean, Ruby *mio,* is that in order to realise my twenty-five-per-cent investment, it seems I have to offer my business expertise. Writing you a cheque after next week and walking away is looking less and less likely.'

Why that thought pleased him so much, Narciso refused to examine.

CHAPTER EIGHT

'I DON'T REMEMBER the last time I sunbathed.'

'I can tell.'

Blue eyes glared at him and his pulse rocketed. Narciso tried to talk himself calmer. No one else was to blame since *he'd* invited her to go scuba-diving with him. *After* another sleepless night battling unrelenting sexual frustration.

'How can you tell? And don't tell me it's because you're a warlock.'

'I don't need otherworldly powers, *cara*. Your skin is so pale it's almost translucent and there are no visible tan lines.'

She glanced down at herself. 'Oh.'

'Here.' He grabbed the sun protection, started to move towards her, changed his mind at the last minute and tossed it to her.

'Thanks.' She sat on the same lounger as last night. But this time, the smell of her skin and the drying sea water made his blood heat.

'Where did you learn to dive?' he asked to distract himself from following the slim fingers that worked their way up her leg.

She smiled. 'I spent a few summers working at a hotel in Florida when I was in high school. I worked in the kitchens and got to dive in my spare time.'

'Have you always known you wanted to be a chef?'

Her smile immediately dimmed and he cursed himself for broaching a touchy subject.

'I knew I had my parents' talent but I resisted it for a long time.'

'I've seen the footage of the contest. You're not a natural in front of the camera.'

One brow rose. 'Gee, thanks.'

'What I mean is, you can easily prove to your parents that they're wasting their time trying to recruit you.'

'It won't stop them from trying.'

He shrugged. 'Then tell them you have a demanding new business partner.'

She shook her head. 'I'd rather not.'

'You want to keep me your dirty little secret, *tesoro?*'

She smiled but the light in her eyes remained dim. 'Something like that. What about you? Have you always known you wanted to be a warlock?'

He laughed, experiencing a new lightness inside. When her lips curved in response, he forcibly clenched his hands to stop from reaching for her. 'Ever since I made my first million at eighteen.'

'Wow, that must have brought the girls running.'

He shrugged, suddenly reluctant to dwell on past conquests. 'It gave me the ammunition I needed…'

She frowned slightly. 'Ammunition. To fight your father?'

'To fight Giacomo, yes.'

'Why do you call him Giacomo?'

He exhaled. 'Because he was never a *father* to me.'

She paused and that soft look entered her eyes. The realisation that he didn't mind talking to her about his past shocked him. He tried to tell himself it meant nothing, but he knew he was deluding himself.

'What about your mother? Is she alive?'

Sharp pain pierced his chest. 'My poor mama is what started this whole nasty business.'

'What do you mean?'

'She died giving birth to me. I was so determined to make

a quick entrance into the world, I caused her to bleed almost to death by the roadside before an ambulance could arrive.'

Her gasp echoed around the sun-dappled deck. 'Surely, you don't think that's your fault?'

'Giacomo certainly seems to think so.'

It occurred to him that Ruby was the first woman he'd actively conversed with. Normally, any conversation was limited to the bedroom. But with sex off the table it seemed *talking* was the next best thing.

'That's why there's so much animosity between you two. He blames you for your mother's death?'

'It may have started out that way, but our *relationship* has evolved…mutated.'

'Into what?'

He started to answer then stopped. 'Into something that's no longer clear-cut.' Shock rolled through him as he accepted the truth. He'd started out wanting to destroy his father. Along the way, and especially lately, the urge to deliver the kill blow had waned. Even toying with his father now no longer held any interest for him.

'So what are you going to do about it?'

Sì, what was he going to do?

Call it a day and cut off all ties with Giacomo? The sudden ache in his gut made him stiffen and jerk upright.

'Enough about me. You have an exceptional talent. I'm officially hiring you to cater my dinner party.'

The compliment brought a smile to her lips. Again, he forced himself not to reach out and caress the satin smoothness of her determined jaw. The urge was stronger because he needed something to blot out his confused thoughts of his father.

'Thank you.' She put the sun protection down and glanced at him. 'Can I get you anything?'

He shook his head. 'No more cocktails.'

Her smile widened. 'Then I have the perfect thing.'

She stood and walked to the chiller behind the bar. To his

surprise she returned with an ice-cold beer. 'Sometimes a beer is the perfect solution to thirst.'

Narciso twisted off the cap with relish and took a long swig, and looked over to find her eyes on his throat. The feel of her eyes on him made his temperature shoot sky-high.

'Aren't you having a drink?'

She indicated the glass of water on the table next to her lounger.

'That must be warm by now.'

Wordlessly, he held out the bottle to her. Her eyes met his and sensation skated over him. Their attraction was skittering out of control but he couldn't seem to apply the brakes.

'You're thirsty. Take it.'

Slowly, she took the bottle from him. Her pink tongue darted out to caress the lip of the bottle before she took a small swig.

She held it back out to him. 'Thanks.'

'So beers are an exception to your don't-drink-much rules?'

'A small drink doesn't hurt.'

'Aren't you afraid you'll lose control with me?' he asked roughly.

'We established that anything between us would be a mistake, remember?'

He stepped deeper into quicksand, felt it close dangerously over him but still he didn't retreat.

Eyes on her, he took another swig of beer. 'Perhaps that no longer holds true.'

Her breath audibly hitched. 'Why? Tell me and I'll remind you when things threaten to get out of hand.'

He couldn't stop the laughter that rumbled from his chest. 'You mean as some form of shock therapy?'

'If it's what works for you.'

His gaze slid down her body. Skin made vibrant by the sun and the exertions of their dive this morning offered temptation so strong it was no wonder he could think straight.

'Don't worry, *tesoro,* I'll try and curb my uncontrollable urges.'

'I'm glad you can. I'm not so sure about myself,' she blurted.

For a moment, he thought his hearing was impaired. 'What did you just say?'

She shut her eyes and cursed as he'd only heard a true New Yorker curse. 'I feel as if I'm skidding close to the edge of my control where you're concerned. After Simon—'

'I am *not* Simon,' he grated out.

She trembled. 'Believe me, I know. But even though I keep telling myself what a bad idea this is, I can't stop myself from… wanting you.'

The blunt delivery made his eyes widen. 'You realise how much power you're giving me by telling me?'

'Yes. But I'm hoping you won't take undue advantage of it.'

Slowly, he set the bottle down. 'Come here.'

'Did I not just mention undue advantage?'

'Come here and we'll see if the advantage is undue or not.'

Ruby stood slowly and stepped towards him, fighting for a clear breath as he loomed large, powerful and excruciatingly addictive before her. Her skin burned where he cradled her hips in his palms.

'What do you want, Ruby?' he rasped.

She looked into his face and every self-preservation instinct fled.

She'd never met a man like Narciso Valentino before. Everything she'd found out about him in the last few days had blown her expectations of him sky-high.

His name might indicate self-absorption but she was learning he was anything but. He could've reported her to Zeus when he'd found out she'd applied to be a *Petit Q* under false pretences. He could've sent her packing after she told him about his company owing her. Stopping himself from seducing her and his generosity with the clothes coupled with his easy companionship this morning as they'd scuba-dived at one of the most beautiful places in the world had shown her that Narciso could be nothing like his name.

Little by little, the traits she'd discovered had whittled at her defences.

And now…

'As crazy and stupid as it is, I want to kiss you more than I want to breathe.'

Dear God, what was wrong with her?

'*Dio mio.*' He sounded strained…disarmed, as if she'd knocked his feet from under him.

She ought to pull back, retreat to the safety of her cabin. Instead, she took his face in her hands, leaned forward and kissed him.

His grunt of desire slammed into her before he seized her arms. Leaning back against the lounger, he tugged her on top of him. Strong arms imprisoned her as he moulded her body to his.

The evidence of arousal against her belly was unmistakable, gave her strength she hadn't known existed. She plunged her tongue into his mouth, felt the stab of pleasure when he jerked beneath her and groaned long and deep.

Firm hands angled her head for a deeper penetration that made her pulse thud a hundred times faster.

He made love to her with his mouth, lapping at her lips with long strokes that pulled at the hot, demanding place between her legs.

Her hands hungrily explored his warm, firm muscle and hair-roughened chest. When her fingers encountered his nipple, she grazed her nail against it, the way she knew drove him mad.

He tore his mouth from hers, his eyes molten grey as he gazed up at her.

'*Cara mia,* this will not end well for either of us if you don't stop that.'

Brazenly, she repeated the action. And watched in fascination as it puckered and goose bumps rose around the hard disc. Before she could give in to the urge to taste it, Narciso was moving her higher, stark purpose on his face.

'One bad turn deserves another.' Roughly, he tugged at her

bikini string and caught one plump breast in his mouth as they were freed from the garment.

The sight of him feasting on her in the dimming light was so erotic, Ruby's nails dug into his chest.

Her hips bucked against his hardness, that hunger climbing even higher as she rubbed against his full, heavy thickness. The thought of having that power inside her made her whimper. When his teeth tugged at her in response, her moan turned into a cry.

Foolish or not, dangerous or not, she wanted him. More than she'd ever wanted anything in her life. For the first time, Ruby understood a little bit of the passion that drove her parents. Of the need that forced two people wholly unsuited to stay together. If it was anywhere near this addictive, this mad, she could almost sympathise…

'Narciso…please…'

One hand splayed over her bottom, squeezed before grabbing the stretchy material of her bikini. He pulled, sending a million stars bursting behind her closed eyelids as the pressure on her heated clitoris intensified her pleasure. At her shocked gasp, he pulled tighter. Liquid heat rushed to fill her sensitive flesh. Almost immediately, she needed more, so much more that her body was threatening to burst out of her skin. She sank her hands into his hair and bit down on the rough skin of his jaw.

He cursed and froze, hard fingers gripping her hips. When the sensation slid from pleasure to a hint of pain, she lifted her head to gaze drowsily at him.

'What…?'

'Before this goes any further I need to be sure you want this,' he rasped.

She looked down, saw her state of undress, saw his hard, ready body.

Instinctively she went to adjust her clothes, her face flushing with heat. 'God, what's wrong with me?'

He stopped her agitated movements with steady hands. 'Hey,

there's *nothing* wrong with you. You're a sensual creature, with natural needs just like—'

'My father?' she inserted bleakly.

Surprisingly gentle hands framed her face. 'If you were like him you wouldn't still be a virgin. Do you get that?'

Tears prickled her eyes. 'But…I…'

'No, no more excuses. You stopped being their puppet a long time ago—you just forgot to cut the strings.'

Her breath stalled and her vision blurred. He brushed away her tears and she fought to speak. 'What does that say about me?'

His jaw clenched. 'That we sometimes spend too much time looking in the rear-view mirror to see what's ahead.'

She moved on top of him because, despite everything going south, her hunger hadn't abated one iota. His hands clamped down harder on her hips.

'What's in your rear-view mirror?' she asked him softly.

'Too much. Much too much.'

His answer held a depth of anguish that cut to her soul. Heart aching for him, she started to lean down but he caught and held her still.

'No.'

She looked into his face and saw his slightly ashen pallor. 'You don't want me to kiss you?'

His chest heaved and he glanced away.

The realisation hit her like a bolt of lightning. 'You stopped us making love on the plane and just now because you don't think you're worth it, do you? Why not? Because your father told you you weren't?'

'Ruby, stop,' he warned.

She ignored him, the need to offer comfort bleeding through her. She caressed his taut cheek. A pulse beat so hard in his jaw, her fingers tingled from the contact.

'*Cara,* I'm a man on the edge. A man who wants what he shouldn't have. Get off me before I do something we'll both regret, *per favore.*'

Fresh tears prickled her eyes, stung the back of her throat.

If anyone had told her a week ago she'd be lying on top of the world's most notorious playboy, baring her soul to him and catching a glimpse of his ragged soul in return, she'd have called them insane.

Her hands shook as she slowly removed them from his face. Levering herself away from him was equally hard because her knees rebelled at supporting her in her weakened state.

Snatching at her bikini top, desperately trying to ignore his silent scrutiny, she tied the strings as best she could and secured the sarong over her chest.

Her hair was an unruly mess she didn't bother to tackle. What had just happened had gone beyond outer appearances.

She looked down at him and he returned her look, the torture unveiled now. She floundered, torn between helping him and fleeing to examine her own confused emotions. Eventually, she chose the latter. 'I have a few things to take care of in the kitchen before I go to bed. *Bona notti.*'

Slowly, he rose to tower over her, and in the fading daylight she saw his bunched fists at his sides.

His smile was cut from rough stone. 'I've awakened too many demons for me to have a restful night, *tesoro*. But I wish you a good night all the same.'

I've awakened too many demons...

Ruby lay in bed a few hours later, wracked with guilt.

She'd pushed him to relive his past, to rake over old wounds because she'd wanted to know the real man underneath the gloss.

To reassure herself he wouldn't hurt or betray her?

Shame coiled through her as she acknowledged that she'd been testing him. But then deep down, ever since he'd turned away from her on the plane, she'd known Narciso was nothing like her father. Or Simon.

And still she'd pushed...

She reared up and gripped the side of her bed. Her head

cautioned her against the need to find out if she'd pushed him too far, if the demons were indeed keeping him awake. But her heart propelled her to her feet.

She went down the hallway and knocked on his door before her courage deserted her.

The evidence that he was indeed up came a second later when the door was wrenched open. He was dressed in his silk pajama bottoms and nothing else.

'What the hell are you doing here, Ruby?' he flung at her.

She struggled to look up from his chest. 'I…wanted to make sure you were okay. And to apologise for what happened earlier. I had no right to push you like that.'

His eyes narrowed for several seconds before he turned and strode back into the bedroom. 'I'm learning that warlocks and demons keep good company.' He picked up a crystal tumbler of Scotch, raised it to her and took a sip.

Ruby found herself moving forward before she'd consciously made the decision to.

Her hand closed over the glass and stopped his second sip.

He stepped back away from her but, hampered by the bed, he abruptly sank down. She took the glass from him and set it on the side table.

'Drinking is not the answer. Trust me, I know.'

Strong hands gripped the sheets as if physically stopping himself from reaching for her and he exhaled harshly.

This close, the beauty of him took her breath away. His chest heaved again, the movement emphasising his stunning physique and golden skin.

Fiery desire slammed into her so hard she reeled under the onslaught.

Before she could stop to question herself, she slid her hands over his biceps. Warm muscles rippled under her touch.

'What the hell are you doing?' His voice was rough and gritty with need.

Her face flamed but a deeper fire of determination burned

within her. 'I have a feeling it's called seduction. I don't know because I've never done this before.'

She leaned in closer. He groaned as her hardened T-shirt-covered nipples grazed his chest. '*Per amore di Dio,* why are you doing it now?'

She placed a finger over his lip and felt a tiny jolt of triumph when it puckered slightly against her touch. 'Because it's driving me as insane. And because I don't want to live in fear of what I might become if I let go. So this is me owning my fear.'

He cursed again and he shook his head. Knowing he was about to deny her, she pushed him onto the bed and sealed her mouth over his.

He groaned and accepted her kiss with a demanding roughness that threatened to blow her away. Encouraged by that almost helpless response, she threw one leg over him and straddled his big body.

Immediately, his already potent arousal thickened, lengthened, found the cradle between her legs. Before she lost her mind completely, Ruby reached out to both sides of the bed and loosened the ties she needed, then she worked quickly before he could stop her.

He wrenched his mouth from hers, and glanced up. Silver eyes darkening in shock, then disbelief. *'Hai perso la tua mente?'*

'No, I haven't lost my mind.'

'Clearly, you have.' He yanked on the binds but they only tightened further. 'Release me, Ruby.'

'Nope. What goes around comes around, *tesoro.*'

Feeling a little bit bolder now she knew he wouldn't easily overpower her or dismiss her, she took a deep breath, drew her T-shirt over her head and flung it away.

'Ruby…' Warning tinged his low growl.

She wavered but the look in his eyes stalled her breath—hunger, anger, a touch of admiration, that little bit of wonder and vulnerability she'd seen earlier on the deck all mingled in his hypnotic eyes.

'I would, but the look in your eyes is scaring me right now. What's to say you won't devour me the minute I set you free?' She trailed a finger down his chest and revelled in his hitched breathing.

'I won't,' he bit out.

She shivered again at the menace in his voice. 'Liar, liar.'

'*Madre di Dio,* do you really want to lose your virginity so badly?'

She shook her head and her hair came free from the loose knot she'd put it into. 'No, it isn't actually that important to me. What I want, what I crave, is to make love with you.'

His eyes darkened. 'Why?'

She tamped down on what she really wanted to say. That he'd shown her another way to view herself. Another way that didn't make her skin crawl for feeling sensual pleasure.

'Do I have to have some noble reason? Isn't crazy chemistry enough? I was absolutely fine before you touched me. You woke this hunger inside me. Now because of some stupid principle, you're trying to deny me what I want. What we both want. I won't let you.'

His chest heaved. 'I won't let you either. Not like this.' The roughness in his tone gave her pause. When she looked into his eyes, that bleakness she'd spotted in the kitchen on their first morning in Macau was back. 'If you want me, release me.'

She wanted to kiss that look away, to utterly and totally eradicate it so it never returned. Leaning down, she did exactly that, luxuriating in the velvety feel of his warm lips. He kissed her back but she could sense the agitation clawing under his skin and she drew back a little. Caressing his chest and shoulders, she touched her lips to his again in a gentle offer of solace from whatever demons were eating him alive.

A rough sigh rumbled from his chest.

'Narciso…'

His lips trembled against hers. 'Release me, Ruby.'

Heart in her throat, she repeated the words he'd said to her in Macau. 'I already have.'

Shocked eyes darted upward. A split second later he was flipping her beneath him, ripping away her panties and flinging them over his shoulder.

Molten eyes speared her as he tugged off his pyjamas, his gaze settling possessively on her damp, exposed sex. 'Sorry, Ruby *mio,* I lied.'

'About what?' Her voice trembled.

'About not devouring you.'

Hot, sensual lips grazed down her cleavage to her navel, the rasp of his growing stubble sending electrifying tingles racing through her body. His tongue circled her navel, then strong teeth bit the skin just below.

Her shudder threatened to lift her off the bed.

One large hand splayed on her stomach and the other parted her legs wider. Watching him watch her was the most erotic experience of her life so far.

She didn't need a crystal ball to know there was more, so much more in store for her.

He bypassed her most sensitive place, lifted one leg to bend it at the knee. Hot kisses trailed down her inside thigh. Again the graze of his stubble added a rough, pleasurable edge that made her breath come out in agitated gasps.

Nibbling his way down, he soothed his bites with open-mouthed kisses that sparked a yearning for that mouth at her core.

But he took his time. Leisurely, he kissed his way down her other thigh, all the while widening her thighs, those molten eyes not leaving her heated sex.

Ruby wondered why she wasn't dying with embarrassment. But seeing the effect the sight of her had on him—nostrils flared as he breathed her in, his fingers trembling slightly as he gripped her knee—she had little room for anything but desire.

'Lei è sfarzoso,' he muttered thickly.

She *felt* gorgeous, a million miles from what she'd always feared she would feel when it came to sex. She blinked back tears and cried out as sublime pleasure roared through her.

Lips, tongue, teeth. True to his words Narciso devoured her with a singular, greedy purpose.

From far away, she heard her cries of ecstasy, smelled the heat of his skin coupled with the scent of her arousal as she writhed with bliss beneath him.

Just when she thought she would burst out of her skin, he raised his head.

'I'd had this thought in my head that the first time I took you I'd torture you for hours with pleasure.' Still holding her down, he pulled open the beside drawer and grabbed a condom. Impatiently, he ripped it open with his teeth. 'But I can't wait one more second, *amante.*'

'I don't want you to.'

Hooded eyes regarded her. 'I can't promise it will be gentle. I could hurt you.'

The slight note of apprehension washed away when she recalled what had happened on the deck earlier this evening. Despite the volatile emotions that had raged between them, he'd never hurt her.

She laid her hand over the one he'd flattened on her belly. 'I'm ready.'

He leaned back and she saw him, really saw him for the first time. The erection that sprang from his groin was powerful and proud. Another testament to how well his name suited him. Judging from the size of him, he had a lot to crow about in that department, too.

Holding himself in one fist, he rolled on the condom and settled stormy eyes on her. 'Are you sure about this?' he rasped.

'Right this moment, my confidence is wavering a little,' she confessed, her voice shaky with the knowledge that he would soon be inside her.

He inhaled deeply. 'I promise to go as fast or as slow as you desire,' he said in a deep solemn voice.

Unable to speak, Ruby nodded. In a slow, predatory crawl he surged over her. Dark hair fell over his forehead in that careless way she found irresistible. She had a second to weave her fingers through it before he was kissing her again.

By the time he lifted his head hers was swimming. The flush that scoured his cheekbones signalled his fast-slipping control. His erection pulsed against her thigh and the very air crackled with sensual expectation so thick, all her confidence from minutes ago oozed out of her like air from a balloon.

'What do I do now?'

He glanced down to where her hunger raged, to the glistening entrance to her body. 'Open wider for me,' he breathed.

Every single atom in her body poised with tingling expectation as she complied with his command and spread her thighs wider. 'Now what?'

Silver eyes returned to hers. 'Now…you breathe, Ruby *mio*.' He took her lips in a quick, hard kiss. 'This will be no fun at all if you pass out.'

Reeling from the sensation coursing through her, she sucked air through her mouth.

'That's it. Eyes on me and don't move,' he instructed.

The first push inside her threatened to expel the air she'd fed her starving lungs. From head to toe, Ruby was soaked in indescribable sensation.

'Oh!' She breathed out again, her hands tightening on his shoulders as her craving escalated. 'More.'

He shut his eyes for a split second, then he pushed in further, carefully gauging her reaction as he deepened the penetration.

The need clawing through her sharpened, deepened. Unable to lie still, she twisted upward to meet him.

'*Dio!* Don't do that.'

'But I like it.' She twisted higher, then gave a cry as pain ripped through her pelvis.

'*Per amore di…* I told you not to move.' His lips were tension-white and sweat beaded his forehead.

He started to withdraw but the pain was already fading. Quickly she clamped her legs around his waist.

'No.' He levered his arms on either side of her in preparation to remove himself from her body. The knowledge that he was holding himself back so forcefully sent a different sensation through her.

Her hand trailed up his throat to clutch his nape, holding him prisoner. 'Yes.'

Tightening her grip, she forced her hips up. He slid deeper to fully embed himself within her and she cried out in pleasure.

'Ruby…'

'Make love to me, Narciso,' she pleaded, because she knew that whatever she was feeling right now, there was so much more to come. 'Please.'

With a groan, he sealed his body fully with hers.

Sizzling pleasure raced up her spine as he set a thrusting rhythm designed to drive her out of her mind. Considering she was already halfway there, it didn't take long before Ruby stopped breathing again, poised on the edge of some unknown precipice that beckoned with seductive sorcery.

Against her lips, Narciso murmured thick, hot words in native Sicilian. Those that she understood would've made her blush if her whole body wasn't already burning from the fierce power of his possession.

His lips grazed along her jaw, down her throat to enslave one nipple in his mouth. His tongue lapped her in rhythm with his thrusts, adding another dimension to the sensations flowing through her.

One hand hooked under her thigh, spreading her even wider. He groaned at the altered angle just as she began to fracture.

He raised his head from her breast and locked his gaze on hers. The connection, deep, hot and direct, was the final straw.

Convulsions tore through her, rocking her from head to toe with indescribable bliss that wrenched a scream from the depths of her soul.

Lost in the maelstrom of ecstasy, she heard him groan deeply before long shudders seized his frame.

His damp forehead touched hers, then his head found the

curve of her shoulder. Hot, agitated breaths bathed her neck as his heartbeat thundered in tandem with hers.

In that moment, she experienced a closeness she'd never experienced with another human being. She told herself it was a false sensation but still she basked in it, unable to stop the giddy, happy feeling washing over her. Her arms tightened around him and she would gladly have stayed there for ever but he moved, turning sideways to lie on the bed.

'I don't want to crush you.' His voice was thick, almost gruff.

'Don't worry, I'm stronger than I look.'

He half growled. 'I guessed as much earlier. Where did you learn to make ties like that?'

'Tying up chickens and turkeys for roasting.'

He grimaced. 'I'm flattered.'

'Don't worry, Narciso. I'll never mistake you for a chicken.'

His laughter caused her heart to soar, the simple pleasure of making him laugh lifting her spirits.

Resting her chin on his chest, she looked into his eyes. *'Grazie.'*

He caught a curl and twisted it around his finger. *'Per quello che?'*

'For making my first so memorable.'

'It was a first for me, too, after a fashion.'

A thousand questions smashed through her brain but she forced herself to push them away. 'Hmm, I guess it was.'

They lay in replete silence for several more minutes. And then the atmosphere began to change.

She started to move but his arm tightened around her. A deep swallow moved his Adam's apple.

'Tomorrow, we'll talk properly, *sì?*'

Heart in her throat, she nodded. *'Sì.'*

'Good. Now I get to show you my favourite knot.'

CHAPTER NINE

'*CIAO.*'

The deep voice roused her from languor and she opened her eyes to find Narciso standing over her lounger, cell phone in one hand.

The midmorning sun blazed on the private deck outside his bedroom suite and Ruby squirmed under his gaze as it raked her.

'*Ciao.* I can't believe I let you convince me to sunbathe nude.'

'Not completely nude.' He eyed her bikini bottoms.

Heat crawled up her neck and she hurriedly changed the subject. 'Was your call successful?'

'*Sì,* but then all my negotiations are,' he said with a smug smile.

'Your modesty is so refreshing. I guess making a million dollars by age eighteen tends to go to one's head.'

'On the contrary, my head was very clear. I had only one goal in mind.'

Despite the sun's blaze, she shivered. 'So it started that long ago, this feud between you two?'

He tossed his phone onto the table and stretched out on the lounger next to hers. Ruby fought not to ogle the broad, firm expanse of skin she'd taken delight in exploring last night. The grim look on his face helped her resist the temptation.

'Believe it or not, there was a time when I toyed with the idea of abandoning it.'

Surprise scythed through her. 'Really?'

'*Sì*,' he replied, almost inaudibly.

'What happened?'

'I graduated from Harvard a year early and decided to spend my gap year in Sicily. I knew Giacomo would be there. And I knew he couldn't throw me out because the house he lived in belonged to my mother and she'd willed it to me when I turned eighteen. I…hoped that being under the same roof again for the first time in five years would give us a different perspective.'

'It didn't?'

The hand on his thigh slowly curled into a fist. 'No. We clashed harder than ever.'

She couldn't mistake the ragged edge in his voice. 'If he hated you being there so much, why didn't he leave?'

'That would've meant I'd won. Besides, he took pleasure in reminding me I'd killed my mother on the street right outside her home.'

Ice drenched her veins. 'What happened to her?'

'She suffered a placental abruption three weeks before I was due. She'd gone for a walk and was returning home. By the time she dragged herself up the road to the house to alert anyone, she'd lost too much blood. Apparently, the doctor said he could only save one of us. Giacomo asked him to save my mother. She died anyway. I survived.'

Ruby reached out and covered his fist with her hand. He tensed for a second, then his hand wrapped around hers.

'How can anyone in their right mind believe that something so tragic was your fault?'

'Giacomo believed it. That was enough. And he was right to demand that the doctor save my mother.'

She flinched. 'How can you say that?'

'Because he knew what I would become.'

'A wildly successful businessman who donates millions of dollars each year to fund neo-natal research among other charitable organisations?'

He jerked in surprise. 'How do you know that?'

A blush crept up her cheeks. 'When I did a web search on you a few things popped up.'

He shrugged. 'My accountants tell me funding charities is a good way to get tax breaks. Don't read more into the situation than there is, *amante.*'

Lowering her gaze, she watched their meshed fingers. The feel of his skin against hers made her heart skip several beats. 'I think we're past the point where you can convince me you're all bad, Narciso,' she dared.

He remained silent for so long she thought he'd refused to pick up the thread of their conversation. Then his breath shuddered out. 'Giacomo believes that.'

'Because you perpetuate that image?'

His smile was grim but it held speculation. 'Perhaps, but it's an image I'm growing tired of.'

Her breath caught.

His eyes met hers and he reached across and took her hand. 'Does that surprise you? That I'm thinking it's time to end this vendetta?'

'Why the change of heart?' she asked.

His casual shrug looked a little stiff. 'Perhaps it's time to force another mutation of our relationship,' he said obliquely.

'And if it fails?'

His eyes darkened before his lashes swept down to veil his expression. 'I'm very good at adapting, *amante.*' He stood up abruptly and pulled her up. 'Time for a shower.'

She waited until they were both naked in the bedroom before she spoke.

'All that with Giacomo. I'm sorry it happened to you.'

His nostrils flared as bleakness washed over his face. Then slowly, he reasserted control.

Intense silver eyes travelled over her, lingering on her bare breasts with fierce hunger that made her nipples pucker. 'Don't be. Our feud brought me to Macau. Macau brought you to me. I call that a win-win situation, *amante.*'

He lunged up and grabbed her. Swinging her up in his arms, he crossed the suite and entered the adjoining bathroom.

'Wait, we haven't finished talking.'

'*Sì*, we have. I've revealed more of my past to you than to any other living soul. If I'm The Warlock you should be re-named The Sorceress.'

Demanding hands reached for her, propelled her backwards into the warm shower he'd turned on.

'But I don't know you nearly enough.'

He yanked the shower head from its cradle and aimed the nozzle in the curve of her neck. Water set to the perfect tem-perature soothed her and she allowed her mind to slide free of the questions that raced through her thoughts.

Understanding the boy he'd been, caught in the hell of a fa-ther who hated the very sight of him, Ruby found it wasn't a stretch to understand why he'd closed himself off.

But she'd seen beneath the façade, knew the playboy persona was just a defence mechanism. His relationship with Giacomo meant more to him than he was willing to admit.

As if reading her thoughts, he sent her a narrow-eyed glare. 'Don't try and *understand* me, Ruby. You may not like what you discover.'

'What's that supposed to mean?'

His eyes met hers and she glimpsed the dark river of anguish. 'It means there may never be enough underneath the surface to be worth your time.'

'Shouldn't I be the judge of that?'

He stepped forward and aimed the shower right between her thighs. Ruby gasped as sensation weakened her knees. She reached out for something to steady her and got a handful of warm, vibrant flesh. He angled the showerhead and she let out a strangled moan.

'No. This conversation is over, *amante*,' he growled. 'Now, open wider for me.'

Despite his clipped words of warning and the blatantly sex-ual way he chose to end their conversation, Narciso proceeded to wash her with an almost worshipful gentleness that undid her. When he sank down in front of her and washed between her legs, tears prickled her eyes.

Hell, she was losing her mind. Right from the beginning, she'd primed herself to hate this skilled playboy for his shallow feelings and careless attitude towards women and sex.

Instead she'd discovered that beneath the glossy veneer lurked a wounded soul, hurting from a tortured past.

She wanted to touch him the way he'd touched her. She reached out, but he grasped her hand in his, surged upright and set the showerhead back in its cradle. Beside the expensive gels and lotions a stack of condoms rested. Her heart lurched as she saw him reach for one and tear it open.

Grasping her waist, he whirled her around, then meshed his fingers through hers before raising them to rest above her head.

'*This* is the only conversation I want to continue. Are you ready?' he rasped low in her ear.

His thickness pressed against her bottom. Recalling the pleasure she'd experienced before, she could no more stop herself from answering in the affirmative than she could stop herself from breathing.

He slid slowly into her, leaving her ample time to adjust to his size. Pleasure shot through her, imprisoning her in its merciless talons.

Her groan mingled with his as steam rose around and engulfed them in a cocoon of rough kisses and wet bodies.

Narciso let pleasure wash over him, erasing, if only temporarily, the cutting pain of the past rehashed. The raw agony of recollection eased as he surged deeper into her and, even though he refused to acknowledge that her touch, her warmth and soft words eased his pain, he hung on to the feel of being in her arms.

She rewarded him by crying out as her muscles tightened around him.

Dio mio, she was unbelievable! And she'd got under his skin with minimum effort. But he'd get his control back.

He had to.

Because this unravelling, as much as it soothed the deep wound in his heart, couldn't continue. For now, though, he intended to lose his mind in the most spectacular way. He slid his hands down her sides, glorying in her supple wet skin. Encircling her tiny waist, he threw his head back and let desire roar through his body.

She woke to a silent room and a half-cold bed.

Ruby didn't need a crystal ball to know regret played a part in Narciso's absence. She felt equally exposed and vulnerable in the light of day at how they'd bared their pasts to each other.

But as much as she wanted to stay hidden beneath the covers, she forced herself to leave Narciso's bed. Shoving her hand through her hair, she picked up the T-shirt she'd brazenly discarded during her seduction routine. Her ripped-beyond-redemption panties she quickly balled up in her fist.

Luckily, she met no one on the way to her own cabin.

Ten minutes later, and freshly showered, she dressed in white shorts and a sea-green sleeveless top, and opened her door to find a steward waiting outside.

'Mr Valentino would like you to join him for breakfast on the first deck.'

Her pulse raced as trepidation filled her.

Yesterday morning hadn't really counted as *the morning after* because after their shower they'd returned to bed and spent the rest of the day making love.

She entered the salon that led to the sun-dappled dining space on the deck.

Fresh croissants, coffee, juices and two domed dishes had been neatly laid out. But her attention riveted on the man flicking his finger across his electronic tablet.

'Morning,' she said, her voice husky.

His gaze rose and caught hers. 'Feeling rested?'

She managed a nod and glanced around. 'Where are we?' The day before they'd moored at the Bay of Placencia after leaving the spectacular Blue Hole.

'We're just coming into Nicholas Caye. Mexico is just north of us.'

'It's beautiful here,' she said, nerves eating her alive at the intense look in his eyes.

'Sit down and relax, Ruby. It will be hard but I can just about stop myself from jumping on you and devouring you for breakfast.'

Heat shot into her cheeks. 'That wasn't what I was thinking,' she blurted, then pursed her lips and pulled out a chair.

Lifting the dome, she found her favourite breakfast laid out in exquisite presentation. Along with her preferred spear of asparagus. 'You made me Eggs Benedict?' Why the hell was her throat clogged by that revelation?

'I didn't make it myself, *tesoro*. I'm quite useless in the kitchen.'

But he'd taken note somewhere along the way that this was her favourite breakfast meal. 'I... Thank you.'

He snapped shut his tablet, shook out his napkin and laid it over his lap. 'Don't read anything into it, Ruby.'

'You keep saying that. And yet you can't seem to help yourself with your actions.'

He picked up his cutlery. 'I must be losing my edge,' he muttered.

'Or maybe you're rediscovering your human side?'

He smiled mockingly. 'Now I sound like a reformed comic villain.'

'No, that would require a lot of spandex,' she quipped before taking a bite of the perfectly cooked eggs.

He laughed, the sound rich and deep. Ruby barely stopped the food from going down the wrong way when she glimpsed the gorgeously carefree transformation of his face. 'You don't think I'd look good in spandex?' he asked drily.

'I think you'd look good in anything. And I also believe you can do anything you put your mind to.'

He tensed and slowly lowered his knife. 'Is there a hidden message in that statement?'

'No…maybe. This is my first morning-after conversation. I may say things that aren't thought through properly.'

Her gaze connected with his. An untold wealth of emotions swirled through his eyes and her stomach flipped her heart into her throat. 'Now you're selling yourself short. You're one of the most talented, intelligent people I know,' he delivered. 'And the waters are treacherous for me, too.'

'Really?' she whispered.

His lids lowered, breaking the connection. '*Sì*. I think we both know we're under each other's skin. It's up to us to decide what we do with that knowledge. What's your most prized ingredient?'

'The white Alba truffle, hands down,' she blurted, reeling at the abrupt question. 'Truffles make everything taste better.'

He slowly nodded. '*Bene.*' He said nothing else and resumed eating.

Ruby felt as if she'd fallen down the rabbit hole again. The conversation felt surreal. 'Why is that important?'

His jaw clenched slightly. 'I need a truffles day to make me feel better.'

'Why?'

'Because I can't wrap my mind around the things I spilled to you yesterday.'

'I didn't force anything out of you, Narciso.'

'Which makes it even more puzzling. So I need a minute and you're going to give it to me,' he stated blatantly.

'How?'

'We're going to spend the day together. And you're going to tell me every single thought that jumps into your head.'

Her brows rose. 'You want to use me to drown out your thoughts? You realise how unhealthy that sounds, right?'

His grimace was pained. 'Yes, I do, but I'll suffer through it this once in the hope I emerge unscathed.'

'And if you don't?'

Silver eyes darkened as they swept over her. The message in

them when they locked on her lips punched heat into her belly. 'Then I'll have to find a different solution.'

Six hours later, Narciso was wondering if he'd truly lost his mind. Although he'd learned everything about Ruby from the moment she'd learned to speak to the present she'd received from her roommate, Annie, on her last birthday, he yearned to know more.

Never had he taken even the remotest interest in a woman besides her favourite restaurant and what pleased her in bed. The fact that he wanted to know Ruby Trevelli's every thought sent a shiver of apprehension down his spine.

He was unravelling faster than he could keep things under control.

Every emotion he'd tried to lock down since that summer in Sicily threatened to swamp him. He gritted his teeth and watched Ruby surge out of the turquoise sea. She walked towards him, clad in the minuscule bikini he'd supplied her with. Her body—supple, curvy and dripping with water—made his mouth dry. When she dropped down next to him on the deserted beach they'd swum to, he burned with the need to reach for her. *Dio,* with the amount of sex they'd had how could he still be this hungry for her?

'So, is the inquisition over?' she asked playfully.

'*Sì,*' he growled. 'It's over.'

Her gaze darted to his and he saw her tense at the coolness in his voice.

'Something wrong?'

'Why would anything be wrong?'

'Because you won the swim race from the yacht and you're not crowing about it. And you're not firing questions at me any more.'

'Perhaps I've had my fill for now.'

'Right. Okay,' she said.

He couldn't dismiss the hurt he heard in her voice. Turning, he watched her slim fingers play with the sugary white sand next to her feet. The desire to have those hands on his body grew until it became a physical pain.

Abruptly, he leaned forward and opened the gourmet picnic basket that had been delivered by his crew. He bypassed the food and reached for the chilled champagne. Popping the cork, he poured a glass and handed it to her.

'What are we celebrating?'

'The end of our beautiful down time. We leave for New York in the morning.'

Her eyes widened. Hell, he was more shocked than she was. His plan had been to stay for a full week. But the restlessness that had pounded through him all day wouldn't abate and he needed to find some perspective before it was too late.

At least once they returned to New York, back into the swing of things, everything would make sense again.

'You've asked my every thought for the last six hours. I think it's my turn now.'

He thought of sparing her the chaos running through his head. Then he mentally shrugged. 'I'm thinking why the thought of being free of you gives me no satisfaction.'

'Wow, you really know how to make a woman feel special, don't you?'

'I don't believe in sugar-coating words.'

'Please, spare me the macho stance. You know how to be gentle. What's going on here, Narciso? Why are you suddenly angry with me?'

He met her cloudy gaze and every thought disappeared but one. 'I'm finding how much I despise the thought of you ever taking another lover.'

Shocked blue eyes darted back to his. 'Narciso—'

'Now I've felt you shatter in my arms, the thought of you with another man makes my head want to explode.'

She gasped. 'Did you really just say that?'

He gave a harsh laugh and shook his head, as if testing his own sanity. '*Sì,* I just did.'

Beautifully curved eyebrows rose. 'And I'm guessing that's the first time you've admitted that to a woman?'

'It's the first time I've *felt* that way about any woman.' He shoved a hand through his hair.

Dio mio, he was like a leaking tap! Yesterday, he'd bared his past and his soul as if he were under the influence of a truth serum; today he was contemplating the future and the ache of not having Ruby Trevelli in it.

He knocked back the rest of his drink and surged to his feet. The crew member manning the launch a few dozen metres away looked his way and Narciso beckoned him over.

'It's time to go.' Reality and the cut and thrust of Wall Street would bring some much-needed common sense.

Unlike when they'd donned their swimming gear and laughingly dived from the side of the boat half an hour ago, silence reigned on the way back to *The Warlock*.

When he helped her up from the launch onto the floating swim deck at the back of the yacht, he forced himself to let her go, to stop his hands from lingering on her skin. As much as he wanted to touch her, weave his fingers through the damp hair curling over her shoulders, he couldn't give in to the spell threatening to pull him under.

'I have work to do. I'll catch up with you later.' With his insides twisting into seething knots, he walked away.

Ruby watched him walking away, a giant chasm opening up where pleasure had been half an hour ago. Things had been perfect. So much so, she'd pinched herself a couple of times to make sure the combination of sun, sea and drop-dead-gorgeous companion who'd laughed at her jokes and insisted on knowing every thought in her head was real.

She hadn't told him every thought, of course. For instance, she hadn't admitted that every time he'd touched her she'd heard angels sing to her soul. *That* would've been nuts. As would've been the admission that she was dying to make love with him again.

No chance of that now...

The hard-assed, enigmatic Narciso Valentino of three days ago hadn't made a comeback—and Ruby hoped against all hope the Narciso who chose to smother away his pain was gone for good—but a new Narciso had taken his place. One who fully recognised his vulnerabilities but then ignored them.

The need to go after him was so strong, she locked her knees and gripped the steel banister. He needed time.

Heck, *she* needed time to grapple with the mass of chaotic emotions coursing through her.

Scrambling for control, she went into her cabin and showered off the seawater. Clad in a long, flowered dress with a long slit down one side, she returned to the bar and lined bottles on the counter. Work would take her mind off her unsettling thoughts about Narciso Valentino.

She was measuring a shot of tequila into a shaker when one of the crew members approached.

'Can I get miss anything to eat?'

She shook her head. He smiled and turned to leave. 'Wait.' He paused. 'Have you seen my phone? I've been looking for it everywhere.'

He smiled. 'Oh, yes. One of my colleagues found it in the kitchen yesterday and handed it to Mr Valentino.'

Narciso had her phone? 'Thank you,' she murmured. She slowly screwed the top back on the bottle she'd opened and put the lemon wedges back in the cooler. Wiping her hands on a napkin, she left the deck.

His study was on the second level, past a large room with a sunken sitting area perfect for a dinner party. Like the rest of the vessel, every nook and cranny screamed bespoke and breathtaking luxury.

He growled admittance after her tense knock.

Seated in a leather armchair behind a large antique desk, he watched her enter with a frown. 'Is something wrong?'

'As long as you can adequately explain why you've commandeered my phone, no.'

'You're expecting a call?' he asked.

'Whether I am or not is beside the point.' She shut the door and approached his desk. 'You've had it since yesterday. Why didn't you hand it over?'

He shrugged. 'It must have slipped my mind.'

Somehow she doubted that. But watching him, seeing his face set in those stern, bleak lines she'd recognised from before made her heart stutter. She'd seen that look before.

She stepped closer, looked down and saw the pictures and papers strewn on his desk. The date stamp on the nearest one—showing that very morning—made ice slide down her spine. 'This is the business you had to take care of?'

He slowly set down the document in his hand. 'No. Believe it or not, I intended to scrap all this.'

'But?'

'But something came up.'

She glanced down at the photos. All depicted Giacomo. In one of them, the one Narciso had just dropped, he was dining with a stunning woman in her late twenties.

'Is that the *something?*' she asked, telling herself the pain lancing her chest wasn't jealousy.

His mouth tightened. 'We're not having this conversation, Ruby.'

'What happened to the man who was going to try to find a better way than this need to destroy and annihilate?'

His head tilted. 'That means the same thing.'

'Excuse me?'

'Destroy and annihilate—same meaning.'

'Really? That's all you have to contribute to this conversation?'

His jaw tightened. 'I told you I was good at adapting, *cara*. So why are you surprised that I'm adapting to the situation I find myself in? And seriously, screwing my brains out does not entitle you to weigh in on this.' He waved to his desk.

'Then why did you share it with me?' she replied.

For a moment he floundered. The clear vulnerability in his eyes made her breath catch. 'A misjudgment on my part.'

'I don't believe you.'

Shock widened his eyes. It occurred to her that she was probably the only person who'd dared challenge him this way.

Slowly, his face transformed into an inscrutable mask. Hell, he was so expert at hiding his feelings, he didn't need a mask at his next ball, she thought vaguely.

'I don't care whether you believe me or not. All I care about, what *you* should care about, is whether you can deliver on our agreement. I can easily find a replacement for you if you wish to terminate it when we get back to New York. Believe that.'

'Oh, I believe you. I also believe you think you can hide behind hatred and revenge to find the closeness you seek.'

'*Madre di Dio.* When I suggested you tell me every thought that came into your head, I had no idea you were a closet pop psychologist or I'd have thought twice. I unequivocally revoke that request, by the way.'

Listening to him denigrate what had been a perfect few hours in her life made anger and pain rock through her. Stepping back from the desk, she glanced at the picture, pain slashing her insides.

'I'll leave you to your machinations.' She rushed out and hurried up the stairs, swiping at the foolish tears clouding her vision.

If Narciso wanted to bury himself in the past, he was welcome to do so.

CHAPTER TEN

'THERE'S A NEW recipe I want to try. Care to join me?'

Ruby looked up as Michel approached the counter she'd been working at for the last two hours.

Her mood had vacillated between anger and hurt, undecided on which emotion had the upper hand. Certainly, the piece of meat she'd been hammering was plenty tenderised.

She set it to one side, went to the sink to wash her hands, and rested her hip against the granite trim. 'As long as it's nothing Sicilian. I've had my fill of Sicilians for the foreseeable future.'

Michel cast her a curious glance, then gave a sly smile. 'No, what I'm thinking of is unapologetically French.'

She wiped her hand on her apron. 'Then count me in.'

'Excellent! It's a *sauce au chocolat* with a twist. You're making *croquembouche* for monsieur's dinner party in New York, *oui?*'

'Yes.' Although right now the thought of monsieur himself sautéed in a hot sizzling pan sounded equally satisfying.

'*Bien,* I thought instead of the caramel you could try using chillies.'

'Chilli chocolate? I love the idea. I always convince myself the heat burns away half the calories.'

He gave a very Gallic shrug. 'In my opinion, you do not need to worry about calories, *'moiselle.*'

The compliment took her by surprise. 'Umm, thanks, Michel.'

He shrugged again and started grabbing ingredients off the

shelves. They worked in harmony, measuring, chopping, straining until the scent of the rich chocolate sauce bubbling away in the pan filled the kitchen.

On a whim, she asked, 'Do you have any fresh vanilla pods? I want to try something.'

He nodded. Opening his spice cabinet, he grabbed the one long pod and handed it to her. Ruby cut it open and scraped out the innards. Then, slicing a few strips, she dropped them into the sauce. 'Let that infuse for a few minutes, and we'll try it.'

He rubbed his hands together with a childlike glee that made her laugh. After two minutes he grabbed a clean spoon and scooped a drop of the sauce. 'As the last ingredient was your idea, you sample it first.' He blew on it and held it to her lips.

She tasted it, shut her eyes to better feel the flavours exploding on her tongue. The decadent taste made her groan long and deeply.

'Ruby.'

Her name was a crack of thunder that had her spinning round.

Narciso stood in the doorway, the look on his face as dark and stormy as the tension thickening the air. For several seconds, everyone remained frozen.

Then silver eyes flicked to the Frenchman. 'Leave.'

Michel's eyes widened at the stark dismissal. Narciso took a single step forward to allow the chef to sidle past before he slammed the door shut behind him.

The sound of the lock turning made her nerves scream.

Slowly, Narciso walked towards her. With his every step she willed her feet to move in the other direction, away from the imposing body and icy fury bearing down on her. But she remained frozen.

She held her breath as he stopped a whisper from her.

'My intention was to find you and explain things better, perhaps even apologise for what I said in my study.'

Her heart lifted, then plummeted again when she deciphered his meaning. 'Well, I'm waiting.'

'Oh, you won't be getting an apology from me *now, amante.*'

He leaned over and looked into the copper pan bubbling on the stove. Picking up a spoon, he scooped up some sauce and sampled it.

'Not half bad. What is it?'

'Oh, I thought you'd recognise it, Narciso. This sauce I've named The Valentino Slimeball Special. It'll taste divine with the freshly made Playboy's Puffballs I'm planning on serving them with. You'll love it, trust me.'

Slowly, he lowered the spoon and speared her with those icy silver eyes. 'Say that again.'

'I'm pretty certain there's nothing wrong with your hearing.'

He tossed the spoon into the sink and leaned closer, bracing his hands on either side of her so she was locked in. 'Say it again anyway. I like the way that pretty mouth of yours pouts when you say *puffballs*.'

Despite his indolent words, his eyes glinted with fury. Her instinct warned her to retreat, but caged in like this, watching the erratic pulse beating at his throat, she knew any attempt at escape would be futile.

He was hanging on to his control by a thread. The sudden urge to shatter it the way he seemed to shatter hers so very easily made her stand her ground.

'You'll have to beg me if you want that.'

'Ah, Ruby, shall I let you in on personal insight?'

'Can I stop you?'

'I think you delight in pushing my buttons because you know it'll get you kissed. Am I right?'

'You're wrong.'

'Then why are you licking your lips like that? Anticipation has you almost insane with desperation right now.'

'You have a ridiculously high opinion of yourself.'

'Prove me wrong, then.'

'I won't play your stupid games.'

'Scared?'

'No. Uninterested.'

'Believe me, Ruby, this isn't a game.' When his hands went to undo the tie holding her dress together, she batted them away.

'Stop. What's wrong with you?'

His laugh was filled with bitter incredulity. 'I walk in here to find you moaning for another man and you ask *me* what's wrong with me?'

'You're *jealous?*'

Right before her eyes he seemed to deflate. His hold on her dress ties loosened. And the eyes that speared hers held hellish agitation.

'Yes! I'm jealous. Does that make you happy?'

Her senses screamed yes. Jealousy meant that she mattered in some way to him. The way he'd come to matter to her. 'Why did you come in here, Narciso?'

He sucked in a breath. 'I told you, to apologise.'

'Because my feelings are hurt or because *you* hurt me?'

He lifted a hand and trailed his fingers down her cheek. 'Because I hurt you,' he rasped deeply.

The breath shuddered out of her. 'Thank you for that.'

'Don't thank me, Ruby. What I'm feeling…what you make me feel, I don't know what to do with it. It may well come back and bite us both.'

'But at least you're acknowledging it. So what happened in your study?' she asked before she lost her nerve.

His lips firmed. 'That woman in the picture you saw. Her name is Maria.'

She bit her lip to stem the questions flooding her.

'She's Paolina's—my housekeeper's—granddaughter. I met her that summer ten years ago. She came to visit from Palermo. Paolina brought her to the house and we hung out. By the second week I'd convinced her to stay for the whole summer. I believed myself…infatuated with her.' His lips pinched until the skin showed white. 'I was young and naïve and respected her see-but-don't-touch edict. Until I found out she was giving it up to Giacomo.'

Shock rocked through her. 'She was *sleeping* with your father?'

'Not only sleeping with him. He'd convinced her to make a sex tape, which he forced me to watch on the last day of my stay in Sicily.' Something in the way he said it made her tense.

'What do you mean *forced*?'

His teeth bared in a parody of a smile. 'He had two of his bodyguards hold me down in a chair while the video played on a super-wide screen, complete with surround sound. It was quite the cinematic experience.'

Her mouth gaped. '*Oh, my God. That's vile!*'

'That's Giacomo,' he said simply.

'So, what is he doing with her in New York now?'

His jaw clenched. 'I don't know. The reason I opened the file in the first place was to tell my investigator to toss the case.'

'But now you think he's plotting something?'

'She's broke. Which means she's the perfect pawn for Giacomo.'

Ruby wanted to ask him how he knew that, but the forbidding look in his face, coupled with the anguish lurking in his eyes, changed her mind.

With the evidence of the two people who'd betrayed him before him, he'd have to have been a saint to remain unaffected. Hell, the thought of the double blow of betrayal made her heart twist in pain for him.

'I'm sorry I condemned you. I didn't know.'

Mingled fury and anguish battled in his eyes. 'What about this, Ruby *mio*? Do you know *this*?' he muttered roughly.

He parted her dress and his fingers were drifting down the bare skin of her belly, headed straight for her panty line, before she could exhale. Warm, sure fingers slid between her thighs before Ruby knew what had hit her.

Her cry of astonishment quickly morphed into a moan of need as his thumb flicked against her clitoris.

'Narciso!'

'*Dio,* how can I crave you this badly when I didn't know you a week ago?'

Need rammed through her and she clung to him. 'I don't know. You forget that I should hate this, too. I should hate you.'

He leaned in close, until his hot mouth teased her ear lobe. 'But then that would mean you were conforming to some lofty image you have in your head of your ideal man. You'd be denying that our little tiffs make you so wet you can barely stand it. I turn you on. I heat up your blood and make you feel more alive than you've ever felt. I make you crave all the things you've denied yourself. I know this because it's what you make me feel too. Close your eyes, Ruby.'

'No.' But already her eyelashes were fluttering down, heavy with the drugging desire stealing over her.

The next moment, his breath whispered along her jaw. 'Do you want me to stop?'

She groaned. 'Narciso...'

'Say no and I'll end this.'

She whimpered. 'You're not being fair.'

He laughed again. 'No, I'm not, but I never claimed I was a fair man. And when I feel as if my world is unravelling, halos don't sit well on my head.'

His fingers worked faster, firing up sparks of delight in her that quickly flared into flames.

'Oh! Oh, God.'

He kissed her hard and deep, then nibbled the corner of her mouth as she shattered completely. He ran his free hand down her back in a roughly soothing gesture as she floated back down. The mouth at her ear lobe feathered kisses down her jaw to her throat, then back up again.

'I'm sorry that I hurt you, Ruby. But I'm not sorry that I make you feel like this.'

The New York she'd left just days ago to travel to Macau was the same. Ruby knew that, and yet it was as though she were seeing it for the first time.

As they travelled through midtown towards Narciso's penthouse on the Upper East Side, the sights and sounds appeared more vibrant, soulful.

Part of her knew it was because she was seeing it through different eyes. The eyes of a woman who'd been introduced to passion and intense emotion.

She wanted to push that woman far away, deny all knowledge that she existed. But self-delusion had never been her flaw.

She'd slept for most of the four-hour flight from Belize City, a fact for which she was thankful. Awake and in close proximity to Narciso, she didn't think she could've avoided letting him see her confusion.

Their intense encounter in the kitchen on his yacht had been highly illuminating. Very quickly after granting her most delicious release, he'd walked away, leaving her replete and alarmingly teary.

She'd stood in the kitchen long after he'd left, clutching the sink and fighting a need to run after him and offer him comfort.

But how could she have when his words echoed in her ears.

I hurt you...I'm sorry...I crave you...

With each word, her heart had cracked open wider, until she'd been as raw as his voice had been.

As raw as she was now...

The need to run from her thoughts was very tempting. Giving in, she activated her returned phone. Several voice and text messages flooded into her inbox.

Three were from the same number. One she didn't recognise but suspected its origin.

She answered Annie's query as to when she would be returning and declined her invitation to a girls' night out when she was back from the West Coast. She wasn't ready to face anyone yet, least of all her perceptive roommate, when her emotions felt as if they'd been through a shredder.

The second message was from her mother, asking her to get in touch. She tensed as she listened to the message again. On the surface, it sounded innocuous, a mother asking after her child

But she heard the undercurrents in her mother's voice and the hairs on her neck stood up. The other messages forgotten, she played the message a third time.

'What's wrong?' Narciso's deep voice cut across her flailing emotions.

'Nothing.'

'Ruby.'

She glanced at him, and her heart lurched. 'Don't look at me like that.'

'Like what?'

'Like you care.'

'I care,' he stated simply.

She sucked in a breath. 'How can you? You told me there was nothing beneath the surface, remember?'

She knew she was probably overreacting but the thought that her mother was reaching out to her because her father had in all likelihood had another affair made her stomach clench in anger and despair.

But unlike the numerous times before when she'd been angry with her parent, Ruby was realising just how harshly she'd misjudged her mother.

From the cocoon of self-righteousness, it'd been easy to judge, to see things in black and white. But having experienced how easy it was to lose control beneath the charisma and magnetism of a powerful man, how could she judge her mother?

Sure, she was aware that part of the reason her mother had stuck around was because she craved the fame that came with being part of a power couple. But Ruby also knew, deep down, her mother could be a success on her own.

A strong, warm hand curled over hers. Her gaze flew up to collide with silver eyes. 'I know what I said but I want to know what's going on anyway.'

His concern burrowed deep and found root in her heart. 'My mother left me a message to call her.'

He nodded. 'And this is troubling?'

'Yes. Normally she emails. She only calls me when something…bad happens.'

'Define bad.'

'My father…sleeping with a sous chef, or a waitress, or a member of their filming crew. That kind of *bad*.'

He swore. 'And she calls you to unburden?'

'And to put pressure on me to join their show. She seems to think my presence will curb my father's wandering eyes.'

His gaze remained steady on hers. 'You don't seem angry about it any more.'

Because he'd made her see herself in a different light: one that didn't fill her with bitterness.

Warmth from his hand seeped through, offering comfort she knew was only temporary.

'I've come to accept that sometimes we make choices in the hope that things will turn out okay. We take a leap of faith and stand by our choices. My mother's living in hope. I can't hate her for that.'

A flash of discomfort altered his expression. 'How very accommodating of you.'

'Accommodating? Hardly. Maybe I'm just worn out. Or maybe I'm finally putting myself into someone else's shoes and seeing things from their point of view.'

'And your father?'

'I can't forgive any man who toys with my…a woman's feelings. Who exploits her vulnerabilities and uses them against her.'

His sharp glance told her the barb had hit home. 'If you're referring to what happened in the kitchen—'

'I'm not.' A lance speared her heart. 'I think it's best we forget about that, don't you?'

I think it's best we forget…

He had no idea why that statement twisted in his gut but it did long after they'd reached his underground car park and en

ered the lift to his penthouse. Beside him Ruby stood stiffly,
her face turned away from him.

He'd expected her to protest when he'd demanded she stay
with him until after his VIP dinner party.

Instead, she'd agreed immediately.

The idea that she couldn't be bothered to argue with him
made another layer of irrational anxiety spike through him.

Roughly he pushed the feeling away, meshed his fingers with
Ruby's and tugged her after him when the lift doors opened.

Paolina exited one of the many hallways of his duplex penthouse to greet him.

Despite being in her late sixties, his housekeeper was as
sprightly as she'd been when he was a boy.

'Ciao, bambino. Come stai?'

He responded to the affectionate greeting, let himself be
kissed on both cheeks; allowed himself to bask in the warmth
of her affection. But only for a second.

Catching Ruby to his side, he introduced her, noting her surprise as he mentioned Paolina's name.

She turned to him as Paolina took control of their luggage
and headed to the bedrooms. 'Would this be the same Paolina
who's related to Maria?'

His smile felt tight. *'Sì.'*

'I…I thought…'

'That I was a complete monster who cut everyone out of my
life because of one incident? I'm not a complete bastard, Ruby.'

'No, you're not,' she murmured.

Her smile held none of the vivacity he'd come to expect. To
crave. He wanted to win that smile back. Wanted to share what
plans he'd put in place before they left Belize. But unfamiliar
fear held him back.

Would she judge him for doing too little too late?

He watched her turn a full circle in the large living room, her
gaze taking in and dismissing the highly sought-after pieces of
art and exclusive decorative accessories most guests tended to
gush over. The location of his apartment alone—on a thirtieth

floor overlooking Central Park—was enough to pull a strong reaction from even the most jaded guest.

Ruby seemed more interested in the doors leading out of the room. 'Do you mind showing me to the kitchen? I'd like to see where I'll be working and if there's any equipment I need to hire. I should also have the final menu for you shortly. If there's anything you need to change I'd appreciate it if you let me know ASAP.'

Again he felt that unsettled notion of unravelling control. But then…when it came to Ruby, had he held control in the first place?

It certainly hadn't felt like it when he'd walked in on Ruby and Michel. Hearing her moan like that had been a stiletto wound to his heart.

In his jealousy and blind fury had he taken things too far? He tried to catch her eye as he walked beside her towards the kitchen but she refused to look at him.

He'd never had a problem with being given the silent treatment. But right now he wanted Ruby to speak, to tell him what was on her mind.

'What I've seen so far of the menu's fine. It's the perfect blend of continental Europe and good old-fashioned Italian. The guests will appreciate it.'

Her only reaction was to nod. They reached the kitchen and she moved away from him.

She inspected the room with a thoroughness that spoke of a love for her profession. Her long, elegant fingers ran over appliances and worktops and he found his disgruntlement escalating.

Dio, was he really so pathetic as to be jealous of stainless steel gadgets now? He shook his head and stepped back. 'I'm leaving for the office. We will speak this evening.'

Four hours later, he was pacing his office just as he had been last week.

Only this time there was no sign of the ennui that ha

gripped him. Instead, a different form of restlessness prowled through him, one that was unfamiliar and mildly terrifying.

He laughed mirthlessly and pushed a hand through his hair. Narciso wasn't afraid to admit so far he wasn't loving being thirty. He seemed to be questioning his every action. He was even stalling on the deal with Vladimir Rudenko. Did he really need to start another media empire in Russia?

Going ahead with it would mean he'd have to spend time in Moscow. Away from New York. Away from Ruby. *Dio,* what the hell was she doing in his head?

Gritting his teeth, he strode to his desk and pressed the intercom that summoned his driver.

The journey from Wall Street to his penthouse took less than twenty minutes but it felt like a lifetime. Slamming the front door, he strode straight into the kitchen. He needed to tell her of his plans. Needed her to know he'd chosen a different path...

She was elbow deep in some sort of mixture. She glanced up, eyes wide with surprise. 'You're back.'

'We need to talk.'

'What about?'

'About Giacomo—' he tensed, then continued '—about my father.'

Her eyes grew wider. 'Yes?'

'I've decided to end—'

A phone beeped on the counter. A look of unease slid over her features as she wiped her hands and activated the message. A few seconds later, all trace of colour left her cheeks. 'I have to go.'

He frowned. 'Go where?'

'Midtown. I'll be back in an hour.'

'I'll drive you—'

'No. I'll be fine. Really. I've been cooped up in here all afternoon. I need the fresh air.'

'Fresh air in New York is a misnomer.' He continued to watch her, noting her edginess. 'Is it your parents?'

Her fingers twisted together. 'No, it's not.' Sincerity shone from her eyes.

He nodded. 'Fine. I just wanted you to know, you have my backing one hundred per cent. After the party, I'll have the papers drawn up to provide the funds you need for the restaurant.'

'Th-thank you. That's good news.' The definite lack of pleasure on her face and voice caused his spine to stiffen. She reached him and tried to slide past.

Unable to help himself, he caught her to him and kissed her soft, tempting mouth. She yielded to the kiss for a single moment before she wrenched herself away.

'Amante—'

'I have to go.'

Before he could say another word she snatched her bag from the counter and walked out of the door.

Narciso stood frozen, unable to believe what had happened. By the time he forced himself to move, Ruby was gone.

CHAPTER ELEVEN

RUBY ENTERED THE upscale restaurant at the stroke of six and gave her name.

A waiter ushered her to a window seat. It took seconds to recognise the man at the table. Shock held her rigid as she stared at him.

Without his mask, Giacomo Valentino bore a striking resemblance to his son. Except his eyes were dull with age and his mouth cruel with entrenched bitterness.

'I knew I recognised you from somewhere, Ruby Trevelli,' Giacomo Valentino said the moment she sat down. 'The wonders of modern technology never cease to amaze me. A few clicks and I had everything I needed to know about you and your parents.'

She tensed. 'What do you want?'

'A way to bring my son down. And you will help me.'

She rushed to her feet. 'You're out of your mind.'

'I met with your loan shark today,' he continued conversationally. 'As of three hours ago, I own twenty-five per cent of your yet-to-be-built restaurant. If you walk out of here, I'll call in the debt immediately.'

Heart in her throat, she slowly sank back into her seat. 'Why are you doing this?'

His face hardened. 'You saw how he humiliated me in Macau.'

'Yes, and since then I've also heard what you did to him. And I know you met with Maria yesterday.'

A flash of fear crossed his face but it was quickly smothered. 'So Narciso knows?'

'Yes.'

The old man visibly paled.

'Give it up, Giacomo. You're out of options because there's no way I'll help you further your vendetta against your own flesh and blood.'

The flash came again, and this time she saw what it was. Deep, dark, twisted pain. 'He's a part of me that should never have come into being.'

She shook her head. 'How can you say that?'

'He took away from me the one thing I treasured most in this world. And he struts around like the world owes him a living.'

Ruby heard the black pain behind his words and finally understood. Deep down, Giacomo Valentino was completely and utterly heartbroken over losing his wife.

A part of her felt sympathy for him. But she could tell Giacomo was too set in his thinking to alter his feelings towards his son.

Narciso, on the other hand, wasn't. Ruby had seen gentleness in him. She'd seen compassion, consideration, even affection towards Paolina, the grandmother of the woman who'd betrayed him. He had the capacity to love, if only he'd step back from the brink of the abyss of revenge he was poised on.

And will you be the one to save him?

Why not? He'd helped her come to terms with her own relationship with her parents. She'd called her mother this afternoon, and, sure enough, her father had strayed again. But this time, Ruby had offered her mother a shoulder to cry on. They'd spoken for over an hour. Tears had been shed on both sides. An hour later, she'd received a text from her mother to say she'd contacted an attorney and filed for a divorce from her husband.

Ruby knew the strength it'd taken for her mother to break free. Taking a deep breath, she looked Giacomo in the eye. 'You probably don't want my advice but I'll give it anyway. You and Narciso both lost someone dear to you. You were lucky enough to know her. Have you spared a thought for the child who never knew his mother?'

'*Ascolta—!*'

'No, you listen. Punishing a baby for its mother's death went out with the Dark Ages. Do you have any idea how much he's hurting?'

Pale silver eyes narrowed. 'You're in love with my son.'

Her heart lurched, then hammered as if fighting to get away from the truth staring her in the face. Her fingers tightened on her bag. 'I won't be a party to whatever you're cooking up.'

'You disappoint me, Miss Trevelli. Before you go, I should tell you that your loan shark provided me with an extensive file on you, which details, among other things, a building on Third and Lexington.'

Panic flared high. '*My parents' restaurant?*'

Giacomo gave a careless nod.

'I swear, if you dare harm them I'll—'

Giacomo put a hand on her arm. 'My request is simple.'

She wanted to bolt but she remained seated.

His speculative gaze rested on her. 'My son is taken with you. More than he has been with any other woman.'

Her insides clenched hard. 'You're wrong—'

'I'm right.' He leaned forward suddenly. 'I want you to end your relationship with him.'

Her mouth dried. 'There is no relationship.'

'End it. Sever all ties with him and I'll make sure your parents' livelihood remains intact. I'll even become your benefactor with your restaurant.'

Frantically she shook her head. 'I don't want your charity.'

His eyes narrowed. 'Do you really want to risk crossing me? I urge you to remember where my son inherited his thirst for revenge from.'

Feeling numb, she rose. This time he didn't stop her.

Her thin sweater did nothing to hold the April chill at bay

as she blindly struck through the evening crowd. She only realised where she was headed when the subway train pulled into the familiar station.

Her apartment was soothingly quiet. Dropping her bag, she went to the small bar she'd installed when she moved in.

Blanking her thoughts, she went to work, mixing liqueurs with juices, spirits with the bottle of champagne she'd been gifted on her birthday. Carefully she lined up the mixtures that worked and discarded the rest. She was on her last set when she heard the pounding on the door.

Breath catching, she went to the door and glanced into the peeper.

Narciso loomed large and imposing outside her door. Jumping back, she toyed with not answering.

'Let me in, Ruby. Or so help me, I'll break this door down.'

With shaking hands, she released the latch.

He took a single, lunging step in and slammed the door behind him. 'You said you'd be an hour, tops.' Silver eyes bore into her, intense and frighteningly invasive.

She forced a shrug. 'I lost track of time.'

'If you wanted to return here all you needed was to say.' There was concern in his voice, coupled with the vulnerability he'd been unable to hide on the yacht.

Knowing what had put that vulnerability there, knowing what his father's lack of love had done to him, made her chest tighten. She so desperately wanted to reach for him, to soothe his pain away.

But in light of what she faced, there was only one recourse where Narciso was concerned. 'I didn't realise I had to answer to you for my movements.'

He frowned and speared a hand through his hair. The way it fell made her guess he'd been doing it for a while. Swallowing hard, she forced her gaze away and walked into the small living room.

He followed. 'You don't,' he answered. 'But you said you'd come back. And you didn't.'

'It's no big deal, Narciso. I wanted to return home for a bit.'

'Are you ready to return now?' he shot back, his gaze probing.

The need to say yes sliced through her. 'No. I think I'll spend the night here.'

He started to speak. Stopped, and looked around. She didn't even bother to look at her apartment through his eyes. Annie had used the term shabby chic when they'd picked up knick-knacks from flea markets and second-hand shops to furnish their apartment. The plump sofas were mismatched, as were the lamps and cushions. The pictures that hung on the walls were from sidewalk artists whose talent had caught Ruby's eye.

'Why are you here, Narciso?'

Narciso walked over to a lampshade and touched the bohemian fringe. 'I tried to tell you earlier. I've called off the vendetta with my father.'

Shock rocked through her, followed swiftly by sharp regret. 'Why?'

He shoved his hand into his pockets and inhaled. 'In a word? *You*. You're the reason.' Again that vulnerability blazed from his eyes. Along with a wariness as she remained frozen.

'I shouldn't be the reason, Narciso. You should do it for yourself.'

He shrugged. 'I'm working my way to that, *amante*. But I need your help. You set me on this road. You can't walk away now.'

Oh, God!

She choked back a sob and fled to the bar. He followed and saw the drinks lined up on the counter.

'You were working?'

'I never stop.'

'What have you come up with?' There was a genuine interest in his tone. For whatever reason, he wanted to know more about her passion.

His softening attitude towards her sent her emotions into panicked freefall. Belize had warned her she was at serious risk of developing feelings for Narciso Valentino. Seeing him in her home, touching her things, making monumental confessions, made her want to rush to him and burrow into his chest, hear his heart pounding against her own. But she couldn't. Not now.

She shoved her hands into her jeans pockets and shrugged. 'This and that.'

He flicked a glance at her. Then he picked up the nearest drink and took a sip. 'What's this one called?'

Push him away!

She took a deep, frantic breath. '*Sleazy Playboy*. The one next to it is *The Studly Warlock*, the blue one is the *Belize Bender*, and the pink one I've termed *The Virgin Sacrifice.*'

He stiffened.

'There's a black Sambuca one I'm intending to call *Crazy, Stupid Revenge*—'

'Enough, Ruby. I get the message. I've upset you. Again. Tell me how to make it better.' He looked over at her and his eyes held a simple, honest plea.

Dear God. Narciso wasn't all gone at all. In fact, right at that moment, he was the single, most appealing thing in her life.

Heat and need and panic and lust surged under her skin as his gaze remained steady on hers. With every fibre in her being she wanted to cross the room and launch herself into his arms.

Giacomo's face flashed across her mind.

'There's nothing to make better because there's nothing between us.'

His eyes widened. '*Scusi?*'

'We had what we had, Narciso. Let's not prolong it any further.'

His eyes slowly hardened. In quick strides, he crossed the room and jerked her into his body. The contact threatened to sizzle her brain. Throwing out her hands against his chest, she tried to break free. He held tight.

'Let me go!'

'Why? Scared I'll prove you wrong?'

'Not at all—'

He swooped down and captured her mouth. His kiss was raw, possessive and needy.

'What the hell's happening, Ruby?' he whispered raggedly against her mouth.

Again her heart skittered.

Briefly, she thought to come clean, tell him where she'd been. Panic won out.

'Dammit, Ruby, kiss me back!' he pleaded raggedly against her lips.

She couldn't deny him any more than she could deny herself what would surely be her last time of experiencing this magic with him.

Desperate hands grazed over his chest to his taut stomach. Grasping the bottom of his T-shirt, she pulled it up. He helped her by tugging it over his head and flinging it away. Eyes blazing with an emotion she was too afraid to name met hers. Stepping forward, she placed an open-mouthed kiss on his collarbone.

His hiss of arousal echoed around the room. Emboldened, she used her teeth, tongue and mouth to drive them both crazy. When he stumbled slightly, she realised she'd pushed him towards the sofa. With a hard push she sent him sprawling backwards. Within seconds he was naked, his perfect body beckoning irresistibly. Driven by guilt and hunger, she stripped off her T-shirt and bra and unsnapped her jeans.

With a shake of his head, he covered her hands with his. 'Let me.'

The slow slide downward was accompanied by hot, worshipful kisses that brought tears to her eyes. Afraid her emotions would give her away, she hurriedly stepped out of the jeans and pushed him back down again and resumed the path she'd charted moments before.

His groan when her lips touched the tip of his shaft was ragged and raw. But encouraging hands speared through her hair, holding her to her task.

Boldly, she took him in her mouth. '*Dio*, Ruby!'

She looked up at him. His eyes were closed, his neck muscles taut from holding on to his control. Taking him deeper, she lost herself in the newfound power and pleasure, her heart singing with an almost frightening joy at being able to do this, one last time.

Tomorrow would bring its own heartache but for now—

'*Basta!*' he rasped. 'As much as I'd love to finish in your mouth, my need to be inside you is even greater.'

He pulled her up and astride him. Reaching for his discarded jeans, he took a condom from his back pocket.

The thought that he'd come prepared dimmed her pleasure for a second. But realising what the alternative would've meant, she took the condom from him, tore it open and slipped it on his thick shaft, experiencing a momentary pang at how big he was.

Silver eyes gleamed at her. 'We fit together perfectly, *tesoro*, remember?' he encouraged gently.

Nodding, she raised her hips and took him inside her.

Delicious, sensational pleasure built inside her, setting off fireworks in her body. His face a taut mask of pleasure, his hands settled on her thighs and he allowed her to set the pace. But this new, deeper penetration was her undoing. Within minutes, her spine tingled with impending climax. She had no resistance when Narciso reared up, sucked one nipple into his mouth and sent her over the edge.

She surfaced from the most blissful release to find their positions reversed. Narciso's fingers were tangled in her hair and his mouth buried in her throat.

When he raised his head, the depth of emotion on his face made her breath catch.

'I need you, Ruby,' he repeated his earlier statement. Only this time, she was sure he didn't mean sexually.

The knowledge that things would never be right between them sent pure, white-hot pain through her heart.

Unable to find the right words to respond, she cradled his face. Locked in that position, his eyes not leaving hers, he surged inside her and resumed the exquisite, soul-searing lovemaking. Eventually, he groaned his release and took her mouth in a soft, gentle kiss, murmuring words she understood but refused to allow into her heart.

Tears sprang into her eyes and she rapidly blinked them away, glad that he was rising and putting his clothes back on.

'I can stay here, or we can return to my place.' Although his tone wasn't as forceful as before, she knew he wouldn't accept a third choice.

'I'll come back with you.' Despite all that had happened, she still had his dinner party to cater for.

They dressed in silence and she studiously avoided the puzzled glances he sent her way.

When he caught her hand in his in the lift on the way to the ground floor, she let him. When he brought the back of her hand to his lips and kissed it, she sucked in a deep breath to stop the tears clogging her throat from suffocating her.

In his car, he pulled her close, clamped both arms around her and tucked her head beneath his chin. In the long drive back to the Upper East side, neither of them spoke but he took every opportunity to run gentle hands down her arms and over her hair.

Unable to stop herself, she felt tears slide down her cheeks.

Dear God, what the hell had she done? Of all the foolish decisions she could've made, she'd gone and fallen in love with Narciso Valentino.

'Qualunque cosa che, oi facevo io sono spiacente,' he murmured raggedly in her ear. *Whatever I did, I'm sorry.*

The tears fell harder, silent guilty sobs racking her frame.

He led her to the shower the moment they returned to his penthouse. Again, in silence, he washed her, then pulled a clean T-shirt of his over her head. Pulling back the covers to his bed, he tugged her close and turned out the lights.

'We'll talk in the morning, Ruby. Whatever is happening between us, we'll work it out, *sì?*'

She nodded, closed her eyes and drifted off to a troubled sleep.

She jerked awake just after 5:00 a.m., fear and anguish

churning through her body. The need to tell Narciso the truth burned through her.

She needed to tell him about the meeting last night. Needed to let him know that Giacomo's thirst for revenge burned brighter than ever.

Her fear for her parents had blinded her to the fact that she was stronger than Giacomo's blackmail threats. There was no way Ruby would do as Giacomo asked.

She loved Narciso, and, if there was any way he reciprocated those feelings, she didn't intend to walk away.

But she had to warn him that Giacomo might come at him by a different means once he found out Ruby had no intention of walking away.

Turning her head, she watched Narciso's peaceful profile as he slept. Her heart squeezed and she sucked in a breath as tears threatened.

She'd never have believed she could fall in love so quickly and so deeply. But in less than a week she'd fallen for the world's number-one playboy.

But there was far more to Narciso than that. And if there was a chance for them…

Vowing to speak to him after the party, she slid out of bed, dressed without waking him and left the bedroom.

Armed with the black card he'd given her yesterday, she went outside and hailed a taxi. The market in Greenwich was bustling by the time she arrived just before six. For the next hour, she lost herself in picking the freshest vegetables, fruit and staples she needed for the dinner party.

Next, she stopped at the upmarket wine stockist.

Narciso had enough wine and vintage champagne so she only selected the spirits and liqueurs she needed for her cocktails.

She was leaving the shop when her phone buzzed. Heart jumping into her throat because she knew who it would be, she answered.

'You left without waking me,' came the quiet accusation.

'I needed to get to the market before sunrise.'

He sighed. 'I'm sorely tempted to cancel this event but I have several guests flying in specially.'

'Why would you want to cancel it?'

'Because it's coming between me and what I want right now.'

Her heart thundered. 'Wh-what do you want?'

'You. Alone. A proper conversation with no disturbances. To get to the bottom of whatever last night was about.'

'I'm sorry, I should've told you...' She stopped as a phone rang in the background.

'*Scusi,*' he excused himself, only to return a minute later. 'I need to head to the office but I'll be back by five tonight, *si?*'

'Okay, I'll see you then.'

He paused, as if he wanted to say something. Then he ended the call.

Ruby was glad for the distraction of getting everything ready for the dinner party. By the time Michel showed up midafternoon, she'd almost finished her preparations.

They talked through the recipes she'd planned and settled on the timing.

'Monsieur tells me you'll be manning the bar tonight?'

'The idea is to divide my time between the bar and the kitchen. I know I can trust you to hold the fort here?'

'Of course.' He peered closer at her. 'Is everything all right?'

She busied herself placing large chunks of freshly cut salmon in its foil wrappings.

'It will be when the evening's over. I always get the jitters at these events.'

His knowing glance told her he hadn't missed her evasiveness. Thankfully, Paolina entered the kitchen and Ruby sighed with relief.

The planning team arrived at four. After that, deliveries flooded in. Flowers, a DJ and lighting specialists who set up on the terrace.

But the most unexpected delivery came in the form of a couture designer bearing a zipped-up garment bag, which she handed over and promptly departed. The note pinned to the stunning powder-blue floor-length gown was simple—*a beautiful gown for a beautiful woman.*

Joy burst through her heart, made her smile for the first time that day.

For the job she had to do tonight, it was severely impractical, as were the silver shoes almost the exact shade as Narciso's eyes, but as she walked into Narciso's bedroom and hung up the dress she knew she would wear it.

Narciso was late. He arrived barely a half-hour before his guests were due to arrive and walked into the bedroom just as she was putting finishing touches to her upswept hair.

He froze in the doorway, and stared. 'You look gorgeous, *bellissima.*'

She turned from the mirror, a cascade of love, trepidation and anxiety smashing through her. How would he take the news of his father's continued scheming?

Remember where my son inherited his thirst for revenge...

Forcing down the shiver of apprehension, she murmured, 'Grazie.'

His eyes darkened with pleasure. 'You need to speak more Italian. Or better still Sicilian. I'll teach you,' he said as he shrugged off his jacket and tugged at his tie.

Then he strode to where she stood. Snaking a large hand around her nape, he pulled her in for a long, deep kiss. Then with a groan he stepped back.

'Give me fifteen minutes and I'll be with you.'

'Okay.'

'*Dio,* I must be growing a conscience, *bellissima,* since I keep dismissing the idea of calling this party off.'

She forced a laugh. 'You must be.'

Shaking his head, he entered the bathroom. She stood there until the sound of the shower pulled her from her troubled thoughts.

She was behind the bar, pouring the first of the cocktails into glasses, when he emerged.

The sight of him in a superbly cut grey suit and a blue shirt that matched her dress made her heart slam into her throat. He'd taken a single step towards her when the doorbell rang.

He rolled his eyes dramatically, then his gaze drifted over her in heated promise before he nodded for the butler to answer the door.

For the next two hours, Ruby let her skills take over, serving food that drew several compliments from the dinner guests.

She declined when Narciso invited her to join them at the dinner table. Although his eyes narrowed in displeasure, there was very little he could do about it, much to her relief.

She was preparing a round of after-dinner cocktails when she looked up and gasped.

Giacomo was framed in the penthouse doorway.

Her gaze swung to Narciso; frozen, she watched his head turn and his body tense as he saw his father.

For several seconds, they eyed each other across the room.

Giacomo sauntered in as if he belonged. Several guests, sensing the altered atmosphere, glanced between father and son.

'Hey, watch it!'

She jerked and looked down to find she'd overfilled a glass and the lime-green cocktail was spilling over the counter.

Setting the shaker down, she grabbed a napkin.

'*Bona sira,* Ruby,' came the mocking voice. 'How lovely you look.'

Her head snapped up and connected with Giacomo's steely gaze. Surprise that he hadn't headed straight for his son held her immobile. Long enough for him to calmly reach across the counter, take her hand and press a kiss on her knuckles.

She tried to snatch her hand away but he held on tight, a triumphant smile playing about his lips. 'Play along, little one, and all your problems will go away,' he said in a low voice.

'I have no intention of playing along with anything.'

'It doesn't matter one way or the other. Narciso is infatuated with you. He'll see what I want him to see.'

With the clarity of a klaxon, everything fell into place.

She'd been played. Giacomo had always intended *this* to be his revenge. By meeting with him last night, she'd only given him more ammunition.

Heart shattering, she glanced over to where Narciso stood stock still, his eyes icy lakes of shock.

CHAPTER TWELVE

'NARCISO—'

'Don't speak.'

Narciso paced in his office, marvelling at how his voice emerged so calm, so collected, when his insides bled from a million poisonous cuts.

'Listen to him, *bedda*. He's prone to childish tantrums when he's upset. Just look at how he threw out all his guests a few minutes ago—'

'Shut up, old man, or so help me I'll bury my fist in your face.'

Giacomo shook his head and glanced at Ruby in a *what-did-I-say?* manner.

'What the hell are you doing here?'

'Ruby told me you were having a party. I decided to invite myself.'

'I didn't—!'

'*Ruby* told you? When?' Narciso's gaze swung to her, then returned to his father.

'Last night, when she met me for dinner.'

'He's lying, Narciso.' He heard the plea in her voice and tried to think, to rationalise what was unfolding before him. Unfortunately his brain seemed to have stopped working.

From the moment he'd seen Giacomo take her hand and kiss it, time had jerked to a stop, then rewound furiously, throwing up old memories that refused to be banished.

Forcing himself into the present, he stared at Ruby. The gorgeous firecracker who'd got under his skin. The woman who'd made love to him last night in her apartment as if her soul belonged to him.

Waking up this morning to find her gone had rocked him to his soul. The realisation that he wanted her in his bed and in his arms every morning and night for the rest of his life had been shocking but slowly, as the idea had embedded itself into his heart, he'd known it was what he wanted.

He loved her. He, who'd never loved anything or anyone in his life, had fallen in love...

With a woman who would meet with his father and not tell him...allow Giacomo to put his hand on her.

No! He couldn't have made the same mistake twice.

Ruby was different...

Wasn't she? Reeling, he watched Giacomo stroll to the large sofa in the room and ease himself into it. His attitude reeked a confidence that shook Narciso to the core.

He forced himself to speak. 'Ruby, is this true?'

She shook her head so emphatically, tendrils fell down her graceful neck. 'No, it's not. I only—'

'You have a spy following me around. I know you do. He reports to you twice a week. Today is one of those days, I believe,' Giacomo said.

Narciso's fists tightened. 'Not any more.'

Surprise lit the old man's eyes. 'Really? You must be going soft. Luckily, I had my own pictures taken.'

Giacomo reached into his pocket and threw down a set of photos on the coffee table.

Narciso felt his body tremble as he moved towards the table. For the first time in his life, he knew genuine fear. He glanced up to see Ruby's eyes on his face.

'Please, Narciso, it's not what you think. I can explain.'

He took another step. And there in Technicolor was the woman he loved, with the man he'd believed until very recently he hated most in his life.

Ironically, it was Ruby who'd made him look deeper into himself and acknowledge the fact that it wasn't hate that drove him but a desperate need to connect with the person who should've loved him.

His legs lost the ability to support him and he sank into his chair. Vicious pain slashed at his heart and he fought against the need to howl in agony.

'Leave,' he rasped.

'I warned you you would never best me,' his father crooned.

Slowly, Narciso raised his head and looked at his father. Despite his triumph, he looked haggard. The years of bitterness had taken their toll. It was what he'd risked becoming...

'She insisted on saving you, do you know that?'

Ice filled his gut. *'Scusi?'*

Giacomo's gaze scoured him. 'Your *mamma*. She had a chance to live. The doctor who arrived could only save one of you. She had a chance and she chose you.' Bitterness coated every word.

'And you've hated me for it ever since, haven't you?'

Giacomo's face hardened. 'I never wanted children. She knew that. If she'd only listened to me, she'd still be alive.' He inhaled and surged to his feet. 'What does it matter? Come, Ruby. You're no longer wanted here.'

Narciso snarled. 'Lay another finger on her and it's the last thing you'll ever do.'

His father jerked in shock, then his face took on a grey hue. Narciso watched, stunned, as Giacomo clutched his chest and began to crumple.

'Narciso, I think he's having a heart attack!'

For several seconds Ruby's words didn't compute. When the meaning spiked, poker hot, into his brain, he reached out and caught Giacomo as he fell.

Behind him he heard Ruby dialling and speaking to emergency personnel as he tore open his father's shirt and began chest compressions.

'*Madre di Dio, non,*' he whispered, the fear clutching his chest beginning to spread as his father lay still.

The next fifteen minutes passed by in a blur. The ER helicopter landed on the penthouse roof and emergency personnel took over.

He sagged against a wall when they informed him Giacomo was still alive but would need intensive care immediately.

'He'll pull through. I'm sure of it.'

He looked up to find Ruby in front of him, holding out a glass of whisky. He took it and knocked it back in one gulp.

It did nothing to thaw the ice freezing his heart.

'Leave.' He repeated the word he'd said what seemed like a lifetime ago.

Shock rushed over her face.

'Narciso—'

He threw the glass across the room and heard it shatter. 'No. You don't get to say my name. Never again.'

He took satisfaction in seeing tears fill her eyes. 'I can explain—'

'It's too late. I told you this thing between Giacomo and I was over. I'd trusted your counsel, taken your advice and abandoned this godforsaken vendetta. But where was your trust, *tesoro mio*? You knew this was coming. And you said nothing!'

'He threatened my parents!'

His expression softened for a split second. Then grew granite hard. 'Of course he did. But his threats meant more to you than your belief that I would help you. That we could fight him together!' He couldn't hide the raw pain that flowed out of his voice.

'I didn't want to fight! And I was going to tell you. Tonight after the party.'

'We'll never know now, will we?' he said scathingly.

'Narciso—'

'Your actions spoke clearly for you. Unfortunately for you, you made the same mistake Maria did. *You chose the wrong side.*'

* * *

Ruby smoothed her hand down the sea-green dress and tried to stem the butterflies.

In less than half an hour, the grand opening of Dolce Italia would be under way.

Two months of sheer, sometimes blessedly mind-numbing, hard work. She'd volunteered for every job that didn't require specialist training in the blind hope of drowning out the acute pain and devastation of having to live without Narciso. Her success rate had been woefully pathetic...

'Are you ready yet, *bella bambina*? The paparazzi will be here in a minute.' Her mother entered, wearing an orange silk gown that pleasantly complemented her slim figure. Despite being in her late forties, Paloma looked ten years younger. With her divorce from her philandering husband firmly underway, she appeared to have acquired a new lease on life. The spring in her step had grown even bolder when Ruby had allowed her to take a financial stake in the restaurant.

She stopped in the middle of the small room they'd converted to a dressing room at the back of the two-storey restaurant and cocktail bar in the prime location in Manhattan.

'Oh, you look stunning,' she said, then her eyes darkened with worry. 'A little on the thin side, though.'

'Don't fuss, Mamma.'

'It's my job to fuss. A job I neglected for years.'

Knowing she was about to lapse into another self-recriminating rant, Ruby rushed forward and hugged her. 'What's done is done, Mamma. Now we look forward.'

Her mother blinked brown eyes bright with unshed tears and nodded. 'Speaking of moving forward, the most exquisite bouquet of flowers arrived for you.'

Ruby's breath caught, then rushed out in a gush of pain. 'I don't want them.'

Her mother frowned. 'What woman doesn't want flowers on the most spectacular night of her life?'

'Me.'

'Are you sure you're all right? Last week you sent back that superb crate of white Alba truffles, the week before you refused the diamond tennis bracelet. I wish you'd tell me who all these gifts are from.'

'It doesn't matter who they're from. I don't want any of them.' She fought the rising emotions back. She'd shed enough tears to last her a lifetime.

Not tonight. With her mother as her new business partner, she'd paid off Giacomo's loan and closed that chapter.

Tonight, she would push Narciso and his in-your-face gifts out of her mind and bask in her accomplishment.

'I'm ready.'

They entered the large reception area to find a three-deep row of photographers and film crew awaiting them. In the time she'd decided to open the restaurant with her mother, Paloma had guided her in how to deal with the press. Where her reaction to them had been led by fear and resentment, now she used banter and firmness to achieve her aim.

With the press conferences and TV junkets taken care off, her mother passed her the scissors and she moved to a large white ribbon.

'Ladies and gentlemen, my mother, Paloma, and I are proud to declare Dolce Italia open—'

At first she thought she was hallucinating. Then the face became clearer.

Narciso stood to one side of the group, his silver eyes square on her face.

'Ruby?' she heard her mother's concerned voice from far away as the heavy scissors slipped from her grasp.

'Ruby!'

She turned and fled.

'Ruby.' He breathed her name as if it were a life-giving force, pulling her from the murky depth of pain. 'Open the door, *per favore.*'

She snatched the door she'd slammed shut moments ago

wide open. 'You ruined my opening. Weeks of preparation, of breaking my back to make this perfect, and you swooped in with your stupid face and your stupid body and *ruined* it.' She found herself inspecting his face and body and tore her gaze away.

'*Mi dispiace.* I wanted...I *needed* to see you.'

'Why? What could you possibly have to say to me that you haven't already said?'

His jaw tightened. 'A lot. You returned all my gifts.'

'I didn't want them.'

He took a step into the room. 'And the NMC cheque? You returned it to me ripped into a hundred pieces.'

'I was making a point. Why did you keep sending me stuff?'

'Because I refused to contemplate giving up. I refused to imagine what my life would be like without the thinnest thread of hope keeping me going.'

She wanted to keep her gaze averted, but, like a magnet, it swung towards him.

He looked incredible, the five-o'clock shadow gracing his jaw making him look even more stunning. But a closer look pinpointed a few surprising changes.

'You've lost weight,' she murmured.

He shut the door behind him and she caught the faint snick of the lock. 'So have you. At least I have an excuse.'

'Really?'

'*Sì,* Michel threatened to quit. We agreed on a month-long vacation.'

'You don't deserve him.'

He grimaced. 'That's entirely true. He wasn't happy when he realised his culinary efforts were going to waste.' He threaded his fingers together and stared down at them. When he looked back up, his eyes were bleak, infinitely miserable. Her heart kicked hard. 'I can't eat, Ruby. I've barely slept since you left.'

'And this is my fault? I didn't *leave*. You threw me out, re-member?'

He paled and nodded, his nostrils thinning as he sucked in

a long, ragged breath. 'I was wrong. So very wrong to believe even for a second that you were anything like Maria.'

'And you've suddenly arrived at this conclusion?'

'No. All the signs were there. I just refused to see them because I'd programmed myself to believe the worst.'

Her heart kicked again, this time with the smallest surge of hope. 'What signs?'

'Your determination to push me away when I came to your apartment. Your tears in the car on the way back home. Your clear distress when my father touched you. Why would you encourage me to reconcile with my father and turn round and betray me?'

'I wouldn't... I didn't.'

He shook his head. 'I know. I condemned you for something that never happened. Something you tried to tell me you would never do. But I was so bitter and twisted I couldn't see what was in front of me.'

'What was that?'

'The love I have for you and the probability that you could perhaps love me, too.'

Her breath caught. 'W-what?'

'I know I've blown all that now—'

'You mean you don't love me?'

He speared a hand through his hair and jumped up. 'Of course I love you. That's not the point here, I meant—'

'I think you'll find that's the whole point, Narciso,' she murmured, her heart racing.

He stopped. Stared down at her. Slowly his eyes widened. Ruby knew what he was seeing in her face. The love she'd tried for so long and so hard to smother was finally bursting out of her.

'*Dio mio,*' he breathed.

'You can say that again.'

'*Dio mio,*' he repeated as he sank onto his knees in front of her. 'Please tell me I'm not dreaming?'

'I love you, Narciso. Despite you being a horrible pain in the ass. There, does that help?'

With a groan, he rose, took her face in his hands and kissed her long and deep. 'I'll dedicate every single moment of the rest of my life to making you forget that incident.'

'That sounds like a great deal.'

'Can I also convince you to let me back Dolce Italia in any way I can?'

Despite the guilt she saw in his face, she shook her head. 'No. It's now a mother-daughter venture. I want to keep it that way.'

'What about your father?' he asked.

'He consults…from afar. We'll never be close but he's my blood. I can't completely cut him off.'

'*Prezioso,* you humble me with how giving you are.'

'You should've remembered that before you pushed me away.'

'I've relived the hell of it every single second since I lost you.'

'Keep telling me that and I may allow you to earn some brownie points.'

He smiled. 'Can we discuss accumulative points?'

'I may be open to suggestions.'

He kissed her until her heart threatened to give out.

'Wow, okay. That could work.'

'How about this, too?'

He reached behind him and presented her with a large leather, velvet-trimmed box. It was far too large to contain a ring but her heart still thundered as she opened it.

The mask was breathtaking. Bronze-trimmed around blue velvet, it was the exact colour of the waters of Belize. Peacock feathers sprouted from the top in a splash of Technicolor, and two lace ties were folded and held down by diamond pins.

'It's beautiful.'

'It's yours if you choose to accompany me on the next *Q Virtus* event.'

'I want to know more about your super-secret club.'

A sly smile curved his lips. 'I could tell you all the secrets, but then I'd have to make love to you for days to make you forget.'

'Hmm, I suppose I'd just have to suffer through it.'

He laughed, pulled her close and kissed her again. She pulled away before things got heavy.

'Tell me what you've done to my mother.'

'She promised to hold the fort on condition I did everything in my power to exit this room as her future son-in-law.'

Ruby gasped. 'She didn't! God, first you muscle in on my opening, then you strike deals behind my back.'

'What can I say? She drives a hard bargain.' He pulled back and stared down at her, a hint of uncertainty in his eyes. 'So will you give me an answer?'

Her arms rose to curl over his shoulders. 'That depends.'

'On what?'

'On whether white Alba truffles come with the deal.'

He pulled her close and squeezed her tight. 'I'll keep you supplied every day for the rest of your life if that's what it takes, *amante*.'

Isla de Margarita, Venezuela

Narciso leaned against the side of the cabana and watched his wife wow the crowd with her latest range of cocktails. Although her mask covered most of her face, he could tell she was smiling.

Music pumped from the speakers strategically placed around the pool area and all around him *Q Virtus* members let their inhibitions fly musically and otherwise.

He raised his specially prepared cocktail to his lips and paused as the lights caught his new wedding ring.

He'd wanted a big wedding for Ruby but she'd insisted on a small, intimate ceremony at the Sicilian villa where he'd been born.

In the end, they'd settled for fifty guests including her

mother, and Nicandro Carvalho and Ryzard Vrbancic, the two men he considered his closest friends.

Although they were working on their relationship, he and Giacomo had a way to go before all the heartache could be set aside.

'So...*last three bachelors standing* becomes two. How the hell are Nicandro and I going to handle all these women by ourselves, huh, my friend?'

Laughing, he turned to Ryzard. 'That's your problem. I'm willingly and utterly taken.' He glanced over and saw Ruby's eyes on him. He raised his glass and winked.

Ryzard shuddered. 'That's almost sickening to watch.'

'If you're going to throw up, do it somewhere else.'

Shaking his head, his friend started to walk away, then Narciso saw him freeze. The woman who had caught his attention was dancing by herself in a corner. Although she had a full mask over her face, her other attributes clearly had an effect on Ryzard.

Smiling, Narciso turned to watch his wife emerge from behind the bar and walk towards him, her stunning body swaying beneath her sarong in a way that made his throat dry.

She reached him and handed him another drink. 'What was that all about?'

'Just me bragging shamelessly on how lucky I am to have found you.'

She laughed. 'Yeah, about that. You might need to pull back on the gushing a bit. You're putting our friends off.'

He caught her around her waist, tugged her mask aside and kissed her thoroughly. 'I have no intention of pulling back. Anyone who dares to approach me will be told how wonderful and gorgeous my wife is.'

His pulse soared when her fingers caressed his collarbone. 'I love you, Narciso.'

'And I love that I've made you happy enough to keep you from sleepwalking lately.'

'That reminder just lost you one brownie point.'

He pulled her closer. 'Tell me how to win it back, *per favore,*' he whispered fervently against her lips.

'Dance with me. And never stop telling me how much you love me.'

'For as long as I live, you'll know it, *amante*. That is my promise to you.'

* * * * *